"IT'S I[N] IN TH[E] OF THE AFTERNOON!"

*   *   *

"Which only adds to the lawlessness. And it's the very best time of day," he said. "I much prefer it to the cover of night, and we've nothing to hide."

Katherine managed to draw away from him enough to move her hand to the bell pull that was near her bed. "This cannot continue," she said. "I shall have to summon Emma."

He held her eyes, his lit with desire and laughter and the challenge that was always there when he was with her. "Do you really care to humiliate yourself by summoning a servant who won't come?"

Katherine hesitated. "As usual, you have arranged everything so that I submit to your wishes!"

"I don't want your submission," he said, stripping off his tunic.

Katherine gasped slightly. "You cannot force me," she said, using her last, shaky defense. "You cannot wish to force your attentions on an unwilling woman."

"Tell me honestly that you are unwilling," he said huskily, "and I shall stop on the instant." He threw back the covers of her bed and gently laid her down...

*   *   *

The Viking's Bride

Julie Tetel

POPULAR LIBRARY

An Imprint of Warner Books, Inc.

A Warner Communications Company

To my mother

The Viking's Bride

____ Chapter 1 ____

York, England
March 1216

Katherine de Lunais escorted her most unwelcome visitor to the street and bolted the oaken door behind him. Leaning against the portal, she slowly let out her breath. It had been a trying interview, one she was relieved to have behind her. It was a further measure of relief to have a full seven days ahead of her before seeing the man again. She did not relish the thought of that next meeting, or the one after that, and she hoped that in the weeks to come, she could keep him at a safe, professional distance. It would be best, of course, to end her association with him altogether, and she knew that it would take all her wits to do so. She reassured herself somewhat wryly that she was always at her best when backed into a corner. To be sure, she was in a tricky corner now.

Now she looked around her and found comfort. The open courtyard of this house in Jubbergate Street was serene in the cool of the late afternoon. Under the eaves in a warm corner a bitch suckled a tumble of pups while a shaggy yard dog worried a bone and a lazy caramel cat dozed atop the rain barrels. A stout stone fountain trickled in the middle of the cobbled yard and was ringed with earthen pots alive with basil and marjoram and savory. A handsome exposed staircase swept up one wall to the gallery, which encircled the half-timbered upper story and whose finely wrought columns bore testimony to the master craftsmanship of the woodwrights of York. The harmonious whole of the house and yard basked gently in the glow of the westering sun, and from the nether regions came the musical clatter of bowls and cutlery and the muffled sound of the high voices of women and children.

Katherine absorbed the quiet scene before her and took heart. She rarely stopped to look back on her life, but the present moment demanded special measures. She paused to remember how she had arrived at this Saxon stronghold flung far in the north of England, a homeless and grieving girl, stripped of everything but her will to survive. Four years before she had been reduced to seeking refuge for herself and her young half sister at St. Clement's nunnery just outside the city walls of York. Now she saw before her the visible proof of all her accomplishments. Her well-tended house and yard reassured her that she had come too far and done too much to abandon her plans. They reduced her present difficulty to nothing more than a small setback. They encouraged her to forge ahead.

Katherine knew that she had cause to feel some fear. Indeed, she would be a fool if she did not. She admitted to herself that the man who had just left had shaken her composure far more than she dared let him guess. He had come, so he said, to offer her friendship rather than to remind her that she owed him a tidy sum of money. Since she had no means of paying him at the moment, she had managed to put him off by arranging to meet him in a week at the castle. He had agreed, but Katherine had heard his menacing undertone. She had observed as well the way his curious, light brown eyes had narrowed, his voice had thinned, and his smile had held the suggestion of a gloat when he said that they would discuss at that time a proposition that would eliminate her debt. Katherine had fought down her distaste and had responded, in the demure manner she deliberately adopted with him, all modesty and maidenly innocence. He had left her with no doubt, however, about her present, precarious position or about the future he had in mind for her.

Katherine took a steadying breath. She had been through worse, she reminded herself, and it would take more of a man than he to stop her now. Nevertheless, she knew that her most effective weapon against the man and the hold he had over her would be the payment of the hard cash she owed him, and this would be hers to give him only when Josef and the ship and the cargo were finally safe in harbor.

She crossed the yard in the direction of the stairs. Josef

was more than a fortnight overdue, and she was becoming more uneasy with each passing day. She had enough experience to know that anything could happen to delay a sailor, even her very dependable Josef. When the sun washed the world clean of worry and the household hummed busily, she was able to name a dozen reasons for Josef's continued absence. But of late, when the night crept down roof and wall to drain a bright world of color, and the mists rolled in from River Ouse to shroud the house in an uneasy silence, her fears leapt from the shadows to remind her that she was in a foreign country, entirely on her own, and enmeshed in a dangerous venture.

Katherine gave herself a mental shake. She would not think of that now, not while the sun was shining and there was still a chance that Josef might return. She would not give up hope until the sun had set, when church bells chimed the compline, and city gates were closed to all newcomers.

Before Katherine had mounted the first step of the stairs, a woman emerged from a low door at the far end of the courtyard and came swiftly forward. She was dressed, as was Katherine, in a kirtle of forest-green sarcenet embroidered at throat and sleeve in the familiar ring-chain pattern, but there the physical resemblance between the two women ended. Emma was ten years the elder and rather thin in comparison to her shapely young mistress, and in contrast to Katherine's curves, the older woman's Saxon stock made her angular, almost squarish. However, Emma matched her mistress in quickness of movement and liveliness of mind, and there was a fine balance between the two of them. When Katherine rushed ahead without regard for the consequences, Emma restrained with a Saxon caution; and where Emma erred in timidity, Katherine dared to take a chance.

The plain, honest features on Emma's face bore an anxious question. Her expression lightened as she drew near to her mistress, but in response Katherine shook her head slightly. "Nothing good to report," she said when Emma had come close enough to hear her low tones.

Emma appraised her mistress. "So he's gone," she said.

Katherine nodded. "Just now."

"I heard the door bell clang in the kitchens and came as

quickly as I could," Emma said. "I thought at first that you might have had good news, judging from your air of unconcern. I had prayed for any kind of a miracle and would not have been surprised to learn that you had performed one on your own."

Katherine smiled at that, a little ruefully. "Then I must have succeeded in convincing myself that there is nothing to be concerned about," she said in an attractive, low-pitched voice that held rhythm not native to Yorkshire speech. "In any case, you know that I dare not show the least sign of trouble. Especially now. We'll have to keep up the appearances for at least another seven-night—and more, if we can manage it. I shall depend on you, as always. And as for miracles...!You must pray for a very specific one: the safe and speedy return of Josef."

"Mauleon had no news of him?" Emma asked.

Katherine shook her head again. "He didn't even mention Josef." She was lost in thought for a moment. When she began again, it was on a puzzled note. "I am convinced that he suspects that Josef has disappeared, but apparently he is not certain. If Mauleon were sure that Josef were not returning to York, he would be demanding payment now—one way or the other."

"One way or the other?" Emma echoed scornfully. "I'm not at all surprised! I've suspected all along how it would be, while you—"

"I've known as well as you what it would come to," Katherine interposed. "We've never denied that it's a man's world."

"—while you have, once again, proceeded without a thought to your personal stake in the matter," Emma continued, ignoring the interruption. Emma did not scruple to hide her opinions, a privilege of trusted retainers, though she wisely aired them in a voice hardly above a whisper. "Many of your gambles have paid off in the end, I'll admit. But this time I fear that you have sailed too close to the wind. Aye, it's a man's world! And I wish by all the saints that you had never gotten involved with this particular man! I know very well how it all came about and how you were not to be blamed, so we won't go into all of that just now. But it's a sad thing to be at the mercy of one like that. He's stirred up a bushel of trouble in York, and he'll be stirring up much more before the country finds its rest, what with all the schemes and intrigues spinning behind those small, darting eyes of his. Why, the man's a—he's a—" Here words failed Emma.

Katherine knew just what he was. "Cedric de Mauleon is a lizard," she said, capturing the image. "But we're not at his mercy, Emma. Not yet. And we can continue to use him to our purposes if all goes well."

"Just as he will use you to his if it doesn't!" Emma replied in some distress.

"We still have a week. I may be able to hold him off even longer if Josef hasn't returned by then."

"But it cannot go on indefinitely," Emma argued. "What if Josef never returns? You'll not be able to hold Mauleon off forever."

"No," Katherine conceded, "but he's not as clever as he likes to think, and I'm not entirely defenseless. We've been over rougher ground than this together, you and I."

"The stakes have not been so high, however."

"All the more reason to find a way out," Katherine returned with spirit.

"Unless Josef returns soon, we will be needing the helping hand of the Good Lord above to find that way," Emma observed.

Emma held a simple faith that Katherine had long ago forsaken; and while Katherine might have chosen to quarrel with Emma's phrasing, she saw that Emma essentially had the right of it. Katherine heartily disliked the helplessness that came with the realization that their fate was now, if Josef did not return, in the hands of a fickle Providence. She had bent all of her considerable energy over the last years in an effort to escape the whims of man and blind fortune. She knew that for a woman no such true independence existed in the world. Nevertheless, it would be lovely, she thought, to be mistress of one's destiny and to be free, as well, of doubt and disaster and ambition.

In the tiny corner of her heart that was still her own, she cherished a vision of her life without a past to haunt her and no future to plan. She wished to be truly what her friends and neighbors in town supposed her to be: the mistress of a plain broidery house. She longed in odd moments to lead the simple life of those prosperous burghers among whom she lived. What a luxury it must be to think only of buying and selling, of marrying and raising children! Such peace and security, however, were not within her grasp. All of Katherine's efforts were devoted to the care of her younger half sister Sybille. Katherine could not lightly break the vow she had made on behalf of Sybille, for the promise of Sybille's care that Katherine had given to their dying mother had been more binding and sacred to her than any oath sworn before the altar.

"We've benefited from good luck before now, Emma," Katherine said bravely, "and it could come our way again any day."

"Let's hope within the next seven days!" Emma retorted quickly, and took just as swift exception to Katherine's first statement. "But was it luck, Mistress Katherine, that we've had? It was your ingenuity that found us this house—not luck! And obtaining the blessing of the archbishop on our humble establishment was nothing less than a brilliant stroke! 'The Lord helps those . . .' I always say."

"Ah, but the ship that came our way a couple of years ago was a piece of purest luck!" Katherine replied. "It put us in business and made us not a penny the poorer!"

Katherine did not often mention this transaction, for its execution had required knowledge of things best left unknown. Emma's brows lowered predictably. "Aye," she said darkly. "Luck and the work of the devil! I wonder if you'll not be paying the lord mayor for the *Jorvik* when all is said and done. One way or the other—to use your own words."

"Not a chance," Katherine replied with conviction. She was struck by another thought. "And the shipment of silks by way of the Viking? Was that not a piece of luck? And very good luck it was, too, to have had the Viking's ship sink before Josef had a chance to pay him. That was the beginning of our real success. When was that storm at sea? Last September?"

"Aye, before the Michaelmas," Emma affirmed. "But

Josef thought that the Viking could have proved even more useful to us in the long run if he had lived. Josef had only just made contact with him the month before."

"That was because we did not have enough trade before then to make us worth the Viking's while," Katherine answered.

"That, of course, is my point!" Emma returned. "Think where we might be now, had he lived."

The Viking had been a legendary figure. As seafarer and trader, he had known the secrets of guilds and taxes, portreeves and mayors, and small, unofficial harbors off England's eastern coast. The news of his death in an unexpected gale had set more than one prominent businessman in the north to grieving, for these tradesmen scorned the present king and traded with the Viking to avoid the royal taxes on foreign commerce. Katherine did not like to profit from another's ill fortune, but since she had never laid eyes on the Viking, she could not find it in her heart to mourn his passing.

"Nevertheless," Katherine replied, "it was a boon to have received that shipment of silk, courtesy of the Viking, as well as to have kept the cash that should have gone to pay for it. With that money we were able to invest heavily in the drapers' guild at a time the wool merchants needed it most. I'm sure the investment will pay off well for us in the end."

Emma demanded once again, "But what if Josef never returns and no miracle occurs? What then? It's unlikely Mauleon will conveniently do as the Viking did and disappear before he's paid."

Katherine faced Emma directly. "No, I am sure that he will not. But he very much mistakes the matter. He thinks to have the money when the ship comes in, or to have me if it does not. If I correctly interpret his leers, then I would say that he plans on having both in the end." Katherine smiled slightly, but her eyes betrayed her uneasiness. "I can assure you that he will get nothing from me but silver. I still have one last source of money left to pursue if all else fails."

All Emma's prudence could be read on her face. "I fear for you, Mistress Katherine," she said gravely. "I think we should prepare to leave York as quickly as possible."

There was a short silence. Katherine had never once considered the chance of complete failure. She refused to consider it now. "Turn tail and run, Emma?" she said lightly with her pretty smile. "Thank you for stating the matter so plainly! Of course, you are right. If worse comes to the very worst, we might do well to leave York—you, Sybille, and I. We have always planned to do so. But I would hate to leave in such a cowardly, abrupt fashion, for our friends in York have been very good to us."

"They have," Emma agreed, "but I am thinking of what is in your best interest and no one else's."

"Thank you again. But you need not, as you well know. So, let us consider again the possibility of leaving York six days from now, if by then our backs are well and truly against the wall. Not yet, though. Not today. Just think! It is so simple: We have only to put our money on the man who will be sitting on the throne next year at this time to have won everything! It is like the game the infidels play. You place your coin on either the red square or the black and wait for the spinning ball to come to rest. Will it be John of England who wears the crown? Or will it be Louis of France?"

"Place your money on red," Emma predicted mournfully, "and black will turn up."

"Dear Emma," Katherine said. She laid an affectionate hand on the older woman's shoulder. "Can you not see that the rewards warrant the risks?"

Emma shook her head. She did not share the visions, past and future, which governed Katherine's every action. After four years of close association Emma still stood a little in awe of her mistress and of her delicate beauty. Katherine's curves were apparent but not too generous, her wrists graceful, her hands slim and white. Her face was delicate with deep hazel-green eyes, a straight little nose, and finely drawn lips that could, by turns, smile warmly or stay firm. Her hair was a dark brown that shone a rich auburn in the sun or firelight. She wore it pulled back loosely into a chignon, a style most becoming to the pure lines of her face. However, there was something more to the whole of Katherine's loveliness than the mere sum of her parts. Emma could not fathom what it was that set Katherine apart from many another beautiful woman, but she knew that it was precisely that quality which Mauleon longed to possess and would never touch.

Mention of rewards and risks reminded Katherine of her sister. "Where is Sybille?" she asked abruptly, looking around, as if hoping to conjure her sister out of the walls. "I haven't seen her since before Mauleon's arrival over an hour ago. Did she go to market?"

Emma hesitated. She had decided to tell Katherine exactly where Sybille had been spending her time of late, but she had chosen to wait until the meeting with Mauleon was over before she spoke. Now was Emma's moment. If she were to dissuade her mistress from pursuing this dangerous scheme to its possibly disastrous conclusion, here was the time, and Sybille was the reason. Emma opened her mouth at last to speak, but the bell over the door clanged and destroyed the opportunity.

Katherine was instantly alert. Relief flooded her. "It's *him*!" she breathed with satisfaction. "I can feel it!"

"Josef!" Emma exclaimed in a tiny voice, and made a movement in the direction of the door.

Katherine laid a hand on her arm to stay her. While her eyes sparkled with a look that said, "You worry far too much, dear Emma!" she kept the mild triumph out of her voice. "No, I want to greet Josef. But stay here. We'll all go to my solar together."

Katherine hastened eagerly to the door. Without checking through the peep window she shot back the bolt and swung the door open wide.

She had expected, of course, to behold a man. The figure looming before her was most uncompromisingly masculine, but it was definitely not Josef.

Instead of looking levelly into Josef's face, Katherine's eyes traveled upward. The afternoon sun was poised on the rooftop of the house opposite hers on the street, just beyond the man's shoulder, so that Katherine's first impression of him was of his sun-struck mane, ablaze with light. His face remained in shadow, but Katherine was aware of his eyes and his slow, deliberate appraisal of her.

She recalled herself instantly and fought down the sharp disappointment at not finding Josef. "Good morrow, stranger," she said evenly. "How may we serve you?"

"Good morrow, mistress," the man replied in a deep, gravelly voice. "I have come about the job."

Katherine's smile was slight and aloof. "The only jobs to be found in this house are for women's fingers."

"I am a sailor," the man explained to this discouraging news.

Katherine's heart began to beat uncomfortably, but her voice was steady. "I repeat, stranger, a broidery house has little use for a sailor."

"Josef sent me" came the reply.

Katherine held the man's gaze a long, nerveless moment. Then she stepped aside and gestured him into her house. He bent his head to enter through the low door, and she closed it behind him so that he might precede her into the courtyard.

In the light of the dying day she saw that the man's hair indeed held the color of the sun and showed a tendency to curl. He wore his plain brown tunic to the knee and shunned all ornamentations, but Katherine's professional eye noted that the cloth was no ordinary homespun but a fine Flemish twill. Cast in vigorous lines, the man was tall with a good pair of legs, hosed and encased in well-worn but excellent boots which Katherine guessed to be of Italian origin. When he turned to look at her, she saw that his face was rough-hewn and remote, as if chopped from a block of wood. Encountering his hard gray eyes, Katherine felt a faint, most odd sensation stir in her breast, and it unsettled her.

Emma came forward immediately, her face a mask of perfect politeness.

"Our guest is come with news of Josef," Katherine told her, and when the man turned to acknowledge Emma's bob, Katherine was surprised to discover that he was startlingly handsome in profile.

"Yes," he said, "I am come in search of Mistress Katherine."

Katherine inclined her head and identified herself. "I will serve you best," she continued in her pleasant voice, "when I have a name to attach to you."

His eyes swept over her again, came back to her face. He owed slightly. "My pardon, mistress," he replied. "I am Eric Shipwright. Of Scarborough."

There was a challenge in the man's manner and voice that was not lost on Katherine. She was aware again of that odd sensation, as if something attractive in the man's presence also warned her that she would be wise to resist him.

She struggled against this contradictory feeling toward her visitor and tried to concentrate instead on the matter of Josef. She would play her part to perfection. "Ah, not from York," she said conversationally. "We have few shipwrights here. You build ships, then."

"That is my craft," he answered, "though my livelihood now comes from sailing."

"But is it not unusual to find a shipwright who is also a sailor? I don't think I've ever heard of such a combination."

"It is unusual inland, in York," he answered. "But on the coast, where a man may easily move from the shipyard to the open sea, it's becoming common practice. Some sailors have taken to traveling with a shipwright on board. Most sailors like to keep at least one shipwright in their employ on land." He grinned. "I save myself that extra cost."

Katherine gave this her consideration. She did not want to appear too knowledgeable about ships; still, she wanted to draw him out. "I gather, then, that your building skill comes in handy after a wreck or a grounding, so that you are able to repair the ship and be on your way."

The shipwright nodded. "There is that, to be sure, and more than once I've needed my craft to make repairs on my vessel. But I've found that my skill as a shipwright has been more important to me in experimenting with new techniques for steering."

She raised finely arched brows. "That must have something to do with the rudder, does it not?"

"Yes, mistress," he said gravely.

Katherine looked speculatively at the man. His eyes met hers, and the gleam of mockery in them convinced her that he was laughing at her. So, he was aware that she was testing him and would not be drawn. She would be glad to be rid of him when she had learned what he knew about Josef.

She sent Emma in search of refreshments for their guest and asked her to join them in the solar. She then bade the shipwright follow her up the stairs, saying coolly, "I would have thought that the shipwrights of Scarborough had all but perfected the rudder by now."

The shipwright smiled at that, and his strong, harsh features took on a more pleasing arrangement. He followed her up the stairs. "The side rudder has its uses—in traveling across wide expanses of sea with men and arms and horses to invade, for example! Lighter, merchant crafts, however, benefit from different steering techniques. For speed and handling I prefer the Chinese rudder."

She led him around the balcony toward a chamber whose door stood open and whose yellow light spilled across the threshold. "You have been to China?" she asked with interest.

"Only as far east as the Volga," he returned. "I learned of the back rudder from the Arabs."

"Then you must have been in King Richard's last, disastrous crusade," she said. She was unable to imagine him a mere foot soldier, but it was equally unlikely that he could have been a knight.

He had been neither. "I don't wage war on the Saracens," he replied, shaking his head, "I trade with them. There's more profit in that. And their merchant ships are equipped with a very effective rudder attached to the stern post. It requires some redesigning of the traditional curled stern, but I've been able to adapt it with success." The shipwright smiled again and said with that same note of challenge, "But perhaps these details carry you out of your depth?"

They had arrived at her solar. It was neat and sparingly furnished with a trestle table and a long, low chest upon which sat bright cushions. A quiet fire whispered on the hearth. Next to the fireplace, the wall was broken by a door that was closed and that communicated to another chamber. The heavy draperies of the solar had not yet been drawn against the approaching evening, and glazed windows filtered the sinking sun into a rose glow. Five or six young women were clustered together before this row of windows, embroidery tambours in hand, their heads haloed in the cir-

cle of light from a large, raised candelabrum. Their eyes
lifted in unison at the arrival of Katherine and the shipwright
on the threshold. Without giving an explanation for this
masculine presence in so feminine a bower, Katherine dismissed the women. They filed out, disappointed, although
Katherine did not miss the fact that one bold-eyed maid used
the opportunity to advantage to flash the shipwright a frank
invitation as she brushed by him.

Katherine continued easily when the women had gone.
"Carried out of my depth? Not entirely. All people whose
trade depends on the sea should know the basics of ships and
sailing. That includes everyone in York—man or woman.
As you know, York prides itself for its inland port. It is
certainly not as large a port as Scarborough, but I think York
is the larger—and perhaps more prosperous—town, is it
not?"

The shipwright agreed to this observation with a deferential nod.

"So. What goods do the infidels offer that are profitable
for you to handle?" she asked, picking up the earlier thread
of conversation.

"Paper," he answered. "The Arab's paper." He paused. "I
handle sugar, spices, dyes too. Cloth as well. All things
small and light and in demand."

The odd sensation that Katherine had felt earlier became
more pronounced and spread to tingle provocatively at the
ends of her nerves. She tried to dismiss the disturbing feeling as the effects of a most hectic day. Emma returned then,
gingerly carrying a tray which bore an earthenware pitcher
and two wooden beakers, and closed the door quietly. Before taking up one of the vacated chairs with its discarded
embroidery tambour, Emma teased the smoldering embers
on the hearth into flames and lit a pair of wall sconces with a
taper from the candelabrum.

Katherine was anxious to have done with this sparring.
With a wave of her hand she invited the shipwright to be
seated at the table. She poured out the two glasses and
placed one of them before her guest. "We keep nothing but
cider here, Master Eric. It is a woman's house," she explained, "but all this talk of sailing reminds me of our good

friend, Josef. A sailor, I believe, and perhaps a trader, too, like yourself. What news of him have you for us?"

"It is not good," he said bluntly.

She drew a breath. "How bad is it?" she asked steadily.

"Josef died in a tavern brawl some weeks back," the shipwright informed her.

Emma looked up sharply and almost immediately resumed her stitchery. Katherine had been steeling herself against just such tidings. Even so, news of Josef's death came as something of a shock. Now was not the moment, however, for her spirit to falter, and so her eyes rested, widening only slightly, on the shipwright's face. He looked, she thought, as dangerous as an unwalled parapet, and she hoped that she could keep her footing.

Katherine crossed herself and said, "Josef was a very dear friend. We shall miss him. Yet I am surprised that Josef should meet his end in so violent a fashion. A tavern brawl, you say? How extraordinary!"

"Not an uncommon end for a sailor," the shipwright said. "The hazards on land far outnumber those at sea."

"Just where did this brawl take place?"

"In Thanet," he said.

"Thanet?" she repeated, as if she had never heard of the place, although she knew it very well from Josef's reports.

"A small inlet known to all sailors who are too poor to pay the portreeves in Scarborough and foolhardy enough to brave the rocky, shallow waters and uncertain tides," he informed her.

Was the man trifling with her? How much did he know? But two could play this game. "And do you belong to the ranks of the poor and foolhardy, Master Eric?"

He did not answer that but said only, "Josef did."

"However, it was not the shallow waters but his temper, it seems, which undid him," she said. "Emma always said that Josef's temper would be the death of him, but I truly did not believe it! He was a very gentle soul for all his gruff ways." She paused to sigh and laid her trap. "I suppose he suffered in the end from the fiery temper which must be the bane of all redheads."

"A violent end may befall the meekest of creatures," he said. "But would you say the color of his hair was red?"

So, he had stepped neatly around it, she thought, picturing Josef's mouse-brown hair. "Well, you're certainly not foolhardy enough to commit yourself to a reading of Josef's character," she remarked.

"I would not presume. I knew him so little."

"Given your slim tie to Josef, then, I am surprised that you bother to come all this way to deliver the news of his death in person," she said. Katherine held out faint hope that the shipwright had come with payment in mind for the information. Although she could ill afford it, she was prepared to pay him off handsomely, simply to be rid of him. "Perhaps you desire a coin to make it worth your while? Am I to know the reason why you have come?"

The shipwright looked at her derisively but said merely, "There are several reasons, mistress. Perhaps the most compelling one at the moment is curiosity."

Katherine was surprised. "Is your curiosity satisfied?"

"Oh, not yet! I wonder why Josef should make such a point—as he did on his deathbed—that you be the one to be told of his end. It puzzles me."

"Does it? We are—were!—in some sense responsible for Josef. We were the only family he had, though we are not related through blood. Whenever he came to York, which was fairly often, he had his bed and board with us." Her voice faltered a little, and she cleared her throat. "We were very close to him! It's natural that he would want us to receive news of his death, so—so that we may mourn him."

The shipwright readily assented to this. "I find it entirely natural that Josef should be attached to a house—and a mistress—of such great attractions."

"So! We have now established that you are neither foolhardy enough to comment on the temperament of a man you hardly knew, nor poor enough to require payment for having delivered these sad tidings," she said. "I would also not have thought that you were much in the way of making pretty speeches, either."

"That depends on the company in which I find myself," he replied easily.

She eyed him with caution. "What brought you here?" she asked, once more, directly.

"Curiosity, as I have said."

"To discover Josef the sailor's attachment to my house?"

He agreed to that with a nod.

She tried to shrug off the feeling that he was not telling her everything, but she could not imagine what he might be hiding. "Did Josef make a deathbed confession of some sort which intrigues you?"

"He confided nothing to me," said the shipwright, "and has taken all personal secrets with him to the grave, as far as I know. Unless they are now safely deposited with the passing friar who was there to attend to him."

"It is a comfort to me," she interposed solemnly, crossing herself again, "that a priest was with him at the last to administer the rites."

"I am sure that it is. I am here, rather, because I thought that Josef had a more official position in your household. Perhaps he was its owner?"

"Josef was a boarder here," Katherine repeated flatly.

"You own the house?"

"I am the head of household," she replied. "Only nominally, if you must know. We live here under a special dispensation from our most benevolent Archbishop of York."

Thick blond brows rose infinitesimally. "You live under the protective wing of the Church?" the shipwright asked.

She met his eye. "Yes."

"Your family did not build the house, then? You are not from York?"

"Are you curious again?"

"I am."

Katherine saw no need to satisfy him. She was aware that in this man's presence her nerves had stretched. She was not yet fully afraid, but a sudden sinking feeling warned her that this man was not so easily handled as her first visitor of the day had been. "What has brought you here, Master Eric?" Katherine asked a third time, keeping her voice calm. "The other reason—beyond your curiosity."

"Can you not guess it, Mistress Katherine?" the man had the effrontery to respond. "You seem clever enough."

Katherine felt as though an obstruction had leapt suddenly into her throat to choke her. She overcame it enough to say in a low voice that wavered slightly, "Who are you? And what do you want of me?"

"I am sometimes called the Viking," the shipwright replied, looking at her with cool gray eyes, "and I have come to collect on Josef's account."

___ Chapter 2 ___

Katherine's eyes locked with the Viking's. She held his stare steadily and took the announcement with little outward display of emotion. Her face was palest ivory in the candlelight, her chiseled features immobile. Her breast rose and fell more rapidly than usual, but there were no other signs of alarm. With a turn of mirthless humor, Katherine wondered silently whether Emma's warning to leave town had not come an hour too late, rather than six days too early.

At first she considered denying any business association with Josef but immediately dismissed the idea. The man opposite her must have had a fair idea of the way things stood for him to have come this far. He might even, somehow, have gathered the full sum of it already. How he came by such information was a riddle she could not at the moment solve, but she was sure that he would not be diverted from the trail at this point. Katherine had her pride. She would not demean herself by feigning ignorance of the Viking's purpose in coming to her.

"Please excuse my surprise! And allow me to congratulate you on your good health," she said. Her voice sounded normal, and she was pleased. "I had believed—and perhaps many others shared this mistaken belief—that you were dead. I can see, of course, that you are very much alive."

The Viking leaned back easily in his chair and stretched his long legs out before him. She looked absurdly young, he thought, for all the cool courage she was displaying. Dispassionately surveying her, the Viking admired the handsome picture she presented. Had the circumstances been different, he might have been deceived by her remarkable beauty and been led astray by her subtle allure. But the circumstances were not different, and he thought, somewhat contemptuously, that her air of innocence might very easily fool other people.

"I am," he replied, "but I wasn't aware that my disappearance had been interpreted for the worst."

"No?" Katherine said. "Were you not in the Michaelmas gale, as so many thought? Or is that another piece of the misinformation?"

"I was in the storm," he affirmed. "My vessel sank, and no cargo was retrieved from it. We managed to save all the men, except two."

Katherine frowned slightly. "But—let me see—that was six or eight months ago already. Why did you wait so long to come looking for Josef? Were you cast adrift all this time?"

"No, I was in prison."

When Katherine found her voice again, all she could utter was "Well!" Then, cautiously, "The Tower of London?"

He nodded.

"So you were finally brought to justice for having cheated the Royal Exchequer out of port duties all these years," she said.

"I am not so clumsy as to be caught at that," he said coolly. "No, it was rather that some of my opinions on King John were considered extreme. Treasonous, in fact."

"And now you have broken out," she said. Her voice held a grudging respect.

"You flatter me." The Viking laughed. "I fear that I obtained my freedom in a most ordinary way. I was released."

Katherine was wary. "You must have friends in high places," she remarked, "to have been released after being charged with treason."

"I prefer to think that it was discovered that I had been falsely accused."

"Then you count yourself among King John's supporters?"

The Viking shook his head. "I could hardly support a king who has made a personal enemy nearly every day of his life," he said with some scorn. "A king who puts a diabolical ingenuity into the performance of familiar royal tyrannies. In any case, I do not think John will remain long upon the throne he no longer deserves."

"Then you side with those who want Louis of France to wear the English crown," she suggested as innocently as she could.

His long, penetrating look brought a wash of color to her pale cheeks. "I did not come here to discuss politics," he said at last, "but money." His deep voice played across her nerves. "Josef owed me a good deal, but Josef is dead. All is not lost, of course, to my way of thinking, for you have always stood behind Josef. I have come to collect."

He dared her with his eyes to deny it. She could see now that evasion would not serve. Her wits would not carry her through this time, and she was unnerved.

There was nothing for it but to meet him head-on. She said directly, "How much did Josef owe you? I fear that I have forgotten."

"One hundred marks." His voice was level. "I do not charge interest."

The silks had been plentiful and of the first quality. One hundred marks, she recalled very well, had been the price, fine and fair. She felt herself sink in deeper than ever. Her one thought now was to face this disaster with dignity. But one hundred marks!

"I do not have it," she said. The words caught in her throat. "Nor anything near it."

The Viking preserved an unnerving silence, his face shuttered, his eyes hooded.

"You must give me time," she continued, trying to keep the desperation out of her voice.

"There is no time," he said. "But you have something else that I want, something I will take in exchange."

Katherine froze. The yellow light flickered across the Viking's face, and what she saw there filled her with fear.

Everything about the man was lean and unyielding, tempered like the keen edge of the dagger he wore thrust in his belt. Katherine lowered her eyes and contemplated her slim, white hands upon the table, one crossed placidly over the other.

She was not to be mistress of her destiny, after all. She had, it seemed, been blissfully unaware of the storm gathering around her in the past weeks. She now saw clearly how events had rushed together, hurtling from all directions, to break over her head with the fury of a North Sea gale. However, she hardly paused to consider her present predicament. Instead, that fateful day of six years before sprang involuntarily to mind. Back beyond her arrival in York, back beyond the filth and sickness of the road that had brought her here, back even beyond the indignities she had suffered at the Royal Court in London, her mind's eye captured the day her long journey had begun. She remembered not the blood flowing crimson, nor the bodies of family and servants littering the castle grounds, nor the stench of decay on that bright, black summer's day in France. Her memory fastened with haunting clarity on the thin thread of a voice, a frail rustling from the depths of her mother's throat, as quiet and dry as autumn leaves, while she lay dying in her eldest daughter's arms: "Keep heart, Katherine. Promise me to do what is right for Sybille."

And it had brought her to this. Katherine knew that there was a price to be paid for everything. She was going to have to pay dearly now if she wanted to continue to protect Sybille from all of life's hardships and rigors, if she wanted to succeed in buying back Sybille's rightful place in the world. Katherine had been clever and nimble enough to have eluded Mauleon all this time while pursuing her goal, but now the Viking had come. He did not look as if he could be put off with feminine wiles or the entreaties of a poor, defenseless woman. Katherine had knowingly accepted the risks of trying to make her way alone in a man's world. It was her misfortune that the Viking had arrived to serve her the final humiliation.

She looked up again and sustained distinct shock at the hard, challenging light in his eyes. She had a quick suspicion that he was daring her to offer herself to him in exchange for her debt. Her cheeks flushed that he would think her so bold, and so it was that she said with a slight tremor, "What is it that you want?"

He smiled slightly and surprised her yet again. "Your ship."

"My ship?" she echoed blankly.

"It is yours, is it not? Aye, so I thought. I have need of a seaworthy vessel at the moment, and one hundred marks will easily buy a share of yours."

Katherine's instincts bristled in protest of this idea. She grasped at the first straw. "Surely you have other ships!" she argued. "After all the tales of the great Viking I've heard over the years, I cannot believe that you do not already own a fleet!"

The Viking cordially invited her to believe what she liked. "My ship lies at the bottom of the North Sea, as I have said, and at the risk of wounding my vanity I will mention that reputations such as mine are usually exaggerated."

He might have also mentioned that she was in no position to bargain but did not. Something was amiss in the Viking's demand, Katherine thought, something that had little to do with her debt or the use of her ship or even her own self. She had recovered a measure of poise. She would not give in, simply at his asking.

"My ship is worth far more than one hundred marks," she said steadily. "I would be a fool to let you have it for a mere trifling."

"A trifling? A moment ago you calculated the sum as far beyond your reach. Have you something else to offer me in payment? Something I might deem worth one hundred marks?" He looked at her in a measuring way, as though he were appraising her worth.

The challenge was unmistakable this time. Katherine fought down the blush staining her cheeks. Enough men in York, eligible and otherwise, had been attracted to her for her to recognize the particular warm look in a man's eyes when they fell upon the woman of his fancy. She had long since learned how to deflect these attentions. However, the Viking did not appear to have fallen victim to her charms, and she did not know how best to counter this man. She was all the more vexed with herself to find that, while warm regards from other men did not have the power to affect her, the Viking's cold evaluation of her assets should so perversely fluster her.

With as much dignity as she could muster she said, "I have nothing else to offer you."

"It seems, then, that we must come to terms," he replied with a cool smile and a maddening hint of mockery in his voice. "I am not an unreasonable man and am not asking you to hand over your ship to me in its entirety. Did I not say that I had come about the job? You need a sailor now, and one hundred marks should buy me a share of the ship and the right to sail it for you."

Again Katherine's instincts warned of danger. Where that danger lay she could not begin to guess. "A share," she repeated. "I am not familiar with the notion."

"I sail for you. We split the profits," he explained. "It is a partnership. Such arrangements are becoming fashionable in these difficult times, I believe."

"But my trade is very small," she protested. "It is hardly worth your while."

"I know just how small an operation you have, and that is what I like best about it," he countered swiftly, then paused before he continued. "Satisfy my curiosity once again, mistress! Josef's business with me last September was the first I had had with him, and I rarely agree to supply before I am paid. He was very convincing—with such an honest face, by all accounts! But now you have no money. Tell me: Did you intend to pay me in the end?"

Katherine's honor was at stake. "Of course," she said at once. "It is only that since then, thinking you were dead, I invested heavily in the drapers' guild. Many of the wool merchants had also lost much in the Michaelmas gale and needed my cash. They have not yet sufficiently recovered, however, for my investment there to have yielded the return I expected."

"Worse luck for you," he commented indifferently. "Now, what name do you trade by in the drapers' guild?"

Katherine exchanged glances for the first time with Emma. "I do not precisely understand you," she said.

His expression was derisive, and his anger lent a frightening quality to his gravelly voice. "Let us agree at the outset not to insult each other's understanding. We both know the ways of this world. So do not think to convince me that you have invested in the guild under the name of Katherine!"

Her anger met his. She would not be cowed. "Do you truly propose to go, cool as you please, to the drapers' guild on the morrow to pick up where Josef left off? Surely you must be known here."

"I rarely come so far inland and never on business," he answered curtly.

"But how can you simply adopt my banner? Or is it that you are still supposed to be dead? Do not tell me that you are not well-known as the Viking on the coast!"

"Not by anyone of consequence," he replied, his anger well pronounced. "I begin to repeat myself, mistress, when I say that I have never made the mistake of exposing myself! Like you, I never do business directly. Circumstances have changed in the past six-month, however, making it necessary for me to come out and trade openly in York. No one knows me here, and I will still be working indirectly, in a manner of speaking, this time through you. Few things could suit my purposes better!" He leaned forward and rapped out, "What is your trade name?"

This time his tone brooked no refusal. Her eyes sparkled a challenge, but her instinct for preservation got the better of her spurt of temper. "Leofwyn," she replied, taking this minor defeat poorly in stride.

The Viking looked curiously satisfied and sat back in his chair. "Very well," he said, and added almost absently, "I will be able to begin again within the next fortnight."

"But what if the ship has suffered damage?"

"Your ship is most likely riding quietly to her anchors in Thanet harbor—a place you know well enough," he replied, favoring her with a keen glance, "and I could repair any damage there might be."

"Ah, yes! I was forgetting the advantages of being a shipwright as well!" she retorted. "And the ship's contents?"

"Looted, no doubt, by now."

Katherine's last hopes of being able to pay Mauleon off anytime soon were dashed. The game had played itself out, and the pieces on the board were stacked against her: She was checked and in danger of losing all. She had no choice, really, but to cast her lot with the Viking.

This much he must have known before he ever entered her house. Without waiting for her reply he made a motion to rise, stating with finality, "The matter is settled."

Katherine rose with him. "Far from it, Master Eric!" she responded with spirit. "You speak of a partnership, and I have agreed to it. I am not so green, however, that I ignore the question of percentages, nor—I am sure you will agree! —does one hundred marks buy anything near a controlling share of the profits. You would do well to settle for a tenth."

The Viking raised a brow at this bold move, but his face gave away nothing of his thoughts. "I am not a charitable institution," he replied smoothly, "and reject out of hand any offers of tithing. We'll discuss the matter when I return. You may expect me within the next two weeks." He slanted her a rapier glance. "Mayhap we will also discuss how it comes that you enjoy the blessings of the archbishop on this house, or how it comes that you run a sailing operation in the first place!"

Katherine was content to defer the discussion of financial matters and so said only, "Don't let your curiosity carry you too far!"

Church bells rang out vespers and the end of the workday. Since Emma was responsible for the household's supper, she rose and crossed to the door. She paused there, waiting for some sign from her mistress.

Katherine did not glance away from the Viking but raised a hand to keep Emma in the room a moment longer. An uncomfortable thought had occurred to her, and she wanted it cleared before the Viking left. "Josef took his room and meals here," she said suddenly.

The Viking looked down at her, his dark face inscrutable.

"His room is taken now," she said.

"A pity," he said. His eyes had narrowed, and the tiny blaze in their gray depths might have been anger. He proceeded to inform her that he had already engaged rooms at the Blue Swan Inn for when he would be in York.

He looked suddenly as if he, too, had some matters to clear up with his new partner, and so he ordered Emma out of the room to attend to whatever needed doing in the kitchen. To Katherine's surprise and irritation Emma quietly obeyed him and left the door discreetly open. When her footsteps had died away, the atmosphere of the room altered subtly, and Katherine had a sense of being bereft and forlorn.

The Viking leaned casually against the table, relaxed and completely at his ease. Katherine felt the full force of the potential for violence in his broad shoulders, in the slate of his eyes, and in the edge of his voice, a violence that was even more menacing to her for being so carefully controlled.

"We need a moment's privacy to discuss things of mutual concern," he said into the unnatural silence.

Katherine lifted her chin. "It could have been said in the presence of my woman," she replied, with a flimsy courage at best.

The Viking shook his head slowly and closed the space between them by a pace. Her impulse was to retreat, but she stood her ground. Her heart beat rapidly.

"She would be a most unwelcome third in this conversation," he said, and with the next breath, "Do not leave York."

Hazel eyes widened. She had already devised several plans, one of which was immediate departure. "The thought had not occurred to me," she lied valiantly.

He looked down at her. "No?" Then, abruptly, "Are you in debt?"

"In debt?"

The Viking placed hands on hips. "Are you in the habit, mistress, of repeating everything I say?"

She found this turn in conversation insulting, but worse was to come. "Why do you ask?"

"That is no answer."

"I know of no reason why I should give you one."

"If I am at the helm of your ship," the Viking said, "it must be unencumbered."

"My debts are my own," she said.

"You misunderstand: I am not giving you a choice in the matter. You must be free and clear of debt in order for me to operate as I wish."

It occurred to her that he could command a larger percentage of their future profits if he were to assume some of her initial debts. She hoped that this thought could not be read on her face when she raised her eyes to his.

"If the contents of the ship have been looted," she said evenly, "then I must suppose that I am in debt."

He confirmed her suspicion with his next words. "The precise figure of which is another item we shall discuss when next we meet! I advise you to deal honestly with me or there will be the devil to pay!"

Katherine had heard quite enough. "Is there anything else?" she asked coolly, feeling sure that all had been said between them.

"One last warning, mistress, since it is apparent from the muddle of your affairs that you stand in sore need of advice," he said unexpectedly. "You would be a fool to let Mauleon know of our partnership."

Katherine was entirely incapable of response. He had slipped in under her guard, and the surprise he read on her face let him know it too.

"There is no mystery to it," he went on in hard tones. "So you may put your mind at rest! I happened to see Mauleon leave this street just as I arrived. I followed him for a bit, until I saw that he was headed straight for York Castle. In all events, you have just confirmed what I could only surmise: He had, indeed, come from this house."

She said the first thing that came to mind. "I thought that you were not well-known here or on the coast!" she flashed. "You have shown me your hand as well, by admitting acquaintance with someone of consequence!"

"I am well-acquainted with many people of consequence, though not in my role as the Viking," he shot back. "You would do well to remember it."

Katherine was goaded now. "Do you threaten me, Master Eric?" she said brazenly. "A word of warning might serve you too! We might rub along better in the future when you come to realize that I, as Mistress Katherine, am not entirely without distinction or protection in this city!"

The Viking put his own construction on these words. His gray eyes were stormy. "Distinguished though the name Mauleon might be," he said, "he'll not bestow it upon you in the end."

Katherine had been so much in the habit of fending off Mauleon's entirely unwelcome advances that the import of these words fell upon her ears with stunning effect. The quick numbness that had come with shock thawed just as swiftly, prickling at her nerves like a frostbitten finger coming back to life. The insult had come so unexpectedly that she was unable to understand fully her reaction to it.

It would have given her the greatest pleasure to have vented her fury with a swift slap across his face and to have aired her opinion of his manners and morals. These desires were followed almost immediately by a resolve to get back at him in some mysterious but highly satisfying way. However, to plead her innocence was certainly no way of doing so, and she knew that it would not be in her best interest to slap his face.

Then she felt tears of chagrin well up in her eyes. Before she could disgrace herself in his presence, she tethered her fury and mastered her voice enough to say, with icy civility, "I see that we understand each other perfectly. I bid you good eventide, Master Eric."

"Then we are off to an excellent start. Good eventide, mistress," he replied, his voice as hard as nails. He favored her with one last regard, bowed slightly, and was gone.

Katherine stood rooted to the spot where he had left her. The tears that had threatened the moment before were suddenly swept away by her anger. She would rather be pilloried on the main square for her trading practices—along with one or two other prominent citizens of York she could name —than shed a tear over that arrogant, insulting, hateful man! A partnership, he proposed. Impossible! Her emotions ran freely from hot rage to profound mortification, but she was unable to decide what angered her more: the fact that she had been in no position to avoid a partnership with this man or the suspicion that had she offered herself to him in payment for the debt, he would have turned her down and enjoyed doing so.

After several long minutes of dwelling on thoughts of revenge against the Viking, Katherine realized that her hands were clenched tightly at her sides. She uncramped her fingers slowly and brought her turbulent thoughts into some order. If tears had momentarily come into her eyes, she reasoned that it was perfectly understandable. Her present state was not a direct response to the Viking, however insulting he may have been. No man had such power over her. No, she reassured herself, she would never have reacted so violently to him had he not come wth news of Josef's death and negotiated—nay, demanded—this outrageous partnership. And all this on the heels of Mauleon's unspoken threat!

However, she had banished Mauleon from her thoughts. An irrational determination to get even with the Viking in whatever way was open to her fully occupied her mind. She would take great delight in showing that arrogant sailor that she was every bit as bad as he imagined her to be and that he had, in fact, drastically underestimated her.

Emma found Katherine some time later staring abstractedly into the middle distance, heedless of the candles burned down to their sockets. Emma registered surprise. "Mistress Katherine! I have been looking all over for you! We've put back dinner to find you! I was worried that maybe you had left or—or—but I did not think to find you still here!"

Katherine turned in Emma's direction but did not reply.

Emma had never seen her mistress's eyes glitter such a brilliant green and could not immediately interpret the look on Katherine's face. Emma chose the indirect approach. "Well! It seems that our Little Anna has fully recovered from her long bout with the grippe! She was still looking very peaked this morning but took a nap this afternoon, and then her appetite almost fully returned at suppertime. She made a very good meal. What do you say to that?"

Katherine, however, had nothing to say to it. She was devoted to the care of homeless and maltreated children, and little Anna was a particular favorite of hers; but for the moment the gross behavior of the Viking possessed her mind to the exclusion of all else.

"I shall serve him out for this, Emma," she replied, her voice quavering with emotion. "Mark my words!"

Emma was slightly taken aback. "What do you mean? I would have said that the miracle we had been hoping for had occurred, after all."

Katherine's abstraction was instantly dispelled. She laughed at what she took to be a fine irony. "Any more miracles such as this last one and we shall be well and truly ruined!"

"How can you say so when the Viking has come to answer all of our prayers?"

It was Katherine's turn for surprise. "You are not serious! Come, Emma. You have always called yourself the cautious one. Surely you are jesting!"

"And what objections do you have toward him?"

"I simply don't like the way he looks."

"I saw nothing wrong with him."

"Neither did Agatha or Bethrica or even Johanna, I warrant. And as for that hussy Maria! I was ashamed at the eyes she made at him. If she did not learn so quickly and have such clever fingers, I would turn her off. But as it is—" Katherine broke off to compose herself and then said more calmly, "That is precisely my point. All the other difficulties aside, I do not think it wise to have that . . . that lion running tame in my house."

"He would not be here much," Emma objected. "No more than Josef was and probably a good deal less, since you denied him bed and board here." Emma paused. "I do not think that he appreciated your refusal of him on that score, when he did not ask it of you."

"No, indeed, and he let me know it—with a vengeance!"

"Did he—did he make improper advances after I left?"

"Improper advances!" Katherine exclaimed. "Oh, no! That is Mauleon's specialty. The Viking's thoughts do not lie in *that* direction."

"I didn't think so," Emma replied, relieved. "Count it as a blessing."

"I will," Katherine said, somewhat doubtfully.

"What else did he say to you after I left?"

Katherine had taken hold of herself now. She recited with

perfect sangfroid, "I am not to leave York. The Viking is to pay off all my debts. I am not to tell Mauleon of our partnership."

"He knows Mauleon!" Emma gasped.

"He has informed me that he knows many men of consequence in York," Katherine retorted hotly.

Emma's plain face was carefully blank. "And he is to pay off your debt to Mauleon?"

"Yes, if you please! That is, I did not say that I was in debt to Mauleon, but I am sure that he must guess it." Katherine paused a moment in thought. "But perhaps I can rectify my debt before next week. Yes, it would be best not to let Mauleon know of Josef's death. I wonder if that will work? If I . . ." Katherine's words trailed off.

Emma recognized Katherine's air of speculative preoccupation but did not probe. Instead, she said casually, "Things could be much worse, by my reckoning."

Katherine cocked a mobile brow. "I'm not so sure about that. A man like the Viking is best handled at arm's length. I would like him almost anywhere but in my employ—such as it is!—and preferably many leagues from York."

"I have never known you to take such prejudice before."

"And I have never known you to be so accepting!" Katherine replied. "The man means mischief."

"How can you say so? I think Josef recognized in him the kind of man we need. He's as good as can be expected to replace Josef. Better, in fact."

"We have no assurance that Josef had him in mind as his successor," Katherine answered firmly, "or that Josef died in a brawl, or that Josef died at all, for that matter!"

"Do you doubt his death?"

"No," Katherine said, shaking her head. "He's dead. The Viking did not come bearing false information. It is not entirely clear to me, however, what he does know or why he came."

"Why can it not simply be that he needs the money you owe him as well as a ship, and that he was with Josef near the time of his death? The Viking heard some things perhaps and, seeing an opportunity, seized it."

Katherine shook her head again. "It does not add up.

Does the Viking look to you like a man who has fallen upon hard times?"

"No," Emma conceded, "but what do you suspect him of?"

"Everything!" Katherine said. "Nothing! Oh, I don't know, and that is the problem."

"But you do know what Mauleon is about, so you may take your choice between the devil you know and the devil you don't."

Katherine considered this. "I still say the Viking means to do us mischief. What it is, I cannot say. And even if he does not, our partnership will prove far from comfortable. He and I are not destined to agree on much of anything, I fear."

"How can you say so? He obviously agreed with what you were saying earlier about it not being a good moment to leave York," Emma said, all innocence.

A militant spark lit Katherine's eye. "That was not for *him* to decide! And, besides, is there anything else we are ever likely to agree upon?" Katherine challenged.

"Well," said Emma slyly, "the Viking does not seem to like Mauleon any more than you do."

Katherine expelled her next breath on a rueful laugh. "All right, Clever Emma, you win. We are better off with the Viking—but only in the short run." Katherine cleared her mind. "Now, what about little Anna? You say she is doing better?"

Emma smiled, satisfied that she had brought Katherine around on the subject of the Viking. "Anna—oh, yes! Her color came back, so right before supper Marta put her in the tub and scrubbed her until she shone. And then, as I said, she ate all of the oatmeal soup and dilligrout that Cook made up especially for her. I'm sure you must be pleased."

"I am," Katherine said. "Very pleased, indeed, and I'll make a special effort to go and tuck her in this evening." With the most immediate of her problems solved, Katherine turned her thoughts to the matter nearest her heart. "And Sybille? Where has she been all afternoon? You were going to tell me something about her just before the Viking's arrival."

Emma affected surprise. "Was I? I thought she went to

market with Marta. That is what she told me, in any case. Come, mistress. Supper has been laid for you these many minutes past. You must have a fair hunger after the trials of the day."

_____ Chapter 3 _____

When rose fingers were spreading across the ghostly gray light of dawn the next day, Katherine was already fully awake. The night had restored her outward calm and brought her counsel. She had decided on a course of action which was sure to infuriate the Viking and which made Emma, when she learned of the errand, shake her head with deep misgiving. Katherine rallied the older woman by observing, "We can afford it now that we're soon to be back in business. It won't harm the Viking to learn a lesson or two, so let's not count the cost."

Shortly after sunup, when the dawn bells had struck, Katherine left her house. She headed to an address she reserved for only the direst emergency, an undistinguished house in Coney Street. She was pleased to meet on the streets at that hour only sleepy maidservants going to the wells with buckets and basins. She left the establishment some time later with a feeling of satisfaction and a purseful of coins and proceeded to the second order of business for the day. Entering the tangle of narrow streets, she made her way toward the center.

York was built to a swarming tightness and packed inside its thick bow of wall. The sun had begun to trace its arc across the sky and was shining down on the merchants who were rattling open their shutters and unbolting their doors to the commerce of a new day. Katherine threaded her way past St. Nicholas Shambles where the butchers were swilling offal and blood into the guttters and skewering their fresh slabs of meat on iron hooks for display. Women in wimples were hanging great sheets of cloth dripping from dyeing vats to dry on lines which crossed open yards. Potters pumped their wheels and brought shapeless lumps of clay to sudden life. Glassblowers fired and blew and twirled long pipes, and blacksmiths sweated and stoked and bellowed white-hot fires. The hammers of the ironmongers and the coppersmiths rang out an arhythmic staccato. She passed painters, paid in advance by the well-to-do burghers of York, who were putting out to dry their glistening wet signs: the crescent moon for the mercer; the camel for the grocer; the bush for the vintner; the three gilded pills for the apothecary; the unicorn for the goldsmith; the dolphin for the fishmonger; and, of course, the ram for the draper. She strode by the fripperers who dealt in rags and old clothes and the rakerers who cleaned the streets, noting that even these poor men, on such a crisp day with the winds blowing away the winter, had shed their bulky cloaks and boasted now wool tabards and tunics.

As she walked, Katherine could not suppress a smile. Wool was king in York and took better care of its subjects than did the hated monarch John. Durable, desirable Yorkshire wool was bringing cash into the drapers' tills from all over the world. York thrived on wool. York teemed with the ram of the draper. York droned with the steady clack of apprentices, working at heddle and shuttle, and reed and treadle, weaving the enduring cloth for the demands of an expanding foreign trade. All of York profited, and the citizens wore their wealth on their backs. The drapers, however, those smug wool merchants, were the most prominent, parading the streets in fine supertunics of burgundy, blue, and yellow, with tallysticks dangling from their wide leather belts to keep track of sales and purchases. Katherine was on nodding terms with quite a number of them. She greeted various of these merchants in the course of her walk through town and paused now and again for amiable chat.

It was easy enough to learn the talk of the town. The topics of trade and taxes, and the rival merits and demerits of King John and Louis of France, bubbled easily to the lips of the merchants when speaking with one of their own. Katherine, with her agreeable ways, was no longer considered an outsider. She had learned through such idle talk in the past twelve-month that many of the wealthy burghers of York seriously entertained the idea of joining the rebel baron overlords in trying to throw John and his brood off the throne and to honor the long-standing claim of Louis to rule the rich island kingdom.

It was an unusual alliance between town merchant and landed overlord, for the self-interests of the two classes diverged so sharply. The overlords declaimed loudly of broken honor and disrespect and the way it should be between liege lord and loyal subject. These rebel barons, among the most powerful in the land, had sought to resolve their differences with the king to whom they had sworn fealty in an honorable way and face-to-face. They had tried the year before, in June of 1215 at the field of Runnymede, to bring to justice the king who had trampled so thoroughly on their baronial rights. They had succeeded in obtaining John's signature at the end of a document called the Magna Charta, but it had been a brief victory. John, in his fury and humiliation, had lashed out with troops, and civil war had erupted.

To the townsmen, however, honor and loyalty under the code of chivalry meant little; and when it came to kings, they had learned since the days of William the Conqueror that one Norman ruler was as arrogant as the next. The merchants attacked instead the ruinous financial policies of the seventeen years of John's reign; and with the universal contempt the king had earned for his cruelties, he could no longer command nor expect respect or obedience from his subjects. The citizens of York, lying far beyond John's easy grasp, had no intention of throwing their good money after bad royal taxes. They would happily line their pockets while John's kingdom crumbled about his ears. Yet these Saxon merchants possessed an instinct for order. They longed for the stability that would come with a respected leader who was supported both by united forces behind him and by gold in his coffers. That man they had decided on was Louis of France.

Katherine had convinced herself that the military force of

the rebel barons backed by the cash in hand of the merchants had every chance of placing the English crown on Louis's head. Although all was not going York's way in the civil war, the citizens of York stood firm in their wish to see John dethroned. The inhabitants of this strategic northern city were a blend of Saxon and Norseman, a strong independent race still unbroken to the yoke of the Norman conquerors who had invaded a century and a half before. Katherine had come to respect these hardheaded, hardworking town folk. She had placed her confidence in her fellow townspeople, and she would not bet against them. How York's fortunes went, so would go Katherine's.

On the day the Cathars had slashed their way through her stepfather's castle, Katherine de Lunais never could have foretold that six years later she would be so close to fulfilling the promise she had made to her mother. She had not achieved her success in York, however, by dwelling on the past. Katherine had all but suppressed the memory of how it had been to hide in a closet with her arms clamped around her young sister, one hand over Sybille's eyes, the other over her mouth, and to gaze, unblinking, at the slaughter in the hall through a chink in the closet door. It was only in her deepest dreams that she relived the long, hot, motionless, suffocating lifetime she spent in that closet waiting; waiting until the scrape of spurs on stone and the ring of steel had died. Only at times of crisis did she recall how she had emerged from her hiding place, to weep and to whimper, weak with horror at the extent of the carnage, and to reach, finally, her dying mother's side.

She had lived a decade in those few hours, witness to the murderous fury that the fanatical religious cause of Catharism had inspired. Certainly bad things had happened to her on the frenzied flight from France. She had lost to fever all save two of her servants who had been spared the Cathars' blades. She had seen the few family jewels she still possessed sink during the Channel crossing. She had lived to suffer the ostracism of the illustrious name Roncevaux at the court of London, for John had no interest in refugees, even very noble ones. However, when something bad happened to her during those two years of flight, she would close her

eyes and see herself in the castle, hiding in the closet, and
what was bad did not seem so bad. Finally, when a series of
good things came her way shortly after her arrival in York,
she began to exorcise from her waking existence those visions of blood and lifeless eyes in heads without bodies.
Deep down she knew that these restless ghosts would not be
properly buried until she had seen Sybille assume her noble
title and position.

That day at Castle Roncevaux changed Katherine's life
forever. The seventeen years of her placid girlhood were cut
off from memory. She was no longer the charming and duti-
ful court maiden who had just been flattered by a very respectable betrothal and who was looking forward to the
satisfying life for which she had been groomed. The events
of history had forced her to use very different and remarkable talents which would have, otherwise, lain fallow. The
twists of fate had taken this lively, carefree girl and forged a
new woman: a woman with a head for cool calculation, a
woman with a flair for business and bargaining and subterfuge and, above all, a woman with an extraordinary capacity
for survival.

Sybille was Katherine's half sister through the same
mother. Katherine's father, Henri de Lunais, was a minor
chevalier from the petty nobility. When Katherine was seven
years old, her widowed mother had made a brilliant marriage to the Duc de Roncevaux and had quickly presented
her new husband with a baby daughter. From the day of her
birth Sybille was the bud of a perfect flower, petted and
cosseted and idolized. The duke easily betrothed her to a
German prince when she was only five years old. She was
destined, so it seemed, for a life as agreeable as Katherine's,
though considerably more magnificent. From the moment
Katherine shielded her sister's eyes from the Cathars' black,
bloodthirsty souls, she had guarded and protected Sybille
with a single-minded intensity. Sybille was not to go hungry
during the two years of vagrancy before settling in York. She
was not to be cold or to be drenched in the cursed English
rains. She was not to suffer. Thus far Katherine had succeeded in keeping her flower sheltered so that she might
open into a perfect bloom. The hoped-for takeover of Eng-

land by King Louis should come at exactly the right time. Sybille was about to turn seventeen, and Katherine was near to buying back Sybille's rightful place in the noble world to which she had been born. Katherine had heard enough of Louis to think that if she solidly backed his cause with all of her disposable wealth, he would reward her by recognizing Sybille.

Katherine had put aside thoughts of regaining her own place in that same world for so long that she never considered her own relatively debased position. If it had ever occurred to Emma to ask her mistress why this was so, Katherine would have replied that at the age of three and twenty, and with two years of flight and degradation and four years of making money and deceiving her adopted neighbors behind her, Katherine de Lunais of Castle Roncevaux was as ineligible now for a return to genteel courtly life as the commonest townswoman.

Very few people in York were aware that Mistress Katherine the Broiderer was deeply involved in both civic and royal affairs. One person who shared a part of her secrets was York's very handsome and most debonair lord mayor. He cut an elegant figure strolling through town with his shock of silver hair and a sweeping black cloak. He met Katherine that morning as she made her way through the streets and bestowed on her his charming, conspiratorial smile. Katherine returned the expression blandly and escaped him at the next corner, the city center.

High Petergate was clotted with market day traffic. The cry of hawkers constantly competed with the rumble and clatter of cartwheels bumping over cobbles and the grunts and squeals of hogs and pigs. Crates of silvery fish were crammed next to muslin sacks spilling yellow-green vegetables and jostled with rush mats displaying golden balls of sweet butter and brown eggs in straw baskets. The smell of fresh bread, hot meat pies, and the sweet-sour scent of brewing permeated the air. Katherine, long since accustomed to the confusion, easily negotiated this busy, brawling marketplace and was almost to her goal when she spied a man whose acquaintance she had a calculated intention to cultivate.

Geoffrey Taverner was a hale, rubicund giant who kept a bright, spruce inn called the Blue Swan. He was engaged in energetic discussion with a greengrocer over the question of weights and honest scales and a tuppence worth of beans. When the business was happily concluded, Katherine arranged to accost the taverner, as if by chance, and he saluted her heartily.

"Now, with the fine traveling weather," Katherine said after they had exchanged the usual pleasantries, "I imagine that the Blue Swan is enjoying good custom. What an interesting profession you have to meet so many of the visitors to York!"

The taverner responded with alacrity to this gambit. "Oh, aye, Mistress Katherine, it is so! Why, just yesterday an impressive fellow came to the Blue Swan. Not but what I thought him a plain lad when I first clapped eyes on him!" the taverner added with a childlike scruple for accuracy. "But, oh, no! Nothing plain about the man, if you're wanting my opinion. He might not dress like some of the town peacocks—who don't have a penny to their name for it!— but he has an air about him. And such a way! Not at all rough-and-tumble, as I had first thought. Not offensively smooth or above himself, either, but forthright, he was, in making his wishes known. Trust a good taverner to size a man up! Yes, an altogether impressive fellow in his own particular way! And with a purse to match it! A silver coin he gave me for lodgings! Oh, aye, an impressive fellow!"

Katherine acted suitably impressed and inquired casually about the man's name and origin.

"Shipwright," the taverner replied. "Easiest thing in the world to remember. By the look of him, a perfect Dane, and what else would he be doing but building ships? Except sailing 'em, choose how! From Stamford Bridge, I think he said. Nay, then, think on, he's from the coast. Stands to reason. Ah! Scarborough. Oh, aye, he's from Scarborough."

Katherine's polite air of inquiry was all the encouragement the taverner needed. He continued on a piece of professional wisdom. "A good trencherman too. You can tell a lot about a man by how he eats. Why, I see it every day. Gratifying it was to see the shipwright do justice to the meal my

Petronella set before him last evening. He came back late—must have attended vespers—and with such an appetite. Nothing left of the baked fish or the savory beans or the small ale when he stood up from the table. For I can tell you that my Petronella sets a very tasty supper, even during this Lenten season. But he couldn't be tempted with a dulcet after the meal. Not even my Petronella's frumenty. An uncommon good dish, if I may say so. Aye, not a sweet eater, the shipwright. You can tell a lot about a man by what he eats."

"Have you never before seen the shipwright in York?" Katherine asked.

"Nay, then. A newcomer. And a good thing it was, too, that he was directed to the Blue Swan with decent Saxon fare and not to Lemoine's," the taverner pursued. Katherine, along with any other inhabitant of York who might have happened to overhear this conversation, could predict to a certainty what was to come next. The taverner lowered his booming voice to a confidential thunder. "Lemoine's!" he exclaimed. "My main competition, as you'll be knowing, mistress. Now, you can't get a meal worth putting teeth to at Lemoine's. His wife can scarce dress a joint of meat fit to eat. She puts cream on 'em. *Sauces,* those Normans call it. Faugh! It's gravy what a body wants to taste with his flesh, say what you like!"

No reply was necessary, for Master Geoffrey continued along the lines of his favorite topic. "It's a good Saxon community, York. And so I ask, what are we needing with Normans? We'll be overrun with them soon enough with Lemoine and FitzAlwin, of course, and deBroc and Pontigny's four sons. Bless my soul! Not to mention the lord mayor. Well, he's mixed-blood, and he's none so bad, seeing as how he's not married and has no issue. Not that York's against outsiders. Why take yourself, Mistress Katherine, being from—where is it? Wales? Oh, aye! Now, I say, let's welcome them that wants to settle here and work for a living, like you do. But the Normans! Can't abide 'em! And not a one of them who can speak a proper phrase of the true tongue. It's like listening, as we say, to a frog croaking English." The taverner laughed from deep inside his chest and wiped his eyes of their merriment, obviously enjoying the jape every bit at this telling as at every other. "And so I ask you, what are we needing with Normans? Let 'em stay in London if they like it there so much. They've no business in York!"

"Very true, Master Taverner," Katherine replied. "But I'm curious. What did the shipwright say he was doing in York?"

The taverner knitted beetled brows. The cloud of a thought flitted across his brain, but the wisp was too high, and the down-to-earth taverner could not catch it. The cloud passed, and the taverner's brow cleared. "Well, now," he said cheerfully, "he must have come for a reason, but I'm not sure he told me."

Master Geoffrey's lively attention was then commanded by the appearance at his side of a boon companion on whose back he bestowed a clap that would have winded a lesser man.

Katherine bid York's garrulous inkeeper good morrow and stepped quickly across the street to the stylish shop of Webster, Webster and Company. She crossed the threshold in the manner of a person assured of her welcome.

Webster's was without doubt the most prosperous of the drapers, very smartly decked out and a little arrogant of its success. The vast salesroom was the result of several expansions, and the bolts of cloth were stacked from floor to ceiling and ranged by weave and price. Dominating the interior was a wide table from which hung bright shears on thin chains. One corner of the table was reserved for a haphazard array of swatches and musters atop which had been carelessly tossed a tallystick.

Katherine waved familiarly to the webster who nodded in return while hovering busily over a client. Master Robert was a stocky man of medium height and swathed in a length of scarlet velvet that swore violently with his ruddy good looks. The webstress herself came from the weaving room at the tinkle of the bell above the door to welcome Katherine personally to the establishment. Mistress Mathilda was a buxom dame in a costly homespun kirtle. Her face was as familiar and inviting as a yeasty bun, with black-currant eyes, licorice hair, and a character leavened with much good humor and fellow feeling.

From the union of the webstress and her husband had come, improbably, a tall youth who was hanging, bored, at the cash counter. Stephen Webster was an undeniably handsome young man who commanded the admiration of every unmarried maid in York and quite a few married damsels too: He was slim, almost willowy, with a pair of beautiful brown eyes, perfectly molded lips, and rings of chestnut gracing a noble brow.

Mistress Webster's eyes strayed briefly from Katherine to her son, for Stephen had flushed guiltily and shifted uncomfortably at Katherine's entrance to the shop. The next instant, Mathilda's eyes had turned again to Katherine, and she was smiling. However, Katherine did not miss the look the mother gave her son, nor did she misinterpret its significance, and she was doubly glad she had come.

Mistress Mathilda and Katherine both had too much restraint to discuss immediately the matter that was uppermost in their minds. They talked first of the embroidery work that Webster, Webster and Company had commissioned of Katherine's women. Mistress Mathilda liked doing business with Katherine. The Mistress Broiderer had, in Mathilda's rather influential opinion, agreeably frank ways when discussing money that blended nicely with her natural, well-bred air of authority; and if Mistress Katherine's background and reasons for being in York were something of a mystery, Mathilda was not one to question the ways of the benevolent God whose many gifts to York included a broiderer who produced superior French stitchery at such reasonable prices.

When the discussion of the embroidered altar cloth that Webster's had commissioned for the new minster was finished, Katherine asked, "And how goes the construction outside?"

"It's a plaguey nuisance!" the webstress responded, taking the cue and clucking her tongue. She drew Katherine in the direction of the leaded windows whose thick, irregular panes threw wavy morning shadows across the floor of polished wood. The webstress unlatched one of the windows and pushed it open with an indignant gesture.

"Just look!" she commanded.

Since Webster's sat upon this main square at High Petergate, the most elevated point of the city, Katherine had a fine view of the flock of swallow-tailed roofs, thatched and shingled, which fluttered gracefully above the winding streets. It was not this sight, however, which provoked the webstress but rather the large construction site opposite her shop. Katherine saw before her a miracle of scaffolding, ropes, and pulleys, forming a transparent hive in which buzzed the best stonecutters and masons in all of Yorkshire, while newfangled wheelbarrows crisscrossed the scene in a flurry of motion. In the middle of the activity, standing quietly, like the calm eye of the storm, was Walter de Grey, the very sere and senior Archbishop of York, surveying the erection of his beloved minster. It was to be the largest cathedral in England and of all Christendom, if the York citizens had their way. Several buttresses, those massive haunches, squatted impressively against a half-finished wall; and the nave, a semicircle facing east toward the rising sun and the Holy Land, appeared like an inverted scallop shell waiting to be fitted with its stained-glass panels. There was a great noise and a bustle with the construction, and everywhere was the dust of quarry-cut stone.

"I sweep three times a day now and dust almost continuously," the webstress expostulated. "There's no end to it! It's as though the dust from the minster seeps in through the walls. We won't be able to open the windows or doors come summer for fear of choking to death!"

"Oh, the disadvantages of having the best location in town," Katherine commented wryly.

The webstress chuckled. Then, in a lowered tone, "Another disadvantage is Stephen's easy access to the market. There's not a thing to be done about it. I can hardly rope him here all day. But——well!" She glanced over to Stephen and, seeing him well occupied with a new customer, continued, "Boys will be boys, as we say. And my Stephen has a roving eye, the fickle young cub! I don't want your Sybille to be hurt in the end. You know how it is!"

Katherine and Mistress Mathilda had arrived at a perfect understanding. Without ever having spoken plain words, they had agreed to quench the little spark that had been lit between Stephen and Sybille. The webstress had brought the matter to Katherine's attention, and Katherine had quickly agreed that this fancy had no future. The webstress stressed her son's fickle nature and volatility, and Katherine responded with murmurs of Sybille's tender years and general unsuitability. Katherine had never mentioned she knew that the websters had all but concluded a match between Stephen and Eleanora, the daughter of the richest brewer in town; Mistress Mathilda never observed aloud that Sybille's beauty would be powerful competition for plain, plump Eleanora. The Websters had their own plans for Stephen.

Katherine, in turn, had a brilliant future planned for Sybille, and it did not include involvement with a webster's son, no matter how prosperous the family may have been. Katherine did not for a moment believe she was harming her half sister, for she did not think that Sybille's affections had been earnestly engaged.

"Do you think they were together yesterday?" Katherine inquired. "Sybille was acting strangely at supper. We ate rather late, so perhaps it was only that she was peckish, but I fear . . . Emma thought Sybille had gone to market with Marta, but I am worried now that Sybille has been making herself a nuisance with Stephen."

"I'm sure of it, from what you say," Mistress Mathilda replied with a sorry shake of the head. "But I cannot say for a certainty that it is Sybille who is the nuisance! My Robert was as cross as two sticks when Stephen showed up late, as well, for his supper yesterday. It was all I could do to keep Robert's hands off Stephen! He was like to throttle the boy, and so I tell you, for Stephen came in spouting verses. 'Take thou this rose, O rose, since love's own flower it is'—or some such thing! Poetry, he calls it! And here were Master and Mistress Brewer already arrived with their Eleanora to take the meal with us. An awkward business, if you see what I mean!"

Katherine did. "What shall we do? Nothing is so attractive as forbidden fruit, and so to insist openly on keeping them apart will only make them go behind our backs!"

Mistress Mathilda nodded in agreement. "Stephen's father has his own solution if the problem continues. He has a mind to send Stephen on a wool-buying journey to the north if he does not begin to behave himself. I admit that Stephen has never had a grain of sense about him when it comes to business, but he's young and there's time yet to learn about the woof and the warp of turning a good deal. But my Robert is not so patient. Oh, no! He's a good man, my Robert, and the best husband and father imaginable. But he's got a flea in his ear about Stephen now, and what he had to say to Stephen's threat of joining a band of those traveling troo-ba-doors could have been heard late last night all the way to Jubbergate Street, I'm sure! And Robert's opinions on rhyming couplets—if that's what they're called—is not to be thought of, much less repeated! Robert says that the corruption of the young is what comes from having let Frenchmen in the city, and now they want to put a Frenchman on the throne again. But that is another matter altogether. Aye! My Robert intends to whip Stephen into shape, will he nill he!"

There was time for no more. A momentary lull in the shop had made Katherine and Mistress Mathilda conspicuous with their whisperings by the window. The webstress escorted Katherine to the door with some final words about the altar cloth.

"Oh, and by the by, Mistress Katherine!" the webstress said as a happy afterthought. "The strangest thing happened yesterday, and I've meant to tell you about it. A man came in here asking for Leofwyn. I was never so surprised! Well, now, I can see that you're wondering what that has to do with you. I was forgetting that Leofwyn was well before your time."

Katherine had looked up rather sharply at the mention of this name. A thrill of alarm ran up her spine. "Oh?" she said faintly at first, and then cleared her throat. "A man came in looking for . . . Leofwyn, did you say?"

"Aye. Leofwyn. The family that owned your house in Jubbergate Street," the webstress informed her. "Before King Richard's time, even before his father's time, bless Henry's soul, there were Leofwyns in York. They were bought out by Baruch—before the riots," she said meaningfully and a little sadly. "But, in any case, the Leofwyn family here died out long ago. A good Saxon name, that! And I'm thinking that there are still Leofwyns aplenty as far north as Tyne and Everic."

Katherine had had time to compose herself. "How interesting! But who was asking?" she queried with a casual interest.

"Eric Shipwright—or so he called himself."

"Or so he called himself?"

The webstress smiled. "Well, now, my Robert spoke with him—it would not have been proper for me to have engaged him in conversation, as much as I would have liked to! But Robert said, after the man had left, that he'd never yet seen a shipwright with such a fine eye for cloth. And the color, why, it was dyed-in-the-wool! From Flanders, his tunic, I'll wager! Though I told Robert that perhaps the shipwrights on the coast are more stylish than in York. The man said that he was from Scarborough." Her dark eyes twinkled. "We certainly don't have any shipwrights like that in York. No, indeed! That is to say, he's not handsome like my Stephen. Never think it. But so—how shall I explain it? The way the man walked in here and spoke with Robert, it was so—he was so—"

"Rude? Arrogant?" Katherine suggested helpfully. "Overbearing?"

Mistress Mathilda was momentarily taken aback. "No, not that. He was so . . . *manly*! That's it, in a word! Manly. Why, if I were twenty years younger and somewhat slimmer —like yourself, for instance—I'd be mighty interested in a shipwright like that. If he *is* a shipwright. But if he's not, I couldn't tell you what he is. He didn't have the manner of a merchant—for I can tell you that I was watching close enough!—or of anyone else I could place. Ah, well."

Katherine was not inclined to enlighten the webstress. She asked instead, "And what did Master Robert tell him? About Leofwyn and the house, I mean."

"That he was two generations too late. No Leofwyns left in York nowadays. Master Shipwright seemed to have a fair knowledge of some of our history and families—why, he would, coming from Scarborough, I suppose, for York is important to the coast and trade. But, in any case, Robert told him that Mistress Katherine the Broiderer lived there now.

"And?"

"And nothing! He merely smiled politely—a very attractive smile I would say, and it changed his aspect entirely—but he seemed to lose interest after that. The talk became general, and very pleasant it was, too, but I surely don't think the man was interested in buying anything. And that's a sight too bad from my point of view, because I wouldn't mind his form darkening my doorstep from time to time!"

The webstress wrinkled her brow. "But the matter went straight out of my mind because Stephen left the shop after that, practically on the shipwright's heels, and we didn't see him for the next few hours. With Sybille, as we've discussed!" Then Mistress Mathilda winked, as if making a joke. "We might have seen the last of the shipwright, but you never can tell. He seemed a knowing one—and with a rare taste in foreign cloth. Why, that's our business to notice such things. But I've heard tell of families who would hide fortunes of silver and gold in secret places in their houses. It could be that the Leofwyns, dead and gone, did such a thing, and the shipwright has heard the rumor somewhere. So don't be surprised if a shipwright comes to your door, trying to gain entry with a smooth story on his lips!"

Katherine's smile had become somewhat fixed. "Thank you, Mistress Mathilda. I won't be surprised," she replied with a certain edge to her voice. "I won't be at all surprised if a man comes to my door with a smooth story on his lips."

____Chapter 4____

Dawn came to Scarborough harbor, dripping wetly from the bristling, bobbing masts raking the fog, hugging to itself in the thick stew of the air all the tang of the brackish sea and barnacles on wet canvas and the faintly resinous scent of slick, caulked wood. Beyond the port, the North Sea churned silently, a vat of sleepy tar, its surface scarcely rippled by the wind which harped across it. The fog, heavy and quiet and gray, showed no signs of lifting before noon and provided an excellent cocoon for a person who might want to avoid being seen. By midday it would have lifted, and the port would be thronged with the crowds come to haggle over the treasures brought from sea to land by merchant ships and fishing knarrs.

A burly blond man stood on the full-length deck of a sleek craft, engaged in running sinewy rigging cables through his great bear paws. He had few claims to beauty, and the heavy frown he wore while executing his task lent him a fearsome aspect. At the pad of a footfall on board, the man glanced up.

The frown vanished. "Eric!" he exclaimed, his voice an involuntary mixture of surprise, pleasure, and reproach.

"I thought I might find you here, Bar," the Viking replied, and returned the wrenching hand clasp.

"Well you might!" Bar answered, and explained his surprise. "The messenger boy you sent me said that I was not to expect you until the morrow."

"I finished my business a day early. I thought it just as well to travel on to Scarborough without delay."

"Better!" Bar said, quick to show his pleasure, and followed up with his reproach. "But what is this all about?" he

47

demanded somewhat peevishly. "You've left us here to twiddle our fingers long enough. Where have you been these past weeks?"

"Most recently, in York."

"You never go to York," Bar replied, reverting to his initial expression of surprise.

"This time it was very necessary. I had to collect on an old account."

Bar took affront. "I like that! *I* take care of all the accounts in York. Can you be doubting me?"

The Viking reassured his henchman on that score. He explained that it was special, the account of a man named Josef.

Bar lumbered through his memory and scratched his blond whiskers. "Josef?"

"The Josef who died some weeks back in a tavern brawl. In Thanet. Did you hear of it?"

"Aye! A stirring set-to it was, too, so I was told," he said with relish, and added on a note of disappointment, "Of course, I haven't been near Thanet in a six-month—your orders—and so I missed it firsthand. There was talk about a body dying, but that's nothing new. Josef, you say? Was that the one I dealt with over the silks all those months ago?"

The Viking confirmed this conjecture.

The heavy frown gathered again and fell on Bar's brow. "I disremember that he had anything to do with York. He sailed the *Jorvic*, wasn't it? I recall right enough that he had not paid us before the *Freya* sank, but I didn't think it worth tracking him down afterward, when you were in London, because there wasn't more than a couple of hundred marks in it for us."

"One hundred," the Viking corrected.

"Is that all?" Bar exclaimed dismissively. "Then why did you bother with it? Was it worth your being seen in York, of all places, for such a slim purse?"

The Viking did not answer that but asked instead, "Tell me, since I never met the man, did Josef have red hair?"

Bar conjured a rather nondescript man with an honest face and indeterminate brown hair and shook his head. "Red hair? No."

"I thought not," the Viking said, somewhat obscurely to Bar's mind.

"Do you mean to explain what you're talking about, Eric?" Bar complained.

The Viking smiled at that. He crossed the wide lime-wood floor timbers to the rail and dropped his hand on an oarlock. He looked out over the water. "Bear with me. A goodly lot has happened since I cooled my heels in the Tower."

Mention of the Tower of London effectively diverted Bar's attention from Josef and money to a topic of much more lively interest. A martial gleam lit Bar's eye, and he bunched his fists into hammers. "Which one of Satan's guards was your jailer?" he asked eagerly. "Ivo the Iron-hearted? Dennis the Damned?"

"Mauger the Murderer," the Viking replied over his shoulder.

Bar grinned his satisfaction and thought his master singularly fortunate to have been honored with the most blood-thirsty of the king's brutes.

The Viking turned back around and propped a boot on a seat plank. "Yes!" he said, easily interpreting Bar's expression. "Mauleon was certainly attentive to my comfort!"

"Damned whoreson!" Bar spat and, in the next breath, demanded to know how the Viking had allowed Mauleon to clap him in irons in the first place.

"Mauleon challenged my loyalty to his beloved King John," the Viking replied, "in the presence of a rather large audience. As a gesture of courtesy, I obliged him with the opinion that John had sown some sour seeds and was raising a bitter crop. I observed, in fact, that he was no longer fit to rule."

"By Thor's Hammer, Eric, you've a tongue! But was it wise?"

"My very existence is a slap in Mauleon's face," the Viking answered curtly. "The moment I knew he had discovered my whereabouts in London, I guessed that he would find a way to garrote me in the Tower—with just cause or without."

"Might as well go for the crime of slander as a false

charge," Bar acknowledged, and then waved a hand, impatient for details. "So tell me. Did you have some fun and knock a few heads together? When I heard where you were trussed up, I gathered together a party—Rannulf, Lars, and the crew from the *Signy*—to storm the Tower. I vow, that would have been sport! Then, the next thing we knew, we'd heard from the usual sources that you'd gone. How did you do it?"

"Not by bending iron grille and rappeling down a length of cold stone," the Viking said with a slight smile. "You will be disappointed to hear that I was released."

Bar's face fell ludicrously. He muttered that he thought this an old-womanish way to make one's way out of the Tower of London. Then a thought struck him. "But who released you?"

"William the Marshal," the Viking answered.

Bar whistled soundlessly, clearly impressed. "William the Marshal? With friends like that you don't have to fret a ha'penny about enemies like Mauleon. Are they not on the same side, though, I'm thinking?"

"I am beginning to doubt it."

"Doubt William the Marshal?" Bar asked incredulously. "I thought he was the last trustworthy man John could count."

"He is, and it is not his loyalty that I question."

"Mauleon's, then!" Bar shook a hirsute head. "Mauleon rode with the Marshal and John *against* the rebel barons at Runnymede. Was that not the final test of his loyalty to John?"

The Viking replied only, "Mauleon is capable of anything."

Bar's beard split wide open with a grin. "And you mean to catch him out at it! Is that why the Marshal released you from prison, then, to go after Mauleon?"

"No, the Marshal is unaware that Mauleon is playing a double game. Rather, he wanted my help to further John's cause."

Bar was justifiably puzzled. "The Marshal wanted help from you? When you had just been thrown in the Tower for treasonous slander against that very king?"

"I agree with you, Bar. It seemed very odd to me at first too."

"Odd? Damned cross-eyed, I call it! You've no love for John, and you've been mortal blunt about it, too, from what you say. I know that the Marshal is getting old, but I had not thought that he had dwindled into a fool!"

"Fool enough to dangle Scarborough lands in front of my nose," the Viking said casually.

Bar's blue eyes widened. The subject of Scarborough demesne and its confiscation from the Viking's father under the reign of John's father, Henry, had rarely been mentioned between them. The Viking had never directly stated his desire to regain his family lands and castle one day. Nevertheless, Bar had a mother wit all his own and did not need to be told the motivations of a man he had known his entire life.

Bar also did not need to be told that the fleet and fortune in the Viking's possession gave him power enough to disregard the wishes of another man, king or not, and so Bar asked, "Well, man, what did the Marshal want of you?"

"He wanted to know if I could sail a ship."

This surprised a crack of laughter from Bar. "Does a fish swim?" he commented. Then, seriously, "Do you think he suspects anything?"

The Viking's eyes traveled up the length of the mast as it disappeared into the low canopy of fog. "The Marshal observed that if I refused him the offer of my services, he would be compelled to inquire more closely into my activities."

Bar gunted. "Did I call the man a fool? A fox, more like!"

"Age has not dimmed the Marshal's wits," the Viking said with conviction, "nor his effectiveness. He's known to have an ear at every door and an eye at every gate."

"Surely we've not been so careless to have left ourselves open to discovery by one of the king's men!" Bar protested.

The Viking thought not. "But the Marshal is canny enough to assume that I have not been idle all these years. He also owns a long memory and remembers my father well, and his taste for the sea. It was easy enough for him to make an educated guess about my probable activities. Added to that, he could hold the bait of Scarborough lands in front of me."

"A very sly fox!" Bar interjected when the Viking paused.

When the Viking began again, it was on a note of humor. "I told you some months ago that John's rule would not survive year's end. Now I think that if John possesses any secret weapon against the challenge from Louis of France, it is William Marshal."

"And the nature of the services he wanted you to perform for him?" Bar asked.

The Viking gave a brief, fluent account of his interview with William, Earl of Pembroke, High Marshal of England. The Marshal had told a roundabout tale, involving York government, the guilds, wool, imports and exports, and hundreds of marks of unpaid taxes. From the story the Viking had concluded that the Marshal was not well versed in the ways of city life. William had not pretended otherwise. The Marshal's expertise was of broadsword and mace and battle-ax, of charge and countercharge, of ambush and sally, of hacking and hewing, of the bright, shining shield of chivalry. To conquer in William's world was, the Viking knew, to brandish the stronger sword. Although the Marshal's grasp of the facts might have been faulty, his perceptions of the situation in York were essentially correct. In sum, the Marshal suspected a conspiracy between townsmen and rebel barons, and he feared that the alliance intended to invite Louis of France onto English soil.

The Marshal wanted Eric, who bore the empty title of Earl of Scarborough, to enter into service at one of the shipping companies in York in order to learn about the inner workings of York economy. Eric would be in a position to discover firsthand all financial matters in this important northern city and its political maneuverings as well. In exchange the Marshal would restore Scarborough lands to the Scarborough family.

"By Sigurd's Sword, Eric, spy for the crown? You've no stomach for it!" Bar said.

The Viking agreed that he was opposed to furthering John's cause. "I would have treated the Marshal's request with the scorn that it merited, save for one circumstance: I had it on good authority in London that if Louis assumes the English crown, he has sworn to drive into exile every man who rode against John at Runnymede as traitors to the king."

This intelligence produced the expected effect. Bar's grasp of the subtleties in the contest between John and Louis was not the equal of his master's, but he understood the implications of Louis's intentions to dispose of the rebel barons. Those men who rode against John at Runnymede represented the richest, most powerful estates in England. If Louis were to install in their places his own cronies, the Frenchman would have the island kingdom well and truly in his pocket.

"By Odin's Ravens!" Bar ejaculated. "That's a fine way of repaying the rebels who invited Louis in the first place. Can you be sure that the Frenchman means to do it?"

The Viking reminded Bar that he had gone to London specifically to contact a certain follower of Louis.

"I warrant the Frenchman has the nerve to do it, but could he truly make the exile legally binding?" Bar asked.

"Louis has the full support of Rome. Remember that the pope has nullified Magna Charta. Louis could punish the barons for having reneged on their sacred oaths of loyalty to John." The Viking's lips curled. "And there is no doubt that Louis would press the issue. We have had enough trade with the man over the years to know that the breaking of oaths is a privilege that Louis reserves exclusively for himself."

"Do we sail with John, then?"

"We are so fortunate, Bar, as to owe allegiance to none in this contest which offers no choice."

"Yet you speak as if you now prefer John."

"Let us say that we would find Louis, given his intentions, far more in our way than John. But I grow weary of their games, for they have cost us enough time as it is."

Bar considered this and then asked cautiously, "Are you so eager to stand in Dane Hall, once again lord and master of Scarborough lands?"

The Viking shrugged. "In truth I do not know. I am well content for the moment to feel a ship's planks beneath my feet after this eternity on land."

Bar nodded in comprehension. The Viking's eyes had narrowed, and his gaze had been drawn out across the sea where a faint breath of wind in the cool dawn trailed tatters of a denser fog. Indeed, it had been many a long month since the *Freya* sank, since he had last stood at the helm of a ship, to soar and to sweep on the roll of the sea with the freedom of a bird. Trapped in the four walls of his dank, vermin-ridden cell, the Viking had not nursed thoughts of revenge against Mauleon; he had not dreamed of the land and castle to which his birth gave him right. Rather, his mind traveled continuously to his first love, for in his blood was his true Viking inheritance, the restless, reckless pulse that urged him always to the sea and beyond; and, given this, Eric, Earl of Scarborough, had done remarkably well in prison for a man who felt best surrounded by miles of open water.

He had longed for days and weeks now to taste again the salty spray of sea, to hear the raucous shrill of gulls and the wind singing in the rigging of his ship as it hissed along the water, and to be on deck, exposed, to feel the sun on his skin, scrubbing it to a deeper bronze. His yearning had grown to a simple, unashamed ache of desire to see the play of light across the water: to witness the dull pewter of the sea at dawn change to pale dun, like a weak, honeyed mead; then to deepest blue in the sun or streaky jade before a storm; and then finally to the dark of shimmering bootblacking with the stain of night. He wanted to ride the sea, that changing beast, with the rest of the world dropped off the edge of the horizon, to see the wind filling the sails to their most billowing curve, to be free and alive again with the passion that had fired centuries of Viking men before him.

"If you did not mean to take up the Marshal's offer," Bar said to the Viking's back, "why did you go to York?"

"Because, during the course of our conversation, the Marshal said something that caught my attention. In discussing the place where I was to offer my services, he suggested a small shipping company in York by the name of Leofwyn." The Viking focused his gray gaze once again on Bar. "Have you ever heard of it?"

"Leofwyn? In York? Never heard of it," Bar said with sure knowledge.

"Neither had I, and it made me curious. That's all."

"Why? It seems that the Marshal simply erred."

"He did not, however. There is indeed a company called Leofwyn in York. Your Josef worked for it."

Bar's face darkened. "The Marshal cannot know more about our own backyard than we do," he growled.

"I did not think it. The Marshal admitted that he has planted many of his men throughout Yorkshire, a good many of them dressed up as priests, among other guises. What had happened was that one of these 'priests' in Thanet was called to Josef's deathbed after the brawl to receive Josef's testament. This testament was wholly unremarkable, save for the fact that Josef insisted that it be sent to Leofwyn Shippers, York. He was probably delirious with fever when he gave the address to the Marshal's spy, for the name Leofwyn is, I have since gathered, very secret. In any case, the spy knew that the Marshal was interested in anything and everything to do with shipping and trade, so the testament was duly sent to Pembroke Castle. Then came the extraneous bit of information, from another unrelated source, that I was languishing in the Tower. The Marshal thought it an excellent opportunity for someone of my qualifications to penetrate the mysteries of York's trading activities."

"How has Leofwyn remained a secret from us?" Bar wanted to know.

"Because it is a secret from most of York as well, and it has not previously been in our interest to know about it. However, all of that has changed. I was so fortunate, when I at last tracked down the elusive Leofwyn in York, to catch sight of Mauleon in Leofwyn's neighborhood. I was then in a position to discover that Mauleon has strong ties to this Leofwyn, who in turn has, I would hazard a guess, a heavy stake in Louis's claim. After all, we have good cause to know the sentiments of the York merchants."

Bar assented readily to this.

"And I would be lacking in manners," the Viking continued with a chilling smile, "to let Mauleon have it both ways. He sits pretty enough if John remains on the throne, but with

Louis, his gains would be enormous! If Mauleon is pumping money into Louis's cause through this Leofwyn and York—as I now believe he is doing—he will be richly rewarded when Louis wears the crown."

Bar put the essential piece in place. "Mauleon would escape the punishment of exile," he said slowly, "since he rode with John and not against him at Runnymede."

"Exactly."

Bar was much struck by Mauleon's perfidy and uttered a highly descriptive and rather vulgar estimation of Mauleon's character and lineage, cursing for effect in the tongue of his ancestors, and summed up the invective with the words, "And if Mauleon's left hand is for Louis, that is reason enough to put our sails behind John."

"So, too, do I think," the Viking concurred, pleased with his henchman's understanding.

"Does the Marshal know that Mauleon straddles the fence of allegiance?" Bar asked.

"Not yet," his master replied, his deep voice resonating with an added note of satisfaction. "I am sure the time shall come, however, for a man of the Marshal's strict sense of honor to know of Mauleon's duplicity. Then, too, I do not ignore my debts and shall owe the Marshal a small favor for returning to me Scarborough lands."

Bar liked the sound of this and brightened perceptibly. He had little liking for grand affairs of state and even less for Norman notions of justice. "That's the spirit, Eric! It's taking matters into our own hands, we are! Shall we get to Mauleon first through Leofwyn? I say, let's go to Leofwyn and show him what-for!"

"That is not possible."

Bar thrust out the bush of his chin and looked distinctly pugnacious. The Viking forestalled the fighting words about to burst forth from Bar's lips by smiling easily and raising a staying hand. "I mean, Bar," he explained, "that Leofwyn is not a man but a woman."

Bar barked a laugh. "Oh! Like Brigit, the widow of Balder the Shipper here in Scarborough? Or Agnes, the daughter of Magnusson and the granddaughter of Magnus the Sailor?"

The Viking's smile was somewhat contemptuous. "I do not think the comparison holds."

Something in the Viking's tone prompted Bar to ask, "What do you mean by that?"

"Our Leofwyn is young—not more than a slip of a girl, although she manages to create the impression of someone more mature and experienced, and her position in the world is, perhaps, not as respectable."

"Who is it, then? Leofwyn's a Saxon name. I know them all in York, by sight or by name."

"Mistress Katherine the Broiderer of Jubbergate Street," the Viking replied.

Bar's features assumed an expression remarkably resembling a stunned sheep. "But—but Miss Katherine? *The Broiderer?*"

"The very one."

"Hela's Teeth!" Bar swore. "Not respectable? She's considered something of a *saint*! She maintains a home for orphans—with the blessings of the archbishop, if I'm not mistaken."

"So I gather."

"A young slip of a girl?" Bar considered this. "I wouldn't call her that because she has the look of someone who knows what she is about. But you're right. She is young." After a moment he added, with a touch of reverence, "And she's beautiful, too, don't you think?"

As a man of wide experience with female charms, the Viking might have conceded that he had found her very beautiful, magnificent even, when her eyes had flashed brilliantly with anger. He said only, "I can understand how Mauleon is attracted to her."

Bar looked ready to take issue with this perspective on the Mistress Broiderer's loveliness but instead chose to keep to the central issue. "What's her lie?"

"No doubt similar to Mauleon's. He's trying to make his future secure no matter who sits on the throne. Why should she not have it both ways as well? She's paid the price."

"I don't believe you," Bar said flatly.

"Do I disillusion you? I had not thought you so easily deceived by an innocent face, beautiful as it is!" the Viking rallied him. "If you know so much about her, perhaps you can tell me if she is a Saxon. I do not think she is from York, or even," he added reflectively, recalling the dusky rhythms of her pleasing, low-pitched voice, "from Yorkshire."

"Aye, I know her! It's said that she's from the south—Cornwall, mayhap. Or is it Wales? She's got the look of the Welsh about her, with her dark hair. But you'd expect blue eyes from a Welshwoman, think on! In any case," Bar continued, standing his ground, "I don't believe she's involved with Mauleon—at least not in the way that you mean it. All of York thinks her a saint."

The patent disbelief on the Viking's face indicated that he thought Mistress Katherine more an Eve than a Mary, but he did not find the subject of her virtue, or any woman's virtue, worth arguing. "So you have said" was his reply.

"How the devil did you associate her with the name Leofwyn, if it's such a secret?" Bar demanded to know.

"A bit of luck and a bit of guesswork. I chanced to drop the name Leofwyn at a drapers' and came up with nothing. The moment I left the shop, however, I was hailed by the son of the establishment, who fancies himself a poet, I believe. He told me enough, quite unintentionally, I am sure, about Leofwyn and Mistress Katherine to add it all up."

"A poet told you about Leofwyn Shippers? Eric!" Bar scoffed, his credulity stretched by this source of York secrets.

"The poet happens to be the particular friend of the Mistress Katherine's sister, I believe," the Viking explained. "He must know of the operation from her sister."

"That's right, there is a sister. The Mistress Sybille," Bar affirmed. "But, by the Valkyries, Eric! You spent but a few days in York, and you learned all this? How do you do it?"

The Viking did not answer that but said instead, "You seem to know a fair bit about Mistress Katherine and her household yourself. If you are so well acquainted with them, then I must assume that they know you, as well."

After an infinitesimal pause Bar admitted, "They know me."

The Viking was alive to the hesitation and acted upon it. "You're not to go to York," he stated.

"I'm used to going to York," Bar retorted, risking insubordination. "Old habits die hard."

"This habit shall die a swift death!" the Viking shot back, quick to assert authority. "The coming summer months will determine whose royal forces shall prevail and you are under no circumstances to jeopardize our position by allowing anyone in York to associate you with me. You have more than enough to do on the coast. I shall look to our interests in York from here on. Any objections?"

Bar studied the tip of his boot. "No, no objections."

The Viking reiterated his command, in terms that left no room for interpretation, that Bar not go near York. "She's a clever baggage, your Mistress Katherine, and you may rest assured that I shall take care of her. She is not, however, the one we need worry about. Far more important to us are her paramour's intrigues in York. We know not to underestimate Mauleon's ability to play both ends against the middle!"

The Viking closed the subject and informed Bar that they had a day or two of sailing ahead of them.

Bar acquiesced by grumbling that there was much to be done to get the ship in shape, for even the brass fittings and suchlike had become, in his words, "duller than Saxon wit" with disuse.

During those same days Katherine had been thinking of the Viking's intrigues in York. She deemed it essential to her safety to discover how he had come to associate her Josef with the name Leofwyn.

When the Viking had first appeared on her doorstep and then apprised her of Josef's death, she had considered the possibility that Josef, on his deathbed, had sent her a replacement in the man Eric Shipwright of Scarborough. She quickly discarded this idea when the man identified himself as the Viking. She imagined that a coincidence must have placed the Viking in Thanet on the occasion of the fateful brawl and that, either by accident or design, Josef had let fall her name. She was even prepared to believe that the Viking had wrested her name from the poor, dying Josef as the person responsible for payment of the debt.

Yet this explanation was belied by the few facts Katherine

had at hand. It was clear that the Viking had not known Josef very well. She surmised, for reasons she could not define, that the Viking had never met her sailor. She accepted the fact that the Viking had come for his money, for these were hard times and he must have suffered with the loss of his ship the year before. Nevertheless, she had to suppose that he had other seaworthy vessels at his disposal or so many of his own contacts that he need not enter into partnership with her to have use of a ship. Then, too, he knew Mauleon, but not in his role as the Viking. The facts did not add up, and she had been confounded by the whole.

Then Mistress Mathilda had passed along the information that the Viking had come to York armed with only the names Josef and Leofwyn—and not, as the Viking had led Katherine to believe, that Josef had divulged her name to him. It now seemed to Katherine that he had not known for a certainty that she was behind the name Leofwyn until she herself had admitted to it. So, the Viking had drawn a bow at venture, had set his sight on the most incredible, truly unthinkable possibility that Mistress Katherine the Broiderer of the impeccable reputation stood behind Josef and Leofwyn. And his aim had proved true.

Katherine was now disturbed far more than she had been previously puzzled. Though she hardly needed more evidence, she knew that in her partner, the Viking, she had a formidable adversary. Emma, however, when she was informed of the Viking's cunning, was inclined to credit him with a fine edge that she had not previously suspected in so blunt a man and declared him to be "one Dane, at least, who does not have both feet in the same boot. Nor does he stop at the obvious. I wonder how he tumbled to us, in sooth! Why, he's the first man in my ken to have matched our women's wits. Compared to him, Mauleon is a poor second!"

To which Katherine retorted, "If that is the case, I would say that for us it's a case of 'out of the frying pan . . .' to quote yourself, Emma!"

Katherine freely acknowledged the Viking's canny guesswork. But could he have so surely concluded that she was Leofwyn simply on the strength of the webster's information that she inhabited the former house of the Leofwyn family?

Katherine did not think so. Thus she set about in a city she knew very well to discover with whom else the Viking might have spoken and where else he might have gleaned any news about her, about Josef, or about her house. Yet she was unable to discover that the Viking had made contact with any townsmen of her acquaintance other than the websters and the taverner. To her dismay she realized that if the Viking had learned anything at all in York, he had learned it at the wharf where Josef had spent many a leisure hour. But where the water began, her trail ended. She could not follow the Viking's tracks farther than the Ouse Bridge.

A woman who enjoyed the reputation Katherine had so carefully nurtured could not enter that most important part of the city that had made York the centuries-old strategic gate to the whole north country. The site of York had been fixed for all time at the confluence of the Rivers Ouse and Foss. The Ouse was a tidal river, deep enough for ocean craft and wide enough for bulky barges of goods. These rivers brought York whitefish from the Hebrides and wheat from the East Riding. They had brought Danish raiders, too, ages ago, sailing unchallenged into the city on lithe and graceful shield-rimmed boats. More recently William the Conqueror had come up from the roiling waters of the Humber to the Ouse and had penetrated York with his Norman warriors. The Conqueror had promptly dammed the Foss for protection of his castle, which he had built to squat on York cliffs. Yet he had not quite succeeded in subjugating this sedentary folk of York, these weavers and shepherds who had for seven generations so stolidly resisted Norman rule.

The joining of the two rivers formed, in fact, the town's visceral center. The piers where an array of sailing vessels bobbed in the deep, murky waters drew all manner of creatures. In the various alehouses and taverns slung along the wharf lounged the affluent or unoccupied of York. Their low-pitched back rooms accommodated the riffraff, as well as the whores, amateur and professional, who came cajoling and bargaining. The wharf was no place for a woman of standing to be seen. Katherine thought, somewhat resentfully, that the Viking would be entirely in his element in such a setting. There was no telling what a man of his obvi-

ous resourcefulness could have coaxed from ale-bitten
tongues.

Katherine was heart-full of courage but kept discretion
the better part of her valor and so did not stray into terri-
tories where her reputation might be put at risk. She much
preferred the ease of movement in town and the information
available to the honest, the seemly, and the respected. She
was sorely tempted to test her skill for subterfuge on this
particular field of contest of the wharf, as she supposed the
Viking to have done, but Emma strongly warned her against
it. Now, with Josef gone, she had no access to the secrets of
the city's entrails, and she knew herself to be at a disadvantage.

Being ingenious and a woman, Katherine had learned to
find the means to weigh in her favor the balance of forces
against her in this man's world. Upon settling within the city
walls of York four years before, she had immediately perceived the differences in a woman's life between town and
castle. Katherine had not really known what to expect from
town life. The village that huddled in the shadow of Castle
Roncevaux had given her no awareness of how prosperous
and independent townsmen and women lived, and she had
been too preoccupied by the matter of mere survival on the
long, miserable flight from France to be interested in the
finer points of life in the towns through which she happened
to pass. In those early days in York she did not fail to notice
that the women of her adopted city stood on a very different
footing with their men than did the women Katherine had
known at Castle Roncevaux. She would never forget the
shock she felt in the first days of wandering through York
markets to see coins flash from women's purses and apron
pockets, to witness money pass through women's hands.
Women did not vote, of course, or hold public office, nor
were their wages equal. Nevertheless, women were very visible and vocal in financial affairs, and Katherine soon found
a snug place for herself.

Even after four years Katherine still enjoyed town life,
and since she always had business to conduct around the
marketplace, she was out and about daily.

Six days after the Viking's first visit to her house Katherine was traveling a side street that issued onto the market at High Petergate when she came, most unexpectedly, face-to-face with Sybille and Stephen Webster. Katherine saw at a glance that they were engaged in deep and flirtatious conversation, for Sybille was blushing charmingly at Stephen's comments. Katherine knew that Sybille had gone to the market with Marta, but Marta was nowhere to be seen.

Katherine wished that this young couple did not make such an exceptionally handsome pair. Nor did Katherine care to see how Sybille glowed in Stephen's presence. Her complexion was as rosy as the first drifts of apple blossoms or fresh peaches. Her tender mouth was the pink of the softest rose and exquisitely shaped. Her nose, escaping the masterful tilt of Katherine's, was perfectly straight, with delicately curved nostrils, and her eyes, which gazed unclouded upon the world, were of a celestial blue and held an expression of wistfulness and the hint of a fugitive smile.

"I give you good day, Master Stephen," Katherine said coolly, and turned to her sister. "Sybille, my dear, I believe that Marta is looking for you."

At the sound of her sister's voice Sybille's eyes flew from rapt contemplation of Stephen's face. "Katherine!" she exclaimed, and had the grace to look guilty. "Marta? Oh, yes! She told me to wait for her right here. She did! And I was not to move from this very spot. And I have not! Then Master Stephen came along and was so good as to keep me company and—and—well, I must say that I did not expect to see you!"

That much was evident, and to cover Sybille's burst of candor Stephen stammered a hasty, "Your s-servant, M-mistress Katherine!" and recalled, somewhat inappropriately, the lines of a *lai* he had been thrashing out in his leisure hours, that in the awkwardness of the moment occurred to him. "O the Parting of two souls, is it not a torment sweet?" he quoted with poetic flourish, "to augment the joy of Chance Encounter when two—er—" Stephen broke off, suddenly recalling that the next word was *lovers*. He flushed in his turn, and improvising rapidly, he achieved a verse that did not also mar the original rhythm, "—when two sisters meet!"

Tactfully ignoring Stephen's hapless expression, Katherine

said dryly, "Quite right," and brought the conversation down to
a more prosaic level by saying, "And now that I have the joy of
this chance encounter with you, Sybille, I have remembered
that I forgot to mention to you and Marta before you left the
house together that we need fresh fennel and dittany to flavor
the Lenten cakes. Can I depend on you to remind Marta to buy
some? You won't forget now, will you?"

"Oh, no! Fennel and dittany," Sybille repeated. "I won't
forget," she assured her sister, and being flustered, she
added on a contradictory note, "Why, here comes Marta
now, and so you may tell her yourself, in case I do forget!"

Marta rounded the corner, looking harassed and worried, as
if she had been looking for Sybille, but Marta was too much the
beautiful girl's slave to betray her to her elder sister. Master
Stephen made a quiet exit from the scene, and the three women
then discussed the shopping needs at some length. When
Katherine was satisfied that Sybille would stay by Marta's side
for the rest of the day, she went on about her own errands.

Katherine did not, however, have the leisure to dwell on
the budding love between Sybille and Stephen. Rather, her
mind was preoccupied with the meeting that she was to have
the next day with Mauleon at the castle. She was reviewing
her position on her debt and its payment, as well as what she
was going to say about Josef, should the subject arise, when
she turned the corner at High Petergate. There she stopped
short at the sight of a tall blond man.

Chapter 5

Across the square Katherine saw the Viking leaning casually at the booth of a spicer. Katherine had not expected to
see him for another seven-night at least. She could not guess
what he was doing back in York so quickly and at the mar-

ket. Nevertheless, there he was behaving for all the world like a merchant, although a commanding air about him distinguished him in Katherine's eyes from every other trader there. She saw him bring a pinch of some powder to his nose and engage the spicer in what looked to be good-natured banter.

Watching him, Katherine was aware of a subtle change in him. Yet she could detect nothing in his outward appearance to confirm this impression. He was dressed, as was his fashion, in an unadorned tunic; it was the color of a moody sea and severely cut, which emphasized the width of his shoulders. He was clean-shaven, too, as on the previous occasion, and his hair glinted gold in the bright sun.

She had observed him a spare moment too long. Just then he waved his hand negligently and smiled a regret to the spice merchant. Before Katherine was able to absorb herself in the throng, he turned unexpectedly in her direction, and gray eyes clashed with hazel.

The Viking inclined his head slightly in acknowledgment of Katherine and then strolled amongst the bustling crowd to meet her. As he approached, she sensed that something was indeed different about the man. He looked hard and fit, as he had before, but she was struck by a change in him, an added air of vitality. It was as if, Katherine thought erratically, he had taken possession of sea winds, fresh and strong and unpredictable, and brought them with him.

To his formal bow she curtsied perfunctorily, and her knees felt unaccountably weak. Since there had been no dignified way to avoid this encounter in full view of the entire market, Katherine had quickly decided to put the best possible face on it. She greeted him with a very proper distance and continued without further preamble, "You told me that you did not plan to return to York before the end of another week or more. Is your early return a good sign?"

"Yes, mistress," the Viking replied, matching her deferential manner. "The unseasonably mild weather inland and on the coast hastened my return. It is a very good sign."

"But to have returned so promptly," she pursued, "must surely suggest that you have business to conduct here—that is, other business," she said without putting too fine a point on her words, since the ears of all of York were drifting by.

"I am always engaged in business," was his uninformative reply, "and speaking of which, we have business of our own to discuss."

The Viking apparently did not consider it at all extraordinary to mention in so public a place the business he had with Katherine. It was true that although he was speaking in a normal voice, the din of the hawking and peddling would render the gist of their conversation unintelligible to the casual passerby. Nevertheless, Katherine was somewhat surprised by this bold mention, and so she said, "Do you mean now?"

"I do."

"But where?"

"Shall we go to Jubbergate Street where we may be private? Unless, of course, you prefer some place closer to the square? I might suggest the Blue Swan, for instance."

Not only bold but impudent as well! She stood her ground. "Surely you do not mean for us to go now together."

"Why not, mistress?" he asked. "There is certainly no need to publicize our arrangement, but neither is there any reason to hide our acquaintance. I shall be in York frequently in the near future, and we are bound to meet on occasion. To pretend that we do not know one another is not only absurd but might arouse suspicion as well. Do you not agree?"

Katherine did agree, and she could not help but compare the Viking's openness to Mauleon's slyness, which she had always disliked. "Very true," she said, "but I do not think we need overdo the association, after all. Is it necessary that we go to my house together and in full view of all of York?"

"I am sure that your spotless reputation," he said blandly, punctuated with another slight bow, "can withstand the brief escort of a shipwright from Scarborough."

His seemingly courteous manner put Katherine instantly on her guard. The harsh words spoken between them at the end of their last meeting hovered in the air. She felt the color rise up her throat, and before she could think of a suitably crushing response, the Viking pressed his advantage. "To Jubbergate Street, mistress?"

Katherine saw no alternative. She nodded agreement, and they made their way together to the alleyway that would lead them from the city center. Katherine was obliged to nod and to smile at quite a number of familiar faces among the market-day bustle, and she was thankful when they turned down the less-traveled lane of Stonegate.

During the short walk to Jubbergate Street the Viking regaled Katherine with such unexceptionable topics as the weather; the drop in the price of wool, determined by the prediction of a particularly plentiful yield; the corresponding rise in the price of the best blue woad and red madder dyes; and the description of the forthcoming Eastertide amusements. She rightly guessed that the Viking had gleaned this last bit of York news from Geoffrey Taverner, who recently had been elected to a two-year term on York's Pageant Council, and she responded in kind to all of these conversational openings.

Soon they arrived below the shingle of the threaded needle in a basket of embroidery silks that was suspended above the door of Katherine's house.

"That is very fine talking for a shipwright," she said, dropping all pretense to civility, "but perhaps, from now on, we can speak much more to the purpose."

"When the occasion demands, mistress," he replied with a mocking solemnity that made her ready to do battle with him, "I assure you that I can speak very much to the purpose."

The massive portal was swung open by Emma, who was enjoying the attention of several youngsters gamboling about her skirts. There was also a spirited game of catch-as-catch-can in progress in the yard, but Emma managed to raise her voice above the gleeful noise to say, "Give you good morrow, Master Eric!"

A storm of children swarmed around the tall blond stranger and pelted him with an array of questions and comments to which he did his best to respond until Emma chivvied her charges into the scullery, recommending to the children not to plague the man who had come to help their mistress. The high babble of the young voices was soon shut behind the kitchen door at the far end of the yard.

Katherine led her guest across the cobbles whereupon they met two apprentice broiderers who were just then descending from the upper story. One of them, the bold-eyed Maria, affected coy surprise to see Eric Shipwright at Katherine's side. She greeted the man with unmaidenly interest, and their brief exchange made it clear that they had seen each other earlier in the day in town.

Maria was indeed a Saxon beauty, from her red-gold curls that escaped her coif to her well-proportioned figure she carried so provocatively; and her honeyed voice had been known to attract many a bee. Katherine saw a red flag of danger wave with Maria's attraction to the Viking and so took the situation quickly in hand.

"Shall you accompany me to my solar, Master Eric?" she invited with an unmistakable nod of dismissal to Maria. She gestured for the Viking to follow her up the stairs, and when Maria was out of earshot, continued, "Let me remind you that we must first establish percentages."

"I have not forgotten," the Viking replied easily, following her up the stairs, "and you may consider yourself fortunate to find me in a receptive mood today."

Katherine halted momentarily on a step and turned to slant her eyes down to him. "Receptive?" she queried. "A change, certainly, from your mood when last you were here. Is the fine weather responsible?"

The anxious note in Katherine's voice was not lost on the Viking, nor was he in any doubt of its cause. His smile was very pleasant. "What other reason for it could there be?"

"I wouldn't know," she replied, thinking specifically of Maria's attractive face and figure.

"No?" Then, "Here is an occasion to make good on the claim that I can speak to the purpose," he said, holding her eye with his compelling gaze. "Your apprentice, Maria, is a comely wench, and since your business dealings have been conducted on a very different rate of exchange from mine own, I understand your concern that business and pleasure might, in this instance, be mixed. But I am a hardened customer, Mistress Katherine, and never tangle the two! Do not imagine that the sight of a pretty face makes me receptive in matters of money. And since Maria is engaged in your household, she holds no further attraction for me. Does that answer your question?"

"It does." Katherine was obliged to swallow his insult about her probable relationship with Mauleon in order to close this difficult subject. She turned back around to continue the ascent. "It is a worthy example you set, your plain speaking, Master Eric. 'Honesty,' as Emma would say, 'reaps a profit tenfold.'"

"Let us keep Emma's wisdom in mind," he commented.

"Yes, indeed," Katherine agreed, and could not resist a last attempt to even the score, "and now, speaking honestly, I am reassured that you will be spared the effort of forcing your attentions on any of the honest maids who work here."

They halted before her solar door. "What makes you think I'm obliged to force my attentions on any woman?" he replied with a devastating smile that she did not doubt had been used with great effect on many occasion.

This remark was plainly beneath reply. She was glad to busy herself with the door, which was locked, and chose a key from the collection that was attached to a tassled cord hanging from the embroidered girdle encircling her slim waist. She bent to fiddle with the lock, and when she stood straight again, she showed a heightened color, but it might have been due to her stooping gesture.

The bolt slid back, and just as she was pushing the door open, she was forced to stifle an involuntary expression of dismay. The realization came a moment too late that she had made a grave mistake in bringing the Viking to her solar this day.

Before leaving her house in the morning to inspect a clip of wool at the usual place, Katherine had been absorbed in the clandestine accounts she kept for the mayor and the wool guild. She had left her work in progress, spread out over the room, with the intention of finishing it upon her return. There were several curling sheets of parchment covering the trestle table, a pot of unfiltered ink, a quill, and a small paring knife, while a sober-looking prayer missal sat atop the sideboard. She did not know what the Viking would make of such evidence, but she knew that his presence had addled her wits, and she could not afford to make such a stupid mistake twice.

Katherine checked her instinct to cover these documents from the Viking's eyes. Any display of concealment would surely make a bad situation worse. Furthermore, the door to her bedchamber stood open to his gaze, and a feminine instinct prompted her to close it before doing anything else. She then casually proceeded to gather together several of the sheafs and to roll them up with deliberation before securing them with neat, black ribands.

Katherine was unaware that one of the parchments had fallen under the table. The Viking bent down to retrieve it while Katherine was occupied with the other parchments, and running his eyes down the yellow sheet, he saw at a glance that John's reign was in far graver danger than William Marshal had ever imagined.

A ruthless gleam lit his eye as he regarded Katherine clearing the table. He had never been fooled by her picture of innocence, but at their first meeting her beauty had baffled his perception of her intelligence. Now, however, his eyes had been opened. Her careless little exposure had shown him that the main objective of his mission to York must surely be the discovery of the schemes that revolved behind her innocently beautiful face.

An instant later, when Katherine had placed the rolls aside and looked up, the Viking's face was impassive. Her eyes naturally fell to the parchment in his grip, and when she stretched out her hand for it, he saw that she was rapidly calculating the extent of her blunder.

The Viking made a minimal gesture, artfully compounded of confusion and hesitation, before placing the sheet, upside down, in Katherine's hand. If his object was to make her think that he did not possess the secret of writing and numerals and was reluctant for her to know it, then he succeeded admirably.

He subtly reinforced that misimpression. Pointing to the parchment, he said, "Your writing material is old-fashioned, mistress. You'd do far better to use the Arab's paper. I think I told you once that I also trade in paper."

"It is very expensive," she replied, turning the page right

side up, "and not readily available. I can always count on a supply of parchment."

"But paper is a product far superior to parchment," he said, "so I am told."

Katherine nodded. "I shall keep that in mind."

The Viking said with careless bravado, "And I am always wary of people who can't keep their numbers in mind."

She glanced at him. "Do you keep all your accounts in your head?" she asked.

"All of them," he stated firmly, as if proud of the fact.

"Admirable," she murmured. Her lips relaxed into a brief smile. She secured this last sheet and arranged it with the others, thinking that she had brushed through what might have been a disaster rather well.

Katherine offered the Viking a seat, and when he had declined all offer of refreshment, she placed her hands on the table and said, "Now, here is what I propose for the equal division of the profits that our partnership shall—"

The Viking interrupted this very promising start. "Equally divide? How shall there be an equal division of profits when we are not on equal terms? You, mistress, are in no position to set the division of any future profits."

"We were agreed," she said evenly, "when last we met, to exchange my ship against your sailing ability."

"But, no! Your debt to me entitled me to a share of your ship. My sailing ability is mine alone, and not in exchange for use of the ship."

Emma came in then, bringing with her a worker candle. Against the setting sun several branches of candles flowered into light. Neither Katherine nor her guest seemed to notice Emma's presence, so the serving woman closed the door and took up her accustomed chair in the corner by the windows.

"Well, then," Katherine was saying, "it is clear to me, at least, that the ship, as a tangible asset, might give me some extra measure of worth coming into the partnership."

Again the Viking took issue. "Your ship," he pointed out, "is idle, and likely to remain so for the entire summer sailing months, if I am not at its helm." He continued without pause, "As I have already told you, I want to base my business in York. It is important enough to me to do so that I am prepared to bar every sailor of my acquaintance from sailing for you."

His voice might have been pleasant, but his words were not, and Katherine felt her heart lurch at this plain threat. "How fortunate I am, indeed, to have fallen upon you in one of your receptive moods," she remarked, managing to keep her voice steady.

"In sooth," he agreed, still with that pleasant note.

"And so, forthright as you are in making your intentions and your estimation of our respective positions known!"

"Following, again, the wise words you shared with me some minutes ago. Honest speaking, we are agreed, is the most profitable course to pursue."

She thought she saw the trend. She was being punished but could not guess why. Whatever the reason, Katherine would not let the Viking manipulate her so easily, and she was determined to show him that she had backbone.

"In all honesty, then, can you really expect me to believe that I am without leverage or claim on profit?" she asked, looking him in the eye.

"But what are your claims? I was not aware that you had anything to offer me except a ship, one that is—if it is indeed the *Jorvik*—in some disrepair and doing you no good while it is anchored in Thanet harbor."

Katherine was provoked. "You must have something to put on the ship," she argued, "and I can supply my ship with the best wool in town. I proceed, Master Eric, according to another piece of wisdom—from the Danes, I believe—that says 'To him the strength of knowledge that muscle cannot match.' Surely you have heard it."

"On my mother's knee," he replied coolly. He leaned back in his chair and folded his arms across his chest and was prepared for her to state her case.

"Then you can imagine that there is no end to the knowledge that even a poor broiderer might possess. Although I cannot sail a ship, I have full command of the wool trade, from start to finish, and it might interest you to know that I have first choice on the raw wool that I buy because one of the most prosperous shepherds outside of town adopted last year two boys reared in my home."

"Thus the reason for maintaining a charitable home for orphans?" he queried acerbically.

"Exactly," she replied with her prettiest smile.

"You astonish me," he said. "You are far better circumstanced than I had realized."

Suspecting the Viking of mockery, Katherine continued, "Oh, yes, I know the best dyeresses, the best cardresses and spinsters, and which of their daughters hold the most dextrous distaff. And I trade with only the best weavers and fullers and stretchers, too, man or woman."

"Are you suggesting that you can close these good markets to me in York if I do not agree to your division of the profits?"

Katherine would not make herself ridiculous by issuing an empty threat. "No, only that my contacts here will cost you something. One hundred marks, to be precise."

The Viking preserved a thoughtful silence and then shook his head. "The fact remains that you have ignored the most important rule of trade."

Katherine raised a brow, her eyes steady on him. "Which is?"

"Never bet the entire company," he stated. "Your whole operation was based on your relationship with Josef. You do not have another sailor in reserve, nor did you put any money aside to hire a new one on your own terms, in the event that you might need one. With Josef's loss, then, you have lost all."

"I am not a half-wit," she said coolly, "and I can see that your position is complementary to mine, for the sinking of your ship last autumn has forced you to seek me out. Our mutual need is, after all, the foundation on which we strike our partnership. Once again, then: It is my ship against your sailing ability."

"Our positions," he said, a thread of amusement discernible in his voice, "are not at all comparable."

Katherine felt her cheeks grow warm but otherwise kept her countenance. "No? I, as you have said, do not have the silver to hire another sailor on my own terms, and so I must presume that you do not have enough to buy yourself a new ship."

"Perhaps I simply do not choose to invest what silver I may possess in the expense of a new ship when I can sail one for the asking."

This observation silenced Katherine long enough for the Viking to continue with an easy smile, "I, like you, am fond of advice. Here's another piece of wisdom, this time from the prudent Saxons: 'Never put all your pennies in one pouch.' Have you heard it?"

"I have heard it," she said, and countered swiftly, "but my business is very small, and I am forced to take gambles that larger shipping companies do not have to take."

"You should not have invested all your money from my account in the drapers' guild," the Viking chided.

That lazy smile did not leave his face. Katherine longed to wipe it off. "You may believe me when I say that events of the past week have shown me the error of my ways!" Katherine returned with spirit. "It remains to be seen, however, whether the investment was an error in the long run. I full well expect it to bring me a large return on quarter day at summer's end."

"Let us hope, for your sake, that it does."

There was something in the Viking's deep voice that struck an ominous note. Katherine felt the chill down to her toes. She did not have time to consider what he might mean, for he was speaking again, his voice once more gravelly and pleasant. "But we wander from the issue. I bargain with my skill as a sailor. You have naught but a ship, and one that is partially encumbered with debt to me. Added to that is my skill as a shipwright, which will always keep me near the sea and most likely seabound. Your needlecraft, as noteworthy as it is, and your easy access to good wool products do not rival what I have to offer you. In sum, I would say that you need me far more than I need you."

Katherine took in breath sharply. "This is indeed plain speaking!"

"'Honesty,'" the Viking intoned, "'reaps a profit tenfold.' Which brings me to yet another difference in our positions, and so I ask you—be honest, if you please—to name the sum of the debt for the looted merchandise which I am to discharge for you."

Katherine was enormously pleased with herself to have obtained her own means of paying off that debt to Mauleon. She permitted herself a smile. "There is no more debt for you to discharge. I have the matter well in hand."

The Viking's eyes narrowed. "You told me but six days ago that you were in debt."

"And I also said that I am not without resources," she replied. "I have since made use of them."

He did not hesitate to put the least flattering interpretation possible on that statement. His harsh features took on a rather saturnine cast. "How did you get the money?" he asked bluntly.

"It does not concern you in the least. Except to say, of course, that had I had it within my power to raise the one hundred marks I owe you, I certainly would have done it. As it was, my debt for the looted merchandise was the lesser amount, so it seemed wiser to discharge it first. Perhaps you would care to quote me an adage to assure that I have done the right thing."

The Viking did not answer that sally. "Tell me where you got the money," he grated.

She could see his growing anger. Far from warning her off her present course, she was encouraged by it. "Keeping in mind the manifold rewards of honesty?" she asked archly. Her laugh tinkled. "Oh, indeed! I shall be open and honest with you when you have had the goodness to tell me—hon- estly!—what has brought you to York and how you came to associate the two names Josef and Leofwyn with my house."

The Viking was, naturally, not prepared to answer that. Katherine continued, smiling charmingly, "You have ex- tolled your skills as a sailor and trader—and I am lost in admiration, I assure you—but you underestimate, I fear, my skills as a businesswoman."

"Do I?" he replied with an unpleasant curl to his lip. "Do I indeed err in thinking what skills a woman must possess to raise a significant amount of cash in so short a time?"

Her hand itched to slap that arrogant face. With great effort of will she forced herself to refrain from it. "You may think what you like," she invited, as if she did not care a straw for his opinion of her, and added, with every intention of reinforcing his poor assessment of her character, "You should not be surprised. I told you that I trade with only the most prosperous businessmen in town."

"I am sure you do," he said, his interpretation obvious. He noted her cool smile but failed to notice the flash of anger that made her eyes glint green, and continued, "The most prosperous businessmen. My surprise comes only from the fact that you are content with them when there are so many aldermen who could help you with your finances and your taxes."

"Yes, indeed! I make fine use of our city fathers for all sorts of favors."

"Why stop at that?" he ground out in a rather gritty voice.

Katherine had thrown all caution aside. "I don't, of course," she tossed back, "for when I really need something, I apply to the lord mayor, and he is always willing to oblige."

Emma gasped.

Heedless of the storm on the Viking's brow, Katherine continued cordially, "Shall we begin again?"

Thereafter the bargaining for percentages did not prosper along polite lines. Katherine defended herself very well, but she did not have much artillery at her command, and the Viking had not earned his reputation for nothing. It was a decided benefit, she was aware, to have a sailor who did not need to brave the hazards of the illegal port of Thanet because he had his own arrangement with the portreeves at Scarborough. However, this only put the Viking in a better bargaining position. Upon learning that he docked in full view of the king's men, Katherine observed, with some asperity, "Well, you don't lack effrontery!" to which the Viking replied in equally harsh accents, "No, I don't lack that!" After some little wrangling, with Katherine losing ground quickly, the bargaining culminated with the Viking's offer to pay her ten marks the shipload.

"Not for all the wool in Yorkshire," she said, and rose to signal the end of the interview. "There is no need for you to berate my poor woman's intelligence, nor to make a May game of me! I shall take heed of your threat to bar any sailor of your undoubtedly wide acquaintance from sailing for me, but I am not desperate and will take my chances without you."

The Viking rose with her, shaking his head slowly. "The keel is laid, as we say, mistress."

"And our ship will be built, I suppose?" she retorted. Her laugh was metallic. "There is nothing more you can do about it."

He took a step toward her and looked down at her through steely eyes. "I am sailing under your banner, and I am not giving you a choice. Do you imagine that you can sail without me? You'll learn to know me better."

Katherine threw her head back to look up at him. "You are ranting, Master Eric. You'll learn to know *me* better!"

"God's Blood!" he snapped, his eyes grown cold as the winter's sea. "I stand in line behind no man, not even a mayor."

He had been deliberately insulting. Katherine knew it but was incapable of controlling her reaction. She felt the anger inside her like a physical ache.

Before she, herself, knew what she was doing, the Viking had grasped and imprisoned the hand that she had raised to slap him across the face. He looked down at her, and she saw the swift flash of satisfaction in his gray eyes, as if he had provoked her to a purpose. They were but a breath away from one another, and Katherine was acutely aware of how the strong sea winds that were his essence had been unleashed and threatened to overpower her. She felt a thrill of fear and dropped her eyes to the strong column of his bronzed throat. She fixed her gaze on the linen chemise he wore unlaced at the neck under the fine wool tunic.

"Our positions are not comparable," he repeated, anger still roughening his voice. His hand tightened on her wrist as she tried to pull it away. The pain of his grip spread up her arm, but she did not try to pull away a second time. "Shall I press the issue?" Then, with a slow shake of his head, "No."

Retort strangled in her throat.

"You are wise to hold your tongue," he commented, this time with the barest trace of amusement. He continued, "You do very well for yourself, mistress. But not well enough. You'll not get another sailor. Not here, not on the coast, and we both know it. I'm a reasonable man and can see that equal risk reaps equal reward. If you get the wool I want by the day after tomorrow, I am willing to split our profits down the middle."

Katherine managed to find her voice but could not control it. "What you will, Master Eric," she said unsteadily and had to clear her throat. "I am satisfied. You will have the wool when you want it."

"Do you need money?"

Was there no end to his insults? "My credit is good," she said through her teeth.

He released her then, and her free hand came absently to cover the maltreated wrist. The marks of his fingers still lingered.

"Very well, then. You'll be able to count a good twenty to thirty marks within the month."

The next moment he was gone.

Emma chased after him to see him to the door, while Katherine was left in her fury to consider that the equal division of their profits was the deal that the Viking had probably intended to give her in the first place, and so she had exposed herself to no purpose. This realization, however, did not make her regret her behavior. In fact, although her pulses were still throbbed with anger and her breast still heaved at his insults, she deeply savored the way she had roused his anger to so dangerous a level.

If Katherine was pleased with the outcome of her interview with the Viking, Emma was not, and when this highly proper serving woman returned to the solar, Katherine was treated to the full force of Emma's shock and disapproval.

"Mistress Katherine!" she scolded in the manner she took with the wayward children in their household, "your conduct was shameful!"

"Shame*less,* more like!"

Emma was not amused. "Either way you were—were—" Emma choked. "I can only say that you deliberately misled him about—the good Lord have mercy!—about all the businessmen, and the aldermen, and the Lord Mayor. You were —you were—"

"Vulgar," Katherine supplied. "I was very vulgar," she repeated with satisfaction, "and I shall be more vulgar still if that man continues to behave toward me in that odious manner!"

"But—but *why?*"

"Why? I enjoyed it! I enjoyed saying all of those horrible things about myself. And he *believed* it!"

"Well, of course he believed it, when you did your best to make him think you were nothing more than the lowest doxy. Upon my word!" Emma gasped again, as if just now coming to a full realization of her beloved mistress's behavior. "And about the children! Mercy! You implied that you housed and fed and clothed them for *business!* I was never so ashamed!"

"That is exactly what he wanted to hear, added to which, it did happen in that very instance that the boys Jonathan and Harold were helpful to me in having that good source of wool."

"But that was *not* why we started this home. You *never* profit from the children. Never! Except, perhaps, in that one instance. And then you were doing the shepherd a favor without thinking what it might bring us. *He* suggested that you could make a little extra money on the side if you bought wool from him to sell on your own without the intervention of the guild. You know that's true."

"Of course I do. But that—that *man* cast the gauntlet down at my feet upon entering this house last week! He had already made up his mind about me before we began. Admit it! Oh!" Katherine cried out in a rage, "If *I* were a man, I would accept that challenge and run him through with a sword!"

Emma was at a loss. "Then what would you do for a sailor?" she asked, somewhat feebly.

Katherine snapped her fingers. "That is what I would do for a sailor. I could get along very well without him."

"But Mistress Katherine—" Emma began in protest.

"I shall frustrate him every step of the way, Emma. He shall rue the day he entered into partnership with me," Katherine vowed.

Emma, who had never seen her mistress in such a temper

and who had certainly never heard her utter any words concerning business that was not always in her best self-interest, was trying to keep pace with Katherine's reactions to her partner. If she were attracted to him—and heaven knew that the Viking was attractive, in Emma's opinion—she would certainly not be doing her best to repel him with her behavior.

"But, my dear, nothing of what you said about yourself is true. He is bound to learn it someday and will think that you have played him for a fool."

Katherine responded with a most unlikely but highly satisfying vision. "And then he shall grovel at my feet in apology," she pronounced dramatically.

The Viking, meanwhile, had stalked away from Jubbergate Street, though not in the degree of fury in which his partner was seething, in enough of a temper to snap at Geoffrey Taverner, who was unwise enough, when the shipwright returned to the inn, to venture a remark on the cool evening weather.

Master Geoffrey, slightly taken aback, hustled back to the kitchen where he nodded sagaciously to his Petronella and recommended her to "bring out the brewet, and be quick about it! The shipwright's here and mortal anxious he is, too, for his supper. Trust Geoffrey Taverner to know when a man's sharp-set. I can't help but wonder at it, though," the taverner continued, mildly puzzled, "for when the shipwright came back to York earlier in the day, I would have said that he had a well-fed look about him. Rarely am I wrong about such things, but where he could have worked up such a hunger in these few hours, I cannot guess."

Although the taverner was at a loss to determine the source of the Viking's appetite, Master Geoffrey's chest swelled with pride when he saw with what relish the shipwright attacked the victuals set out before him.

The Viking, however, hardly tasted his food. His satisfaction in the meal derived principally from the mental review of the names that he applied to his new partner, and among them, Bar's estimation of *saint* most certainly did not figure. Indeed, the thoughts he cherished about Katherine were fully as unkind as any she indulged toward him. Although the Viking's temper was hot and imperious, it was by no means ungovernered, and he could recognize that she had stood up to him far better than he ever would have imagined. If he had begun this day with a desire to use the lovely Mistress Katherine to get to Mauleon, he had ended it with a firm resolve to ruin the heartless jade herself, and vowed, unconsciously following her own example, not to be out-done by a beautiful strumpet with the morals of an alley cat. Not that he believed the half of what she had implied, but since he did believe that she would stop at nothing to gain her ends, whatever they might be, he did not doubt her con-nection with Mauleon. He had also derived a gritty satisfac-tion at her bald admission of her liaison with the lord mayor. He might have underestimated her before, but he had her full measure now. She was beautiful, she was intelligent, she was dangerous; he would bring her to her knees and very much enjoy doing it.

The ruthless train of the Viking's thoughts was presently interrupted by the taverner, who was eager to gauge the Vik-ing's reaction to the meal. Master Geoffrey hovered about, straightening a bench, wiping invisible crumbs off a neigh-boring table, refilling the pitcher of ale that stood at the Viking's right hand, until the Viking chose to end the sus-pense by complimenting his host on the excellent repast. Then the abrupt request: "Tell me about your mayor."

Geoffrey Taverner could not have been better pleased. "Well, now. It's the lord mayor you're wanting to hear about. Not a bad fellow, and so I say. Not a bad fellow at all. Well liked in York, too, and we've just elected him to his fourth term this February past. On St. Blaize's Day, given that wool is our patron saint, as you'll be knowing. But the mayor is none so bad. Oh, he has humble beginnings. Very humble! But there's nothing to hold against a body in that. Why, it's not his fault that his mother was never married— though she was quite a beauty, so I'm told."

The taverner leaned forward. "And that is why his father was a Norman lord. That's the rumor. A high and haughty one, too, which accounts for the fact that Fitz Osbert— that's our mayor. Godric Fitz Osbert—and there's no need telling you that there's a name for a Norman by-blow, if ever there was one! And that, you see, is why our mayor was educated in a monastery and speaks French like one of them." There was a disapproving tone in the taverner's voice, but he was a practical man before all else, and so he appended the observation. "Not but what his ability to speak that tongue isn't a good thing for us in York when all is said and done. Bless my soul, it's good to have one of our own represent us and make our wishes known with no mistake. But, as I was saying, the mayor is a pleasant enough fellow with a sense of what is best for York. A handsome man, too, and a bit of a dab with the ladies. Not that I approve of his mode of dress. Never think it! Not at all what I care for, although it suits his station as mayor, I suppose, and apparently the womenfolk think him as fine as a shiny brass trivet. It queers me, though, that he never married."

From this broad opening the Viking drew the loquacious taverner out on the subject of York guilds and trade. After chatting at length on the scandalous taxes imposed on the good citizens of York and a helpful hint on how Master Shipwright might avoid a levy or two himself, the taverner declared, "But it's the drapers what suffer the most, bless my soul! And with the wool we have, it's the drapers who should by all rights be the richest, what suffer the most. Oh, yes! We've had the drapers' guild since the days of King Henry when the weavers banded together to form what they called a monopoly, but they couldn't pay the guild money, steep as it was, year after year, and so they got deep into debt with the Jews. Very deep debt! Why, York used to have many a Jewish family, and right good citizens and neighbors they were, too. They lived in Jubbergate Street and Coney Street. But that was before the trouble, and I'm ashamed to think that suchlike ever took place in York, bless the Virgin Mary"—The taverner shook his head mournfully—"and there's been no monopoly since. A good thing, I call it! More than one draper had gone under before the trouble against the Jews, and as for the rest of them—well, *their* debt was wiped out at the deaths of their creditors. You've heard the story?"

The Viking nodded.

"Then you'll be knowing that it's a shame that York has

had to live with for many a year," the taverner said with a deep rumble of emotion, for the memory of the final curse on "the pig-eating Christians," spat out by the Jews before their massacre that the young Geoffrey Taverner had heard twenty-five years before, could still rend him to his very soul. "And for all you could have heard 'Death to the Unbelievers!' in the streets of York during those riots, I'll never come to think that the massacre of the Jews was to avenge the death of Our Saviour on the cross. And if *that's* what it means to be a Christian," he confided, "then I'll stay by the Saxon gods who have served us long and well and with no bloodshed. And so I've told the archbishop!"

Master Geoffrey wiped his face with his apron and recovered himself. "But you know, as a kind of atonement for that tragedy and the black mark it has left on York, let me tell you that our archbishop, in all his wisdom, has made the house of the richest moneylender, Baruch, into a home for orphans. Now, Baruch, who lived in Jubbergate Street, and who, by the by, bought out from Leofwyn, oh, years ago it was, too—though that's of no interest to you—survived the tragedy and left York for parts unknown. It's said that he has returned, but ah well! I know nothing about it. But as I was saying, his house is now in the hands of a Mistress Katherine the Broiderer, who, in addition to the fine service she performs for the community, is an outstanding needlewoman. Very devoted she is to the care of homeless children, too, seeing as how she was homeless once herself, not so long ago."

Something in the Viking's sudden, penetrating glance caused the taverner to ask his guest whether he knew the mistress in question.

The Viking answered in the affirmative.

"Well, then. That's a good thing! I admire the Mistress Katherine myself. Oh, yes! My Petronella is very fond of her, too, and thinks her a very good needlewoman and housekeeper. So is my Petronella. That is, my Petronella's a fine housekeeper and an excellent cook. Not much with a needle, but who's to care when she dresses fish, flesh, and fowl equally well! But if my Petronella has a fault, it's that she likes to think that she rules the roost." Master Geoffrey held up a hand and winked broadly. "My advice for handling women," he informed a man of singularly wide experience, "is to let them think they hold the whip, but in fact"—he nudged the Viking meaningfully—"it's the man who rides the filly and not the other way around. But as I was saying, the Mistress Katherine is a fine woman. One of the best there is. Ah! Mistress Katherine! Why, she's an *angel*!"

Master Geoffrey had hardly begun to sing the Mistress Katherine's praises when, the next thing he knew, the shipwright had thrust his horn of ale under his nose and demanded a refill. It seemed that all confidences were at an end. There was no accounting for the shipwright at all, the taverner thought, for the Dane did not appear to want to hear anything more about a perfect saint of a woman but looked ready instead to make it a night of hard drinking.

_____ Chapter 6 _____

The next day Katherine accompanied Sybille to market. Marta's feelings were hurt, of course, to have her beloved charge taken away from her for the morning, but Katherine wanted time alone with Sybille. Since Katherine knew that Sybille enjoyed the shopping, Katherine thought it strategic to be engaged in that housewifely activity while she dropped gentle hints into Sybille's ear that Stephen Webster's attentions were neither to be sought nor encouraged.

The morning went well. Sybille was indeed in her element at the market, and she had surprised Katherine over the years by the zest with which she applied herself to the mastery of her role as a free townswoman of York. Upon turning sixteen Sybille had acquired from Marta the rudiments of shopping skills but had quickly surpassed her teacher. Sybille had honed on her own a sharp eye for watered wine,

blown-out meat, bread with too much yeast, stale fish red-
dened with pig's blood, and cheese made to look richer by a
soaking in broth. She had learned, too, which of the
butchers mixed tallow with their lard, which cutlerers
trimmed the bone handles of their knives with silver and sold
them as ivory, which chandlers did not observe the proper
measure of wax to wick, and which tailors would repair
cloth ruined by faulty cutting.

During their various commissions Katherine hinted gently
about Stephen Webster's probable future, and because Sybille was as sweet and modest as she was beautiful, Katherine's carefully worded suggestions about Master Stephen's
interest in Eleanora Brewer were not being met with resis-
tance. Sybille was a little surprised and crestfallen, perhaps,
Katherine thought, but Sybille was not displaying any real
hurt, and so Katherine was encouraged that this little talk
had not come too late to be effective.

When they turned on Stonegate on their way home, however, Sybille said seriously and with not a trace of the foreign accent that was discernible in Katherine's speech, "Do
you really think, Katherine, that Stephen's affections are engaged with Eleanora? I would not have said so."

"I cannot tell you when a man's affections are taken,"
Katherine replied in English. It had become such a habit
with them to speak English in public that now they spoke it
even in private. Katherine continued thoughtfully, "But only
a very foolish person would wear his heart on his sleeve,
don't you agree? The fact of the matter is that Mistress
Mathilda was telling me just the other day that Stephen is
very intent on Eleanora." Katherine paused again, for effect,
and added, "You sound surprised by this."

"I am, a little," Sybille confessed.

"How so?" Katherine asked. "Eleanora is a very well
brought up young woman with much to offer Master Stephen, and she's very attractive too!"

"Oh, yes!" Sybille agreed warmly. "I like her very much,
and she has such pretty clothes! But are you saying—do you
think he means to marry Eleanora?" she asked.

"Why, I am sure he does, my dear," Katherine said, as if
the answer were obvious.

The faintest hint of stubbornness set Sybille's rosebud lips. "But, marriage! Oh, no! It is just that I was beginning to think that he rather liked—that is, when you told me, oh, a week or two ago, I suppose, that I was not to make myself so forward with Stephen or to plague him with my presence. Well, I do not think that I am the least bit a nuisance to him. You see, I was beginning to think that he liked my presence and that *he* was seeking *me* out and—and—he says such pretty things to me!"

"Of course, love, he is a poet, and poets always say pretty things," Katherine argued, adding quickly, "but he's a webster first and foremost, and as a tradesman, he is looking to settle down and make a good match."

Sybille wrinkled her brow in consideration. Even a frown could not mar her loveliness, and Katherine could imagine that her sister's fragile, porcelain beauty might well have inspired Stephen Webster to some of his most extravagant poetic flights. "I can see what Stephen's attraction to Eleanora might be," Sybille said thoughtfully. "Truly I do, Katherine. She would make someone an excellent wife. But, you see, I thought that Stephen had formed an attachment to me, and now you tell me that he is making up to Eleanora, and I cannot believe that he is so inconstant!"

Katherine laughed gently. "Can you not? He is a man like any other. Do I need tell you? Young, old, handsome, homely: they are all the same. *Fickle,* I believe, is the word the Saxons use, and men are notoriously fickle."

"But you said that Stephen was intent on Eleanora," Sybille said, brightening a little, "and I thought you meant that his—his emotions were engaged. I do not think he will marry where his heart does not take him."

The time for subtle hints was over. "Eleanora is a rich young woman, and Stephen knows it," Katherine said bluntly. "You'd do well to realize it too!"

Sybille looked hurt, and because Katherine could not bear for her sister to suffer even the slightest wound, she tried to soften the blow. "You might think now, Sybille, that you feel some attachment to Master Stephen. He is a handsome boy, I own, and he might have given you to think that he feels something toward you. Nevertheless, you are both very young, and these calf loves do not last. Just a passing fancy, as Emma would say. You may depend on it, for I know what I am talking about!"

Sybille asked, in all her innocence, "But how can you know about it, Katherine, when your heart has never been taken? Why, Daniel Goldsmith has been wanting to marry you for years, and you have never given him a second look. Or any other man in York!"

Katherine would have liked to ask Sybille how she came by this particular piece of information. Katherine, herself, had never mentioned to her younger sister the highly eligible Widower Goldsmith or his persistent courtship of her, but she did not now want to digress from the matter at hand.

Before Katherine could answer, Sybille continued, "And don't tell me that it has anything to do with your fear of losing your respectability, because I should think you have established that long since!"

Sybille was right. Katherine had irrefutably established her respectability. Upon arriving in York as a woman of some nineteen years without male protection, Katherine had not at first been sanguine about the prospects of making a decent life for herself and her sister. Katherine saw that the moral code within city walls was as stringent as within castle walls and could not be breached, particularly not by a young woman alone in the world. Since all could be lost with even one longing glance at the wrong man, Katherine had taken extreme care in all her dealings with the male half of the population. This, added to the excellent personal and professional relations she enjoyed with the women, had won for her the respectability she desired.

Katherine would have received the blessing of York had she wanted to marry the widower; but she did not, and mention of the Master Goldsmith's attentions served Katherine's point.

"Certainly you can see how unsuitable a marriage between me and Master Goldsmith would be, my dear," she said at last. To Sybille's wide-eyed appeal Katherine continued on a gentler note. "He would do well to fix his desire on any number of the young women in town who would be pleased to reciprocate it. Mistress Sarah, for example, would do very well for him." Katherine paused. "Just as Eleanora will do very well for Master Stephen."

"But he is not in love with her!" Sybille insisted.

"Love? Oh, yes. The beating of two hearts as one," Katherine said prosaically. "Love is the figment of a poet's imagination. That much we learned from the most elegant Aquitanian *trouvères* who would travel to Roncevaux! And now that it has come up, I certainly hope that Master Stephen has not, what with all the pretty things he has said to you, talked of love or anything else of an indecorous nature!"

"Oh, no, no, no!" Sybille protested readily. "Never that! He is all that is proper. And so good!"

"Well, *that* is a relief," Katherine said in her most matter-of-fact manner. "I would not like to think that Master Stephen is making up to one young lady while on the verge of offering for another."

"Oh, it's not fair!" Sybille cried, betraying now all her youth and hurt.

"No, it is not," Katherine replied firmly. "Few things that have happened to us thus far have been fair. We have been over all this before, my love! Our purpose here and now is to make an attempt to balance some of the unfairness with our own plans, and it looks as if our very best chance is coming soon. We might never regain our home, but I intend to come close enough."

"York is my home," Sybille stated simply.

"I am glad that you have adjusted so well," Katherine said quickly. "I know that it hasn't been easy for you, our new life."

"But I love living in town! I don't want to go back to castle life."

"Court life," Katherine corrected. "It was what you were born for." Further words of denial were bubbling to Sybille's lips, but Katherine stopped them by saying, with some difficulty, "You are the daughter of the Duc de Roncevaux. There is no denying it or forgetting it." She added silently, "Our mother's spirit cannot rest peacefully until you are reestablished."

"Oh, I know! Indeed, I do, Katherine! You are right. You

have done so much for me, and I am so very grateful. Truly! But it is not easy."

"It will go much easier for you if you do not attach too much importance to the home we have made for ourselves in York, or to any of your friends. Do you understand that?"

Sybille was all obedience. She nodded. "I do. Truly I do! I'll stay away from Stephen from now on. I'll never speak to him again."

"You need not stay completely away from him, my dear, and if you see him on the street and you are with Marta or one of your friends, of course you must greet him and exchange words as acquaintances do. But no private talk!"

Sybille's heavenly blue eyes filled with misty tears. She murmured that she understood and would do as Katherine bid.

"I only want what is right for you, my dear," Katherine said. "It is not just a whim of mine, you know."

Sybille blinked away a tear. "I know that, too, Katherine. And I promise not to add to your problems when you have so many other ones just now."

Katherine laughed and dismissed this. "Not at all, love! Everything is going along just fine. Well, there are problems that come up in the course of the day but nothing out of the ordinary."

"I wouldn't call Josef's death ordinary," Sybille countered.

Katherine was conscious, once again, that Sybille was growing up. Although Sybille necessarily possessed the essentials of Katherine's business, Katherine had always taken care to shield Sybille from the details of her dealings, and Katherine had scrupulously avoided all mention in the past two weeks to anyone but Emma her worries with Mauleon and Josef and her newest partner. Katherine had confidence in Emma's discretion, but Sybille had eyes in her head and knew without being told of the general comings and goings of their house in Jubbergate Street.

"No, but I have taken care of all that now," Katherine said lightly.

"I know that too," Sybille said, "and I saw Master Shipwright in town this morning."

"*What*?" Katherine exclaimed, taken off-guard, but fortunately they had just turned down Jubbergate Street and there was no one about to hear her cry out.

"Why, yes," Sybille replied, blinking in surprise at the unaccustomed violence of Katherine's reaction. "I know that you do not like to discuss your trade with me, but is there some reason why he should not be in York today?"

"Not at all," Katherine replied hastily. "He returned here yesterday, as you know, and I expect him to stay a few more days. Two or three, perhaps, until we get the first shipment established. My—my surprise at mention of his name comes only from his association with you. You have not been indiscreet, have you?"

"What do you mean?" Sybille asked cautiously, flushing.

"I mean, of course, that it would not do to have Master Eric associated too closely with our house, under the circumstances. He does not have quite the same relationship to York as did our Josef. It is one thing for me to be seen with him parading the streets and another to have him engage you in conversation. Did he speak with you?"

"Oh, no," Sybille replied, recovering her complexion. "It would have been most unseemly for me to speak with a man like that. Besides, he did not look particularly interested in me and did not even really recognize me when his eye fell on me, although I met him only yesterday evening in our courtyard, just as he was leaving our house. Emma made the proper introduction, but he was so fierce-looking that he put me in a quake. But today in town, it was as if I did not exist, which is what you would like, is it not?"

"You only saw him, then," Katherine said, feeling relief.

"Yes, he was engaged in conversation with Stephen, you see, and afterward Stephen told me—" Sybille clapped her hand to her mouth and blushed beautifully. "But Marta was with me. Stephen and I had no private conversation, I swear to you, Katherine!"

Suddenly indulgent toward Sybille on the subject of her latest meeting with Stephen, Katherine prompted, "And Stephen told you afterwards . . . ?"

Sybille squared her shoulders and said with a touch of defiance, "They discussed Stephen's poetry, I believe, and

Master Shipwright seemed not to—to laugh at him the way all the others do. It makes me think the better of him, I can tell you, for when I met him yesterday, I would have said that the shipwright is a very rude man."

Katherine smiled unexpectedly when they arrived at their door. "So, Master Eric Shipwright has a turn for poetry, does he? Well!" Then, reasonably, "He is bound to meet people in York and speak with them, and Stephen is as harmless a connection as any. All right, now, enough of this. We are agreed what is best for you—enough said! Tell me instead all about little Anna's recovery."

Once inside, Sybille was proud to say that Anna was progressing wonderfully. Sybille had personally undertaken the little girl's care, and while Anna had been grievously ill for quite some days and could not hold down her food well, Sybille explained that the worst was behind them and that Anna would be playing with the other children in no time at all. Katherine heard the details of Sybille's ministrations on the way across the courtyard. There she saw little Anna herself, intently watching from a sunny corner of the yard a game of closh with ninepins being played by a group of the older children. Emma was presiding over the contest.

After a few minutes of observation Katherine came over to Emma and said brightly, "Well, I'll be off now."

A shadow momentarily darkened Emma's straight brow. "Do you know what you are going to say?"

"I've rehearsed it a dozen times: I have the money to pay off Mauleon, and there is no reason to inform him that anything has changed in my way of doing business. As far as he might be concerned, Josef still lives. It is a risk, but one I must take."

Emma nodded approvingly. "The chances of his having heard of Josef's death are slim. I've done what I could to put it about in certain quarters in town that if any questions are asked, particularly by Norman lords, Josef's prolonged absence from town is nothing unusual. Mauleon would, of course, have no access to the talk, but you never know about the lord mayor."

Katherine pursed her lips. "I have the felicity of seeing our lord mayor first, as you know," she said. "A pleasant interlude before the delight of seeing Mauleon again. Although between the two of them I much prefer the mayor to Mauleon."

"Take a care," Emma said low.

"I shall," Katherine replied, gathering together her courage. " I am reasonably confident of the outcome."

"And the prayer missal?" Emma reminded her mistress.

Katherine blinked. "By the apostles! I nearly forgot." She smiled ruefully. "Did I speak of confidence? Overconfidence, more like, if I am to go about with my head cut off. I can hardly see the mayor without the prayer missal, can I?"

Emma offered to fetch the object in question, but Katherine declined, saying that she had stored it in a new place. Katherine returned to her solar and used the occasion to adjust her starched coif in the small hand mirror she kept in her bedchamber. Two minutes later she was in the street with the pious prayer missal tucked under the arm of her cloak and wending her way toward the castle.

Katherine made her most direct way by skirting toward the defenses surrounding the town proper. She passed presently in the shadow of Walmgate Bar, one of the four main gates into York, whose towers, curved, square-toothed, and crenellated, stood mute sentry to the city. From Walmgate Bar she turned onto Friar's Walls Lane, which ran along the River Ouse to the city's main fortifications. From this lane she had direct sight of the one structure high atop its motte of earth that rose above the city, a potent sign of royal authority. She soon found herself at the foot of the menacing bulk of the castle and trod the long, steep flight of steps to the main portal at a pace eloquent of grace and confidence.

Godric Fitz Osbert, Lord Mayor of York, happened to be outside on the bulwark watching her ascent, another slim figure in his shadow. The mayor was a suavely handsome man, dramatically clad in a rich ebony mantle, one panel of which was cast over his shoulder and secured by a large and very handsome silver clasp to expose the length of crimson tunic beneath. A black hat, which came to a sharp point in front and adorned by a curling plume, was set at a slightly rakish angle on the mayor's thick silver waves. He wore one black glove and held the other in the same hand, together with an extremely heavy-looking trousseau of keys. From under the narrow brim of his hat a pair of light brown eyes were looking enigmatically down on Katherine. Their expression, along with the Gallic nose and the exquisitely shaped mouth that was saved from femininity by a decidedly square jaw, combined with the mayor's sartorial perfection to give him an air of elegance and urbanity.

When Katherine had mounted the last step and turned toward him, his face was wreathed in a smile of welcome.

"*Votre servant, demoiselle,*" he greeted her, bowing over her hand with punctilious grace, and continued in English, "You may well stare to find me out of doors on such a day. Here I am standing in this disagreeable wind when you know very well that I am not at all of the robust constitution that so many of our pure-bred Saxons enjoy. Ill winds have a way of ferreting me out, and my colds always descend upon my chest. But Piers, the dear boy, persuaded me that although the winds were freshening, they had shifted from the north quarter to the south and that I would be entirely protected from them by the bulwark. And I did so want to put my new cloak to the test. I find that I have not the least chill and am enormously pleased! But do you think," he said, casting a critical eye over the mantle, "that the effect is perhaps too— how should I say?— funereal?"

Katherine had not at all been wondering why the mayor was outside, and being used to his gentle eloquence, she was able to reply that it was a becoming creation, adding, accurately, that she detected the hand of Samuel Taylor. Her eyes moved around the mayor to a fair, gentle youth with hardly the down of a beard on his chin and said, "Good day to you, Piers."

"Mistress Katherine," the youth murmured in return with a respectful nod, and after a few more desultory remarks on the weather the mayor dispatched Piers with a silken voice to the performance of one of the many ill-defined but apparently entirely necessary offices the young man executed to justify being in the mayor's employ.

When Piers had melted into the shadows of the creamy limestone battlement, sparking white in the late March sun, Katherine handed the prayer missal to the mayor with the words, "The accounts are finished and should satisfy, once again, the sheriff, when he comes next to collect the revenues."

"Ah, Katherine," Godric said in dulcet tones, accepting the black leather-bound book and smiling his singularly compelling smile. "How you relieve my mind of care. Positively you do."

"Our arrangement is of mutual benefit in that respect, sir, is it not?" Katherine returned sedately.

"Is it? Why, yes, it is of mutual benefit for the ends we both hope to achieve, but your motives, my dear, are by far the purest. I confess that I envy you your purity and your determination."

"My determination would be sadly insufficient were it not for you," Katherine answered for the sake of form.

The mayor bowed with a flourish. "I invest for you in the guilds. It is nothing. The easiest thing imaginable for a man in my position. An insignificant nothing compared to the work you do for me. But then," he said, considering the disparity in degree of difficulty of the services they performed for one another, "women are accustomed to these unequal accommodations."

Katherine preserved a demure silence.

"Do not think that I do not understand your position," Godric continued. "I understand perfectly. Most assuredly I do! You are convinced of my sincerity, are you not? Otherwise we could not work together in such harmony. Nevertheless, women do not, in general, achieve what you have achieved. Such a very unusual combination of gifts you possess, my dear! Your head for numbers, for example," he said, gesturing minimally with the prayer missal, "must surely be unique among women. Not, of course, that I intend to disparage the rest of your sex, for I do not have the genius for numbers, either. The way you are able to conjure columns of these numbers makes me think, at times, that you are a witch."

Katherine smiled slightly. "There is no secret to my ability, as you well know, sir. The task is greatly simplified when one has mastered the numerals the Arabs have devised. They are far less cumbersome than the system that you were taught."

The mayor lapsed into memory. "How my spirits would quail when confronted with a sum to be reckoned in the Roman numbers. If the sum were beyond twenty—no! Quite beyond me. It was perhaps that, more than anything, that made me realize that I was most unsuited for a monastic existence. That must, of course, remain one of life's ironies. One would have thought that I would have been eminently suited for the life of the monastery."

"Your talents are better used as mayor," Katherine said. "I have benefited."

"Yes," Godric replied affably. "I plume myself on the talents that come naturally to me and that make me so . . . useful in York. But we were discussing your talents my dear, not mine. It seems that you have a natural head for numbers. I stand in awe!"

Katherine thanked him prettily for the compliment.

"You have never divulged, you know, how you learned the Arabs' system for counting. Of course, I hardly need ask, for no doubt, somewhere along the way in your varied career you learned from a poor, itinerant scholar with whom no one else would care to speak and got the lessons at bargain rates. In addition to your talent with numbers I have observed that you have a positive gift for seeking out unusual people and using them to good advantage. Not that you do not do so charmingly, I own!" Godric plainly did not expect a reply to these observations because he continued without hesitation, "And speaking of your unusual connections, you have come to see my brother, have you not?"

"Yes, sir, I am come to see Lord Mauleon at the quarter hour."

"How stand your affairs with him?" Godric inquired casually.

"My ship has come in at last, sir" was Katherine's response, "and I am back in business. I have come, in fact, to pay him what I owe him."

Godric Fitz Osbert's eyes flickered with something that Katherine could not quite fathom. "I am glad of it, my dear," he said. "Truly I am glad of it. My dear brother—or should I say, more accurately, half brother?—wants finesse. There is a certain coarseness of mind about him that I deplore. Not that I am one to find continual fault. He cannot help it that he is liverish, after all, and he has been so much the worse ever since he was denied the one and only thing he ever truly desired, I believe. Far too much indulged as a youth. He does his best to smooth over the rough edges, but the effort does not come naturally to him. Yet he is the one with birth and title and land, while I—" The Mayor broke off again, more artfully this time. "But that is another of life's ironies. Run along now, my dear. I am inclined to congratulate you on your narrow escape from what I can only call my dear brother's clutches. Indeed, my conscience smote me that I put you on to him in the first place, but I knew that you were having difficulties making ends meet, and I was also aware that you would never presume too much on your relationship with Baruch. My dear brother seemed the perfect stopgap for you at the time, but I seem to have miscalculated. I was truly sorry that when I began to realize the new difficulties that his intervention presented to you . . . but, ah, well, I have done well for you and Leofwyn, have I not?"

Katherine felt at the moment that the mayor would have done better not to have had her use the name Leofwyn to trade by in the guild, but she held her tongue on her unfortunate partnership with the Viking and merely nodded.

Dismissed by Godric's words, Katherine entered the gate house, her passage past the guards assured by a negligent wave of the hand from the mayor. She traversed the barbican, looking neither right nor left, and penetrated the castle proper through a wicket in the huge wooden gates by which people could be let in or out. The main hall was poorly lit, but as it gave onto a gallery that faced west, there was enough natural light to guide her steps. She climbed a narrow, winding staircase carved out of the wall of a round turret and felt the wind swirling up that cavity. She soon arrived at a high-vaulted chamber. The exterior wall of that chamber rose out of the curtain wall of the castle and formed the most imposing fortification. This wall, high above the moat created by the damming of the River Foss, was broken by three arched windows fitted with mullioned green glass. The room was hung with palls of tapestries to block the drafts and to absorb the heat of the leaping fires that were laid in the two capacious hearths that faced each other across the wide expanse of room. Several functionaries, liveried and official-looking, moved in and out of the room, keeping busy.

Hardly had she entered this room than she heard a voice at her side. "Your prompt arrival," it said in French, "encourages me to think that you are eager to be here." Katherine's slight start caused the voice to continue, on a faint note of satisfaction, "Do I surprise you?"

Katherine stepped back from the figure that had crept up on her from behind. "Good day, sire. You do surprise me," she said coolly in the language of the nobility. "I am eager, as you suggest. I had expected to be here first and most likely would have been had I not engaged in conversation with the lord mayor."

The voice had a face. It sneered. "And you were transported with joy to speak with him, were you not? But since he could hardly be accused of detaining a woman to practice the art of dalliance, I must assume that your eagerness to arrive here was not on his account."

"No, sire. On yours."

"Ah, *demoiselle*! You have had a change of heart!"

"A change of fortune, rather," she replied, and gave the conversation a literal turn. "The closing of an account—yours—is always reason for eagerness. I have come to pay you my debt."

Something unpleasant sprang into the face but was quickly masked behind a thin smile.

The sight of the man always jarred Katherine. From the circumstance of his being one of the most powerful barons in all the land and enjoying the reputation of a knight of unquestioned chivalry, he assumed in her mind rather more magnificent proportions when absent than in the flesh. He was Cedric de Mauleon, Lord Arcachon, Earl of Wessex, but his physical presence seemed ill suited to bear these noble titles.

He was clad in a velvet tunic trimmed with fur, as befitted his station in life, but his eye for fashion was imperfect. He was booted and properly spurred and displayed the physique of a knight well trained. Nevertheless, for all his muscles, there was a narrowness about him, and it amused Katherine to imagine that his shoulders might droop under the weight of mail.

"You have come to pay me, *demoiselle*?" Mauleon asked. "Now it must be said that you surprise me!"

Katherine was prepared for this and on her mettle. "There is no cause for surprise," she said. She reached into her cloak, withdrew a heavy purse, and extended it on an open palm. "Here are the twenty-five marks which you so kindly lent me, and a little more," she said, lowering her lashes, "for it would be remiss of me not to include a gift to you, sire."

Mauleon did not immediately take the proffered purse. "A gift, *demoiselle*? Of money?"

"Why, of course, the gift is monetary. How could it be otherwise?"

He laughed indulgently. "Very easily. I did not expect it."

"It is the custom in business," she pursued, "to repay the debtor for use of money."

"Such talk!" Mauleon exclaimed with distaste. "Debt! Loans! Gifts! It is like the taste of lemons." His eyes narrowed. Their color, light brown, was the only feature that might possibly have indicated a bond of blood to Godric Fitz Osbert, but their expression was so very different from the mayor's languid regard. Mauleon was unaware that Katherine knew of the relationship between him and the mayor; if he had known, it would not have unduly troubled him. "Do you forget that you speak to a peer of the realm and not to one of your merchant friends?"

"Not at all, sire," she replied respectfully, "and that is why I have offered you a gift instead of calculating the interest on a loan, as I would for a banker."

Mauleon narrowed his eyes and switched tactics. He took the purse. "After all, that is the game you play," he said, as if to himself. "And to think that some women pine for flowery phrases."

"Sire?"

Mauleon waved his hand impatiently. "Tell me about this unexpected payment, I beg of you."

Katherine nodded, as if happy to converse with him on the subject. "Indeed, sire, but it is hardly unexpected. I learned that my shipment had arrived safely on the coast shortly after your departure from my house last week. Of course, then it took several days to receive the vouchers and then the conversion into currency, but I have it now, and I was able to weather the rough times, thanks to your help and patience. For that I thank you."

"My patience, *demoiselle*, has yet to be rewarded."

"You speak in riddles, sire," she countered.

"Since you will have it in the plainest of terms, I mean that I do not view our relationship in the light of creditor and debtor but of man and woman."

Katherine said evenly, "Were you not a married man, I would understand you better."

"Married?" he ejaculated.

"Do I misunderstand? Are you not married?"

The light brown eyes narrowed again. "I cannot begin to guess why my marital status should have any effect on our arrangement."

Katherine maintained her position. "It is only that I had thought that the proposition you mentioned last week— well, now, sire, upon learning of your marriage from the mayor, I fear that you meant the proposition to be dishonorable."

"There is a little dishonor attached to one such as I desiring one such as you."

"But—but," she said, as if foundering in confusion touched with embarrassment.

"Surely you did not build false hopes, Demoiselle Broiderer," Mauleon said, the scorn like a whip in his voice.

"I did not know what to think, sire. Honor and marriage go together. It is the custom."

Mauleon sneered. The expression came easily to him. "The burghers and their customs!"

"They are the only customs I know, sire," she said, affecting mortification.

"And how is it, then, that you speak such excellent French?"

"I have the ear for it. I have found it useful in business, and did I not have it, I could not deal with you."

There was something elusive about the woman that maddened and incited Mauleon. He had not expected her to pay him. Nor had he expected her to balk at what he anticipated would be a very agreeable arrangement between them. He was unused to moral scruples attending a lady's coy denial before her ultimate capitulation. The novelty had its charm, but he was growing impatient.

"Back to your ship, *petite bourgeoise*," he said. "I had heard of trouble on the coast. I thought that your sailor might have been in it. At least Fitz Osbert seemed to think so when he first mentioned you to me."

"Oh, yes, I heard of it, too, and was sick with apprehension that Josef was involved," she answered readily. "Fortunately he was not harmed in the brawl, if that is the trouble you are referring to. Oh, he was a little the worse for having been in the fight, but he has returned and I can go along again most comfortably."

"I can add to your comfort, my dear, if you could overcome your scruples to allow it," he suggested silkily.

Katherine could not imagine that her position could be any less comfortable than it was at present, finding herself caught as she was between the Viking and Mauleon. She replied lightly, "Oh, no, sire, my affairs are quite satisfactory!"

Mauleon crudely phrased the suggestion that Katherine had all the satisfaction she needed from her sailor.

Since Katherine's thoughts were still with the Viking, her quick blush was entirely genuine. "Hardly, sire," she managed.

Mauleon noted the flush and was reluctantly convinced that there was nothing between her and her Josef. He paused to consider the various aspects of his interview with Katherine. "How do I know you speak the truth?" he asked at last.

Her face was properly shocked. "I am an honest maid!"

He was suddenly impatient with protests of her virtue. "No, I mean about Josef's return."

A pulse began to beat in Katherine's throat.

"Well, *ma petite*?" he prodded with a nasty undertone that came from his disadvantage in the conversation. He should have paid more attention to the details, he thought. Really, he should have, but he was not expecting her to extract herself from the debt, and he had gotten nothing from the stupid Saxons he had tried to converse with earlier in the day on the wharf.

"But you must have seen Josef on the wharf in the past week," she said with a daring lie. "He is gone again now, of course. Did you not go to the wharf to see him?"

_____ Chapter 7 _____

"I went to the wharf," Mauleon answered somewhat derisively. His voice was dull and opaque, like wax. "But don't all Yorkshire sailors look the same?"

The ploy had worked, and the danger point passed. Katherine's laugh betrayed none of her relief. "Not to me, sire."

"Then I must surely make a point of meeting your hardy Josef so that I may become accustomed to the fine distinctions in Yorkshire physiognomy."

"By all means," she replied. "You have only go to the wharf and ask for him by name. He will return next week, no doubt."

"Ah, but I do not stay the week."

"No?"

"No, *ma petite bourgeoise*, I do not stay," he said. "Is that dismay I read in your lovely face?" He laughed. "I will be back in a month or so."

"After the Easter celebrations, then," she stated. "You travel to London?"

"So much interest in my movements! From another

woman I might preen myself, but from you, *ma petite . . .*
Yes, I go to London, and from there to the coast."

"You mean the southern coast, sire? Go you to Dover,
perhaps?"

Mauleon looked mildly surprised. "I do mean Dover. I
must return your very flattering interest in my person. Tell
me, why might you think I head for Dover?"

Katherine would use this unpleasant interview to good
purpose. "Because Louis of France is reported to be amass-
ing a fleet and heading for the English shore at Dover."

The curious light brown eyes flicked over her. "Is mind
reading another bourgeois custom—like modesty and marriage and monetary compensation?"

Katherine shook her head. "One has only go to York
market to hear the latest of the movements concerning Louis
of France and John of England. Surely, as one of John's
staunchest supporters, you are aware of Louis's movements." Katherine, like her partner the Viking, had surmised
that Mauleon was hedging his bet on who would successfully lay claim to the English crown. She had reason enough
to believe that he, as she intended, was investing in Louis's
cause through his half brother, the lord mayor. Like every
other tradesman in York, she had taken an intense interest in
the events on the field of Running-Mead on the Thames the
year before. "You rode with King John against the rebel
barons, did you not, sire?"

Cedric de Mauleon had indeed ridden with John to Runnymede. It was a day of color he would not soon forget: the
lush, green field and the blue-and-gold pavilion where John
had signed the Magna Charta. Bright sun had lit the banner
of a blue sky above and the fluttering pennants of every
proud English baron below. It had glinted on helmets and
breastplates and lances held erect to display the colors of
those barons open in their opposition to King John. Those
same barons, Mauleon remembered, who had refused to follow the king on his continental forays and whose hatred of
him it had taken to bring them out united and in full force
against him. Proud men, honorable men, foolish men, Mauleon thought. Let them choke on their pride and honor. Sure,
he had ridden with John, along with William the Marshal,

the Earl of Warenne, and a few other lustrous names from the days of the conquest. Only a fool would not have supported John. Only a fool openly challenged a king. And Louis, when he came to wear the English crown, would exile the rebel barons for their folly.

"Naturally I was there," Mauleon said. "But I had not thought the villeins of York to be so informed," he said, "and—"

"Citizens, sire," she corrected.

Mauleon paused. "Faith, how times have changed! The humble Saxon serf has come a long way since the days of my forefathers," he jibed, for he rarely missed an opportunity to enhance his own exalted position, particularly at the expense of others. "The York citizens, if you will have it so, seem to take an unwarranted interest in the doings of their betters."

"They have much at stake in the contest. Trade is our livelihood, and it would be bad business to ignore the contest for the crown or not try to influence its outcome."

"Jésu! Trade! Is that all you think about?" he cried out.

"No, sire," she said, lowering her lashes with the humility demanded by her role as a petty bourgeoise, " I think long and hard about the salvation of my soul."

"Very proper," he said with a twist to his thin mouth, and patted her on the shoulder where his hand rested. "Others of us must concern ourselves with merely the salvation of the kingdom. And in these matters for whom do you pray, I wonder?"

"The citizens of York are for Louis. 'Tis no secret I divulge to you, for you could hardly spend a day here without learning it for yourself. The citizens have some cash in hand and consider it a sound investment to put it behind the man who will soon be wearing the crown."

Mauleon smiled, not troubling to hide his satisfaction. His hand lightly caressed her shoulder. "And if Louis prevails, will you be a part of the York entourage to come to London for his coronation?"

"I hope so, sire," she answered. "But shall Louis prevail? Surely *you* do not hope so."

"Who can say? Your Louis has a fine advantage over

John at the moment. It is rumored that the Frenchman has loaded his ships with the trebuchet. Have you heard of it?"

Katherine had indeed heard of the trebuchet. She knew it to be a more accurate and more powerful version of the catapult, for this latest advance in the engines of destruction had been used with deadly success in the storming of Castle Roncevaux six years previous.

"No, sire," she said demurely, "I have the head for numbers, not for warfare. But does it give Louis an advantage?"

"Most definitely, and when he prevails, I will be pleased to receive you in London, my dear," he said. With the thought of dazzling her with the magnificence of his position in the reign of Louis, his hand traveled from her shoulder down her back, and from there he insinuated his arm around her waist. Katherine willed herself not to recoil in revulsion.

"But sire," she protested, "if Louis prevails, that must spell disaster for you."

He laughed indulgently, as if at a simpleton. "My naive little merchant woman! Do you not know that there are some lords who are above the passage of kings?"

Katherine's eyes widened innocently. "Are you truly so powerful, sire?"

"Truly," he stated, and with that his hand came to rest on the curve of her hip.

There was something reptilian about the man that made Katherine's flesh crawl. "Your hand has become lost, sire," she said.

Mauleon disliked her tone. He had become aware that they were in a public place. Pages scurried to and fro, eyes were upon him. He removed his hand. It crossed his mind that Katherine had chosen this place on purpose, for he could not bodily remove her from the hall without seriously damaging his credit. Not that he cared a flick of his fingers what this lot of Saxons thought. Still, he had a certain reputation to maintain, and he had agreed to this meeting place when he had seen her last in Jubbergate Street only because he had thought her securely in his net.

But he did not have her. He could not quite understand how this little broiderer had eluded him. She should have been easy prey, Mauleon thought acidly, and she was not even the kind of woman who usually attracted him. In the past he had preferred the slim, blond, blue-eyed Nordic beauty. But now he found that Katherine the Broiderer's hazel eyes and rounded curves, her coloring so like the noble Frenchwomen he knew at court, were haunting him and inflaming him. He remembered Godric's taunt: "You must do your best, Cedric, dear brother, to file those rough edges." Mauleon's face soured considerably. He would bide his time, but he would have this little broiderer in the end.

"My hand lost?" His voice had thinned. "I might suggest that you would *find* it pleasurable if given the chance."

She did not reply. She was waiting for him to dismiss her, and he was angered by her lack of response. He had envisioned an entirely different outcome to this encounter. He looked at Katherine once again. He had to leave York on the morrow and did not have an extra day to woo her. He had already waited a week, thinking to be rewarded in the end, but now he felt a fool. Of all things, Mauleon liked least feeling a fool.

"I will see you in a month," he said, the waxy quality of his voice having grown pronounced by his frustration.

"Yes, sire," she said, and could not resist adding, "Perhaps then we will be able to do business again."

"We shall see. I would not call it business, however." He took her hand and raised it to his lips in a gesture designed to fill her with longing.

The loathing she actually felt at his touch lingered long after he had left her standing in the counting room. She had escaped this repugnant man for the moment, but she knew she walked the thinest of lines between having him as ally or enemy.

Katherine found her way out of the castle with no further glimpse of Mauleon. Nor was the mayor anywhere to be seen, although she exchanged a few words with the handsome Piers before descending back into the town.

She needed to clear her mind. It was late afternoon and she did not know well this outer part of the city that ran by the River Foss. She traversed it, anyway, somewhat aimlessly, content that she would see no one she knew. She crossed, unseeing, several invisible boundaries, the parishes that divided the city and that were marked by a stake, each parish having its own church with an imposing gateway and great crossbeams with angels suspended from the roofs and even a chained red devil held at bay under the eaves, each parish having its own city father to whom it was answerable. Katherine had kept to the river, and so she strayed at last into a liberty, or enclave, where the city's authority could not penetrate.

It was a particularly noisome, depressing quarter of York, but Katherine was so lost in thought that she did not immediately notice it. The stink of dung heaps, the penetrating odors of the tanworks, of brine-soaked fish and of the river which took the effluent of dyers and fullers of the cloth trade, where sausage-makers washed skins and fishermen gutted their catch, mingled with the dust and chaff of the streets and with the ever-prevalent tang of wood and peat smoke. Katherine became aware of her surroundings all at once and looked up and down several dirt lanes to find her bearings. She oriented herself to cut back to the center of town, and when she turned a corner, her steps were halted by the drama going forward down a dingy alleyway.

A child, surely not more than six or seven years of age, covered from top to toe in filth, was cringing in terror and whimpering much like a wounded kitten before a tall, gaunt man who, mittened and cloaked, was raining the child with blows and curses. From the man's mode of dress and general demeanor Katherine determined that he was a muckraker and that the urchin he was flogging was his chattel. A scattering of indifferent existences littered the unswept doorsteps of the alley and were taking a sullen interest in the beating.

Instinct warned Katherine that the raker was both vicious by nature and slightly intoxicated. She also determined that she could expect no help from the ragged audience in attendance, but these circumstances did not deter her from her intention of rescuing the boy. It did not particularly trouble her that she herself would come into peril. She was confident that she could either outwit the drunken man or overpower him physically—that is, if she could first trick him into dropping the stick he was waving about. She had had more than her fill of swaggering braggarts for the day, but even without the recent contact with her least favorite bully, Mauleon, to inspire her to action, she would have been moved to save the lad.

Katherine looked about for the largest and most jagged rock she could find at hand, bent down, still unnoticed by the man, and concealed it in the folds of her skirts. Then the hissing birch stick slashed a wicked smile of bright blood across the boy's cheek, and Katherine stepped forward.

"Leave the boy alone," she said in a clear, fearless voice.

Several unwashed heads turned around toward her at this unexpected interruption but effected little change of expression to witness so well dressed a young woman alone and in their untraveled section of town. The gaunt man looked up, gestured impatiently in Katherine's direction, as if he were swatting an annoying fly, and returned to his main occupation.

Katherine took several steps toward the man. "Leave the boy alone," she repeated in firm, authoritarian accents.

This time she succeeded in drawing the raker's attention. From the malevolent gleam in his eye it was certain that he was not disposed to acceding to Katherine's command. He looked her over in the light of a new and possibly more interesting object of abuse. "Well, now, missy," he said in a cracked voice, "and what business is it of yours?"

Katherine did not answer that. She took another step forward so that she was within striking distance of him but outside the circle that he could circumscribe with his stick. "Is the boy your son?"

"What's it to yer?" he replied, and appended a rather crude form of address in referring to her person. Katherine was in blissful ignorance of the cant of this class, but she guessed his meaning well enough.

"I asked you if the boy is your son, and I expect an answer."

The raker chuckled unpleasantly and thought, what with the fine audience, that he would play the scene for what it was worth and humor the hussy before disposing of her in whatever way the fumes curling in his brain took him. "He's mine. I bought him with good money and treat him just like

me own, if yer wanting to know," he said with broad sar-
casm.

"He is not your son, then," Katherine insisted.

"And just what do you intend to do about it?"

"I intend to take him with me to my home," Katherine
stated flatly.

The raker cackled. The urchin was looking up at the goddess who had come, it seemed, to deliver him from his misery and was regarding her in blankest incomprehension. His
experience with the wimpled sex had always been through
the intermediary of a broom handle. He knuckled his eyes
with grimy fists and thought it likely that he had died and
gone to heaven. His hazy notions of paradise had previously
included only a clean room, fresh bed, new clothes, and
enough to eat. He saw now that this conception had fallen
woefully short in that it had lacked a beautiful lady with the
most musical voice he had ever heard. So absorbed was he
in contemplation of this new vision that he had stopped co-
wering.

"Is that the way it is, then, missy?" the raker spat back
derisively. "You come as if you own the place and think to
take what's mine from under my nose. If that isn't just like
you high-nosed bitches to think that whatever is there is
yours for the taking." Perceiving another angle on the situation, the man continued, "He's mine, I say, and wouldn't
think of parting with him—except for a very good price."

"I'll not pay you a pence for him," Katherine said. "I
suggest that you hand him over to me now."

"On whose authority, missy? Your own?" The sweep was
enjoying this now.

"On the archbishop's."

He whistled rudely. "On the archbishop's?" he mimicked.
"Don't you know that you're in a liberty? Damned bitch!" he
spat. "The archbishop's word is nothing here. He has nothing to say to me about my boy here, and he'll have nothing
to say to me when I'm through with you!" The raker came
toward Katherine, suddenly angered by her self-righteous-
ness, and decided that he would take great pleasure in slash-
ing her unmarked skin.

Katherine did not fear the murderous look she read in the

raker's face. Instead, she was planning to use his anger to her advantage and was rapidly devising her plan to disable the man with her rock, then grab the boy and run. She raised her arm to aim her missile, he brandished his switch to stripe her face, and what happened next, neither combatant could have predicted.

A longer, broader shadow had darkened the alleyway. Before the raker had delivered himself of a long string of foul names he was spewing at Katherine, and before he could bring his stick down across her, he was pulled bodily off the ground by the scruff of the neck and thrown effortlessly into a gutter choking with refuse. The raker was to explain to a very appreciative audience later that evening that the human form that had towered over him looked like one of those Viking devils come to life from the stories his granny used to tell to scare little children into minding her, with chips of steel for eyes, molten gold for hair, and sledgehammers for arms.

Katherine registered a mechanical surprise to see the Viking haul the raker to his feet then and boot him soundly out of the alley. She frowned slightly, laboring through the thought that the Viking had followed her, for it was singularly unlikely that he was in this godforsaken liberty on his own business. She consigned the matter to later consideration. Her full attention at present was bent on the urchin who, having no very clear idea what it was all about, was clutching his protectoress's skirts with a single-minded intensity.

Katherine knelt down in the filth of the street and, carefully prying his fingers loose, took the boy's claws in one hand. With her other hand she abstracted a handkerchief from the sleeve of her cloak and began to dab at the clotting wound on his face. He winced at her ministrations but submitted docilely. She gentled him with soothing words, and when she felt that he had accustomed himself to her, she asked him his name.

The boy remained dumb.

"Can you speak, lad?" she asked.

He nodded, his hungry eyes drinking in Katherine's face. "Aye," he croaked a moment later in a small, scared voice.

"Good enough. Now tell me your name."

"Ole Rake called me Ben," he said.

"Old Rake? Your owner?"

The boy cringed slightly and looked warily over at the formidable figure of the Viking looming over them.

Katherine did not even look up at her partner but said, "He won't hurt you, Ben. And neither will the raker ever hurt you again. You have nothing to fear from him now, for I am going to take you to my home with me. Would you like that?"

That vision of paradise shimmered before Ben's eyes, and he was transfixed by it. However, his young life had not been marked by mercy or generosity, and so his face was torn between an expression of joyful anticipation and one of suspicion and terror.

Katherine saw the conflict and guessed the reason. She patted his ragged hair with a gentle hand. "You must not be afraid of me. I promise you that I will not hurt you or let Old Rake near you again. Is that what is troubling you, my dear?"

Ben nodded again. "I'm afeard. Mortal afeared," he confessed, adding, prompted by some dimly understood precept of politeness, "mistress."

Katherine smiled, thereby further enrapturing her young adorer. She looked down at the remains of the braes that covered his skinny legs and at the rags that swaddled his feet. "Did Old Rake not clothe your properly? Does the cold frighten you?"

"That was none so bad," Ben replied, being resigned to accepting life as it came. "It were the rats what scared me most. Big rats at the river where we shoveled the muck!" He shuddered in recollection.

Katherine had had her own memorable experiences with rats on her flight from France and so accepted this statement in its proper light. She frisked him gently for bites or swellings produced by contact with the rats and, finding nothing but the bruises and scars from sundry beatings, decided it time to leave this liberty with no further waste of words.

She got up off her knees and shook out her skirts. Only then did she turn to the Viking, who stood silently at her side, and glancing up and down the empty alleyway where evening shadows were lengthening into weird forms, she said conversationally, "You certainly cleared the street in a hurry. I had not expected to have had such an easy time of it. But I am not sure that Ben can walk—or at least not with any speed or stamina—and we've got the whole of the city to cross. Perhaps you should carry him. I am not sure that I could bear his weight, even underfed as he is."

With a nod in Ben's direction the Viking replied, "Can you do this?"

"Who's to stop me? The raker?" Katherine answered defiantly.

He shook his head. "He'll not be back. No, I was wondering whether your arrangement with the archbishop allows you to adopt any child at will."

"I'm allowed a limit of twelve children," she said, her mind absorbed more by her present charge than by her quarrel with her partner. "I'm at that figure now, but when I go on the morrow to register Ben with the archbishop, I don't expect any trouble. Walter de Grey owes me a favor, as it happens."

Without further remonstrance the Viking picked up the urchin as if he weighed no more than a feather, and the oddly assorted trio left the liberty for more hospitable parts of town.

Katherine examined Ben's wounds as they walked and spoke aloud and at random about the plans for the boy's rehabilitation, which included principally a bath, nourishment, and a liberal application of basilicum ointment to his wounds. Their passage through town was uneventful, since no slit-purse prowling the streets after the chiming of vespers dared to tempt his fate with so imposing a man as the Viking. At Katherine's door in Jubbergate Street he bundled Ben into Katherine's arms and rang the bell. Moments later the judas window slid back to reveal Emma's disembodied eye, and the next second the door swung open to the serving woman's expressions and exclamations of surprise and query.

The Viking bowed slightly and withdrew. Katherine did not see him again until the next day and at the appointed time. She spent the next morning arranging matters for little Ben with the archbishop and set in motion the relay for the first shipment of wool and notions that the Viking was to retail under her banner. These tasks naturally commanded her concentration, but some other part of her mind, the one that was never free of the struggle for survival, was at work sifting through the unexpected encounter she had had with her partner in that dirty alleyway in the liberty. She could not believe that blind fortune had guided his steps. He must have been trailing her, but she could plan no sure way of trapping him into admitting it. Nor was there any way of asking him outright what he had been doing in such a place at such an hour, for he could easily turn the question around and pose the same of her.

She had no clear recollection of the few words they had exchanged at the time, but she did not think that she had divulged anything sensitive to her security. She appreciated the fact that he was nothing if not able in a pinch and had not argued with her about her actions or intentions. She was aware that his decision not to impose his own ideas of what to do with the boy had allowed him the better to observe her in the situation. It also occurred to her that this strange passage had broken the storm that had raged between them at their last meeting. The circumstances in the liberty had offered neither time nor place to wrangle over business or to trade insults. She was encouraged to think that they had reached a stalemate. Their partnership simply could not survive the continuous pitched battle of hand-to-hand combat.

She was soon to discover that the contest had not ended, neutrally, in a stalemate, but that it had come rather to a temporary cessation of hostilities and was a heavily armed truce at that. The Viking, duly escorted by Emma, arrived later in the day at Katherine's solar while she was involved with some stitchery with a new prentice. She had had the foresight to have sent Maria and the others to their lodgings for the evening. Upon Master Eric's arrival Katherine excused the new prentice and signaled to Emma that the door might be left open.

The topic of little Ben could hardly be avoided, and Katherine had already decided how she was to dismiss it.

To her partner's question, which came after the few preliminary remarks, she said, "The lad goes on very well, thank you."

"I am glad to have been of service," the Viking replied with that lurking, challenging manner.

She would not thank him for his intervention. She had not asked him for it, and she did not think that she would have ultimately needed it. She merely inclined her head and said with a pleasant smile, "Yes, you helped me to insure my future. In Ben I may have a future shipwright or sailor, perhaps. He will be happy to follow my orders when the time comes, as long as I bathe, clothe, and feed him properly. He looks to be an obedient type, for he has already submitted docilely to all my wishes."

"You are long-headed, mistress," the Viking answered, accepting without demur this explanation of her motives for rescuing the child. "But I am hardly convinced that he has submitted without protest to all your wishes. His bath, for instance," he commented lightly and unerringly, and closed the subject with the demand to be apprised of the quantity of wool he was responsible for and where he was to get it.

Katherine allowed the turn in conversation, and they remained civil throughout the discussion of the particulars. Katherine did not even rise to the provocation of the Viking's hard questions about the quality of the wool. She knew it to be of the very finest, and in any case, it was his perfect right to ask.

When the Viking was satisfied with the arrangements, he said, "Then I shall see to the tides in the Ouse and begin with a barge which I shall accompany to Scarborough. In the near future I shall arrange to bring the ship directly into York. At present I am obliged to come and go on horseback. A waste of time! I shall head for now from Scarborough to Amsterdam, if that's acceptable to you. That's to avoid Flanders now that Louis has taken to patrolling the coast from Calais to Ostende."

It might have been that he was baiting her with this morsel. Katherine paused and then answered with a tidbit of her own. "One hears that Louis will be landing shortly at Dover. I suggest that you avoid the eastern English ports as well. I would certainly dislike losing two sailors in as many months."

"I do not fear Louis in England," he said carelessly.

"Then I assume that you do not know him."

"You assume much, mistress, as I have remarked before. What makes you think that I do not know him?"

"Because I would think that a prudent man—you are prudent, are you not, in matters that relate to your pocket? —would have undertaken to follow Louis's intentions concerning England. The fleet roaming the coast that you desire to avoid is probably bound for Dover."

"And what is there to fear in that?"

Katherine took the question as a feint, which it was, and so parried, daringly, "One hears as well that Louis carries a good deal of weaponry with him, perhaps even the trebuchet."

"Then I repeat that the news does not give me overmuch to fear" was the Viking's nonchalant response.

"Ah, yes. I recall that you have told me that you prefer trade to warfare and have taken part in no Crusades," she bantered. "But I would have thought you conversant in the ways of the new weapons, at least. Do I assume too much now in thinking you ignorant of the trebuchet?"

He accepted her mild taunt with equanimity. "I do not claim expertise in the art of warfare, but I do know about ships. Louis might carry as many trebuchets as he likes across the Sleeve, but he'll not make it up the Thames with them, if his object is to take London. The tides there are contrary to the type of ship he has in his fleet to begin with, and all the more so with the load he will be carrying."

An appetizing piece of information, that. "Then you do not favor Louis," she said.

"Not in the skirmish that will take place in these next few months."

Katherine considered this. "Then why is Louis attempting to cross the water and invade, if he's bound to fail?"

"Apparently because he does not know enough of the Thames and did not have the wit to consult me on the issue."

"And if he had, would you have given him your opinion?"

"For a price."

"Ah!"

"Yes, mistress. I am a businessman, start to finish, and give nothing away. You, of all people, should know it well enough from your vast and varied experience with the breed."

Dearly would she have loved to retaliate in kind but kept, as he had guessed when he handed her the insult, to the central issue. She had the distinct impression that he was watching her again, as he had in the alleyway the day before. He was watching her, but she did not know whether he was also lying in wait for her. She had not gotten this far, however, by continually looking over her shoulder and so asked, "But even if Louis loses the skirmish, do you think he will lose the war?"

The Viking smiled enigmatically. "For twenty marks I'll tell you."

"Then unless you are bluffing and do not have a winner in mind," she countered, "I would say you are involved in the matter."

"Every man is involved when a crown is at stake," he replied. "I might have chosen a winner, but I did not say that I had a preference."

"It is all the same to you, then?" she pursued. "Louis or John?"

"What do I stand to profit from one or the other? Or lose, for that matter?"

She did not stop to consider why it was that this man could so irrationally rouse her anger. "Nothing more nor less than I, perhaps," Katherine replied with irritation, and brought the entire meeting to a summary end by adding coolly, "And as we were speaking of tides when we began this digression, I was of a mind to inform you of them myself. There is hardly a person in York better acquainted with the secrets of the Ouse than I am! It is not easy sailing—mark my words! But on second consideration I can see now that I would be singularly foolish to let you have the information for less than twenty marks. Good day to you, Master Eric, and I shall look forward to your return a month from now."

The Viking was soon to be seen striding the streets by Sybille and Stephen Webster, who were together and alone in a secluded corner of King Street.

The Viking passed them with only the curtest of nods. He did not evince the least surprise to see them together, nor did he appear to care, but even his palpable indifference did not reassure the guilt-ridden Sybille, and so, after his passing, she whispered into Stephen's ear, "Oh, dear. That was Master Shipwright. And he saw us together! Do you think he will tell Katherine?"

Stephen was not attending and so answered absently and with unintentional accuracy, "I rather think not," and because he was in the throes of a poetic fury, Stephen continued, "But tell me! What rhymes with *swift*? The lines as I have them scan: To the smile that comes on bird's wings swift/So is a lover its captive . . . Its captive *what*, I ask? Its captive sift, rift, thrift, gift? But, no! There is nothing that fits!"

"If *swift* does not have a suitable rhyme, you must try some other word," Sybille said at random. "A different word that means the same thing."

"Ah! A synonym!" he said knowledgeably.

"I don't know about that," Sybille answered doubtfully. "I was thinking more of a word like *quick* or *fleet*."

Stephen was much struck. "Fleet! Yes! That is it!" He moved his lips wordlessly and then broke into speech: "To the smile that comes on bird's wings fleet/So is a lover its captive sweet." Stephen's handsome face was lit with satisfaction. "Fleet and sweet. Oh, that is famous! Sybille! You are my inspiration! Would that I could place—let me see . . . yes!—a swansdown kiss on your gossamer cheek. That is a lovely image—but I cannot. I dare not! Oh, Sybille, Sybille!" He reached out a hand to touch, tentatively, her shoulder but resolutely dropped it to his side.

Sybille thought him very noble and loved him all the more for the restraint he showed her, and she was always pleased when she could help him with his verses; but at present her mind was rather more on other matters. "Stephen," she said, "you must give me your attention. The shipwright has just passed, and I very much fear that he will tell Katherine he saw us."

"The shipwright? Oh, yes!" Stephen came down from the dizzying heights of invention. "Well, you know," he said practically, "I cannot help but think that it's no concern of his whether or not we're together. And why should he make it his business to tell your sister? Besides, he did not seem to take the least interest in us."

"No," Sybille agreed, "but that is because he is a very rude man. And he looked so fierce as he passed. I do not know how Katherine has the courage to talk to him, much less manage him. But since he is sailing under her banner now and must be having conversation with her, he might just mention having seen us."

Stephen shook his head. "He doesn't look the man for idle talk, and I don't think your sister would have told him that we should not be together, so why should he find anything mentionable in having seen us? I agree with you, though, that he was looking fierce just now. Put out by something, I would have said. But as for being rude... Never think it! Why, when he came into the shop last week looking for Leofwyn, he could not have been better mannered. And although my father has not the wit to appreciate the finer pursuits in life," said Stephen darkly, "he thought the shipwright a very smooth customer. And my mother! She was all eyes from the moment he walked in. But then he asked for Leofwyn, and I can tell you that I was never so surprised. Bruiting the name about like that! You may rest assured that I gave Master Shipwright a piece of my mind right after he left our shop. He took it in good part, too, I own—perhaps it was my commanding manner, although I would not like to flatter myself—and I sent him straight to the Mistress Katherine, before he could do more damage."

"That was very good of you, Stephen." Sybille sighed.

"I try to be helpful on your behalf, whenever I can," Stephen said with simple pride.

"Just as I try to help you," Sybille returned dreamily and a little breathlessly.

"Yes, O my inspiration!" Stephen concurred. "And now back to our verses. We were working on rhymes for *amour*."

Stephen deeply felt the deficiencies of the Saxon tongue for proper expressions of poetic love, but he was not allowed to pursue this favored topic, for just then Sybille said urgently and in a low voice, "Hush, Stephen. Here comes Marta. And no one is supposed to know that you know that I am French."

___ Chapter 8 ___

April came to Yorkshire with the promise of spring. The fresh, sweet breezes whirled and whispered that soon the land would be leafy with larch and birch and beech trees and green with meadows dappled by a fugitive sun. Soon bluebells would carpet the fields. Soon apple and pear orchards would be aureoled with blooms, and rolling hills would shimmer in a haze of larkspur blue. Brooks would rush and gurgle, and lilac would hang over stone walls, heavy with buds, waiting patiently for the warmer weather of May before they would open.

Showers came to drench the woods and fields and fells of Yorkshire. Bands of sheep roamed: rams with thick, sodden fleece; and silly-faced ewes heavy with springtime lambs who would be born to skip and grow the much-sought-after English wool. Always a shepherd was there with a crook and a clever, heel-nipping Border collie to keep them moving.

In the villages song-sweet bushes lined rutted paths between straggly hedges scattered over manorial estates. They were just huddles of thatched-roofed cottages, with only a weather-beaten cross to mark their boundary and crowded with small gardens soon to be filled with yellow and brown wallflowers and rank-smelling cabbages. Fat sows and piglets wallowed in rain puddles. The villeins plowed their long strips of land, running straight as arrows to the green shaws in the distance and hinting of new life.

In York town preparations were going vigorously forward for the Easter celebrations. The archbishop, Walter de Grey, took a solemn interest in the proceedings of the Pageant Council and called a special meeting in early April at the parish church of the Holy Trinity in Goodramgate to assure that the Fourteen Stations of the Cross to be enacted in the streets of York during Easter week were properly erected. Dennis Baker, with his hands on his knees and his belly in his lap, nodded acquiescently throughout the meeting and was generally remarkable for nothing but being dull and pompous and chairman of the committee. And since all the members had been required to attend this special session, Geoffrey Taverner also made an appearance; that is, all members were there save John Mason, who had been called that morning in an emergency to fix an old brick wall in Peaseholme that a goat had butted through and who had then, in celebration of its freedom, proceeded to wreak havoc on that sleepy suburb.

Master Geoffrey's election to the Pageant Council had been to insure representation of the wishes of that large constituency of York citizens who, holding hard by the old religion, had at one time or another entertained the bitter reflection: "Why, now they're trying to bring the new religion into *Easter*, of all things!" Thus the taverner came to the meeting full of ideas for the traditional diversions. At the first opportunity he gave it as his opinion that this year the Easter celebrations would benefit from a more organized (though pagan-inspired) Egg Roll, to be held on Pasch Monday, the day after Easter. Halfway through the exposition of his rather elaborate plans, which included the coloring and decorating of the eggs, Mastery Geoffrey noticed the quelling eye of the archbishop upon him and manfully met this austere spiritual leader's eye. "Oh, yes, Archbishop! *I* know!" The taverner's tone was reassuring as he dutifully recited, "Father, Son, and Holy Ghost! The Resurrection and the Agnus Dei! Let us not forget it!" With the hope of further gratifying the archbishop he continued, somewhat chattily, along the lines of doves and candles and other symbols of an imperfectly absorbed Christian catechism and concluded with the extremely ill-advised remark that Easter was by far his favorite of the holy days because it meant an end to the Lenten fasting which severely limited the scope of his menus.

After the meeting Master Geoffrey unburdened himself further to a number of very sympathetic ears, saying that it was all very well to celebrate their Savior's Resurrection, but if they were to celebrate Eostre, the Saxon Goddess of the Dawn, they had better do it right. Carl Cartwright was heard to say in response that his own mother had never held with this idea of the Resurrection in the first place and had thought it a sacrilege to associate the sacred rites of spring with the newcomer Jesus Christ because this business of rising from the dead so directly defied the laws of nature.

For Katherine, Easter presented a very different kind of paradox. It was a time for her to renew her faith in herself and her conviction in her purpose; it was a time for her to despair of life, for she had seen her God brutally murdered that day at Roncevaux and did not expect Him to rise again, now or ever.

Everyone took it as a good sign when Easter morning dawned bright. It was a jeweled day with the sky a vault of azure and sparkling air that turned the soaring spires of York into dazzling, blinding towers of silver. Soft breezes lifted the wimples of the women in their Easter finery and the mantles of the men as they flowed into their parish churches. Katherine attended hers with Emma and Sybille and Cook and Nurse and all thirteen children, scrubbed and shining pink and anticipating the treats that were in store for them after the service.

Having been expedited by favorable winds, the Viking had returned, successful, to York on Easter Eve and chose to attend the Holy Mass at Katherine's parish. St. Deny's was a small, stone church, around the corner from Katherine's house in the lane of Feasegate, not more than a chapel, really, with thick tendrils of ivy rambling over its exterior and dark and cool in the interior. He had arrived only moments before the heavy iron-studded portals had been closed, so that one might throw them open again joyously at the end of the mass, after the benediction. As a result of his tardiness he could find only standing room in the narthex with the rest of the latecomers. With his height, however, he commanded a good view of the whole of the small church and easily could have espied Katherine and her entourage on their stools, had he been looking for her; but apparently he was not, for he took to leaning against the wall and seemed to be only mildly engaged in the proceedings.

Katherine had not seen him enter. She knew of his intention to attend her church this day because he had personally informed her of it upon his return. She was not thinking of him, however, nor of the money she had received from his hands the evening before, nor of their properly businesslike exchange of words. Her thoughts were elsewhere as her eyes roamed the great banner of silk suspended from the cross-beams. It depicted the Lamb of God, a welcome symbol to the shepherd folk of Yorkshire, serene and poised mid-step before the red-cross pennant affixed to a standard that was itself topped by another cross. It was a most beautiful banner, a study in white and red and silver, and one she herself had helped to stitch. Her eyes traveled to the paintings that filled wall and ceiling, paintings accomplished by proud York artists who populated their canvases with golden-curled, golden-haloed angels in jewel-encrusted vestments, hovering above the flat surface of the earth.

Katherine's thoughts would have been impossible to determine from her composed countenance as she gazed at the illuminated paintings. She never used these quiet moments of prayer in church to dwell on her peaceful childhood, for she had long ago discovered that there was no greater pain than to remember those happy times. She used this Easter morning to mourn Josef's death, to knit up bits of her reflection that constantly threatened to unravel in the pull of her double life, to make whole her thoughts that could so easily spin off the tilt of her activities, like thread off a carelessly held spindle. Her despair and her memories she kept hidden away, treasured them even in the unlit depths of her heart.

The sun slid from behind a fugitive cloud and lit the church in sudden splendor. Patterns of crimson and cobalt and canary streamed on beams of light through the stained, leaded glass of the gracefully arched windows. The color and the warmth of the sun through the glass gave Katherine such an extraordinarily strong surge of hope in her imminent success that she was compelled to regard Sybille at her side.

Sybille's head was bent piously in prayer. In profile and bathed in filtered sunlight, Sybille was so delicate and so exquisite that Katherine's expectations for the girl soared. Katherine did not doubt that once she had gotten her sister to court in London, Sybille, with her beauty and all of Katherine's accumulated wealth, would make a magnificent match. Katherine contemplated her sister's face for a moment and then transferred her gaze back to the celebrants of the mass. But her thoughts had already traveled far away from Sybille to London and, even farther, to the southern coast, and she spent the rest of the mass standing and kneeling, reciting and responding, all the while weighing the respective merits of John against Louis, Louis against John. There was Mauleon's participation to account for as well, and from there she came to consider the part that the mayor played, the rich burghers, the price of wool, the weight of the trebuchet, the unusually clement weather, and the uncertain seas. In fact, her thoughts roamed far and wide but in so devious a fashion that she could avoid thinking about the more subtle, the more incalculable, and perhaps the more real obstacle that stood between her and the accomplishment of her goals. Finally she could hide from it no longer. She had to confront the Viking's stake in the matter, but then her thoughts became immediately tangled, and she was at a loss to decide the reason. Was it because he could so easily provoke her into an unaccustomed anger that had no place in the cool execution of her plans, or was it that the many unexplained circumstances of his appearance in her life gave her just cause to be wary of him?

The same light that fell on Sybille had also fallen on Katherine. The Viking, from his vantage point, had an unobstructed view of Katherine at the moment she had turned to regard her sister. Katherine was illuminated, Madonnalike, by the blue and yellow rays of sun that filtered through the scene commemorating "The lion hands the scepter to the doe," and her ivory skin seemed to glow from some inner source. He was obliged to confess that she did indeed radiate the self-absorbed serenity that all of York chose to interpret as the beauty of her angelic, otherworldly soul.

The Viking had never denied her beauty, but he was far too wise in the ways of women not to appreciate in her particular beauty the attractions of her earthly body. He saw, as well, the intensity of Katherine's gaze as she looked upon her sister. His brows drew together. He had seen a similar look on her face the month before, in that dingy alleyway of the liberty. She had shown then a remarkable front of self-possession and calm fearlessness. And for what? The defense of a boy who could be of very little real use to her in the near future, if ever. Her behavior had seemed extraordinary to him at the time, and after reviewing all of what he knew of her from their various encounters, he had had to admit that her defense of the boy when she herself had so much to lose had not only been unexpected, it was also inexplicable.

The Viking had been trailing her that day the month before and had seen her entrance into the castle and had awaited her exit. Katherine was entirely correct in her suspicion that he was watching her, and he was doing so far more closely than she realized. He had not originally meant to interfere with her progress through the back streets that day, but he could see that she had gotten herself into serious trouble, and he would not stand idly by when she was so directly threatened. When he had considered it afterward, he decided that her actions had been inspired by her belief that she could best the drunken muckraker in a physical contest. The Viking was sure, however, that in this confidence in herself she had gravely overestimated her strength. Whatever her lack of physical prowess, though, he could see that she did not lack for courage. She seemed, in fact, to possess an uncommon amount of it, and a seed of doubt about her and her motives had been planted in his mind.

He accepted, cynically, her claim that she used the children she housed to suit her own ends—their principal use being that her good works enhanced her aura of saintliness—but conceded that Katherine's home did provide the children with a better life than they would know in the streets. He had also been scornfully pleased during their last meeting that she had tried to draw him out on the subject of Louis and had divulged her knowledge of the Frenchman's plans, for this valuable information about Louis's intended invasion at Dover and his surprise use of the trebuchet could have come only from her paramour, Mauleon. She had, furthermore, lost no time in raising his ire with her swift counter to his own attacks by her impudent dismissal of him on the issue of the tides in the Ouse.

To be crossed so consistently, and by a beautiful young woman, was a new experience for him. From the circumstances of his unmatched knowledge of the seas, of his unrivaled trading acumen, and of his ability to sail through the political winds that blew as skillfully as he could navigate those on the North Sea, he had been used for a good decade or more to arranging things to his liking in this northern part of England. In addition, his own masterful disposition made him entirely accustomed to absolute obedience from those men he employed and to a very different kind of acquiescence from the women in his life. From the very beginning Katherine the Broiderer had set herself at odds with him and was herself neck-deep in intrigues that conflicted directly with his own interests. After their last meeting he had only redoubled his desire that she should pay very dearly for her continued intransigence.

Nevertheless, that look on her face of fearless, implacable determination to save an insignificant little boy, now coupled with the look she gave her sister, which carried with it something far more than ordinary sisterly devotion, gave him pause to think again. His contempt for her methods of doing business, his rage at having to deal with such a lovely, lowly creature in the first place, struggled with the first tiny shoots of that seed of doubt in his mind.

When the happy worshipers had filled the little square in front of the church at the end of the mass and had set about the serious business of greetings and gossip before their Easter dinners, the Viking scanned the crowd for Katherine and her entourage. He espied Sybille and Emma in general conversation with their neighbors, but Katherine was not immediately to be seen. He looked around the square again and chanced to glimpse Katherine as she slipped around a corner to a street that did not head in the direction of her house.

Since he was not burdened by acquaintances in York, he was not delayed in conversation and so set out to follow, once again, Katherine's movements through town. He kept a discreet distance behind her but had his difficulties in keeping up with her because of her rather circuitous course. Wherever she was going, he quickly realized, she was not taking the most direct route. She would turn right, then left and left again, doubling back on her path in an almost random fashion. He did not, however, believe that her direction was aimless, as he thought it might have been the month before when she had ended in the liberty. Her gait did not appear to be purposeful, but he could not believe that she did not have an objective this Easter morning to have taken herself off so immediately after the service. Although she did not look over her shoulder once or indicate in any other way that it was of any importance that one might see where she was going, he had the distinct impression that she was scrambling her trail deliberately, in the event that she was being followed.

The Viking did not, in fact, discover her destination. She had a way of losing herself in the crowds of people who were swarming in the squares before the churches of the various parishes which she traversed, only to emerge again from the throng to travel down an unexpected street. He saw her stop and speak with several acquaintances during her peregrination, but she always managed to extract herself from any lengthy talk, calmly and most gracefully. She paused somewhat longer in the yard of St. Martin's parish church, in the vicinity of High Petergate, where she was engaged by an older woman whom the Viking remembered as the wife of the webster. Katherine smiled and spoke with the webstress, leaning close to her ear in order to be heard above the buzz of conversation around them and the incessant tolling of the Easter bells from all quarters of the city. The next moment she was absorbed in a milling mass of people, and her prim wimple and straight back were momentarily lost to the Viking's sight, and by the time he had crossed the busy square in the direction he thought she was headed, she was nowhere to be seen. He paused a moment, then abandoned her trail and retraced his steps to St. Deny's.

Since not more than a quarter of an hour had elapsed during his trailing of Katherine through town, he returned to St. Deny's to find Emma and Sybille still in the yard in front of the church enjoying a fine gossip with a good part of the parish neighborhood, which showed no inclination to hurry home for the midday feast. He retired to one corner of the yard to await events, and within the next quarter hour Katherine returned to greet and speak with her friends and neighbors as if she had not left them for a moment. When her party appeared ready to depart for Jubbergate Street, he made so bold as to join Katherine's group and drew her to the side for a moment to inform her of his desire to leave for Scarborough on the morrow.

"On the morrow?" Katherine replied, surprised. "Why this sudden change? You told me that you would not be leaving until five days from now in order to take care of the cloth I have just ordered and to catch the outgoing tides."

"It's a waste of my time and trading opportunities for me to travel from here to Scarborough on horseback, as I've said. I've wanted to bring my own ship into York from the beginning, and now I've the means to do it. If I leave York on the morrow, I reckon that I shall be able to return in four days' time with my ship for the cloth and the tides."

Katherine smiled prettily. "With all due respect, I might point out that if it is your object to travel up the Ouse in order to arrive in York four days from now, you are sadly out."

The Viking, clever sailor that he was, knew precisely what he was about. "Oh?" he said, achieving a look of bland inquiry.

"With the moon in its present quarter," Katherine continued, "you will arrive from Scarborough, by my calculations, at York city walls after nightfall, which means, of course, that the nets will have been hung to bar nightly river traffic. And if you cannot dock, I assure you—no matter how skillful a sailor you may be—that by morning you will be unable to withstand the tides that will carry you out to sea again. I warned you, I believe, some time ago that the tides in the Ouse are a tricky business."

"You did" was all the Viking said to this most informative bit of news, but with a glint in his eye that Katherine failed to perceive.

Caught up in her little triumph, she bubbled on. "Is this an example of your knowledge of inland water travel? I do not doubt your ability on the high seas, but inland navigation is very different, isn't it? If your familiarity with the tides in the Thames is no better than with those in the Ouse, I don't wonder that Prince Louis did not think to consult you on the matter of sailing his ships with the trebuchets into London. Now that I reconsider the matter, however, I think he might stand a very good chance of success with his plans for invasion with the trebuchet and that I should put my money on the Frenchman, after all."

To this unwise speech he said, "Did I neglect to mention that I have made a deal with the netmen in York for the night I plan to return?"

Katherine, who had for the past several years desired to negotiate such an advantageous arrangement herself, felt the color flood her cheeks and said tartly, "You did neglect to mention that small detail."

"Then I beg your pardon! I credited your intelligence with all the powers that I would have thought you credited mine. I naturally presumed you would prefer that I enter York under cover of night and that I would take the necessary steps to do so. Indeed, I can see now that I was not wrong. What I did not know was that you considered yourself a supporter of Louis. Am I to infer now that I am in partnership with a sympathizer of the rebel cause?"

Katherine saw that she had spoken without thinking and had sailed into uncertain winds. Her partner's provoking nature was, however, no excuse for her unconsidered speech. She attempted to jibe but got tangled in the hasty riggings of her argument. "Not at all. However, thinking that you had miscalculated on one issue simply convinced me that you erred on another one that we had discussed in a similar context. Then, too, there are the well-known sentiments of the citizens of York who favor Louis, and you have no doubt heard this. But between what I have said and York's political leanings, you need not jump to the conclusion that I care— any more than you do—who sits on the throne."

"Of course not," he said with blighting mockery. "You have given me no reason at all to jump to such a conclusion."

Katherine opened her mouth to retort but thought the better of it. She knew that he was repaying her for her dismissal of him on the very subject of the tides in the Ouse. Her bosom swelled with indignation. "I suppose you are thinking," she said with a kindling eye, "that my ship won't float and that I've been washed ashore on the drift of bad reasoning."

"No, mistress, you're only becalmed," he said with a maddening, charming smile, and added the equally provoking reassurance, "But you'll come about again!"

Thus having so effectively snatched the wind from his partner's sails, he took leave of her and went about his business that day in an excellent frame of mind.

The next morning, upon his departure from York, he was afforded another very satisfactory exchange, this time with a man whose score with the Viking was of much longer standing and of a very different nature.

It was an unusually cold morning that day after Easter but the mild weather that had been holding throughout the springtime was likely to prevail by midday. The unexpected chill of a raw dawn and the threat of rain were not sufficient deterrents, in any case, to keep the Viking within city walls. At sunup he was already at St. Clement's nunnery, just outside the walls where he had stabled his stallion. He was involved in lashing gear to his Arabian's mighty flanks.

A riding party of three arrived at the nunnery. Voices, the jingle of bridles, and the scrape of spurs on stone entered the stables behind him, but the Viking did not turn around.

There came a pause and then a softly spoken, sneering comment that passed from one newcomer to the others.

"What an age we live in," the sick voice said to the Viking's back, "to find a horse with a more impressive pedigree than its rider." Soft, derisive laughter accompanied this witticism.

The Viking detected a loose strap and cinched it, satisfied. Only then did he lift his head from his task and turn to face the threesome. "It's a pleasure to see you, too, again, Mauleon," he replied with a glance and a nod at Cedric de Mauleon's two companions. He stroked the steed's neck. "And I agree with you. Magreb's a beauty."

"Scarborough!" Mauleon exclaimed. His voice held a mixture of real surprise and contemptuous dislike. The next moment, he had recovered himself sufficiently to say, with a hint of slyness, "If I had known it was you—"

"Then the insult you offered just now would not have been gratuitous," the Viking finished bluntly.

Mauleon smiled thinly. It was a rude, most displeasing shock to find his old adversary a free man again, but Mauleon was quite sure he could turn this unexpected meeting to good account. "You are far too quick to wrong me, Scarborough. Indeed, you are! No, had I known it was you, I could not have compared your lineage unfavorably with that of your horse. But how could I tell? When I walked in, all I could see were your hands at work. Since you wear no gloves, I drew the obvious conclusion. As the son of an earl," he taunted, "you are entitled to gloves, you know."

"Fur-lined cloaks, too, jewels and the rest," the Viking responded without heat, running his eye over Mauleon's sartorial magnificence. "Surely after all this time you have determined my taste in such matters. You should be able to recognize me anywhere—even from the back."

"Your disregard for the clothes of your station in life is well known to me," Mauleon replied. "However, if I mistook you, it is because I hardly expected to find you here."

"No? And why not?"

"When last I heard, you were in prison on the charge of slander against the king."

The Viking bowed. "And as for my very pleasant stay in the Tower, it seems that I stand in your debt."

Mauleon's eyes narrowed. "Oh?"

"I must thank you for having so well attended to my comfort by providing me with the jailer who goes by the name of Mauger the Murderer."

"You are most welcome," Mauleon replied acidulously. "I

am so glad that he provided you with an entertainment I had not calculated. You seem to have overpowered him and escaped."

"He's a fearsome lad, I'll grant you that, but far more impressionable than I would have expected or dared hope for."

"So it was not brute force but clever talking that led to your escape? You've a mortal busy tongue, Scarborough, to get yourself both into and out of prison."

"It was rather that Mauger the Murderer has no head for dice. He lost a deal of money to me that bought me my freedom. Remember that in the future."

"I shall, but do you customarily extract yourself from prison by casting dice with your jailers?" Mauleon asked silkily.

"Only when I lack the means to get them drunk," the Viking explained.

To this exasperating remark Mauleon said threateningly, "There are no doubt several people who should be apprised of your escape."

"By all means," the Viking replied with utmost cordiality. "Inform whomever you deem it necessary to know of my, ah, freedom."

The Viking's nonchalance brought something murderous into Mauleon's light eyes. Mauleon would have derived great satisfaction at just that moment to have unsheathed the sword clasped to his belt and to have run his oldest adversary through. "William the Marshal, for one," Mauleon replied, his lips tight. "And I have witnesses."

It was the Viking, however, who drew blood. "Witnesses? What, Mauleon, is your word not good enough? Will you not be believed on your word alone that I am once again a free man?"

Mauleon's hand went automatically to the hilt of his sword. "Would you care to challenge that?"

The Viking smiled, but feeling that a sword and a smile were always better than a smile alone, he laid his fist on the butt of the dagger thrust in his belt. "My pleasure! But not at your leisure. I have better things to do today than to help you defend your honor."

"Yes, we have not yet learned what you are doing here in York," Mauleon said.

The Viking affected surprise. "But I am from the north. Had you forgotten?"

Mauleon had not forgotten, nor was he likely to forget it anytime he looked at the Earl of Scarborough. Mauleon saw his enemy with the blond hair and Nordic bearing, and he thought inevitably of Scarborough's beautiful sister, whom Mauleon had wanted so desperately seven years before. Mauleon might have even lowered himself to offer marriage to the dispossessed Scarborough noblewoman, so much did he want her, but her brother Eric had made it clear that he would bar any association of his sister with Mauleon, proper or improper. It was enough to rouse Mauleon's enmity that he had been denied the one thing in this world he had ever truly wanted, but the Dane's attitude toward the illustrious house of Mauleon had been a slap in the face from which he would never recover.

Mauleon viciously hated the man before him. "I had not forgotten," Mauleon replied waxily.

"And being from the north country, I am naturally curious to know what business brings you to York."

Mauleon adopted a rather superior attitude. "Nothing that concerns you, I am sure. I have many interests here—and many pleasures."

The Viking's features became saturnine. He and Mauleon were far from being finished with one another, and the score was only getting longer. He mounted Magreb and reined the steed in a mincing, sideways step across the hard-packed earth and beaten straw of the stable. He leaned down over the pommel of his saddle. "Then I leave you to your interests and pleasures, Mauleon, and wish you joy of them."

Chapter 9

Southerly winds prevailed for the forty days between Easter and Ascension and promised to blow kindly during the summer months to come. They also insured good profit, and Katherine's profits had been good, a little too good. Since the Viking was doing so well by her, she began to wonder, once again, why he had chosen to sail under her banner. She knew by now, of course, that whatever schemes were in her partner's head, they would not be revealed to her at her asking. Thus she decided that a trip to the port of Scarborough was in order before the summer was over. She had no assurance that she would learn anything about how he operated there, but it had become clear that no information was going to land conveniently in her lap while she remained sedentary in York.

She laid the groundwork for her trip to Scarborough at the first meeting with her partner since Easter. Shortly after sundown on a warm May evening, when all of Katherine's broiderers had left for the day, the Viking arrived at the doorstep. He was ushered into the house and up to the solar with a warm welcome from Emma, and even Katherine was ready to humor him first with the good news on her ledger sheets.

The Viking gave his approval to the figure at the bottom line with an indifferent nod. "Very well," he said. "That was what I had expected—to the penny."

Katherine resisted the impulse to rally him with the words *And you keep it all in your head*? but replied instead, "You do not sound pleased."

"I am not displeased," he answered, and helped himself

to the cider and nuts that Emma had provided for the occasion.

"I consider a profit of, what, twenty or thirty percent, very respectable."

"Twenty-four," he said, and won a sharp glance from Katherine, but she held her tongue. His smile was charming, lazy. "Yes, mistress. I keep the figures in my head."

"Is that a warning?" she asked.

"If you choose to read it so. But you should not make it a practice to off round your numbers. There's a vast difference between twenty and thirty percent."

Katherine, with her own excellent head for numbers, plucked the feather from the squat, black pot of ink on the table. "Would you care to help me with the figures, then?" she asked, offering him the pen.

He smiled again and shook his head. She was beginning to know this mood of his when he returned from the sea. He was always the same yet different, and upon setting eyes on him that evening, she had put up stout defenses against the effect of the powerful set of his shoulders under a stark tunic; the glint of unruly, sun-lightened locks; the sea-gray eyes; and the deep rumble in his voice.

She did not think she could get the better of him in this humor, and so, when he declined the offer of plume and parchment, she said, "No? Well, then, it seems that I shall just have to console myself with the round profit of twenty-four percent."

"You are easily satisfied," he remarked.

"Hardly that. But I cannot complain with our present earnings. It is better than I have done in a long while."

"So I should imagine, but it is a long way from satisfactory to me."

"I am not so greedy," she retorted.

"The word is *competitive,* I believe," he said, "and I would not know what you are. But the profit you show on that sheet is evidence only of how cheap are English goods on the continental market."

"That cannot but be in our favor."

He shook his head again. "England is very much in the second class of trading countries," he said matter-of-factly.

"We have a long way to go before we are on an equal footing with the crafty Italians and the aggressive Flemings. We have the wool and the industry but little silver in English tills to seek out more profitable markets—or to bolster prices and improve profits, if it comes to that. The leavings from the Italians' table alone run our trading economy." He glanced down at Katherine's careful arithmetic. "No, the situation is far from satisfactory."

"Where are the better markets, then?"

"Turkey, for one," he said. "Arabia, for another."

"Why don't English merchants exploit those markets?"

"It's one thing to get there, quite another to trade there," he answered.

Katherine understood the difficulty and laughed, a little ruefully. "Our merchants are not famous for their fluency in foreign tongues."

"Very true."

A blinding realization struck Katherine, and she averted her gaze to hide it. "You told me once that you speak Arabic," she said, casually looking out the solar window.

Her partner did not immediately reply. Then, "Tolerably well. Enough Turkish, too, to acquit myself respectably in the marketplace, if you must know, but I do not recall having mentioned it."

"You have forgotten, then, for how else could I have known?" she countered. She had a sudden, visceral intuition that he commanded a perfect fluency in French as well, but she would not venture a question on that subject at such close range where she, herself, would be left open to direct counterattack. She said instead, "But if these markets are so good and you are able to trade there, I wonder that we do not explore these better markets now. Your last trip was to Flanders, the next one to Denmark. Modest journeys when all is said. I do not think you're accustomed to staying so close to home." She paused. "And I recall very well Josef's telling me that the *Jorvik* would be most worthy on the high seas."

"We were agreed on a six-month plan when we began our partnership in March," he reminded her. "There's a time for the long journey to reap a large profit, but the present market is very good for short forays and smaller, quick profits. And you have just told me that you are well satisfied with your margin. By the way, we did by far the best on small steel goods. You should consider increasing the next purchase."

To this turn she replied quite civilly that she had already taken care of the matter the day before with a sizable increase in purchase of nails and had run into some very interesting needles and bodkins in the bargain. She returned, without missing a breath, to the subject of the merits of long journeys versus short.

Well accustomed to deceptively careless banter, the Viking tossed the subject about easily, all the while alive to the undercurrents of their conversation. The lovely Mistress Katherine had a shrewd head on her shoulders when it came to business, as well as a ready tongue. She had furthermore given no sign of the smug satisfaction she must have felt at having come off so well on the business of the nails and needles. He slowly found himself, most reluctantly, taking a more than passing interest in the workings of his beautiful partner's mind.

"I still prefer the shorter journeys for now," he said smoothly to her suggestion that he try a compromise journey to the Iberian peninsula after the short voyage to Denmark. He explained that the preparations for a trip to Spain in June would mean that he would miss the upcoming summer fair in York. "I've heard its fame for many a year now, and here at last is my chance to attend. There's more to life than turning a profit, after all."

"Of course," she said, as if accepting at face value his reasons for wanting to stay close to English shores in the coming months, although she did not for a moment believe that he cared more about the summer fair than business. Here was her own chance to introduce the plan uppermost in her mind. "The subject of quick journeys reminds me," she said, "that I had not mentioned to you that every summer I take a trip to the coast. It is quite a ritual with me. Call it a pilgrimage. In the past, of course, it was to help Josef out. Little things, to be sure. But it's attention to the details that makes for good business, don't you agree. And I like to keep abreast of all sides of the business."

"Naturally," he replied cordially. His gray eyes were suddenly keen. A trip to Scarborough? Now what was she about? Did she think she had fooled him with her professional airs and cool demeanor? The Mistress Katherine had, for once, disastrously miscalculated. "By all means, you must travel to Scarborough," he continued pleasantly. "Why not make it in August, after my midsummer run?"

"August. Excellent," she replied. "Yes, I can see that the shorter journeys serve both our purposes better than the longer ones. Very good. I suppose, then, that we are to look for your return from Denmark at Whitsun."

He raised a brow. "The winds are good but not that good. You may look for me in three weeks, after the Trinity," he amended. "But that will still give me time and to spare before the fair."

He left her, a prey to doubt, for Denmark. She did not truly think an all-consuming desire to attend York's justly renowned summer fair kept her partner from exploring distant markets. She felt quite certain, in fact, that he simply did not want to be away from English shores for any length of time in these coming months, and she would not have been at all surprised to learn that his real reason for staying close to home port was related to the contest between John and Louis. In odd moments she would even admit to herself that his interest had something to do with York economy and her own dealings, but since this thought made her distinctly uneasy, she tried not to dwell on it.

She was not left in much doubt, however, about his particular attraction to the summer fair, and the reason had red-gold curls and a honeyed voice.

A short, handsomely profitable voyage to Denmark brought the Viking back in time for St. Barnabas's Day, on June 22.

York was justly proud of its summer fair, held on the day of the sun's summer solstice, and children chanted cheerfully through the streets in the weeks before: "Barnaby bright, Barnaby bright, the longest day and the shortest night!" The weather proclaimed the event as well, by warming up to an early summer heat.

The crowds that came from all over Yorkshire to attend

the fair began to swell the streets of York days in advance. The congestion that it created was enormous, but the members of the pageant council had unanimously agreed this year to put Idiot Tom, commonly known as Toodle Tom, in charge of the traffic. It had long been noticed, and indeed was a remarkable fact, that the town half-wit was unusually good at directing traffic, particularly on market day. Toodle Tom was the unquestioned king of the streets that third week in June.

The pageant council had also decided, somewhat less harmoniously, to approve the production of *The Hard Creditor* for the fair's evening entertainment, it being a personal favorite of Mistress Mathilda Webster, and of almost every other dame in town. This well-known romance survived strong competition from the colorful and slightly fantastic comic adventures of the hapless, affable squire in *The Kite*, whose bumblings landed him in every sort of fix, amorous and military, from his liege lord's bed complete with the liege lord's lady, to a drunken brawl in an enemy camp, and ended with his somewhat miraculous attainment of the gilded spurs. But the winsome charms of *The Hard Creditor*'s Portia won the day, and *The Kite* was sure to be the front-runner for next year's fair.

The stage for Portia's triumph over her hard creditor was duly set up in Petergate Square before the half-shell of the minster. The platform was very cleverly devised by York's woodwrights, who placed several dozen planks of unfinished wood athwart a series of strategically placed carpenter's horses. A box of nails, a short morning's work, and the thing was done. A maze of lanterns strung the square, booths sprang from nowhere, streamers and pennants fluttered from every roof and cornice, pies cooled on every window ledge, hens and ducklings and rabbits turned on roasting spits in every open yard, kegs of ale and bock and weiss beer spanked smartly down every cobbled thoroughfare, city gates at all four of the bars were thrown open, taverns and inns filled to bursting, and money changed hands in the days before at a very brisk pace.

The sun gave its blessing to the celebration of St. Barnabas. It rose that day to illuminate a cloudless sky and found Geoffrey Taverner and several of his cronies on the pageant council already out and about, it being their invariable custom to prowl the dawn of any feast day and to retail gossip.

Master Geoffrey inhaled deeply and gave it as his opinion that the hour before the prime was the only time of the day left when a body could catch a breath of fresh air and have a moment of peace and quiet. "For I've never made it a secret, as you'll be agreeing with me, Carl and Dennis and Thomas, that since we were lads, the air of the city has gotten worse and worse—not to mention the noise! No, I'm thinking that between one thing and another, a body can hardly sleep at night anymore. Why, after the shearing, we'll not be catching a wink, what with the bargeman's call of 'Through!' all the night long. Disturbing the peace, I call it. Not that all the wool isn't good for trade," he conceded magnanimously, "and we're all of us businessmen ourselves—and proud of it! But I can't tell you which is worse, the traffic on the river at night or the clanging of the church bells all the day. It's as if we couldn't see by the position of the sun when it's time to eat—or by the grumble in the belly, think on! And that's not the worst of it. At least none of us live in the neighborhood of the smiths. The noise from their hammers on top of the rest would be unbearable, not to mention that it would be fatal to the digestion, and there you have it."

After thoroughly thrashing out the ill effects to good health of the constant racket of city life, the men turned their attention to the poor quality of the air, which absorbed them for quite a while, Carl Cartwright concluding the conversation on the observation, "For part of the day today, at least, we'll be outside the walls and in the fresh air of the sporting fields, and I've seen to it myself that no cows have grazed there for a month."

St. Barnabas's Day Fair opened, as tradition demanded, with sports and games. The populace turned out to trample the outlying granges for the better part of the morning and early afternoon, baskets of food hooked onto elbows and flagons of ale in hand. Boys frisked over the field with crooked sticks to bandy a ball about, while smaller tots and girls danced around the beribboned maypole or balanced gleefully on the merry-totter or put gay kites aloft to dance in the same warm breezes that billowed wimples, skirts, and tunics alike. Women spread out vast coverlets for the food and settled into gossip, and men bowled on prepared greens or played closh with ninepins. Spirited badger-baiting and bull-running and shooting at the butts provided high entertainment for the male population of York.

The Saxons—these square, heavyset men—had conceived a fondness for the mighty longbow and were accustomed to the feel of bow and arrow in hand at an early age. They took to the archery grounds gladly, and from there, later that morning, loud laughter and approving cries of "Shotten!" rose to accompany the thud of arrows soundly striking the clout. For the fair, the citizens of York were not content with the everyday marks at which their youths would aim by the hour in leisure time. They took willow wands for the day instead, fashioned rose garlands for targets, and even devised the special popinjay for their mark, a brightly plumed artificial parrot.

Bob Forrester, at the braw age of seventeen, was considered the best shot in York and expected to walk away with the purple ribbon this year, as he had for the past two years. His first real competition appeared on the field in the person of one Master Eric the Shipwright of Scarborough, who, being land-bound for the seven-night, sought relaxation in a sport he found particularly pleasurable. They were an even match, the square-shouldered young Bob with his bow as long as he was himself, and the tall, keen-eyed Dane from the coast. Bob was giving a very good account of himself, although trailing a little, until a disastrous accident befell him in the second-to-last round. The leather shield protecting his left upper arm became dislodged, and the heavy, thwanging string of his bow badly burned his skin straight through his tunic and shirt. The contest was halted while the surgeon-barber, who wore three stripes of red on the arm of his white coat, was called in to attend to the wound. This experienced medic put a vile-smelling poultice on Bob's arm, and a swarm of children tore themselves away from their merrymaking to watch it fizzle. Bob put on a fine display of stoicism, but his main opponent, at least, could see that his vanity had suffered far more than his arm.

Bob was inclined to retire form the lists after that; but since it was not the Viking's purpose at the fair to draw attention to himself by taking the ribbon, he encouraged the young archer, in a comradely spirit, to finish the contest. Bob was delighted (and somewhat surprised) to find that when the final tally was called, he had won the event by a full twelve points, although something in Master Shipwright's graceful loss momentarily abated young Bob's conceit. The mayor, Godric Fitz Osbert, resplendent in a rich black tunic with silver lacings and topped by a dashing black hat, took all in with his slightly sardonic eye and proclaimed that the shipwright had made a good enough showing to win for himself a chine of pork for his dinner. The Viking thanked this city father with aplomb and at the same time caught the come-hither look from Maria, who had been watching the proceedings with unmaidenly interest and whose warm regard promised a reward of a very different kind.

Katherine had, of course, been informed of her partner's intention to attend the summer fair, but she did not intend to concern herself with his activities. She spent the morning on the other side of the archery field engaged in a comfortable coze with the Mistresses Webster, Brewer, Wainwright, and Taylor, while Sybille and Eleanora Brewer and Kate Taylor were a few feet away, deep in their own conversation.

These were the influential women who had helped to establish Katherine. These were the women who had bought the family linen that Katherine had been forced to sell off the day she had decided to stay in York four years previous, the day she had realized that she could depend no further on the charity of St. Clement's nunnery. These were the women who had recognized that Katherine's fingers held the secrets of the finest stitchery in Europe and who had helped to set her on her feet as one of York's premier broiderers.

It was not to be supposed that so interesting a man as the shipwright from Scarborough would be ignored in the mistresses' conversation that morning of the summer fair. When the talk moved away from fond commentary on the virtues of Kate and Sybille and Eleanora, Mistress Mathilda herself turned the topic to the attractive, intriguing Dane from the coast and scored a hit with the news that the man had been in her very own shop. Mistress Wainwright then asked if she had not seen Mistress Katherine several months back in company of the shipwright in the streets of York. Katherine had no ready answer for this. She opened her mouth to make light of this encounter with the shipwright but was forestalled by a comment by Eleanora Brewer's mother.

Mistress Brewer was an arch, inquisitive woman and the daughter of the late chief engineer for York's minster. During the conversation she had been keeping a sharp eye on the various fields of sport and had noticed that one of the needlewomen from Katherine's establishment was showing an absorbed interest in archery that morning. Mistress Brewer thought it her duty to point out to Katherine the bold broiderer's attraction to the longbow. Mistress Brewer's moment came when the subject of the shipwright entered the conversation. Before Katherine had a chance to reply to Mistress Wainwright's observation, Mistress Brewer interposed, "My dear Mistress Katherine, is that not one of your prentices over there watching the contest?" thereby directing Katherine's gaze and everyone else's to the archery field at the very moment that Maria flashed the Viking her provocative look.

Even across the yards separating Katherine from the field, she was able to intercept the warm regard that passed between her needlewoman and her partner. Katherine imagined that Maria's voluptuous sensuality bridged the distance between her and the Viking like a rainbow. Katherine blanched and felt a strong, unnamed emotion stir in her breast. She made some comment in reply but afterward was unable to remember what it was.

The reference to the field of archery was, however, a good one from Katherine's point of view, for the ladies' interest was diverted from the Viking to Bob Forrester, who had begun to strut the fields with the ribbon pinned to his proud chest.

Mistress Brewer had misread Katherine's reaction. When the talk moved on to the inevitable and absorbing topic of herbs and the various medicinal uses of hyssop, rue, mallow, nightshade, and borage, Mistress Brewer drew Katherine aside.

"My dear Mistress Katherine," she said. "I can see that you are having quite a time of it. How you have accomplished what you have done, I shall never know. I stand in great admiration of you. But it cannot be easy for you to be in charge of all that goes forward in an establishment of the size you keep with no man's hand to guide you. Why, I saw your face when you noticed your prentice—Maria? Maria, then—over at the field of archery. And I can guess at the surprise and dismay you must feel to see her behave so, so . . . well, so openly. And I can see that her interest in archery is as obvious to you as it is to me, and perhaps she is the reason why the shipwright made your acquaintance in the first place. Making up to the mistress of the establishment in order to fix an interest with one of her workers. Why, it's an old story."

Katherine colored up in spite of herself and was able to respond in convincing accents that she would have to have a talk with Maria, for this kind of behavior would just not do. Since she did not think that Mistress Brewer cared profoundly about Maria and the stranger from Scarborough, Katherine wanted to bring the discussion of it to the quickest end possible and direct talk to the topic of Sybille and Stephen Webster.

Katherine said first, "And I hope that if I drop a word in Maria's ear about her conduct, that will be sufficient. I cannot have her harm my business, after all. I would hate to have to turn her off, since her fingers are so talented. And all the more so, since I can readily imagine that Mistress Olivia would be more than happy to engage her. It would go against the grain for me to be giving away the valuable prize of Maria to my main competition." Mistress Brewer, no partroness of the expensive needlework of Mistress Olivia, laughed and agreed.

"And, yes, you are right," Katherine continued, "it is difficult at times to maintain order in my household. Especially now that Sybille is coming of age. I would not be frank with you if I were to tell you that she does not worry me."

Mistress Brewer needed no better opening. She was not an architectural engineer's daughter for nothing and liked to study her strains and stresses before hazarding herself. She asked, most politely, in what ways it might be that Mistress Katherine had cause to worry about Sybille. From Katherine's response Mistress Brewer easily inferred that Katherine did not countenance Sybille's attraction to the young Master Webster and would not be promoting a marriage between them. Completely satisfied, Mistress Brewer was left, at the end of the conversation, with the general impression that Katherine was an excellent young woman and that Mathilda Webster had been right about the Broiderer all along.

If Mistress Brewer and Katherine were pleased with the outcome of their little talk, they would have been far less satisfied with the state of affairs had they known of the idyllic little tryst that Stephen and Sybille had arranged for the early afternoon. They were to meet in the leafy, green cool of the riverbed where Stephen was fishing. Marta guessed it but did not want to trouble her mistress on such a fine fair day, and so the serving woman thought to make amends by keeping a quelling eye on Sybille during the enactment of the play on the main square later that afternoon.

After the morning's exertions and the midday repast in the open air, the folk drifted back into the city for the gala. In addition to the burghers and merchants, there were in the throng the peasants and their wives who had taken the day off and arrived on foot by midday. A few knights and their ladies graced the crowd as well, and enough French could be heard in the streets to prompt Geoffrey Taverner to say to his Petronella that the sound of it was in a fair way to maulding his innards. The bulk of the fair-goers, though, were townsmen, from Yorkshire and environs, and from even farther away. The burr of the Scotsman and the flat accents of the Londoner could be caught by the sharp ear, and a few foreign tongues as well.

All had come to find a bargain, or to sell an ell of cloth, or to see the sights. Since buying and selling was the main business of every other York day, the pageant council saw to it that the summer fair would draw the most people for its sights. There was no lack of diversions, but shilling was strictly outlawed for the day. Dancers and jugglers and acrobats, mummers and minstrels and monkeys on chains strolled the streets. Shaggy bears in cages yawned in sleepy captivity on street corners while jongleurs sang on church steps. Farmers gawked at this exotica with much the same curiosity as the Bedouin in the Levant who first laid eyes on fair-skinned Crusaders in bright mail. York citizens, accustomed to the event and rather proud of their worldliness, took it easily in stride.

The pageant council knew its audience well, and *The Hard Creditor* was an unqualified success. The benches set up around the three-sided stage that filled the square were crammed long before the sun had started its downward arc, which would bring on the beginning of the play. Lucky were the people who had shops on the square itself; their chairs had been pulled to second-story windows from which excellent vantage point the play could be watched. Katherine took a standing place with Sybille and Emma and Marta at the back of the square, near the opening to an already crowded side street, and observed that the Brewers, with Eleanora in the center, had places at the Websters' windows. From the distance where she stood on the square, however, Katherine could not read the look on Stephen Webster's face. Katherine did note, with approval, that Sybille kept her eyes conscientiously averted from the Webster's windows.

Katherine had tried to give herself over to the enjoyment of Portia's alarums and excursions on stage. This fair heroine was played, of course, by one of the lads that every acting troup engaged for female roles. His voice was high and sweet and carried well over the square. Katherine loved the theater and these productions, but she was unable to keep her mind on the action for any length of time.

"'Do unto others,'" Portia was quoting piously midway through the first act.

"Before they do unto you," the villain (a dishonest sausage merchant) answered, rubbing his hands with anticipation that Portia's debt-ridden father would soon be forced to pay with Portia herself.

The audience roared with appreciative laughter, and Katherine's wandering eyes and attention were brought back to the stage. She kept with it from that point to the end of the third act and chuckled over the hero's wise observation to Portia's father that "One spends one's life in innocence, or one trades with a Norman merchant!" Thereafter, however, her thoughts were otherwise, and the felicitous circumstances by which the hero saved the heroine passed in a blur before her eyes. She missed as well the punch line at the end of the last act, after the villainous sausage merchant had been exposed and pilloried. One of his former, faithful (and extraordinarily slow-witted) customers confessed to a neighbor that he had traded with the sausage merchant for seven years. "Seven years!" exclaimed the neighbor. "And you're still alive?"

The players took their bows amid a good deal of laughing and applause but were whisked off before the clamor had fully subsided. The crowds were directed off the square and lured to the side streets where kegs of strong drink were being pegged and food was appearing on trestle tables hastily set up to line the narrow passageways. The square was cleared of benches and refuse by a very efficient team of young boys, and the stage was dismantled as cleverly as it had been erected to make room for the after-dinner dancing. Minstrels drifted in and among the streets to tune and to practice during the brief, noisy respite of the eating and drinking. With the sun slowly sinking on this longest day of the year and the shadows lengthening across the city, the real business of St. Barnabas's Day was about to begin.

Those in a position to do so donned fine feathers for the evening's festivities. Katherine and her household returned to Jubbergate Street for supper, and the children were bedded and left in the care of Cook and Nurse, and Katherine, Sybille, and Emma returned to the square sometime later that evening after the dancing had begun.

Torches had been set to blaze, lanterns had been lit to spangle the square, and an exotic tangerine moon was already hanging high in the sky. The square was crowded with persons of fashion who, while not necessarily possessing a desire to join in the dancing, all flocked to Petergate, some with the sole intention of being there, others, elaborately decked out, for the purpose of drawing admiring glances;

and a few (not all of whom were young, unmarried men) hovered on the edges of the milling crowds in the hopes of discovering adventurous young maidens. Amongst this throng was to be seen Bob Forrester, puffing off his prowess and looking rather cock-a-hoop, displaying the twin badges of his purple ribbon pinned proudly to his chest and the bandage of the grievous wound on his arm. Off to one side a number of older boys, for whom dicing and betting were always interesting and worthwhile pastimes, had congregated to cast the bones across the cobbles. The established merchants of York, represented by Dennis Baker and Dick Brewer and Carl Cartwright, who sat to one side and bent their energies over red-and-black-checkered gaming boards, looking heavy-eyed, as well they might, having begun their drinking early in the morning; by Robert Webster, in desultory conversation with his brother-in-law; and by Geoffrey Taverner, who was still having a grand time of it, busily exchanging recipes with a number of fellow taverners from the backwoods he met once a year on fair day. Their better halves were keeping strict eyes on their older daughters and sons, who were showing a marked predilection for dark corners and shadowy side streets, while the smaller fry were swapping sweets they had hidden in their sleeves and giggling over the pinches and kisses exchanged in secret by their elders.

Katherine had decided to be very gay that evening. She left Sybille to seek out her girlfriends and then promptly forgot about her younger sister. Katherine knew that Sybille and her friends would spend the evening chafing under the combined gazes of Emma and Marta and a battery of mothers.

Katherine was just concluding a conversation with Petronella Taverner when Mistress Mathilda came up and laid a hand on Katherine's arm. Mistress Petronella had a friendly salutation for the webstress and moved on.

"Something on your mind, Mistress Katherine?" Mistress Mathilda inquired.

"Why, no! Why do you ask?" Katherine laughed.

Mathilda smiled, crinkling raisin-black eyes. "Oh, I don't know. But I'd say that you've not been in good spirits all day. Now, don't tell me you've been chirpy as a lark, for I've eyes in my head. Not that you've been precisely out of spirits today, either, for you're not given to ill-humored tics. You never let anyone see your worries, but I've known you long enough, my dear, to see that there's something on your mind—and to make so bold as to ask you about it."

Katherine shook her head. "Just tired."

Mathilda correctly interpreted this polite lie and continued. "Well, it can't be business that's troubling you, since York has fared uncommon well of late, and Mistress Brewer has just informed me this evening that she has a large commission that she will be wanting you to undertake. I don't think there has been a round of sickness since winter, so none of your children are ailing. And I'm quite sure you would tell me if you had any concerns about Sybille."

Katherine looked quickly around. "Where is she?"

Mathilda indicated a group of girls. "With her friends, of course, and between me and thee, I think we've done the trick. Stephen has been most amiable to Eleanora all day, and we're to be announcing a wedding for the autumn any day now." Katherine offered congratulations, but Mathilda waved them away by asking with motherly concern, "Tell me what's the matter, my dear."

Katherine met her older friend's gaze. "A late case of spring fever, I suppose," she confessed. "Call it summer fever. It's such a warm evening."

Mathilda nodded wisely. "Restless, are you? I would be, too, if I were young and as pretty as you, and there was a fine, unmarried shipwright from Scarborough in the crowd."

Katherine flushed a little at that comment and asked lightly how Mistress Mathilda came to know the shipwright's marital status.

"My Robert asked him," the webstress replied readily. "Came right out and asked him. That and other things. Mr. Robert's had quite a few conversations with him, here and there. The shipwright's a sailor, as well, in case you did not know it. Keeps close to himself, though. Like you. All in all, my Robert thinks well of him." Mathilda regarded Katherine shrewdly. "And so, it seems, does your Maria."

Katherine kept her countenance and even laughed. "And

what do *you* think I should do about it? Mistress Brewer, I believe, finds Maria's open pursuit of the man potentially harmful to my business."

"Do about it? I think you should offer Maria a little competition. Give her a run for her money, as we say here in York. You're far too modest and circumspect. I understand your position and sympathize, but for one night in the year, at least, you should have a little fun."

A faint gleam of humor came into Katherine's eye. "Are you suggesting, Mistress Mathilda, that I make a spectacle of myself in front of all of York?"

"Well, now, I cannot imagine you conducting yourself with anything less than decorum. Or creating a spectacle— why, no! I've never seen anyone handle a man as skillfully —and with as little spectacle—as you've handled the Widower Goldsmith. Why, you've preserved your dignity and even managed to prevent him from making a blooming fool of himself, while it has been plain as day to me that he's deep in love with you. You certainly do have a way about you!" Mistress Mathilda winked broadly. "But consider me a friend. You've had a rough load these past years and should have some enjoyment. Now, the shipwright's the man for my money—far, far more interesting than the goldsmith and I think you've been wise to wait—and if I were you, I'd not let Maria steal the show."

The gleam in Katherine's eyes became pronounced. "A little fun, you say? I admit that I love to dance. It suddenly seems that I have not done so for a long, long time. But if I join in, am I at least allowed my own choice of partner?"

"The shipwright's the one, my dear," Mathilda reiterated. "He's a bit of a mystery, like you. But I don't mean anything personal by it, and your life is your own. Go on, dance! It's the one night in the year that we've so many foreigners in town, so no one will be bothering with what you do. And if it's the wagging tongues you're worried about, never you mind. *I* know how to handle it."

Thus encouraged, Katherine thanked her friend and plunged into the crowds. A carole was forming in the center of the square, and the minstrels were plucking the opening lines to announce the next set. Katherine quickly spied the man she sought, and without further reflection on her actions she went up and asked boldly for the next dance.

The bored eyes of Godric Fitz Osbert widened a trifle at Katherine's very beautiful face. He knew a moment's hesitation and threw an unreadable glance at Piers, who stood, not far away, in the shadows.

"Almost, my dear," the mayor said suavely, "you tempt me."

___Chapter 10___

Lutes and mandolins strummed. Tambourines shallied. The air, sweet and warm, pulsed to the rhythm of the bells calling the dancers to their places. Flames danced to tempo atop their torches. Lanterns flickered in an answering counterpoint. When all had joined hand over hand to form the large circle, Katherine was in her place next to Godric Fitz Osbert.

She had finally secured her dancing partner with a lilting smile of promised adventure. After a moment's hesitation the mayor had chosen to accept Katherine's provocative invitation with the observation, spoken in a low voice and not without a taste of pungency in his dulcet tones, that her efforts were quite wasted and would have been better appreciated by his dear and titled brother, Cedric de Mauleon.

Godric Fitz Osbert's decision to dance with Katherine was prompted by his awareness of the currents and countercurrents swirling in and throughout the day's activities. His unerring intuitions informed him that some very interesting things were going forward in his city, and he was certainly amenable to obliging the Mistress Katherine's sudden desire to join the dancing. It seemed that she was stirring a brew of her own, and Godric was not above allowing himself to be used as her tool. The pretty little broiderer with her skill for numbers, her excellent French, and her well-bred ways had always intrigued him. If Katherine had dared ask him what the young man waiting in the shadows would think of Godric's momentary lapse, the mayor would have said that Piers, the dear boy, would simply have to understand.

The freedom of the fair and the dance caught up with Katherine. She was feeling light-headed after her talk with Mistress Mathilda. "But my efforts are not at all wasted," she replied to the mayor's quip as they found their places in the ring, "since you have accepted to dance with me."

"Flirting, my dear?" he queried.

"I know better than to flirt with you, sir," she replied demurely, but her eyes danced prettily.

"I am neither so vain nor obtuse, child," the mayor said mildly, still sotto voce. "I did not mean that you would flirt with me." Katherine looked up at him with a knowing twinkle in her eye. "We are both of us aware," he continued, "and to our mutual benefit, I suppose I should add, that I sit on the other side of that particular fence. Your knowledge is one of the foundations, after all, of our financial arrangement."

"Yes, sir, but nothing that you have said should prevent us from enjoying a dance together," she said in the brief interval while the musicians were still readying themselves.

Godric nodded. "Indeed not. You dance wonderfully well and are so light on your feet. I have observed you on the rare occasions in the past that you have joined in the Saxon dances. But I do not think that a true desire to dance with me has inspired your kind invitation. Do I unnecessarily underestimate my manly charms with that suspicion?"

"Why, Lord Mayor, I hardly know how to respond."

"Honestly, if you please, my dear! I assure you that my vanity will not be mortally wounded."

"If you must have it, then," she said, teasing, "the answer is no. I love to dance but have a reputation to maintain, and so I have chosen you as the safest of all men here."

Godric accepted this gracefully. His eyes scanned the ever-milling crowds. Just as the opening beats of the dance sounded, he said slyly, "Ah! Do you imply that there are dangerous males present?"

"I do not intend to find out," Katherine replied primly.

"Speaking of men," Godric said smoothly, pacing slowly in the circle, "that is, we are speaking of men, are we not? Yes! Well, then, it has occurred to me more than once of late that your Josef has not been seen in York in the past several months. Oh, I have heard various stories about him in my strolls along the wharf, but you would know nothing of those stories, would you? Nevertheless, I find his continued absence most interesting. Does my memory fail me or do I not recall quite clearly that you told me that he had returned?"

The interlaced arms and hands broke. Partner faced partner. "I did indeed tell you that he had returned," she said, looking him straight in the eye.

"And his absence," Godric continued, "coincides with the appearance from time to time of a shipwright in town during these past months. He is from Scarborough, I believe, or so he told me on the one occasion we spoke together at the wharf."

"What a startling association the lord mayor makes," Katherine said, preserving her light tones. "A startling but —how should I say?—somewhat improbable association to make. Why should Josef's absence and a shipwright's presence be linked?"

"That I don't know. And the association is so entirely improbable that I am surely the only one in town to make it. Nevertheless, it fascinates me."

"And I am equally fascinated to know why you would mention it to me," Katherine said.

"Only perhaps, my dear, to drop a word of warning in your ear." Godric's hand dropped to Katherine's waist, and he turned her around.

"Do I need one?" she tossed back. Her feet did not miss a step.

"I don't know. You are such a clever, independent young woman. In this instance, however, you would do well to protect yourself—or find someone to do it for you. You might be playing with fire."

Katherine looked up at him and felt inclined to say that the mayor did not know the half of it and that to have someone protect her was her most ardent desire of these past months, but she refrained. She said instead that if he was referring to his brother, the Sire de Mauleon, she thought she had that situation well in hand.

"Oh, I am sure you do! He was most put out on his last two visits to our city to find that you were inaccessible to him. I am sure that you can expect a third before the summer is over. He is not a patient man, as I am sure you must know, but all this is quite beside the point."

"Is it?" Katherine said. The dance was quickening. "When do you expect him again?"

"In August, if I were to hazard a guess."

"And how should I avoid him if I were of a mind not to see him? I fear that I have run out of excuses," she said.

"The only solution seems to me that you would have to leave town, but I know that is hardly an easy thing for you to do, for where would you go? But that is entirely your own problem, my dear, and we were speaking of the shipwright and your Josef." He looked down at her enigmatically, as he turned a second time. "No, I am sure that we understand each other well enough to elaborate no further on the subject." He smiled. "But do not fret, child! We have agreed that you are safe with me, and I have no cause to betray you." He patted her hand. "I confess that I have an odd liking for you, my dear."

There was time for no more. The beats of four had gathered pace, and a new series of patterns had begun.

A few brows raised to see this strikingly handsome and unexpected couple join in the dance, and the owners were surprised or satisfied or disappointed, according to their dispositions, to see the stylish, unattached mayor squiring the lovely young and virtuous broiderer in a dance. The mayor had never been known to single one lady out from the many who would have enjoyed his favors, and only Mistress Mathilda could have told them that it was Katherine who had invited the mayor. Did it signal, the curious wondered, some serious intention toward Mistress Katherine on his part? Could he at last be thinking of settling down? But he had always made his bachelorhood, charmingly though firmly, a matter of course. Just as the Mistress Broiderer had amiably established her spinsterhood. Well, then, perhaps nothing could be read into the matter. It was only a dance, hardly a proposal of marriage, and what was one carole, after all?

The Archbishop de Grey might have informed the interested that even one dance carried deep and immoral suggestions and should not be tolerated. This stern religious shepherd of York was standing soberly to one side of the square when the mayor led Katherine in the circle. He was frowning down on the heathenish bodily exercise on display, his presence necessary, so he thought, to insure that the occasion did not lead to other fleshly transgressions.

Nothing in this particular carole should have provoked in the archbishop any deep displeasure. Though the dance increased in speed as it progressed to finish on a lively note, it was a pattern dance, and as such, the participants were required to maintain a certain decorum throughout in order to execute the intricate steps. Katherine enjoyed the movement and desired nothing more than to give herself up to the weaving hands and arms. She whirled with the tune of the gay pipes and plucking strings, clasped hands in the center with the women to form a feminine circle, broke to swirl in smaller stars of five dancers, and returned at intervals to lock elbows with her partner.

In the pleasurable, measured abandon of the dance Katherine should have been able to get her mind off the subject which had vexed her for most of the day. Katherine did not, of course, display her thoughts on her face. No one at the fair, save perhaps the Mistress Mathilda, would have thought by looking at her that she was not enjoying herself very well. The truth was that while Katherine's feet tapped and skipped, her mind was elsewhere. That most irritating man, the Viking, had consumed her thoughts for most of the day, and her distress was in no way alleviated by the realization that the more she saw of him, the more he intruded in her well-ordered and businesslike mind.

Throughout the various activities of the fair it seemed that Katherine had only to look around her to spy the Viking's leonine mane somewhere in the crowds. She was surely not on the lookout for him. Never that! His leisure activity could not have been of less concern to her. Nevertheless, he was conspicuously tall, and his stature alone drew the eye, and thus when she did catch sight of him, she inevitably glimpsed Maria's red curls as well. On each of these inexplicably frequent occasions (really, the man seemed to be constantly in her line of vision), Katherine felt an unaccustomed twisting in her breast for which she could not satisfactorily account.

Katherine would have been far happier to have believed that her concern for the association between Maria and the Viking derived from a worry that Maria might indiscreetly expose something important about Katherine's household that she, Katherine, would prefer her trading partner not to know. However, Katherine was confident in her belief that Maria had no suspicion about Katherine's affairs and knew less, therefore, than what the Viking had already determined. It simply did not occur to Katherine that the Viking would have to discover Maria's ignorance of Katherine's affairs for himself, if he were of a mind to find something out about Katherine through such a source. She had no way of knowing that once Maria had attached herself to the shipwright for the day, the redheaded broiderer was difficult to shake off. Katherine had no reason to think that the Viking's interest in Maria was other than amorous.

Neither did Maria. Nor did she suspect that the Viking's interest in her did not survive his rather rapid discovery that Maria knew little of her mistress's life before coming to York and even less of Katherine's political and business activities since.

The Viking, on the other hand, was most cynically impressed with Mistress Katherine's demeanor during the fair. He could see that she enjoyed the friendship and goodwill of the most influential women in town. She apparently enjoyed their custom, as well, for he had extracted from Maria, in his lazy, unassuming way, a long list of the various commissions that the Mistress Broiderer's establishment was paid to execute. Maria, a little swollen with pride in the shipwright's interest in her day-to-day life, divulged a good deal along the way about her mistress as well but nothing more than he already knew.

Maria's prattle also led the Viking to dismiss privately the needlewoman as a pretty, curvaceous creature without much sense or spirit; and while the tenor of a woman's conversation had never before affected his appreciation of her more tangible assets, the fleeting thought came to him that he preferred women with more strength of character.

He did not stop to consider the matter at length, however, since he had spied Katherine taking part in the carole with the mayor. His lip curled. He wanted to expose the lovely Mistress Katherine and to drive a wedge between her and the mayor. By the time the music was reaching its final, lively pitch, the Viking saw the perfect opening and made his excuses to Maria and was wending his way toward the ring of dancers.

When the final note had throbbed wistfully in the warm, velvet night, Katherine looked up, breathless, at the mayor and received a shock to see the Viking standing just beyond the mayor's shoulder. Katherine felt the full force of the Viking's cool, challenging smile, of his gray eyes which only flicked Katherine's flushed, upturned face, and of his hair, burnished bronze in the torchlight. The mayor, still holding her hand, was aware of her slight start and turned in the direction of Katherine's gaze. The mayor smiled with a kind of feline pleasure to behold the man whose occasional visits to York, he had so recently admitted, were a source of fascination to him.

"Ah, Master Shipwright," Godric said smoothly, "I have not had a moment to speak with you since this morning's contest on the archery field. I trust you recovered from your small loss to the Forrester lad and have been able to enter into the spirit of the rest of the day?"

Master Shipwright replied, with no evidence of wounded pride, that the loss had not impaired his enjoyment of the festivities.

"But you are most proficient with the longbow," the mayor pursued. "That much was evident from the very first round, and I should imagine that if Young Bob were of a more reflective nature, he might wonder how he came away with the ribbon. But he is not, and neither would one expect it. Just as—if I may say so—one does not generally expect such excellent marksmanship in a shipwright. You possess an unusual combination of talents, it seems. Something I have recently said of Mistress Katherine, in fact."

"I have always considered the longbow a sport of relaxation," the Viking replied with a speculative glance at Katherine.

"Relaxation!" the mayor exclaimed, and ran his eye over the muscles rippling just below the Viking's tunic and chemise. "And I can well imagine that you would find jousting with lances equally diverting, were that form of sport open to you."

"It isn't," the Viking replied, and added, for good measure, "But a round or two with the small sword is, and provides me with entertainment when the longbow cannot be practiced."

"Dear me! Such pastimes!" the mayor said. "It is such a violent age we live in. I have often remarked upon it. But I forget myself. Allow me to introduce you to my most charming companion, Mistress Katherine the Broiderer."

"Mistress Katherine and I are already acquainted," the Viking said with the hint of a bow to Katherine. His glance fell to her hand, which was still in the mayor's possession, and although his eyes did not linger there but reverted directly to the mayor, Katherine felt the need to withdraw her fingers from Godric's light clasp.

She was powerless to prevent the color from warming her cheeks but achieved a steady voice. "Yes, indeed," she replied with aplomb, "we have already met. Good eventide to you, Master Eric."

"Already known to one another?" the mayor queried. "But of course! You have been to York on several occasions over the past months, have you not, Master Shipwright, and thus you have had a chance to meet a wide variety of our citizens. Let me see, now, when was your first visit to York? During the Easter season in April?"

"The month before," the Viking corrected. "In March."

"So long ago already," Godric said mildly. "I had not realized it. But tell me again what has brought you to our city. When we spoke together on the wharf some little time ago, I believe that you told me that you were engaged in ship repairs or some such. One would not think otherwise, but I fear that I have quite forgotten."

"Have you?" came the response. "Is it not the case, then, that after I had completed a replanking in the hull on one of York's wool barges in April—that first time when you and I met one another, I believe—you returned to the wharf to inquire of the dock warden if my work had met with satisfaction? That is what the warden told me, in all events."

The mayor paused. Katherine held her breath. "Such a thorough man you are," Godric murmured. "Yes, and now that you bring it to mind, I recall very well that I did just that. I was told, by the by, that you did excellent work. But I am put in mind of someone else as I speak with you now. Yes, there was a man here last year—a stranger to York, like yourself—who purported to be a—what was it now?—a peddler of poultry. Quite!" Godric turned to Katherine. "Do you remember him? A small, dark man with an accent that, to my untrained ear, held the sounds of London. Yes, I see that you do remember him, my dear. Well. He was a thorough man, like yourself, Master Eric. Inquisitive, as well. As it happened, one thing led to the next, and sure enough, he turned out to be an agent of our beloved King John! Come to poke his nose in our tax records, as if we did not turn them over to the sheriff who comes around with such depressing regularity."

Godric held up a finely manicured, dead white hand, so that the black sleeve of his overtunic slid back to permit a glimpse of peacock-blue lining. "Please stop me if I chatter on to no purpose. But to make a dull, tedious story short, I found that his presence could no longer be tolerated in York, and he has not peddled his poultry here since." Godric sighed. "But King John, I am told, never gives up, and his spies are reportedly everywhere."

Katherine's heart had skipped a beat. Did the mayor suspect her trading partner of being an agent of the king? Could he possibly be? She could not quite believe it; it did not add up with the rest of what she knew of him. Yet one must suppose that a spy's most valuable asset would be his very unlikeliness. Katherine dared to look at the Viking and saw that his face was closed and grim.

"Is that an open threat of your intention to expel me from York, should the fancy take you?" His deep voiced rumbled a chilling challenge.

There was a short silence while the two men regarded each other. The mayor broke it with a soft laugh. "Not an open one, in all events," he said gently. "You have already informed me that you find the longbow and the small sword forms of leisure diversions. That defies my imagination, as I myself am the mildest of creatures. No, if I suspect you of something, I assure you that I will not deal with it openly. Such is the advantage of the title of mayor. But do not fear that I will abuse my powers. Oh, no! I would not dream of depriving our wharves of a skilled and apparently much-needed shipwright, unless I had very good evidence that it was in York's best interest to do so. But there are so many gaps in the fabric of free town life through which unwanted eyes may peer. And what with the uncertain political climate, one can never be sure that a—forgive me!—shipwright is a shipwright and not something more."

"Or that a beggar is a beggar."

The mayor's face showed polite inquiry. "Is there some meaning behind that statement?"

"The beggar who haunts High Petergate," the Viking said, "and can sometimes be found on Stonegate. I have seen him on the wharf, as well, and near the castle. If I were to suspect someone in town to be one of John's agents, it would be that beggar. Have you not noticed him?"

Katherine felt a profound, if misplaced, relief. It seemed that the Viking was not sent by the king, after all.

Godric's light brown eyes were sharp and interested. "My vanity prompts me to inform you that I have suspected him all along," he said, thinking the matter through. "But my civic conscience will not permit me to allow this rare occasion to slip through my official fingers. Compliment me on my unfailing sense of duty. But it seems that I must admit—reluctantly—to having suspected the wrong man these past months. The beggar has entirely escaped my notice. Tell me, if you please: What proof do you have that he is an agent of the king?"

"None, but I have seen him in London, at the Royal Court, and not in the habit of a beggar."

"I suppose that it would be impertinent of me," Godric said affably, "to wonder what business you had at that very same court?"

"It would. But you have said that I have an unusual combination of talents," the Viking reminded him.

"Yes, of course. Why should I find it odd that a shipwright such as yourself visits the Royal Court? But do you advise me to rid York of this beggar's presence?"

"Immediately."

"With all your good counsel I cannot help but also wonder if you have not been dispatched to York by our French friend, King Louis," Godric continued. "To play on our sympathies, one might say. York is a rich, strategic city, and the influence of our . . . ah, sympathies is no doubt important to the man who wishes to wear the English crown."

The Viking told him bluntly that a mere quarter hour at York's market sufficed to inform anyone who spoke the English tongue that the citizens' sympathies were behind Louis. "But I would not throw my money after the Frenchman."

"No?" queried Godric.

"Not with the trouble he has had sailing up the Thames. He has run himself aground, it seems, and is having to retreat to France for the summer months to regroup his forces." The Viking did not so much as glance at Katherine when he made this statement. "It has something to do with having overloaded his warships with weapons and miscalculated the tides in the Thames."

"Thorough and informed, as I have said," the mayor said softly. "You do not side with John. Neither do you side with Louis. My dear Master Shipwright, just what *are* you doing here?"

"Is not my interest obvious?" the Viking asked directly.

"Have I outlived my usefulness in my position as mayor?" Godric wondered aloud to the night air. "I have not previously thought of myself as a dull-witted fellow, but these past few minutes have revealed that I am become afflicted with a most unfortunate rash of obtuseness. The good citizens of York have overestimated their confidence in me, I fear," he mused. "Or perhaps the malady is seasonal and I shall recover by summer's end." Then, to the Viking, "You have left me entirely in the dark."

"I have come to dance with the Mistress Katherine," the Viking replied, and turned to Katherine with a glint in his eye she had never before seen there. She was instantly wary and at a loss to understand his tactics or to formulate a reply.

She was fortunately spared the necessity, for Godric said smoothly, "Ah, I am quite better already. I did indeed overlook the obvious. What could be more natural than your desire to dance with Mistress Katherine?"

"Unless you feel opposed . . . ?" the Viking pursued.

Godric felt nothing but delighted surprise in this byplay, for he had detected the steely note in the shipwright's voice, and his curiosity pricked up its ears. Katherine was consternated. It was plainly too late now for her to warn the mayor that she and he were supposed to be intimately linked and that Godric would do well to show some sign that Katherine belonged to him.

The mayor responded with unflattering alacrity, "Opposed? My dear man, of course not!"

The opening notes of another dance drifted over them, this time a wilder, foolish tune. Minstrels strolled and strummed throughout the moving crowds and beckoned the dancers to formation.

One minstrel stopped at their group and diverted the Viking's attention by engaging him in some inconsequential raillery. The resonating notes of the musician's mandolin, whose strings he was vigorously strumming as if they itched, provided a useful cover for the mayor's whispered words to Katherine: "My fascination in the man deepens, my dear."

The minstrel moved along. "Then I have your permission to dance with Mistress Katherine?" the Viking continued when he had turned back around.

"It is not my permission you need," Godric said on a note of refined relish.

The Viking regarded Katherine. She saw there a look that

could only mean mischief. If her trading partner was laboring under certain misapprehensions and was trying to catch her out at her own game, she had only herself to blame. She flushed in spite of herself.

"I beg the favor of a dance, Mistress Katherine," he said with a slight bow and a bland politeness that did not deceive her.

She took refuge in her most unencouraging manner. "What can you be about, Master Eric?" she asked.

Master Eric was unabashed. "A dance, mistress."

"But, my dear," Godric protested, with a soft clucking of his tongue, "you will give our visitor a very odd idea of York hospitality to refuse so charming an invitation. Especially in light of the fact that he has so thoughtfully alerted us to the presence of a most unbeggarly beggar in our streets. Do not delay," the mayor prodded, "to join in the fun."

The ring of dancers had assembled itself in the middle of the square. Katherine glanced over at it and then back at the Viking. She had a visceral intuition that he was trying to come between her and the mayor. But he was tempting, tantalizing her too. Her blood stirred in response to the gay lilt of the pipes and lutes. Her feet urged her to dance, but the gleam in his eye and the quirk of his smile prompted her to read caution. She drew back infinitesimally. The Viking felt her hesitation and was irritated by it.

Mistress Mathilda, watching the ill-assorted threesome from afar, shook her head at the unencouraging look she saw on Katherine's face and decided, with a swell of her matchmaking heart, to give Katherine a push in the right direction.

The redheaded beauty, Maria, noticed the exchange between mistress and shipwright as well, but she, senses sharpened, came to a far different plan of action.

The Viking appealed to the mayor. "I demand something in return for having alerted you to the beggar," he said with a dangerous glint in his eye.

"Quite right, Master Shipwright," the mayor murmured. "Katherine, my dear, you must show a little more readiness for fun."

Katherine shook her head. "No," she said baldly.

"You insult our guest," Godric chided softly. "This will not do!"

The Viking had his own methods for dealing with the insult. He bent an engaging smile on Katherine. "Oblige me, Mistress Katherine," he said smoothly, "for I shall confess to you an irrepressible sense of curiosity."

It worked and she was drawn. "Your curiosity?" she replied, recalling quite vividly his very first visit to her house and the curiosity that he had put to so sure a purpose.

"Aye. I would not have thought you stingy with your favors, mistress. And I am curious to learn for myself what the mayor already knows." Katherine looked doubtful of his implication. "But there's an adage known to men—you are fond of adages, are you not?—that inspires my curiosity, and your friend the mayor can fill you in on it at the next appropriate opportunity."

Katherine had no knowledge of the allusion and imperfectly understood his drift. She felt only regret that she had so carelessly taunted the Viking with her nonexistent relationship with the mayor and was indignant that he should fling it back at her in so impossible a situation.

Godric, on the other hand, had understood the Viking's meaning perfectly, and his world-weary eyes had widened. A deeper, most provocative current had entered the conversation, for the couplet that sprang instantly to his mind was the one that exhorted men to "Dance, dance with Eve to the tune of pretty measures/So that you may judge her skill in other pleasures."

Godric Fitz Osbert had never before found himself in the position of having to defend an insult to a lady's honor, even one so oblique as this, and thus did not invest the office with the chivalry that, say, a Stephen Webster would have deemed necessary. The mayor chuckled softly. "An attempt to draw me into a contest that requires the use of the small sword?" he queried.

The Viking shook his head. "An attempt only to meet Mistress Katherine on equal terms," he replied gravely but with a maddening note of mockery that made Katherine long to best him and made Godric think that York had lacked a certain sort of something before the shipwright's arrival.

"I'm easily satisfied, however," the Viking continued, "and we can call it even if she dances with me. We have already missed the opening round, but the best is yet to come in the galliard, and so all is not lost." He turned to Katherine and held out his hand. "The dance," he commanded.

"Do join in, my dear," the mayor encouraged silkily.

There was nothing for it but to accept the Viking's outstretched hand with as much good grace as she could summon. "With pleasure," she murmured, but she could not meet his eye, which, she suspected, was full of devilment.

The galliard was a country dance that the Saxons had imported from their Norman overlords and adapted to their own sense of rhythm. It was gay and quick with a hint of abandon and not at all the sort of dance one would expect to find the Mistress Katherine executing. Indeed, she had never before danced it. She was obliged to observe her partner's steps closely at first until she had grasped the proper rhythm, and she was quite sure that he was aware that she had never danced it before.

The tempo increased little by little, and Katherine was not immune to the contagious spirit of the dancing. She was vaguely aware of something between the two of them as they came together at intervals and broke apart, something barely concealed beneath the homespuns and the twills, a stirring of blood, a stirring to life, as if the world suddenly extended no farther than the tips of his fingers on hers and was circumscribed by his hands circling her waist as he twirled her indecorously off the ground. She caught his eye on one occasion and had the fleeting sensation that something had been lit inside of her.

The Viking was a bright and dangerous fire, the mayor had said. Katherine had known from the beginning that she would do well to have a caution, but she had chosen to see the danger in terms of the harm he could do to her business. Now, with the physical intimacy of the dance, she realized that she was playing with a fire of a very different sort.

When the dance was too quickly over and he made his way to return Katherine to the mayor's side, her pulses were throbbing with an unsteady, erratic pace—but surely this was only a simple result of her exertion. She looked up, and when she read the laughter and pleasure in her partner's eyes, she was suddenly so afraid that she took refuge in her tongue. "You shall not succeed, Master Eric," she warned him in a low voice, and experienced a mixed relief and regret to see his warm regard instantly replaced by the look of uneasy antagonism that she knew so well.

The Viking did not have a chance to respond to her challenge, for just as they returned to the mayor, they were hailed by a new voice.

"Mistress Katherine!" It was Mistress Mathilda, who, in her own opinion, had arrived at an opportune time. "How nice that you have joined in the dancing with two such delightful partners this evening." Mathilda paused to salute these two partners, bending a particularly warm smile upon the attractive shipwright, and since her mind was on matchmaking, she continued to praise Katherine, in a good-natured, motherly fashion, for her graceful dancing and was about to ask the shipwright some searching, pertinent questions when Mathilda's plans were utterly foiled by her own husband.

Master Robert Webster accosted the group just then, his face suffused with a dull beet-red, and put an end to all discussion by informing the group that he was in a fair mood to tan Stephen's hide. "It's not enough that our son," he said to his wife, "has mooned the day long over the fact that I wouldn't let him join the minstrels in the streets. As if I, Robert Webster, would permit my son to make a perfect donkey out of our name and craft—three generations of Websters in York! By St. Blaize's Body!—I beg pardon!—spouting poetry for the amusement of the whole of the town. To which Stephen cries out, 'Oh Cruel Fate,' as if I had beaten him, which I've a mind to do, 'to have bestowed a pater so unfair!' Pater!" Master Webster spat. *"Pater!* Not that *father* is not a perfectly good word to use. Oh, no! For that is what *pater* means, or so he said, when I threatened him with the belt for using such language in my presence."

Master Robert cast a perfunctory glance around the group and bid them a collective good eventide. His strong sense of propriety warred with his anger. His anger gained the upper hand. "But that was not enough for Stephen for the day," he went on, unable to contain himself. "Oh, no. I have just seen him in the shadows with Mistress Sybille, and, begging your pardon, Mistress Katherine, I know that you've done everything in your power to bring this—this—I don't know what—to an end, but there he was with the Mistress Sybille and practically under Mistress Brewer's very nose! And so I have come straight away to you, Mathilda, for I do not trust myself within ten feet of the boy, and so I say!"

The Viking's moment for any further exchange with Katherine was over. He was not sorry, for something unexpectedly intriguing was happening before his eyes. He seized with interest on the evident fact that Katherine did not countenance a match between her sister Sybille and the son of the richest weaver in town. Or was that another of her ploys to gain the friendship of these influential people? He watched the seemingly genuine play of concern across Katherine's face and admired her smooth interaction with the Websters. It was swiftly decided among the three of them that Katherine and Mathilda would take matters in hand, and so they took themselves off, leaving behind the three men.

The trials and tribulations of young love could not have bored Godric more profoundly, and so he found his earliest opportunity to bow himself away from the discussion that was sure to ensue between the two remaining men.

"Well," said Master Robert, manfully meeting the Viking's eye, "I suppose that my Stephen is not the only member of the family to have made a spectacle of himself tonight. But it was either coming here and venting my anger or killing the boy with my bare hands! Stephen fancies himself a poet, as you've gathered, and fancies himself in love. A fatal combination. Well, and it wasn't the worst thing that Mistress Katherine was also on hand to lend her support in the matter. A fine woman, the Broiderer!"

The Viking reassured Master Robert that his interruption with the domestic crisis was of no moment and that it would, he hardly needed to say, go no further than the group.

Master Robert was understandably embarrassed by the situation and was somewhat reassured by the shipwright's apparent lack of interest in either his son's career or his love life. "I thank you for your discretion, but I'm afraid that the whole of York already knows about them. Or soon will! Drat that boy!"

The Viking smiled indulgently.

"Oh, your time will come," the webster rallied him, "when you settle down to marry and have sons."

The Viking did not answer that but asked instead, "And you say that Mistress Katherine is not in favor of the match between her sister and your son?"

"She knows what's proper, Mistress Katherine. A fine woman, as I say, and a friend to my Mathilda. And Mistress Sybille is a taking little thing. A real beauty, as a matter of fact," the webster amended truthfully, expelling breath, "and I'm thinking that Mistress Katherine has other plans for her, and I hope she can comfortably settle her."

The Viking merely cocked a brow at this disclosure.

Master Robert continued with some strong statements about keeping his nose out of other people's business and ended with the observation, "This country's headed for ruin. I'm hoping York will keep her head above the stormy seas. Politics is a strange thing, and none of us can escape it. But I hope Mistress Katherine will weather it with us. A fine woman, but I know little more of her life than I do of most newcomers to York."

The Viking judged his moment. "I'm from Scarborough, as you know," he said, meeting the webster's eye. "And as for my politics, I tell you that I'm neither for Louis nor for John. If I may be counted as anyone's man, I'm for the Marshal. William the Marshal."

The webster was impressed. The name of William, High Marshal of England, had been the only one to escape the taint of John's reign. The Marshal, the webster knew, was an old man now, and one of the few who had ridden with John at Runnymede. The Marshal's name went hand in hand with a staunch adherence to the feudal code. The Marshal, it was known, who would never desert the king to whom he had sworn fealty. For Master Robert, a townsman devoted to free trade and to the adherence to bourgeois customs, it was, paradoxically, the Marshal's old-fashionedness that inspired the webster's respect.

For the Viking, on the other hand, it was the Marshal's

vision of the future for an independent, united England that had swayed him to undertake the Marshal's bidding. "The Marshal," the Viking repeated. "He's one of John's men, aye, but John's not long for this throne. He'll be ousted soon. Perhaps even before summer has faded. Who is to know? But I would gamble the whole of York's wool money that John will be gone before year's end."

"That leaves only Louis to take over, then. Not a bad substitute, in my opinion," Master Robert replied. "He's a bloody sight better than our wasted line of Angevin rulers— if one can call them such!"

The Viking shook his head. "A far sight worse. You may believe that I know what I am saying."

"Neither Louis nor John? Who's to rule, then? The Marshal can never wear the crown."

"No, but with John's son, Henry..." The Viking held up a hand. "I know! He's naught but a lad. With the Marshal behind him to guide him, however, the country will weather the storm. The Marshal is for England. John and Louis are for themselves."

The webster considered this. The Viking had said enough and left the subject to speak of this and that, to return, in due time, to a subject that interested him more than he cared to admit to himself.

Mistress Katherine and the lord mayor? Master Robert scratched his chin and shook his head. "He's a good man, our mayor, make no mistake! Some would call him a ladies' man, but I don't know about that! He has never married, nor is he, in my Mathilda's opinion, like to tie the knot anytime soon—if ever."

Master Robert continued in this style for a few more minutes, oblivious to the narrowing of the shipwright's eyes as they had scanned the crowd and came to rest on the mayor with the slim, handsome Piers in his shadow. By the time the webster had finished expressing his puzzlement over the mayor's bachelor status and looked up once again at the shipwright, the Viking had come to his own conclusions about the mayor and Piers, and hard on that realization came a reevaluation of Mistress Katherine and her boast about her relationships with that city father and with every other businessman in town.

One thought had taken possession of the Viking's mind: That only Mauleon was left!

___ Chapter 11 ___

Katherine's first feeling upon sight of the port village of Scarborough was one of blessed relief. She had been for four days on the road from York to the coast with a small group of York nuns with whom Katherine had a slight acquaintance, but it was not from her traveling companions that Katherine sought escape. Their wit and well-informed minds had, in truth, made the encounter surprisingly pleasant, while the two burly outriders graciously provided by the Archbishop of York had assured the journey's safety. It was the ripe, unrelenting sun of August that had rendered the travel difficult, and each day Katherine would long for refuge in the cool of night when the moon came to conquer the sun and to soothe the sky. During the day she had dutifully worn her woven, wide-brimmed hat and the cotton gloves that Emma had sewn to prevent any unattractive tanning. While these aids had screened her from the direct rays, they could do little to allay the chafe and irritation and beastly heat of high summer.

As the tired mounts of the traveling party slowly trailed up the last wave of earth before land gave way to sea, the fresh tang of maritime breezes reached out to ruffle neck and face, and Katherine found the sensation stimulating and agreeable. She dismounted with the nuns near the shrine at the crest of the rise to bend a knee at the weather-beaten cross and to look down into the great inverted shell of land that formed the harbor. A few hardy bands of sheep that thrived on salty tufts of grass could be seen straggling over the neighboring hills. Lambs, as dazzlingly white as boiled linen, flocked the rocky, green hillsides.

The village lay below them. In mid-morning a light fog was nestled in the harbor, a cloudy, opalescent mist, perched daintily on thatch and treetop alike, that transformed the coarse, gritty stone of the houses into shimmering pearl. Beyond stretched the deep gray nacre of the North Sea. The sun and sea on an August day, the cawing of circling birds, and the bracing air gave Katherine her sense of relief.

There was more. Katherine's initial apprehensions before the journey, the displacement and physical discomfort of the last days on the road, heightened her relief. They gave her an expected lift that she had not previously known, as if it were enough to have come this far and to have filled her lungs with this new, most extraordinary air.

She frowned. This was not the moment for sentiment. She would not lapse into the kind of soft-minded poetic imaginings that had addled Stephen Webster's wits and seriously undermined Sybille's as well. In the past days Katherine had been very reluctant to come to Scarborough and had, even the week before, called off the trip, stating that she did not want to leave York because of Sybille. It was only now six weeks after the disaster of the St. Barnabas's Day Fair, and Katherine was not yet convinced that Sybille and Stephen had learned to behave themselves. However, Emma had insisted that Katherine make the journey to Scarborough, as originally planned. Emma had waxed confident that she would keep a stern eye on Sybille.

Katherine was taking no chances, and in her opinion the safest course would be for the Websters to tie the knot with the Brewers with no further delay. Mathilda and Katherine had dispensed with subtlety between them and had discussed quite frankly that a public betrothal between Stephen and Eleanora before the end of August would be a very fine thing for everyone. Stephen had seemed subdued in the past weeks and Sybille sufficiently chastened. Still, Katherine had her doubts and did not like leaving York when she could not be easy in her mind that Sybille would behave.

However, Katherine's trip had been so commodiously arranged by Godric Fitz Osbert that it was virtually impossible

for her not to go to Scarborough. Godric delighted, it
seemed to Katherine, in attending to the details of the journey whose complications had threatened to keep Katherine
in York. He arranged to have her safely entrusted to the
company of the several *religieuses* from York's St. Clement's nunnery, who were preparing a visit to a sister priory in
Scarborough; and he took a special care in mounting Katherine with a gentle mare.

As for the irritating, unpredictable man, the Viking,
Katherine had only to think of him to feel some ill-defined
alarm. This feeling came not entirely from his behavior toward her at the fair, maddening as it was; he had since, in
the two meetings that they had had in the past six weeks,
retrieved his position as her hardheaded, hard-tongued business associate. She had known from the beginning that he
was watching her and that she must be wary of him, but
there was something more in his eyes now when they rested
on her. She refused to admit to herself what it might be, and
she was unnerved.

Katherine and the sisters remounted their horses. They
picked their way gently down the slope of the vast bowl and
encountered no difficulty passing village gates.

Scarborough town was neat and solid, presenting a bold
face to the rigors of life in daily confrontation with the sea.
Stone prevailed as the main building material, but there were
half-timbered buildings, tucked with wattle and daub, and
long-and-short masonry as well. The wide stone and cobble-
paved wharf defined the boundary between earth and sea,
with a row of warehouses, the heavy shutters thrown open,
on the land side. This wall of buildings was punctuated by a
tavern or two which essayed a note of hospitality with
benches on each side of the door for the summer months
when the howl and fury of the wind gentled to brisk breezes
and the weather calmed down enough to permit repose out-
of-doors.

Along the waterfront were the great stone bollards, heavily scored where ships's ropes had moored vessels on the
quay, and everywhere could be seen ropes and cleats and
masts and hulls and canvas. Gulls sat in rows on the warped
planks of the short dock and peered for scavenge. Houses

lined narrow streets running parallel to the water and provided barriers to the winds whipping off the watery depths of the ocean.

Mid-morning in summer, this thriving port town was alive with activity. There were cranes and scaffolding and pulleys in front of the warehouses to fill the second stories, and boxes and crates and loose goods to be sold or stored for further shipping. Great frames stood on the docks over which vast fishing and cargo nets had been cast for repairs. Katherine's first impression of the inhabitants, bustling around the waterfront, was of blond hair and blue eyes, this distinctive combination being much more prominent in Scarborough than in York. Katherine followed the nuns through the town to a small priory on the outskirts to the north where Katherine was to be given lodging for the week that the sisters planned in Scarborough before their return trip to York.

St. Agnes's priory slumbered peacefully in the shelter of a berm and a beach scarp, and boasted, as a consequence of its position, a little orchard. There she shared bread and cheese and olives and watered wine with the sisters before going into the village.

Katherine traveled the quay a short distance to the center of activity. Judging from the great, broken loaves of bread strewing the docks flanked by salty vats swimming with smoked fish and flagons of ale that were there for the taking, Katherine surmised that the dockworkers kept working through the midday repast. She picked her way in and among the men and women, and no one seemed to remark the presence of a strange woman in town.

She saw no immediate sign of the Viking. His broad shoulders were not to be seen among the hands on deck of the moored sailing vessels or at work on the nets or in the throng at the warehouse. Then it came to her where she would find Master Eric Shipwright.

Beyond the wharf, at the opposite end of town from the priory, was the shipbuilding yard. It was protected from direct wind by a stockade fence to the sea side but otherwise was open to the town and with a vista down the coast to the south. As she approached the site Katherine could see through the steady hum of activity that there were three ships under construction, in various stages of completion. She noted also, as she came closer, that women swarmed over the yard, dispensing food and drink. Her presence was therefore unremarkable. Katherine came to stand next to a neat stack of cut and planed timber planks bleached white by the sun and which still smelled of fresh resin. It took but a moment for her eye to come to rest on the Viking.

He was bent with hammer in hand, fitting keelson to garboard, to shape the frame of the ship mostly recently begun. He kneeled over the frame that stood on a platform raised a few feet off the ground. He was stripped to chemise and chausses in the hot summer sun, and a light film of perspiration made the linen of his shirt cling in places to his broad, muscular back. His work was interrupted once by a fellow shipwright, apparently asking a question. The Viking gestured and pointed and briefly explained whatever it was and went back to his rhythmic hammering. His face, all crags and hollows, was deeply tanned. He paused to look up again, not in Katherine's direction but down the southern coast.

His profile outlined against rock and sea, Katherine saw him gaze at the tempting horizon. His brow held a distant, restless look, the same one his ancestors—that untamed, incautious race of men—must have worn before their roaming. When he shook his head slightly to return to work and thrust a hand through his curls, she saw that his hair was spangled with sweat. The sudden image came inescapably to mind that his hair was the color of sun-gilded creek sand. She had not previously noticed that before, but as she looked at him now, she realized that there had always been a familiar look about him. It was his hair: the color of the sand in the creek bottom, bright-streaked by a high, scorching sun that had glinted through the rippling water on those hot, lazy summer days she had known as a young girl in France. It was an errant memory, of peace and serenity and childhood.

She did not have a moment to consider it. He turned again and met her gaze directly. He smiled slightly, in welcome, and gestured her forward. She took several steps in his direction and looked up at him.

"So you came," he stated in his gravelly voice, and she wondered why its resonance should make such a strong impression on her at just that moment.

"I came," she returned, with a slight smile of her own. "Did you doubt it?"

He hung his hammer on a cross plank of the ship frame. "Yes," he said, bounding to the ground beside her, "and no." He leaned against the platform. "I did not know."

"I know that I changed my mind once or twice . . ." she began.

"Once or twice?" he said lightly. "I received no less than three messages from your errand boys in the past fortnight with changes of plans and dates."

"Did you think that the hardships of travel for a woman should prevent me from making the journey?" she asked.

"That, perhaps, and other things."

"I'll have you know that Godric, the lord mayor, arranged everything. That is, Godric and the archbishop between them. I was in company of a party of sisters traveling from York to Scarborough, and we were protected by two outriders. We encountered few hardships as a result. A most enjoyable journey, in fact, save for the abominable heat."

"Ah!" was her partner's reply to this news.

She looked at him speculatively. Was that a gleam of humor lurking in the depths of his eyes?

"And your accommodations in Scarborough?" he asked.

"The priory. St. Agnes's."

"Do I take it that you did not come on foot?" he asked.

"Of course I did not come on foot," she replied, surprised. "Godric provided me with a well-behaved young mare as well," she added, and saw that he was indeed silently laughing at her. Pray, why should he find her reference to the mayor amusing? It had always had quite a different effect on him before.

"The lord mayor is attentive to your wishes," he murmured.

With an effort she bit back the retort that rose to her lips. She confined herself to saying, "He is."

"It is unusual for a townswoman to ride," he remarked,

apparently finding the topic of the mayor of no further interest.

She instantly disclaimed any skill on a horse and went on to say that she had so little practice (although she had, in truth, sat a pretty saddle as a young girl) that she had felt every bump along the way. A most uncomfortable ride, she assured him.

"I thought you said that it was only the heat that had caused discomfort."

Well, really! What was the man's mood today? "That and being sidesaddle on a horse for four days. Perhaps I should have mentioned that first, since it seems to trouble you."

"That doesn't trouble me at all."

Katherine met his eye squarely. "Only my reasons for coming here."

"I would not say," he said slowly, "that your reasons for coming here trouble me."

She did not understand him. She felt again that change in him toward her, the subtle alteration in their relationship that had been so vague and intangible but present, nonetheless, and had, when she came to think about it, so little to do with business.

"I have a right to come, do I not?" she answered. "Surely you can appreciate my reasons for wanting to see the *Jorvic*. I still own the controlling interest in it, after all, and I have been wanting for some time to see the general lay of things here in Scarborough. I made my way in York by learning everything there was to know about the wool trade and making the best deals I could. I intend to do the same here. It's only fair that I have as free access in Scarborough as you have in York. Or have you something to hide here?"

"Not at all. But did you consider simply asking me what you wanted to know about Scarborough? It might have saved you the heat—and the bumps."

She smiled prettily. "How do I know that you would not lie to me?"

"Don't judge me by yourself, mistress!"

"We have discussed the merits of truthful speaking on a previous occasion, I believe," she retorted. His eyes rested on her lingeringly. She felt her color rise and was compelled to speak. "So tell me. What were the other reasons—besides the hardships of the road—that you thought might keep me in York?"

"Speaking truthfully," he answered, "it was your sister."

"And what interest do you have in my sister?" she demanded.

"None. I was referring rather to your own interest. I observed that you do not approve of a match between her and York's most promising poet, and I wondered how you could leave her unattended in York at this time."

"She is hardly unattended," Katherine replied. "Emma is there. Marta too. And I have faith in Sybille herself. Deep down she knows what's right."

"No doubt she does," he said dryly.

"What do you mean by that?" she replied immediately.

"I have seen her on more than one occasion, alone and unattended, with the webster's son. I would have said that she had already decided what was right for her."

"That must have been earlier in the summer when you saw them together. All that has changed now. The Websters will be announcing Stephen's betrothal to Eleanora Brewer upon my return to York next week. And that will be the end of that."

"Will it?" The Viking laughed. "You are a very clever business woman, I own, but I predict that you will fail as a sister. The announcement of the betrothal will be fatal to your plans for Mistress Sybille—whatever they are. Nothing could be better calculated to send a young woman into the arms of her fair swain than to announce his betrothal to someone else."

Katherine had said something of the sort herself to Mathilda Webster months ago but was in no mood to hear it now from this man. "Mistress Eleanora is a virtuous young lady who will make Master Stephen a very fine wife and who will become an excellent Mistress Webster. Stephen will not fail to see the wisdom of the match in the years to come—and so will Sybille."

"You have committed that pretty speech to memory very well. And once again I am impressed by your longheadedness. But correct me if I am wrong: Is not Mistress Eleanora a rather plump maiden with little to recommend her beyond her virtue and her father's purse? She can hardly be expected to compete with your sister's charms now or in the future, as you say."

"And just how do you come to know so much about Mistress Eleanora and Master Stephen—or my sister, if it comes to that?" she demanded, feeling her temper rise.

"As I told you and your mayor, a morning in York market is all that is needed to apprise the interested of the latest in local gossip."

"You learned all this at the market?" Katherine exclaimed involuntarily. "I knew that some people in town were aware of Stephen's particular interest in Sybille, but I had no thought that it was common knowledge."

He shook his head. "Robert Webster mentioned the proposed match to me some time ago, and the Brewers are prominent enough to be mentioned here and there at the market, even if one doesn't ask. And I told you that I have seen your sister and the poet together on several occasions. Incidental encounters that I would not have noticed, had not been associated with your house in the first place."

"Well, yes, that is true," she said, a little doubtfully.

"And don't forget that I was there with you at the fair when a problem between your sister and the poet arose," he reminded her, and added on a provocative note, "After our dance together."

Instead of responding to the disturbing memory of that dance she presented him with a sweet smile that sheathed the barb beneath. "But how do you know so much about the motivations of maidens and their swains? I would not have thought that you had much experience with young, virtuous girls."

"I have three sisters," he said with something resembling a grin. "All younger and all of them—thank God!—married off by now."

Katherine was genuinely taken aback. She had not once considered that her partner might belong to a family. It was natural, of course, but the thought of him as a brother left her momentarily speechless.

"Does that surprise you?" he queried.

"Not at all," she replied, recovered. "I have a sister. Why should you not have one—or three—yourself? Or a brother, even."

"No brothers," he answered briefly. "But why are you against the obvious advantages of a match between your sister and Stephen Webster? I confess that it puzzles me."

"Does it? A match between the Websters and my house is out of the question! A perfect simpleton could see that!"

"Shall I acknowledge the rebuke with a civil bow? Or simply point out that I am less than a perfect simpleton?"

"The match is entirely inappropriate," she said impatiently. "All of York would think so!"

"You're observing the proprieties?" he said with exaggerated surprise. "How could I have guessed? I had not supposed that such considerations weighed with you. At least not for yourself. But if it comes to the appropriateness of a match, you could dower your sister well, if you chose to do so, and secure her an honest future."

She took immediate offense. The courtesy of their exchange, precarious at best from the start, rapidly dissolved. "I have other plans for her. That must be equally obvious."

"It is. But I have not yet learned what they might be, if it is not an advantageous marriage," he said with heat.

"And I have not yet learned what business it is of yours to know!" she retorted, her own anger bubbling up to the surface.

"I am merely trying to understand in my own simple terms what you are doing here in Scarborough at this time," he said.

"I have many things to do here," she replied. "You would think me a fool if I did not make at least one trip to see how things stood here."

"*Fool* was not the word I had in mind for you. But now that you are here, how may I help you go about learning what you want to know?" His tone was anything but cordial. "I can direct you to the best gossips in town, if you think it would serve. We've our Geoffrey Taverners and Mathilda Websters. Fine citizens! And they offer a wealth of information. But perhaps that is not what you're after?"

She could not imagine what it was about the man that

should arouse in her a perverse spirit. "Thank you. But I have my own methods of obtaining information, and considerations of propriety do not constrain me, as you have pointed out. I am, in your considered opinion, at least, no fool, whatever else I may be. So why should I bother with gossip when I can learn far more interesting things by seducing the portreeve!"

A hard glint came into his eyes. "Do not let me stop you!" he snapped. "I perceive that you must be about your work. Such things take time, I am sure, even for a woman of your experience. Surely they cannot be accomplished in the space of an afternoon. Or can they?"

She did not trust herself to speak. She took herself off with an angry flounce and was so absorbed with black thoughts about her infuriating partner that she did not notice a man she had cause to know rather well. Fortunately for himself, the Viking's henchman, Bar, saw Katherine before she saw him, and so he was able to slip away and out of sight. Katherine had already decided not to investigate Scarborough on the day of her arrival and so repaired to the quiet confines of the priory's orchard in order to reflect on her undignified behavior. Once again, instead of finding anything objectionable in her pert responses or resolving to mend her tongue, she found that she was rather pleased with herself and spent the greater part of the afternoon discussing in perfect amity with several nuns some of the latest papal bulls issued from Rome.

A thick fog wandered in from the sea after sundown, shrouding the town in misty white cotton and making the future around every corner very murky. Bar found his master on board one of his ships, checking the oarlocks for signs of disrepair.

"Everything in order?" Bar asked as he alit.

The Viking did not immediately look up or respond. He had found a loose screw and was tightening it. "Almost," he said finally.

"Do we leave by week's end?"

"There's no hurry."

"Do you sail with us, Eric?"

"Perhaps not this time. I'd like to stay in Scarborough

through the week. If I've a mind to take to the sea then, I can always sail with the crew that leaves for Holland in ten days' time."

Bar paused. "I saw Mistress Katherine in town today."

The Viking bit off a laugh. "I did too." Then, sharply, "You're not to go near her or let her see you."

"I know that. Not that I would have wanted to today when I saw her. In a rare taking, she was! By Freya's Hand-maidens, she's a beauty when she's angry!"

"She's a saucy baggage with a well-filed tongue who will come by her just desserts one day soon," the Viking replied with enough savagery in his voice to raise Bar's brows.

The heavy fog hid Bar's smile. "What is she doing here?"

"She's come to see her ship, among other things" was the reply.

"She'll like what she sees, then. The *Jorvic* is in good repair and as pretty a decoy as one could imagine. Do you think she'll know that we don't use it?"

"No," he said briefly.

Bar waved the issue aside. "It hardly matters. It's not a bad vessel, all in all, but I know you prefer to sail ships you've built yourself. You'll be taking Mistress Katherine on a tour of it, I'm guessing, if she's wanting to satisfy her curiosity."

"Mine is far from satisfied."

"Oh?"

"I've a suspicious nature, as you well know, Bar."

The burly seaman scratched his beard. "About what? I don't know what you're thinking she's doing here other than minding her own business. Why, that's *exactly* what she's doing, think on!" Bar said, pleased with his turn of phrase.

"There's more to it than that," the Viking stated.

"Than what?"

"She didn't come here just to inspect her ship," Bar's master said. He held up a hand. "And don't, I beg of you, bleat her praises. You will tell me that she has come for a simple purpose, and I will tell you that I know she has other things in mind, as well."

"By Loki!" Bar chuckled. "I'll tell you nothing of the kind! There is always mischief afoot with a woman."

The Viking was not diverted by this piece of wisdom. "All the more reason to remain suspicious."

Bar merely chuckled again and said that whatever Mistress Katherine's other reasons for coming to Scarborough might be, she was certainly wise to see firsthand the goings-on here, as any businessman would do; and with rare diplomacy Bar forebore to mention how many times his master had urged the men he traded with to come to Scarborough during the summer months to learn what there was to know about sea trade.

Further discussion about Mistress Katherine did not prosper. Bar had been with the Viking long enough to know when his master wanted to be alone on board ship, a tool in hand, to hammer out a problem that might be exercising his mind. Bar also knew that his master was closely monitoring John's campaign through the countryside and Louis's difficulties with sea travel. The Viking had predicted to Bar that the contest between John and Louis would come to a head in the next several months, and that he, Eric, was doing what he could to insure that Louis would not ascend to the throne. York merchants, with their much courted cash, could likely sway the outcome, one way or the other.

Bar knew that these considerations weighed on the Viking's mind, and thus Bar did not find it unusual for his master to have returned to the wharf after the evening meal to tend to details. Bar presently left the Viking to his own thoughts, but since it was high sailing season, Bar had work of his own to accomplish along down the wharf, and in any case, it was his habit to sleep on board his own ship in the summer, since houses and beds and domestic routine had a tendency, he often proclaimed, to unman him.

Much later the Viking laid down his tools and was ready to go back into town. The fog was a dense, ghostly white in the late evening, but he knew his way so well that he was in no way troubled by it.

It may have been that never quite dormant itch between his shoulder blades that warned him of danger. When he stepped from the ship's deck to the solid stone and cobble of the wharf, he felt it down his spine and checked his step. The fog swirled, and weird shapes and shadows crouched in and around the moored ships and great bollards. The Viking's fingers closed over the handle of the dirk in the belt slung at his waist. Instinct warned him against retreating to the ship where he could be ambushed. He took several assured steps toward town.

One nearby shape suddenly took the form of a man and attacked him from behind. He was prepared, turned quickly, and warded off the blow. There was a muffled groan. Two new shadows leapt from the billowing, wet white fog, and the dull flash of steel penetrated the mist. The Viking's own blade swept a circle before him, and the two shadows jumped back. Blows rained on his head and shoulders and arms, all from seemingly different directions. He uttered a low curse, parried the blows, and shot out the short steel of his dagger. Contact with a body was made, and the blade came away red.

Then confusion. The Viking knew only that he must distance himself as much as possible from pier's edge, or he could end up unconscious and left to die in the water. Three, possibly four, attackers were on him now. He was far from winded, but his strength could not last forever in this unequal contest. His attackers were on the receiving end of an occasionally well-placed fist, but he was beginning to catch the worst of it. Gasps, hot oaths, the scrape of steel pulsed in his ears. The fog worked with him while he wrenched away from the unsure grasp of a foe. Then the fog worked against him as he fell backward into the knuckles of another assailant.

Farther down the wharf a deep, gruff voice called out. It was Bar. "Hey, lads, let's join the fun," he cried, as if to an accompanying band of men, and the quick pad of boots on stone was muffled, making the number of running feet indistinguishable. Eric's attackers were surprised by what sounded to be a host of reinforcements and began to thrust wildly before they could disappear into the mist. One blade found the Viking's back, and the last thing he knew before blackness descended on him was a sharp, stabbing pain near his heart.

Bar's shouts and hoots scattered the band of ruffians. He moved swiftly for so hulking a man and, kneeling over his master, quickly found the ooze of blood. Bar did not move the Viking as he lay on the cobbles but remained for an almost interminable space of time, applying pressure with his fist to the wound until he was satisfied that it was beginning to clot. It was clean, Bar judged, though deep. It would need a proper binding before too much longer, but Bar was reassured by his master's steady breathing and relatively strong pulse. Only inches had spared the knife thrust from proving fatal.

The Viking groaned and murmured thickly. Bar lifted him slowly to his feet, propped his master's arm so that it fit firmly about his shoulder, and half carried the Viking through the deserted streets of the town. Bar knew just where to take him and kept up a determinedly cheerful patter of conversation the whole way. Bar knew it was important for the Viking to maintain consciousness until Bar could get him comfortably fixed. Bar remarked humorously on the hazards of late-night fog that made attack by roaming bands of ruffians so attractive and thought it a mean trick of nature to find that the fog was beginning to clear now that the harm had been done.

A good many arduous minutes later, Bar was heartily relieved to see his master in a comfortable bed and in safe hands, his wound washed and dressed. A cup of strong wine was brought to his lips. The Viking roused enough and cracked his eyes. A circle of concerned faces hovered above him. He accepted the wine with little protest.

His eyes fastened on Bar. He seemed to want to speak. A woman's hand came down on his brow.

"Don't speak, love! You're here with us now," a soft, feminine voice said. "Do you know what has happened to you?"

The Viking nodded.

"You're going to be all right, love," the woman continued. "We're going to let you rest before we plague you again with wine or food. Close your eyes and get some sleep."

The Viking was agitated and began to struggle.

"Don't talk, love," the woman soothed.

"He has something to say." This, from a man's voice. "Let us try and find out what it is."

The Viking nodded.

"What is it that you want, Eric?" the man asked.

The Viking moved his lips. Pain engulfed him, but still he made the effort to speak. "The priory. Fetch Mistress Katherine the Broiderer"—his voice was low and halting but held an ominous note that boded no good for the broiderer —"so that she may survey her night's handiwork."

___ Chapter 12 ___

The anxious tingle of the galilee bell over the priory door did not penetrate Katherine's slumber. Neither did the shuffle and scuffle of hurried slippers on stone, nor the hushed, grave voices beyond the makeshift curtain which had been hung to provide privacy for Katherine's sleeping pallet in the small dormer room. Even when the curtain was pulled back and the yellow light from the lantern fell across Katherine's cheek, her only reaction was to try with a sleepy, ineffectual hand to wipe the bothersome patch of light from her face. It took a voice in her ear and a quiet shake of her shoulder to rouse her.

Then, fully awake, she sat up abruptly, her heart pounding irregularly and fearing the worst.

"Mother Superior," she whispered respectfully, and then drew herself to her feet.

"You have a visitor, mistress," the head of the priory told Katherine, and then, handing the lantern to the woman who stood behind her, disappeared behind the curtain.

Katherine saw before her a tall young woman in a golden spill of light. She was remarkably beautiful in the Nordic fashion and had apparently hastily clothed herself, for her hair hung in two thick, blond braids to her girdle, and she wore no coif. Her face struggled for composure, but she was visibly upset.

"You are Mistress Katherine?" she said on the heels of the mother superior's departure. Katherine nodded. "My name is Gwyneth. Come with me," she said with low urgency. "To my house. Quickly. I'll explain on the way."

Katherine did not argue. Her first pang of fear that tragedy had befallen Sybille had receded. Katherine groped for her shoes and slipped them on, but when she began to search for a coif to cover her hair which, like her blond visitor's, was braided for the night, Gwyneth motioned impatiently to Katherine to follow her. Again Katherine offered no protest and slipped quietly into step beside the tall young woman.

The fog had lifted, and the night was crisp and tangy. All remaining corners of sleep in Katherine's head were instantly cleared. Outside the priory wall a great, muscular beast of a man stood ready to escort them through the town. They set a fast pace. Gwyneth took a deep breath and said, "It's Eric."

Katherine experienced a wild jumble of emotion. "Eric?" she repeated.

"Yes. He's going to be all right. He asked for you. I am not sure that a visitor is the best thing for him right now; but it seemed important to him that you come, and so rather than upsetting him, we thought it wisest to come get you. We were not at all sure what he meant about you, although he did not seem dazed. Are you a schooled in physic?"

"No."

"Well, I seriously doubt that there would be anything more you could do for him at the moment, even if you were. He's at my house. Almost the other end of town from here. The other end of town from the wharf, too. It was very bad for him to have been transported all that way, losing blood. He's perfectly safe now, of course, and well tended. He's going to be all right," she repeated, as if to reassure herself more than Katherine.

Katherine was having difficulty assimilating all of this. "Eric?" she repeated stupidly. "Master Eric Shipwright?"

"Yes. Or Eric Knudson if you prefer. Of Scarborough." Gwyneth wrinkled her brow. "Do you not know him?"

"I know him," Katherine affirmed. "Pray, excuse my

dull-wittedness. I have hardly understood a word you have said. You say that he has met with an accident?"

"Hardly that," Gwyneth replied, low and with force of emotion. "Attacked and stabbed! I nearly wept when I saw him, but tears are of no good when someone so dear to you has a desperate need of you. He always comes to me, of course, and so I am used to seeing him in various conditions —but never as bad as this. I tell you, seeing him tonight was like experiencing death myself." Gwyneth's voice quavered at the memory, still painfully fresh. "The bruises made it seem much worse than it is, I suppose, and once we got him cleaned up and into bed, I realized that it was not so very dire, after all."

Katherine lowered her eyes from Gwyneth's beautiful concerned face. "You say that he will recover?" Katherine asked as steadily as she could.

"Yes. He has only a very low fever, almost nothing in fact, and he seems very aware of what has happened to him, which is a good sign. He had not spoken much as yet. We don't want him to. Except to mention you, of course. We turn here at this corner, and then my house is straight ahead. This is the Jarl, by the way," she said, pointing to their protective beast. "He's Gustaf's son." As if that should mean something to Katherine. "What would I do without him—and all the others who have helped my Eric. Oh, he's given me plenty of frights, but this one was by far the worst. And so unexpected! Right under our very noses, here in Scarborough!" Her voice took on a rough, scolding, loving tone. "Eric had better settle down before much longer. And he will, if I have anything to do about it!"

Katherine spoke carefully, as if she were stepping on eggshells. "Are you betrothed?"

"Me?" replied Gwyneth, somewhat surprised. "Why, no! I've been married for, what, six years already and have two children. Why do you— Oh! Eric's my brother," she explained in a lighter tone. "I thought you must have known that! I'm his middle sister. There are three of us, but I'm the only one who stayed in Scarborough. Here we are."

A large two-story house stood at the end of a lane. Cracks

of light squeezed out through chinks in the downstairs shutters, while upstairs, the shutters of one window had been shoved open, transforming the window into a dimly illuminated yellow eye. The house itself floated as an oasis of light in the midnight black of the night. Katherine saw several men, of roughly the Jarl's size and proportions, standing outside the front door. Katherine had the impression that they were guarding it. It was no doubt, Katherine told herself, the overall feeling of safe haven that emanated from the house that allowed her to view it suddenly with such a clear heart.

Gwyneth paused to speak with the men at the door and then ushered Katherine through it. She paused to add, "I'm the miller's wife, by the way. My husband, Morten, is upstairs with Eric. Go on up. He's expecting you. I'll be up presently."

Katherine mounted the narrow stone corkscrew of stairs and tiptoed soundlessly into the room whose door stood open. She had vastly underestimated her reactions to Gwyneth's various disclosures on their walk through town and would have said, if asked, that she naturally felt some surprise at the news of her partner's attack and that this initial reaction was followed by mild relief. Thus she was entirely unprepared for the shock and the fear and something else again that surged through her upon sight of the Viking, Master Eric, his gray eyes closed, so quiet and pallid in the large four-poster bed.

Her heart leapt into her throat, and she closed her eyes to steady herself against a feeling of nausea and dizziness. She took a deep, ragged breath and opened her eyes again. With effort she recruited her forces and said low, "Good eventide, Master Miller. I am Mistress Katherine the Broiderer."

The Viking stirred in the bed at the sound of her voice.

The miller looked up from his contemplation of the patient, and a worried frown cleared form his brow. "Good that you are come, mistress," he said in equally hushed tones, and rose from his bedside chair. He was a large man, distinguishable from the other men Katherine had seen this night by his raven-dark hair and beard. "We are sorry to have disturbed you, but—God's Body!—it seemed important."

The Viking shifted uncomfortably and groaned slightly.
The miller looked down at him and lowered his voice to a
bare whisper. "For the life of me, though, I can't figure out
what he wants from you. A strange thing he said! But I see
you've suffered a shock," he said, noting her stricken face
and moving quickly to her side. He led her to the chair at the
head of the bed. "Eric's never mentioned you before, to my
knowledge, and you're not from Scarborough; but have you
known each other long?"

Gwyneth entered the room then, so Katherine was
obliged to say only "Not very long" in response to his question. Gwyneth and her husband then discussed how the rest
of the night should pass, now that Mistress Katherine had
come. The Millers were puzzled by the request for the broiderer's presence; but since their concern for the wounded
man's well-being overrode every other consideration, they
did not delve too deeply in the reasons for her presence.
They decided on a vigil to rotate among the three of them, if
Mistress Katherine would agree.

Katherine could scarce keep her mind on the conversation. She nodded absently. Her eyes were resting on the
Viking, his bright hair drained of color and sunk into the
snow white of the pillows, his mouth a grim line of pain, his
broad shoulders bruised and unnaturally still against the
merciful softness of the mattress. His eyelids seemed to
move with their conversation; she thought he was listening
to them.

Fear that fever might still set in was uppermost in Gwyneth's mind. Katherine stretched out a hand to feel the Viking's brow. There was no sign of unusual warmth, but he
moaned in response to her touch, and she quickly removed
her hand. She dropped it on the bedcovers near his side.

"I think he wants to say something," she said, still looking at him.

"I wish he would not try to speak," Gwyneth whispered.
"It costs him so much just now."

Katherine shook her head. He suddenly looked very agitated. "I don't think he wants me here. Perhaps you misun-
derstood him. I think that my presence—that I am
disturbing him," she said. She made a movement as if to

rise. "Shall I wait downstairs for a while until his sleep is deeper?"

Before she had even left her seat, the Viking's hand shot out and caught her long, cool fingers in a firm clasp. Katherine's heart lurched and then began to drum anxiously in her breast. Master Morten and his wife exchanged alarmed glances. Katherine, held immobile by surprise, remained where she was.

The Viking's lips moved.

"Don't speak, love," Gwyneth said, bending over her brother.

Despite the recommendation, the wounded man tried again. "Stay," he croaked. The command was apparently directed at Katherine.

Gwyneth looked over at Katherine and nodded vigorously. "I'll stay," Katherine said, her low voice pleasant and soothing. Eric nodded slightly, as if satisfied by these words, but the effort caused a quiver of pain to chase across his face.

Silence reigned in the room for several minutes. The Millers stood, immobile, at the head of the bed across from Katherine, intently watching the Viking. Katherine's hand lay unresisting under her partner's. When his grip began to slacken, she tried to pull her hand away very slowly, but his fingers immediately tightened again.

Katherine caught Gwyneth's eye. "I think that it would be best if I stayed for the first watch." She glanced down at her imprisoned hand. "I cannot go anywhere for the next little while, and there is no reason for all of us to lose sleep. I am not a bit tired now, so why don't you come and relieve me in three or four hours? I can return to the priory then and will come back here after the matins to see how he is."

The Viking had seemed to be sleeping, but this brief speech provoked another flicker of agitation in him. Katherine thought that she heard him breathe a flat "No." She was at a loss to understand what was in his mind, but she knew that he was trying desperately to communicate something.

"I won't return to the priory, then," she said to the Millers, who were regarding her with a puzzled look. "Perhaps that is what he wants. I don't quite understand. I feel that I must ask him." She addressed the Viking very quietly. "Would it be acceptable to you if your sister were to fix me up a pallet downstairs?"

Again no, and he would not let go of her hand.

Gwyneth felt his brow for fever but shook her head, as if she could not understand the cause of this strange exchange.

Master Miller tried a turn with his brother-in-law, since it was evident that he was conscious enough to follow the conversation. "Eric," he said, "it's Morten. Mistress Katherine is with you now. She will stay here with you for the next few hours. Then Gwyneth will come to relieve her. Mistress Katherine will need her sleep, too, if she is to be able to help you."

"No help" came the weak response.

"She's here to help you," Master Morten insisted.

The patient shook his head slightly. "No help," he repeated. "Not leave . . . this room."

Morten strove for a light touch. "Eric! You make us think that she is your prisoner rather than our guest."

The Viking's grip on Katherine's hand tightened. He nodded and had a look of satisfaction. He had been understood at last. "Yes. Prisoner," he murmured thickly. "This room."

The rest of the night passed uneventfully. He became warm but not feverish. He was strong enough to fight off infection, but awareness of his ironlike constitution did not entirely relieve Katherine's mind of worry, nor did she leave the chair at the Viking's side. Toward dawn she surrendered to her exhaustion and stretched her head and arms across the bed next to her wounded captor. Gwyneth and her husband took turns keeping watch on the other side of the patient.

Gwyneth had made apologetic noises about her brother's extraordinary and inexplicable statements about keeping Katherine a prisoner, but Katherine had dismissed them and told her partner's sister that they were of no moment. She could have told Gwyneth that her brother's high-handedness was entirely typical of her relations with him but did not. Katherine had said merely that she would submit to his wish and stay in the room. He had drifted minutes later into sleep.

Katherine's last thought before succumbing to her own

weariness was that this rare submissiveness on her part was the least she could do for the man she depended upon to sail her ship, but she would give him to understand, as soon as his senses were restored, that it would not be repeated.

The next thing she knew, it was morning. She shifted and stretched and tried to recapture sleep, but it eluded her. She suddenly remembered where she was, and when she opened her eyes, it was to find the Viking's regard fixed on her.

She sat up. He was propped against several fat pillows, with Gwyneth at his side, looking steadily at her. Katherine noted with a pang that the hollows beneath his eyes were deeper than when she had last seen him the day before, strong and fit, in the shipyard, and that his skin was still ashen beneath his tan. She thought, irrelevantly, of her own disheveled appearance and would have liked, womanlike, to have her comb and brush at hand. She was, in point of fact, still pink from sleep, rumpled and vulnerable and very beautiful.

Nothing in the hard, unappreciative gaze that riveted her indicated how desirable she appeared. As he continued to stare at her, her eyes turned a chilly green in response, and she tried to assume as cool a demeanor with her captor as the circumstance of having spent the night in the same bedchamber with him permitted. She was about to speak when the Viking shifted his eyes to Gwyneth and said in a deep voice that lacked its customary vigor but was still authoritative, "The Mistress Katherine may be excused to perform her morning toilette, and you may accompany her. Call Morten and the Jarl and Olaf to come to me. I shall need some help." He tried to raise himself on one arm as he spoke but failed and sank back into the pillows, spent with the effort of talking and moving. Gwyneth clucked and cosseted and then ushered Katherine out of the room.

There was, of course, no sign of Bar to be seen around the house, for when he heard that Mistress Katherine the Broiderer had been summoned, he told Morten, somewhat cryptically, to inform the Master that he, Bar, would keep "hisself to hisself and entirely unsuggested."

The two women returned to the Viking's room some time later. Fresh bed linens had been spread, the wound newly dressed, and the patient bathed and put into a clean chemise. A hot broth was being fed to him when the two women entered the room. Gwyneth immediately took over the task and shooed the men out.

Gwyneth had kindly lent Katherine a clean kirtle of a becoming Kendal green and had wound the braids of Katherine's thick, glossy hair across the crown of her head in the Norse fashion. The style emphasized the delicate shape of her face and her youth and made her look much less the prim townswoman. The Viking was in no mood, however, to admire her particular beauty. He pinned her with fierce eyes and looked as if he had something to say to her but managed only, "Sit." Then he closed his eyes and slept for the greater part of the day.

Katherine was confined to the room. Gwyneth stayed with her for most of the time, and they broke their fast together and spoke low and at random but very pleasantly, avoiding all but the most common of personal subjects; and although Katherine was aware that Gwyneth regarded her with some puzzlement, Katherine liked the Viking's sister very well and found that she was not bored by the inactivity. Katherine refused to examine the reasons why she was content to be in one small room, a virtual prisoner of a man who irritated her beyond all reason. She used the hours to show Gwyneth several new stitches. Together they passed the afternoon embroidering household linens, something Katherine had not done, it seemed, for years. The windows were open to catch the healing maritime breezes, and the sounds of the busy town at work drifted in to accompany the women's industry.

Toward the end of the working day, when shipwrights were laying down their hammers and fishermen were hanging their nets to dry, the Viking roused in full possession of himself and in a strong voice stated a desire for real food. Gwyneth could not have been better pleased and went to the kitchens. Katherine sat atop homespun cushions in the window embrasure and watched him warily. He did not address her.

When the Viking had dispatched with appetite a large veal shank, salted herring, jellied neat's tongue, buttered salsify, boiled beans, black bread, and a tankard of malt beer, he handed the tray to Gwyneth and said, baldly, that if she had other things to do in the house, she was at liberty to perform them. Gwyneth left without a word but not without shooting Katherine a lively, very curious glance.

"Now, mistress," he said ominously. "Come here."

Katherine did not like his tone, but she was too unsure of his condition to argue with him. She rose and came to the foot of the bed.

"Here, I said," he repeated, indicating the chair that she had occupied throughout the night.

Katherine did not move. She saw his gray eyes, clear and bright and strong. "You can see me well enough from here, I think."

He shook his head. "Oh, no," he said in a low and wrathful voice, "not well enough. You do not comply? I see that I shall have to call the Jarl, who stands outside to assist you." He turned his head to the door to summon his man. Katherine, thinking that any physical contact between herself and the Jarl would lead to indignity, hastily came around and sat down at the Viking's side. Their eyes were level.

"So, let me look at you," he said. Although his voice was not as strong as usual, it rumbled deeply and held stinging contempt. "I thought I had your measure, but I was mistaken. I knew from the moment I laid eyes on you, despite the image you present to the rest of the world, that you had something strongly in common with the lowest strumpet from the taproom, but now I find that even a drab from York's most disreputable liberty could learn a trick or two from you!"

Katherine blinked. Was he feverish? "What do you mean?" she asked inanely.

"Have I not made myself plain?" he said with biting force to his words. "You are an intelligent woman and can easily interpret what I say. Perhaps too intelligent for your own good, since you obviously do not know where that lies. And you are beautiful—I grant you that! Even your outrage becomes you, but you may spare me your wide, innocent eyes, for I know you to be treacherous to the bottom of your heart. But I did not suspect—even *I* had underestimated the degree to which you are false! Do you stop at nothing to gain a farthing? And at no man? Do you treat them all to your favors? I would heartily like to know what you think you shall gain."

"Now I know, at least, that you are back to normal," Katherine flashed in response, almost choking on her words in her anger, "after spending an entire night of worry and dread. Are you irritable in your convalescence and in need of a fight? You shall have one, Master Eric, for I shall be happy to oblige!" Her eyes darted green fire. "I shall avail myself of the example you so forcefully set and freely air my opinion of you. My one regret is that you should be incapacitated. Nothing would afford me more pleasure now than to slap your face!"

"What is to stop you?" he taunted harshly.

She rose from her chair and made a movement toward him. With resolution she kept her arms at her sides. "Yes! You goad me when I cannot retaliate!" She stalked away from the bed and then whirled around. "I can hardly hit a man who has been at death's door but a few hours before, and so to sling insults in my face, even allowing your condition, is beyond what is fair!"

"Fair! God's Love, that's rich! Do you call being set up by four men fair?"

"Of course not," she replied. "And I would call it cowardly, besides."

"Then who were the four cowards, if you please? Can you tell me that?"

"How should I know who they were?" she said, surprised.

"How, indeed!" he mocked. "Tell me instead if you paid them in coin or with your very large favors!"

"What! You *dare* say these things to me! The minute you are on your feet I've a mind to run you through in earnest and finish off properly someone else's most excellent idea. I never knew how good until this very moment!"

He laughed bitterly. "Someone else's excellent idea! At that admission I should think you would even want to come forward to take the credit you deserve."

"The credit I deserve?" she echoed, mystified.

"Who else but you could have put the men on to me?" he rasped out. "I would not normally have been in Scarborough this week if it had not been for you. Your visit to Scarborough altered my sailing schedule, as you well know, and with the many changes in plan this fortnight past, only you and I knew where I was to be yesterday. You told me at the yard that you had many things to do in Scarborough—one of which, apparently, was to put your men on to me, for no one has dared attack me in Scarborough before. This bold move I can only lay at your address!"

Katherine gasped. "You think that I— Oh, *infamous!*" She stamped her foot and then abruptly began to pace the floor to vent her fury. "It is not as if I came to Scarborough to see my ship—which I have *not* seen, by the by, thanks to having spent the entire night and day in this room, worrying about you. Oh, no! I could not have wanted to come here, according to you, for any perfectly sound business reason." She hardly paused for breath. "A pretty opinion you have of me! But that has been clear from the start. Not only am I a woman to take to bed every man in York—"

"Except the mayor," the Viking interposed.

"Well, of course, except him," Katherine agreed dismissively without thinking, "but in addition to being a woman of unmentionable reputation, you supposed me to have set four men on you to kill you? For what end, pray? I confess that my motives escape me."

"You were acting at the instigation of your fine London lover."

"I have so many that I cannot conceive which one you might be referring to," Katherine said between her teeth.

"Can you not?" he shot back.

"I fear that you shall have to—" Katherine began, and then everything fell into place. She blanched and whispered, "It must have been Mauleon."

"Yes, Mauleon," he agreed.

The Viking was watching Katherine's face. His own harsh features were impassive and unreadable.

"Only Mauleon would think to set four men against one!" she exclaimed, diverted by this new thought. Her brow darkened. "The coward! And I doubt that he was one of the four.

Bullies do not usually do their own work. Oh, that is him, start to finish!"

"You informed him of my whereabouts, never thinking that he would come after me with a purpose?"

Katherine looked at him, magnificent in her scorn. "I told him nothing. I haven't seen the man in months—since April or May, at least. Mother Mary, half the reason I left York was to avoid seeing him! I had run out of excuses, and even Godric let me know in his own inimitable and oblique way that leaving the city was quite possibly the only way I could escape—" She stopped short.

"Escape? Escape what, mistress?"

A flush crept into her cheeks. She did not finish her statement but said again, "I told him nothing."

The Viking let her unfinished thought pass, but he did not miss the significance of her impetuous words. He took another tack. "And he simply guessed your whereabouts—and mine?"

"No! Godric must have told him where I went. Or perhaps Mauleon forced the information out of him! For all I know, Godric might have told him voluntarily, just to have a little fun at my expense. I do know that Emma would not have said a word about my whereabouts, no matter how he threatened her."

"The mayor?" he asked, interested. "Why? Why should Godric Fitz Osbert and Mauleon have anything to say each other or discuss your movements?"

Katherine paused at length. "Because they are half brothers through the same mother," she said slowly, "and it was Godric who introduced Mauleon to me. Godric had the idea to use Mauleon to pay off my creditors, who were wanting the money from the shipment I lost when Josef died. It was a risk I was willing to take, and Mauleon's money did save me from possible exposure in the guild, since, as you know, I do not invest there under my own name."

"Naturally not," he commented. "It sounds a reasonable solution."

"Does it? I would say that it ranks among one of Godric's worst ideas, but I did not know it at the time, of course."

She dared to look at him. "That was just days before your first visit to my house."

"And you never told Mauleon of your partnership with me?"

"That would hardly have been in my best interests," she exclaimed.

"So you agreed with me."

"Only on that one point," Katherine replied swiftly. Then, "Godric suspects something, however, and might have told Mauleon that I had come here to see you—although I told Godric that I was coming at Josef's request. No one officially knows of Josef's death yet, but again, I feel that Godric guesses that something has happened to him. But I have no notion of how much he told his half brother."

"I see. So Mauleon came here to kill two birds with one stone," he said, adding casually, "Nevertheless, it seems somewhat extreme on your part to have fled York simply to avoid seeing Mauleon."

She had already said too much, but this was not a subject on which she could speak with any moderation. "The man makes my flesh creep," she said with extreme distaste.

The Viking turned something over in his mind, and a gleam of humor came into his gray eyes. "But now, let me guess. You were in debt to Mauleon on the day of my arrival in York. However, after our partnership assured you of future income, you discharged your debt to him by applying to one of York's bankers and borrowing money at an outrageous rate of interest. That debt you paid back—if I am not mistaken—on Easter morning." He smiled. "I did offer at the outset to assume any of your outstanding debts, and I told you then, as well, that I do not charge interest."

She had thought herself so clever to have scrambled her trail on Easter morning when she went to repay Baruch in Coney Street, but now she saw that the Viking had arrived at the correct result in spite of all her precautions. "There is more to the matter than money and interest," she replied evasively.

"Oh? And you have led me to believe this whole time that you are a competent businesswoman! Yet you must have borrowed quite a sum to get out of a debt that could have been settled more cheaply. As little as you like Mauleon, you must have disliked doing business with him at such a price."

Katherine saw the amusement hovering around the corners of his mouth and met his challenging regard with a kindling eye. She was backed into something of a corner. "Not half as much, I can assure you, Master Eric, as I dislike doing business with you!" she retaliated with spirit.

"I return the compliment," he said cordially, "and can only hope that the interest you paid was worth it."

"Every penny, and it was at a fair rate," she said with dignity. Then, to change the uncomfortable subject, "But what do you mean by Mauleon's coming to Scarborough and killing two birds with one stone?"

"It's very simple. Presumably he came here to find you, and as a matter of convenience, since he knows well enough that I live here, he thought to do me in at the same time."

"He certainly got to you!" she exclaimed. "And it seems that his intention was to murder you! He's a very ill-humored man, you know. Godric calls him liverish, and I'm inclined to agree."

He laughed at that, somewhat grimly. "You have the general idea. However, I would have other names to call him."

His earlier insults still rankled, so she said with heavy irony, "Why waste your delicacy on me? You are surely not too polite to mention what must be very foul names to a—what was it, now?—strumpet from the taproom and a drab from the stews?"

If she was hoping for an apology from him for his harsh words to her, she was to be sadly disappointed. He favored her with a look that brought the blood to her cheeks and said that if she replied to Mauleon in such a saucy fashion, it was no wonder that he was after her as well.

That observation drained the blood from Katherine's face.

"Yes," the Viking went on. "To find you, we must suppose, was Mauleon's original reason for coming to Scarborough. His attack on me simply filled the time before he could find you." He paused. "This morning there was a raid on the priory at dawn. The Jarl told me about it, since he was out patrolling most of the night, but he arrived a few minutes too late to prevent it. No one was hurt and nothing was stolen, so that it was not clear to the sisters what it was all about. I cannot help but wonder now, of course, if Mauleon has not lost patience with you and raided it with the thought of finding you there."

Katherine felt fear. She had stalled as long as she could. The lines were surely drawn now, and she had won Mauleon as an enemy. If his disposition could bring him to attempted murder in the case of the Viking, what might it cause him to do to her when he finally got his hands on her? What was worse, here she was miles away from the relative security and comfort of her friends and her own four walls in York.

She sat down in the window seat and cast a glance out the open window to the brilliant streaks fired across the sky by the setting sun. "You do have guards outside your house, do you not?" she said in a low voice. "Those men I saw last night when I came. They appeared to me to be guards."

"They are. But they are there to guard me."

She cocked a slim brow at his tone. She perceived that he was baiting her, and her momentary fear of Mauleon was replaced by a warm irritation provoked by the man in bed in front of her. Did he think she would ask to be protected by him? She would rather cut out her tongue than fling herself on his kindness.

"That is reassuring, in all events," she said with cool dignity, "and since Mauleon has already raided the priory and I am no longer your prisoner, I presume, I must suppose that I am at liberty to return there for the night." She said sweetly, "Perhaps you could spare one of your men to escort me through town?"

"The Jarl also told me this morning that he did not think the attackers had left town but had only retreated to the hills," he informed her. "There is no reason to think that they will not try again in the hope that you will return there confidently thinking the coast is clear."

Katherine considered her options and then drew a long breath. "I shall have to ask your sister for shelter here until my traveling party is ready to return to York."

"She never does anything without my approval," he said lazily.

"Even in her own home?" she said with pointed incredulity.

"Even in her own home," he answered. "And now that you mention your return to York, do you think it wise to travel in a small party of nuns?"

"We have two outriders," she said, "as I told you yesterday. Provided for us by the mayor and the archbishop."

He laughed. "Wonderful protection! You, yourself, have mentioned that our bully Mauleon never prepares for a fair fight. As we both know from past experience, he likes to weigh the balance heavily in his favor, so that he has no chance of losing."

"But I cannot stay here indefinitely," she protested. "I'm needed back in York for a variety of reasons—not the least of which being our business concerns, do not forget!—and so I will take my chances."

"No," he stated, "you will not take your chances. You'll return with me and my men when I'm well enough to ride again. I've a desire to scour the countryside for Mauleon and his band now, and hope that they won't have flown the region before I'm on my feet again!"

This plan did not find favor with her. She stood up abruptly. "You will understand if I decline your generous offer. I shall return to York in whose company I came, and I shall have my lodgings at the priory for the rest of the week. I am perfectly capable of taking care of myself."

"That," he said, with a low, angry rumble, "is apparently what you are not able to do, mistress! You make a habit, I have observed, of underestimating the danger in which you continually place yourself! Although I've no cause to save your pretty neck from Mauleon, I will see you safely back to York while I still have an interest in Leofwyn Shippers."

"The precise nature of that interest—which is more than monetary, I have always thought—you shall no doubt divulge to me in the near future."

"Assuredly! If Mauleon hadn't gotten to you first and you're still around to discuss it with me," he tossed back.

In the face of these arguments Katherine fell back on pure

defiance. "I will return to the priory—without an escort, if you will not grant me one—and find my way back to York on my own. And you can do nothing to stop me!"

"Oh, can I not?" His voice was clear and strong and hot. "Given the fact that you have no idea about your own safety, I shall have to take matters in my own hands. For all the rest of the house knows, you are still my prisoner, and I do not intend to tell them any differently. You'll not be leaving this house until I give the order."

Katherine made a sound like an angry kitten and shook her fist at him. "I'm through with you!" she cried, and made her way to the door.

His voice, clean and sharp, stopped her. "You and I have not yet begun," he threatened with unmistakable meaning. "And when we do, it will be on my time and on my terms."

Katherine swept out of the room, her color high. "He is recovered," she informed the Jarl, who was standing sentry outside the bedchamber door.

___ Chapter 13 ___

Relief may have attended Katherine's arrival in Scarborough, but it certainly did not accompany her departure from the port village. The weather was stiflingly hot and heavy and as oppressive, she thought, as her traveling companions. Having suffered a humiliating defeat in a test of wills, Katherine was not returning to York in the company of the delightful nuns with whom she had come to Scarborough. Rather, she found herself in the highly uncomfortable presence of the Viking and a half dozen of his men. The wife of one of them had come along to "observe the proprieties," as the Viking phrased it with obvious malice.

Katherine had not succeeded in returning to the priory,

either, but had been forced to stay at the home of Master and Mistress Miller. Once it had been made clear (through the intermediary of Gwyneth, no less!) that Katherine was not to leave the house, except for a short daily walk in town and in the company of Gwyneth and two bodyguards, the Viking had had nothing more to do with Katherine. Their rather heated exchange of words that announced the beginning of his recovery had been their only conversation during Katherine's stay with the Millers. The Viking convalesced during the week without once summoning her. Not, of course, that she wanted to see him for any particular reason, for he had never been anything but insulting to her. But since his health was vital to her business concerns (just as he had said her safety was important to him as long as he had a share in Leofwyn Shippers), she kept abreast of the news of his health. Reports of his excellent progress came regularly from Gwyneth, who was always happy to speak of her brother.

Katherine had not seen the Viking again until their early-morning departure for York eight days after his attack. Even then they exchanged no conversation, for she was put immediately in the company of the dame named Margotta, who had come to serve as Katherine's chaperon.

The party of the seven men and two women rode out into the bright dawn and scaled the steep rise that reared behind the village. The hills were clothed in a deep summer green, well watered by the series of recent, sudden downpours. The crest attained, Katherine looked back for her last glimpse of the village. It shone, morning-fresh and jewellike, on the shore. The sea beyond was fretted by small, white-crested waves. Katherine drew the last breath of fresh ocean air she was to have before they rapidly moved to the interior. Five of the men, the Viking at the head, fanned out in front of her, already descending the slope of earth that led inland. In this open country the two backriders maintained a distance of half a league behind the women. Katherine remembered with a smile how, at the point of departure, Gwyneth had admonished the backriders to close their distance to Katherine in the many wooded areas they would traverse.

Katherine had come to like Gwyneth. In a fair-minded

spirit Katherine chose not to hold against her hostess the fact
that she possessed a perfectly abominable brother. Gwyneth
was apparently quite blind to her brother's imperfections and
spoke of Eric in terms nothing short of wonderful. Katherine
generously excused Gwyneth this misperception but privately condemned the way Mistress Miller, and half of Scarborough village, so it seemed, jumped to the Viking's
decrees. Katherine could not imagine why he should enjoy
such absolute authority, but the man had been much spoiled
by it and needed a lesson in manners. She was not allowed
an opportunity to deliver that lesson, however.

Instead, her fast-recovering captor had mischief on his
mind during his week of idle convalescence. Shortly after
Katherine's stormy interview with the Viking, Gwyneth had
been summoned to her brother's bedside.

After Gwyneth's talk with her brother she sought Katherine out and greeted her with a warm smile and the words,
"Well, now! Eric had the goodness to explain the whole
thing to me. That is, he did not explain it, really, but I've got
eyes in my head and can guess. I'm *very* happy how it has
turned out, and you need not be embarrassed with me, and
so we need say nothing further about it, Mistress Katherine!" Her voice was breezy and held a note of relief. "I must
say, I'm not entirely surprised. It was bound to happen one
day. I know Eric well, and I can't think of another woman
who has *dared* to treat him so, and now your presence here
makes perfect sense. So I am glad that we have it all behind
us. Or, rather," she said with a wink, "you and Eric have it
all ahead of you. But enough of that. I would be very happy
for you to show me now the secret of the pearl stitch that we
spoke about yesterday afternoon."

Katherine would have been less than human had her curiosity not been mightily piqued. Gwyneth had made it difficult to pursue the topic, and Katherine let the matter rest.
Whatever the Viking had told his sister, it apparently had not
been unflattering to Katherine. She was accorded respect
and treated with warmth and genuine hospitality. She and
Gwyneth spent an amiable week together.

Gwyneth's final words to Katherine were equally intriguing. Gwyneth hugged Katherine to her and said, with a

broad wink, "I am delighted to have gotten to know you, my dearest Katherine, and mind you, I think my brother is very sly, but he has not fooled me for a minute. I am sure to see you again soon—and you must let me know your news. Riding can be dangerous now, and I will make sure that Eric looks after your comfort."

Master Eric did not, however, take the least interest in Katherine's comfort during the early stages of the journey. Katherine remained supremely indifferent to the fact that her partner did not see fit to have conversation with her on that first day of travel. He was a rude man, as she had known from the beginning, and she wanted nothing to do with him. She was to have her wish, for the first overnight stop had been prearranged, and since Katherine was appropriately quartered with Margotta, she saw nothing of the Viking that first evening, either. That suited her just fine. Thus, when toward the middle of the afternoon of the second day the Viking rode back from the head of the party and reined in beside her, she firmly decided not to feel gratification or pleasure.

If anything, annoyance was uppermost in her mind upon seeing the man so recently wounded mounted gracefully on his powerful stallion as he drew near her. The Viking motioned the chaperon away with a wave of his hand, and when Margotta had ridden ahead to meet her husband, the Viking ran his eye over Katherine's fine seat and easy hand on the reins but said nothing of her horsemanship.

"How are you faring with the bumps?" he inquired. "They made for rough going on your journey over to Scarborough."

They were in an open stretch of field now, the trail badly rutted. It was indeed rough going. The day was smothered in heat and humidity, and the low haze kept a lid on the sun's scorch. The dust from the road mingled with the heavy air to cloy the skin. In another month the high tide of harvest would be upon them. The sky above would be clear and crystal, the surrounding fields would be barbered and stubbly, and the threshing would bring the glorious smell of chaff to fill the air. Katherine did not know what had made her suddenly remember the harvest which she had not fully experienced since taking up city life in England.

She turned her mind back to the heat and the discomfort and her quarrel with her partner. She replied with perfect honesty, "I hardly know which is worse: The bumps, the heat or the pace," she confessed. "Three days is rather demanding, since I am not accustomed to the saddle. We came to Scarborough in four and a half days, you'll remember, and even then I was exhausted."

"Such a slow pace would fret my men. Three days is a compromise. I'm sorry."

She did not think that he was sorry at all, and because she was out of sorts, she said somewhat waspishly, "And you've ridden back now to prevent insurrection among your ranks? I assure you that I am too tired to protest your decision physically—though I still have enough breath to say that your orders are far too uncritically accepted, Master Eric."

He slanted a keen glance down on her. "And to demonstrate to you what a clever administrator I am, I will not answer in kind, mistress. I will simply say that I had hoped Gwyneth would have explained the riding schedule to you."

"Oh, she did, never fear! You have an excellent sister. Far better than you deserve. Gwyneth explained that you usually prefer to ride straight through or, at most, camp out one night. And speaking of Gwyneth, what exactly did you tell her about me—that day when you summoned her to 'explain' everything?"

He cast his eye over her. "It is a hot day, mistress. One not conducive to discussing such things."

"Meaning, I suppose," she said warmly, "that I would not in the least approve of the story you concocted and that you are trying to protect yourself from a much-deserved tongue-lashing."

The Viking laughed. "You could offer me no better evidence of the wisdom in keeping the matter to myself," he observed.

Katherine was disgusted. "You do not mean to tell me?"

"Not in your present mood."

"On the grounds that I'm a shrew?"

He laughed again. "Fencing with me, mistress? It's no use. I won't be drawn."

Katherine's humor was not improving. "I should have guessed you would have a glib answer ready."

"Yes," he said, "you should know me well enough by now to have guessed that."

Katherine found herself a little breathless. It must have been the heat. She recovered herself and managed to laugh, although a little shakily, and to concede, "Wise man! But my tongue has served a purpose over the years, and of late it has kept Mauleon at bay."

"A woman's tongue cannot forever ward off a truly determined man," he commented.

Was he referring to Mauleon? "Of course not," Katherine agreed, feeling less confident than her words, and added, "But it has been the only weapon available to me over the years. As you know, I do not enjoy the protection of a brother."

The Viking was acute enough. "Are you hinting at something, mistress?"

"Oh," she said carelessly, "I was thinking of your sister. She could not have been nicer to me, and I like her. But I became aware, from something she mentioned, that she has not had to use her tongue to defend herself. On one occasion, at least, you were on hand with your sword."

"And what occasion might that have been?"

"It seems that our special friend, Mauleon," Katherine said with an acrid taste in her mouth at the name, "was desirous of marrying her some years ago but that you put a stop to it."

"Did Gwyneth mention him by name?"

"No! Somehow I gathered that it was he. I also gathered that it was a painful subject for her and best not to speak his name."

"We never mention his name to her, and so I must thank you for your forbearance."

"You're very welcome. But is my deduction wrong that it was Mauleon?" she asked.

The Viking paused. "No, it was not wrong."

"I had been wondering what it was between you and

Mauleon!" she exclaimed with a certain triumph and a hint
of satisfaction, for she felt she could now score some points.
"And yet, not but a week ago you wondered why I did not
choose to make an advantageous match between Sybille and
Stephen Webster when you prevented your sister's alliance
with Mauleon. A more brilliant marriage could not have
been made."

"But Gwyneth's affections had already been engaged with
the miller, and she did not care at all for Mauleon," the
Viking explained.

"That I can well understand."

"And so the two situations cannot be compared," he went
on, "because Mistress Sybille's affections are engaged with
the young webster. Why protest when fortune and inclination coincide?"

"Oho! So you hold inclination over fortune?" she asked
entirely skeptically.

"Indeed, I do."

Inexplicably Katherine blushed. "Well, I do not believe
that Sybille's affections really are engaged," she rallied.
"She is too young to know her own mind."

"You know your sister best," the Viking murmured.

Katherine cocked a brow. Her arguments were not going
the way she would have liked. "Fighting shy?" she needled.

"Why, yes," he admitted, unpiqued. "I won't cross
swords with you today, mistress. I am in need of rest and
comfort, not hard words. You forget that I have been recently wounded."

"You don't look it," she complained, and then asked testily, "And just where is our friend Mauleon? In that thicket
of trees just ahead? Do we need worry about an ambush
from him?"

"No such luck," her companion replied. "We rode out on
several patrols last night, but not a trace of him was to be
found. My men are spoiling for a fight. Since they figure
that Mauleon has not been foolish enough to linger in the
neighborhood, they're hoping for at least a band of ruffians
to attack us."

"Hoping for?" Katherine echoed, astonished. "I thought
the object was to avoid them."

"We are not city-bred men," he commented simply. "However, I'm not entirely lacking in city manners, and so I shall ask you how you and your children fared in the past weeks. Emma mentioned to me, I believe, when I was last in York, that you had planned several outings with them."

Katherine was cross but took her cue for polite conversation by telling him all about the two excursions that Emma, Sybille, and Katherine had taken with the children. She described two trips to the countryside, one in July and one in August, and how nice it was for the high-spirited little ones to see the animals and to run free over the fields. She admitted that she had had little time for the children in the past six months or so and regretted it. She hoped to make up for lost time in the near future.

Launched now on safe topics, their talk wandered desultorily over this and that for the next league. Katherine was looking forward to entering the cool of the forest that lay just before them and was about to mention how she welcomed relief from the sun when one of the Viking's men rode up to them. Master Eric said that he would be parting company with her now.

"No sign of them?" the Viking asked when the rider came abreast.

The man shook his head. Katherine recognized him and recalled that his name was Rannulf. Katherine gathered from the ensuing conversation that Rannulf had seen someone of interest on the Scarborough demesne through whose southern corner they were traveling. She had only a hazy notion of the history of the large and rich Scarborough lands and knew them to be in the possession of a Norman lord. So interested was she in getting to the shade of the forest that she did not pay any particular attention to what was being said, nor did she notice that the Viking and Rannulf were speaking in guarded, oblique terms. She caught only the last of Rannulf's comments.

"That's why Lars and I thought you should be told," Rannulf said. Katherine had attended too late to the conversation to understand his meaning.

The Viking nodded, considering this information. He looked at Katherine and then back at Rannulf. "Very well," he said. "There'll be a change in plans. I was going to ride ahead here and summon Margotta back to Mistress Katherine while you and Lars kept to the rear. It would be a bad idea for me now to skirt the woods, as I had planned to do."

Katherine entered the conversation. "Is it Mauleon?"

The Viking laughed derisively. "I'll wager that Mauleon is far away and safely on the road back to London. This is someone else . . . of no importance."

"The master of the estate, then," Katherine said. "We're on Scarborough lands, are we not?"

"Accurate, as usual, in your deductions, Mistress Katherine," he said.

"Are we not allowed the right of passage?"

"We are."

"Then why the wish to avoid the seigneur?" she asked.

"Merely a dislike of meeting Norman lords," the Viking answered curtly, "on their own lands." He changed moods suddenly and smiled down at her charmingly. "Which means that you shall have to bear my company for another few leagues. Can you abide me for so long?" Without waiting for a response, he turned to Rannulf. "Tell Lars to have Margotta meet us halfway into the woods so that Mistress Katherine shall have her by her side by nightfall. Is everything arranged for this night's lodgings?"

Rannulf nodded and said that it was and that he would give Lars the message, but he expressed some doubts about the weather holding for the rest of the day.

The Viking narrowed his eyes against the sun's rays that penetrated the low, gray clouds. The sky was pied, haze blue and thunder black. "It's hard to tell," he said at last. "Rain is in the air. Perhaps it will hold off until nightfall, as it did last night. If it doesn't, it's likely to be one of the quick drenchings we've been having for the past several weeks. It's not likely to slow us down for long."

Some parting remarks and Rannulf was off with a flurry and a cloud of dust. The Viking considered Katherine a moment but said nothing.

They entered the dense growth of trees. The shadows were deep. The clop of the hooves was instantly padded by a thick carpet of pine needles, and to a person standing but a few feet outside the forest, their forms were quickly swallowed up and out of sight in the snarl of vines and bushes, brilliant with burnished summer berries shining through the underbrush. The path was just wide enough to travel side by side, so that their horses jostled one another. There reigned a silence so profound that neither one chose to break it with words.

At length they reached a partial clearing, and the path widened. It was cool and inviting. A stream, swollen by the recent rains, wandered through this portion of the woods. It was not an unknown corner, for there was a hand-hewn bridge with shaggy railings arched over the stream. Hardly aware of stopping, Katherine paused on the bridge to contemplate the water. She looked down on a fat old spider weaving silken ropes from twig to twig. She watched him as he craftily avoided a dunking. Under the bridge the water crooned and hummed and sang as it tumbled over moss-slick boulders, purled over broad, flat stones, tinkled over pebbly bottoms, and eddied in dark pools beneath overhanging oaks. The banks of the stream were gay with color, flames of purple asters, huge nuggets of goldenrod and a riot of bog myrtle, while clumps of crowberry crowded against a towering backdrop of tall, straight pines.

It was a glorious world, Katherine thought suddenly. One that she could not reconcile with the clutter and choke of the weeds of her long struggle for survival. Clear thoughts of that desperate day at Castle Roncevaux, however, escaped her. She felt that her mind had been turned upside down and that memories of the old days, her childhood, came slipping through, like grains of sand in an hourglass. An unfamiliar center had overturned in her, and she remembered all that was pleasant and peaceful from the days of her youth.

She took a deep breath. Her face lit with delighted discovery. "Mint!" she exclaimed to her companion. "I have not smelled wild mint in the woods like this in an age! Almost forever, in fact!"

The pungent fragrance was an elixir in her veins. It ran so deep that it began to break up the ice of her buried grief and pain, much as a spring breaks up a frozen stream. A tide of

happy memories came flooding back to her, and she wa▪
enchanted by them.

"'Tis a pleasant spot," her companion agreed.

Nothing more was said. They moved on at an unhurrie▪
pace. The pulsing silence of the forest became hushed an▪
still, foretelling the coming storm, but neither rider seeme▪
to take particular notice. The air was crunchy with bugs, an▪
the shadows deepened to pitch green.

Then the drizzle began, slowly and softly at first but gath▪
ering in density until it became an earnest rain. They halte▪
in the leafy bower of an old, gnarled tree to wait out th▪
worst of it. From under the tree Katherine thought that th▪
pelting rain against the wan daylight resembled a stream ▪
polished rice. This initial, happy impression did not las▪
The rain steadily worsened until it had become a thick cu▪
tain of dirty gauze. Even in their shelter Katherine and Eri▪
were getting progressively wetter.

"This thrice-accursed rain," he muttered with a scowl. "▪
should have predicted it and followed the original plar▪
Margotta should have come back to you while I took up th▪
rear with Lars and Rannulf. They could have accompanie▪
me through the forest instead of traveling around it. An▪
Margotta knows her way well enough."

Not understanding where his thoughts had led him ▪
make such a comment, Katherine replied reasonably that h▪
should not worry himself on her account and that she wou▪
be getting just as wet in Margotta's company. "What har▪
could a little water do me, after all?" she asked. "I wo▪
melt."

Eric ran an eye down the dampened kirtle that was begi▪
ning to cling to Katherine's neat curves and then trained h▪
gaze on a far corner of the woods. "No, but your starch h▪
been drained," he said with the barest suggestion of humo▪
"It's almost worth the soaking to see you so."

The rain was still warm and caressing, and so Katheri▪
could laugh at that statement. "This is hardly the worst rai▪
have endured since being in your England," she said. ▪
betrayed nothing of his thoughts about her particular phra▪
ing but merely agreed that the damp, bone-chilling rains ▪
late autumn were far worse.

"And in any case," she appended, "it can't last much longer."

As if in protest of Katherine's confidence, the heavens opened up and poured out their fury. It had become a drenching. After an interminable interval with no abatement of the rains, what little daylight had been able to penetrate the dense forest and the dark clouds began to wane. Katherine suddenly became aware of the prospects for her immediate future.

The Viking sensed her shiver and knew that he did not have any choices left. "You're getting cold," he observed.

The earlier warmth of the rain was indeed cooling quickly with the approach of evening, but that is not what had caused Katherine's tremors. "Nothing significant," she replied with a shrug, but added on a determinedly brighter note, "But where do you think the others are? Do you think that they have already reached the night's lodgings and are awaiting our arrival? We shall be a little late now that night is falling and the downpour is continuing, but, well," she said in rallying tones, "it's none so bad. I'm good for another two or three hours, at least."

She dared to look up at him. In the fast-descending darkness of the night he was looking rather grim and shaking his head. It must have been a freak of temper on her part, for her earlier crossness had deserted her, leaving her in surprisingly good spirits. Her companion was now the one suffering from a decidedly bad mood.

"You're soaked to the skin," he said with an undertone of savagery, "and good, at most, for the next half an hour. We've wasted far too much time here. It would be futile to try to find the others or to gain our original destination." He paused and did not speak for a long space. Then, bluntly, "We must look to our own shelter for the night."

She suddenly remembered that he had suffered a near fatal stabbing hardly the seven-night before and that he was no doubt in far weaker physical condition to withstand the rigors of the chill and travel at night than she was. She thrust to the back of her mind the highly uncomfortable thought that they might be spending the night together alone. She concentrated instead on the importance of her partner's health.

Katherine saw that he had the right of it. She replied that they would have to do what he thought best.

He lifted a brow at that but said merely that the cottage of a woodcutter and his family would be the closest shelter.

"It's the only roof that I can recall in the immediate area," he said. "I am not sure that I can find it in this weather, but you need shelter before too much longer."

Katherine nodded, her eyes wide with conflicting emotions. At length she accepted the terms of their predicament and said, "Very well. But just for the sake of accuracy let us agree that it is your health that must be guarded, not mine. You have recently been at death's door, so if we are to hurry, it must be on your account." She ruined her effect, however, the next moment by sneezing.

Without further ado the Viking lifted her into her saddle, sodden skirts and all, and swung onto his. He displayed none of the debility of the recent wound that had caused Katherine's concern. They trudged out into the porridge of the trail and the soup of the air, heads bent against the steady stream of water. Despite the obvious discomfort of their situation and the drawbacks that would necessarily attend the nighttime sleeping arrangements (if any were to be found), she felt safe with the idea of the woodcutter and his family. Katherine was, in fact, curiously unconcerned. For the very first time in years she was not shouldering the burden of the problem of immediate survival. She did not know what lay ahead of her, she did not really worry about it, and that was very pleasant. Her main sensation at that moment, besides a thorough wetness, was lightheartedness.

They plodded forth, shrouded in their watery cocoons, for an indeterminate length of time. At last the Viking turned his head around and nodded ahead. "Here's our shelter, but it is not the woodcutter's house. It's only a way station, but we are in no position to search further."

Her companion apparently had very keen eyes in the dark and was used to traveling at night, for it took Katherine several more paces to discern the outlines of their salvation.

It was a rough structure, she saw, certainly not a house;

but at least it promised protection from the ever-falling rain. As they approached, she also saw a little lean-to wobbling on shaky walls several feet from the cottage. Before she knew what she was about, the Viking had already dismounted, tied his horse to a rail, and come to help her down off her mare. His hands were strong and warm as they encircled her waist. They did not linger there.

She followed him into the little cottage to be engulfed in a bat's-wing gloom thicker and fuzzier than the rain-laden air outside, but the one room was warm and dry.

"It smells of smoke," she said into the blackness.

She heard his movements ahead of her, presumably at the hearth. "Yes," he replied. "The woodcutter must have spent last night here and left, perhaps as recently as this afternoon. With luck I might be able to make something of the fire."

She heard some scraping and the shifting of logs and then his comment. "Good. There are several dry logs, a little kindling, and I've found the flint."

Katherine could not stay at the door forever. She moved forward into the room timidly, guiding herself across the packed dirt floor by sound rather than sight. She almost bumped into him when he bent in an unanticipated movement to position the logs. Katherine averted bodily collision but grazed him slightly and quickly stepped to the side. He did not react.

"You've left the door open," he said expressionlessly after a moment. "You'll have to close it if the fire is to have the proper pull up the flue."

Katherine made her way easily back to the door, which glowed a deep blue rectangle against the black of the interior. By the time she had closed the heavy plank and turned back around to lean against it, a flame flared on the hearth, and the yellow glow illuminated the handsome, finely etched profile of the man bent over the fire. He stirred the hearth with a stick so that one flame became two and then many, and they shot up the hood and up the flue, their light painting orange the old stone walls cobbed with mud and heather and bringing the low rafters and thatched roof out of somber hiding. Shuttered windows flanked the door. Save for the cobwebs festooning the walls, the room was completely bare.

The Viking straightened up and looked around at Katherine. He said nothing but merely strode past her, leaving the cabin to return some moment later with an armful of damp straw. "From the shed," he explained tersely, and went out again for another armload. Katherine made herself useful by spreading out the straw to dry in front of the fire, taking care to keep it far enough back from the hearth, out of range of any chance sparks flying off the flames. When she had done, the Viking had returned a third time with the rain-soaked gear that had been lashed to the rear of his steed. Katherine's mare had not been similarly burdened. Her personal belongings were far ahead on Margotta's horse.

He unrolled the blanket, which contained tunic and chausses, some smoked meat in a cloth bag, a knife, and a skin of water. He spread the blanket on some straw and stripped off his wet tunic. He laid it atop the blanket to dry. His linen chemise beneath was thoroughly soaked as well, but he did not remove it. Instead, he drew up the spare tunic and shook it out before the fire.

Katherine was standing to one side of the fire, rubbing her hands absently, transfixed by the hot, leaping flames, trying not to think how they were completely alone together. At last he turned on her and broke her spell by saying in his deep, resonating voice, which startled her by its quietness, "Take off your kirtle and unbind your hair."

Words of instinctive protest died on Katherine's lips when her eyes flew from the fire to look at him. She saw the gray depths of his eyes lit with determination, and the set of his lips and chin informed her that he would entertain no gainsaying the evident necessity of divesting herself of her wet clothing and of drying her hair.

"You do not need my help," he stated when she made no motion to remove the sodden kirtle.

She betrayed all of the nervousness of an insecure young maiden when she replied, far too quickly, "Oh, no, no!" and was only thankful, the next moment, that the flickering firelight on her face would hide the fierce blush she felt creep up her neck. She might have spared herself her embarrassment, for her companion had already shifted his eyes back to the fire, where they unswervingly remained. He absorbed himself in contemplation of the flames, holding the spare tunic out to their drying warmth. For all the movement he made, he might have been turned to stone.

Her coif had been lost hours before on a low-hanging tree branch. She had only to reach up and feel for the pins that kept in place the heavy knot of hair at her nape. The black banner uncoiled itself down her back. Katherine then took a deep breath and began to unlace her sleeves, her progress marred by the wet threads and her suddenly clumsy fingers. She momentarily lost the struggle for composure and lapsed into self-disgust that she should be reduced to an awkward girl, which did not improve her manual dexterity.

At last she freed herself of the kirtle, feeling both relieved to be rid of the clinging, chilling weight of the dress and exposed in her sheer, damp shift, which left none of her rounded curves to the imagination.

Before she had a moment to wonder what she was to do with herself in her near nakedness, her companion thrust the tunic he held in his hand at her with the curt command, "Put it on."

It had not occurred to her that he would be drying it for her. A rallying, defensive comment on his gallantry rose to her lips but was swallowed by a sniffle and a sneeze. She settled for accepting the garment with a murmur of thanks. It was far too large for her, nearly dry and very warm.

Her hand smoothed down over her hips the fabric that fell well below her knee. She examined what she could of the weave in the dim light, trying to think of anything other than the fact that she was surrounded by the feel and smell of him. She took a second look at the material that covered her and said on a surprised, professional note, "Yorkshire homespun, and it's new."

Only then did he look at her again. A thick, blond brow raised itself in a bare hint of mockery and challenge. "I'm a poor sailor, and we both know the prices of foreign cloth these days."

"You're a good businessman," she countered, "and cannot help but flatter our drapers when they encounter you in the streets dressed in your local finery."

"Remind me to put it on when we reach city gates."

Standing next to him before the fire, the cold and wet draining out of her, Katherine did not dare look at the Viking. But she was aware of every breath he took, every small movement he made, and felt his flesh and blood presence so tangibly that she felt she had become conscious of every bone in his body.

Since she feared the fall of a silence, she took him up on his offer and said, "I shall remind you and hope to witness Master Webster's pleasure when he sees you. The first time he laid eyes on you, I gather that you impressed him with your taste for Flemish twill."

"My first trip to York?" he echoed, apparently amenable, in the situation, to idle chat. "Ah, yes. But never let it be said of me that I took credit for another man's taste. That tunic was not originally mine."

"You are saying, I suppose," Katherine said with an attempt at humor, "that you stole it."

"Not at all. I won it in a friendly game of dice."

"I should think with our profits of the past few months," she replied with a hint of disapproval, "that you might be able to afford to buy your own clothing now."

"Of course," he replied smoothly. "This homespun, for instance. But just before my first trip to York, I was in the Tower," he reminded her. "I was kindly relieved of all personal possessions upon being imprisoned and was left to my own resources at my release. Fortunately for myself, a rich and fatuous peer of the realm could not resist an evening of gambling, after which I was decently clothed and mounted and able to be on my way."

"You won your horse too?"

His teeth flashed a smile in the firelight. "Not bad for an evening's work, I agree."

"If you had needed money and a mount, you might have applied to your sister or any number of your men in Scarborough," she said, and then, daringly entering a dangerous territory, "or to whomever it was that released you from prison."

He did not answer that but cocked an ear to the sounds of the night. "The rain. It's easing up," he said, deliberately ignoring her comment, "and speaking of horseflesh, I'll bed ours down for the night."

He left the cottage. Katherine busied herself with tending the fire and drying the blanket and clothing. She should have been irritated that he had avoided answering her on the subject of his release from prison, but she was bone-weary and feeling warm and woozy from the chill she had received in the rain. She could not concentrate on anything that lay beyond the present reality of being alone with him for the night. She had no idea how they were to fill the hours before daybreak.

Her thoughts traveled inevitably back to those many sleepless nights filled with grief and hunger and terror on her flight from France, during which she had defended herself and her sister and their few worldly goods from outside attack. She was struck now by the profound differences between the dangers of those many nights and this particular one. This night, she suddenly realized, all danger would lie within the four walls of the cottage, within her very heart and soul, and she would have to stay awake to defend herself from her dimly admitted attraction to the man who shared the cottage with her and the strange, incomprehensible stirrings of her own desire.

The Viking returned with the information that the rain had stopped. He gazed a moment into the fire and shifted a log with the tip of his boot. Then he reached for the skin of water along with the bag of dried meat and, extending a slice to his companion, sat down cross-legged on some dry straw.

She accepted the offering and sat down beside him, tucking her legs under her. "Well, if the rain has stopped," she began hopefully, nibbling a corner of the salty meat and noting the way his hair had dried in curls and how his chemise no longer clung to his broad torso, "and we are warm enough now—"

"We're not going anywhere tonight." His voice sliced evenly across hers. "The mud is knee-deep. Here we're warm and dry."

A taut silence fell. Katherine searched desperately for

something to say. "The meat is good," she said shakily, and drew a nervous breath. "Too bad the woodcutter who passed by here last night did not think to leave a crust of bread."

He handed her the water. "He could not have known that people would be here later. To leave food around would only invite the rats."

Katherine choked slightly on the water and looked around her. "Rats?" she breathed.

"Surprised?" he queried. "You surely have experience with rats."

"What makes you say that?" she asked warily.

"The way you treated the lad you picked up that day in the liberty," he replied easily. "He mentioned contact with rats, and you treated the admission as matter-of-fact."

"Oh," she said, relieved. "That's the way it is when you house poor and abandoned children. I'm used to all manner of things like that."

"Accustomed but not reconciled."

"One does not, I think, become reconciled to living with rats." She shivered, but whether or not it was at the thought of rats invading their cottage was not clear. "Horrible!"

"Afraid?" he asked. It was a leading question.

"Well, it's no pleasant thing to be in a situation like this. Anyone would be afraid."

She caught her breath sharply. She had blurted it out unthinkingly, and there was no unsaying it. The threat he had issued to her from his sickbed only days before suddenly loomed large in her mind, and she was sure that her exclamations must have called that threat to his mind too.

They did. He was looking into the depths of the fire, but at her words he turned the full force of his gaze on her. "You have nothing to fear," he said harshly.

To convince him of the unconcern she did not feel, she rushed into speech. "That's not it! I know that you must be very tired and in need of rest—just like me—and then, added to that, I figured that since you've been recently wounded, you wouldn't be—that is, you would be wanting only to rest. I mean, of course, that you wouldn't be thinking of—wouldn't be needing—"

She broke off, cursing her tripping tongue for only making things worse, entirely incapable of finishing the explanation of what she could possibly think he would or would not be needing. For the life of her, she could not remember the last time she had blundered so badly.

She cast him a cautious look through lowered lashes and saw the look on his face of uncompromising masculinity mixed with a ruthless amusement that she had come to know so well. This time there was something else again there that she did not dare define. Her heart raced away, and she knew that in this particular contest with her partner she was entirely at his unpredictable mercy.

"Rest? I think not," he said in low tones that did nothing to mask their violence. He stood up abruptly, breaking the tension that bristled between them. "I'll be outside."

He left her. Her thundering heart and the awareness of his volatility kept her at first very far from the tranquillity of sleep. He did not return, and at length the seconds stretched into a limitless flow of time and the tiredness of the journey seeped into her bones and overcame her. She nodded off, warm and dry, her limbs dissolving into the cushion of the straw, her head finding the edge of the blanket.

The depths of sleep, however, provided her little comfort. The dreams that came to haunt her were unsettling in their newness and held nothing of the paradoxical security of the searing memories of her dying mother, the slaughtered castle folk, and her driving ambitions for Sybille. A tall, blond Viking had swept these images away, had invaded and conquered her dreams, the very heart of her own sanctuary, and had taken possession of her sleep with the power of his vitality. She cried out an ineffective protest but did not awaken.

Leaning against the outside wall of the cottage, arms folded across his chest, the Viking heard her fragile, muffled cry, but its cause was hidden from him, like a cricket. He straightened up and pushed the door open. He did not enter. He saw her shift restlessly in her sleep, and his eyes lingered a moment on her. The embers, still smoldering, provided warmth with no threat of fire. Satisfied that nothing was amiss, he closed the door again and took up his posture against the outside wall.

The clouds parted to reveal the full moon ruling the midnight sky. The air was sharp and clear after the rains and showed the Viking's face set in grim lines, frowning against the bright, elusive moonlight. He did not like his thoughts. Had Katherine been able to read them, she would not have been able to sleep at all, even uncomfortably. She had suggested that he was tired and in need of rest. His lips curled at the thought that she could be so naive, but he was not smiling, and he was not amused. Recently wounded but still very much alive, he might have told her, and rest was far from what he was needing.

He began his pacing again around the cottage. So, they were at the heart of the matter, he and Mistress Katherine, after having avoided the issue for so long. Once having arrived there, he did not think retreat was possible. Nor would he believe that Katherine was unaware of it. His frown deepened. He could not go on much longer in this fashion, trading words in such close proximity with his beautiful, desirable partner. He would bring her to his way of thinking, but now was certainly not the time and he had not yet won his terms.

___Chapter 14___

They left the woods behind by noon of the next day and caught up with the rest of their traveling party well before nightfall. Katherine had risen at dawn, changed into her dry kirtle, and bound her hair before emerging from the cottage to find the Viking walking the horses back from a source of water where he, himself, evidently, had just rinsed his head. He nodded her in the direction of the stream, where she made the best of her morning toilette. She returned to him his tunic. They finished what was left of the meat and water and took to the trail immediately thereafter.

It was a beautiful morning. Birds chirped and quarreled and flirted their tails. Squirrels danced and flipped on thick trunks and branches. The sun was brilliant and the temperature ideal. Neither rider was in the mood to be diverted by the beauties of nature, and if they had, neither would have commented, for they exchanged nothing but the most necessary of conversation along the way. He set a hard, punishing pace and did not ask after her comfort. She did not complain.

When Lars, Rannulf, Margotta, and the others came into sight, the Viking thundered ahead to meet them and sent Margotta trotting back to Katherine with a comb, coif, clothing, and more substantial food to break her fast.

The faces of the men were alive with expectant curiosity, but one look at their master's countenance informed them that any of the witticisms they had bandied among themselves about the previous evening's sleeping arrangements would be uttered now at grave personal risk.

The Viking did not approach Katherine again until they arrived at Monk's Bridge over the River Foss. He told her then that he would call on her in Jubbergate Street later that day or the next and did not wait for her approval.

This curt announcement did not improve Katherine's humor, and so, by the time she finally reached home, she was in a temper. She was greeted by Emma, whose face held much the same lively expression that the Viking's men had worn the day after their master had spent the night in the woods with the beautiful young broiderer from York. Emma expressed animated concern and sincere dismay over the Viking's attack at Scarborough and concurred wholeheartedly with the conclusion that the dastardly deed had been devised, if not also executed, by Mauleon.

Emma listened with attention to a retelling of the amusing stories told by the sisters with whom Katherine had traveled, to the descriptions of the priory of St. Agnes and the fascinations of the port, and to Katherine's high praise of Gwyneth, the miller's wife, but she felt that an essential piece was missing from the account of Katherine's two weeks away from York. When Katherine came to the end of her recital, Emma asked the not-very-innocent question, "And well?"

Katherine replied coolly, "And well what, Emma?"

"Well, I mean," Emma said, seeing that her mistress was going to be difficult, "that you surely have not told me everything, have you?"

"But I have. What else could there be?"

"Why, Master Eric, mistress! You've hardly said a word about him!"

"But, my dear Emma," Katherine replied with a very convincing laugh, "there is hardly anything more to say about the man. He was attacked and is now, I would say, fully recovered. Not a thing to be troubled about. Although the first night was a bit worrisome, I'll admit, when he was so pale and still. But to look at him now you would never know he had suffered more than a scratch."

"And when shall I look at him?" Emma inquired eagerly.

Katherine rolled an amused eye at her serving woman. "Not you, too, Emma! He has the whole of Scarborough eating out of his hand. It is most vexatious. I cannot tolerate the thought that he has wrapped you around his little finger along with every one from here to Scarborough. Why, the way he orders me about is—is—well, I've no doubt that he thinks *he* is running Leofwyn Shippers now!"

Katherine was working herself up into a little tirade but put a firm guard on her tongue. "But that is nothing to the point," she said, striving for a calm note. "To answer your question: He will be here today or tomorrow, most likely tomorrow, and then you shall see him for yourself and ask him anything you think I may have left out. And now I refuse to discuss him any longer, for I have come to realize that he is a thoroughly overindulged man. Not at all worthy of the attention given to him. Pray, let us speak of something else!"

Emma was not to be diverted from the subject at hand. "But you must have had private conversation with him during his period of convalescence or on the return trip."

"Oh, yes, now let me see," Katherine replied, as if giving the matter her full attention. "He did call me in to see him —once, it was—just after he recovered his senses following the attack. Now, the aim of that interview was—yes, I do believe it was to insult me. I must suppose that he was feeling cranky, in his early recovery, poor fellow," she said with a sweet smile that did not deceive Emma, "and in need of an object upon which to—how should I say?—vent his spleen? I served wonderfully! And then, on the return trip—" Katherine began, and then colored up.

Nothing would induce her to recount to Emma that night in the woods. Katherine had only to picture the Viking standing before the fire, his strong face and broad shoulders set against the flames, for her thoughts to go disastrously awry. His existence had so invaded her well-ordered, well-aimed life that he had come to dwell—drat the man!—almost continuously in her thoughts; and she did not want to examine too closely how he had achieved this effect on her. It was probably due to the fact that she had been on her own for so long, or perhaps it was a lapse into weak-mindedness.

"Well, on the return trip," she managed at last, "I can assure you that we exchanged very little conversation. Now, tell me about Sybille."

This time Emma allowed the change in subject and, having noted the flush, decided that all was going as well as could be expected.

Sybille, Emma recounted, had become weepy and taken to languishing about the house, sighing and sniffling and lavishing affection on all the children to such a degree that even little Ben, who, Katherine knew, lapped up all the kisses that came his way, was moved to dismiss, with distaste, all the caressing and coddling as "girl stuff."

The news of Sybille's maudlin behavior had an unexpected bracing effect on Katherine, who was more than happy to turn her attention to a matter whose aims were clear to her. She summoned Sybille to the solar and was presently edified by her younger sister's suffering but brave face. Sybille had that rare feminine ability to cry beautifully (which activity she had of late much indulged), her heavenly eyes resisting the ugly red that ruined many another pretty woman's weeping, her tears not splotching the lovely peach bloom of her cheeks.

Katherine saw this beauty and launched at once into a speech intended to fortify Sybille's weak emotions and to explain the importance of Sybille's true position in the world. For some reason Katherine lost the thread of her arguments and stopped abruptly in mid-sentence. When she began again, it was in French, and she found that she suddenly felt much more comfortable in that language and was pleased with her own eloquence.

Sybille, however, remained unmoved. At the end of her elder sister's discourse Sybille suggested sulkily, and in English, that Katherine go to court and make the brilliant match herself, if she liked the idea so much. Sybille had the great good fortune to be spared Katherine's very pertinent reply to this piece of insolence by the clang of the door bell belowstairs.

Sybille was standing by the window and had full view of the street. "Why, it's Master Eric," she said, peering down, and added, quite naively, "He frightens me." Sybille regarded him as he waited for Emma to open the door to him. "Although he looks almost approachable at the moment. But you know, I have noticed that he often leaves here under a cloud." Sybille turned back from the window. "What is it that you do, Katherine, that always makes him so angry?"

Katherine, thoroughly distracted, did not answer that but instead asked Sybille to fetch Emma to her immediately. Sybille replied reasonably that Emma was no doubt already at the door, and then the sounds of the visitor in the house drifted up through the open door to the solar, confirming Sybille's guess.

Katherine was suddenly vexed. She had not expected the Viking to come today. She was not properly coiffed and made a small fuss over her dress, which was not her most becoming. Sybille was slightly surprised by Katherine's agitation but was given no chance to consider the reason for it. She was shooed out of the room and almost collided with the Viking. Sybille bobbed and murmured an excuse.

The Viking brushed the pardon aside, hardly heeding her. He dispensed with Emma's presence as well with a curt, dismissive words of thanks for her escort to the solar.

Katherine was turned away from him but felt his presence behind her and turned to look at him. Their eyes held each other as though at sword point.

The Viking, Katherine noted, was freshly shaven and

clean and in full command of himself. She was never more aware of the contradictory feelings he had produced in her from that first moment she had laid eyes on him: how his masculine presence attracted her; how that unknown part of him threatened her and cautioned her that she would be most wise to resist the attraction.

Katherine could not find any words to keep him at a proper distance, and so she held her tongue.

The Viking broke the silence. "Mauleon was seen in York several days before my attack in Scarborough," he said. He took several paces into the room. He did not take a chair but stood, leaning slightly forward on his arms with his hands spread on the tabletop, as if holding down the shaft of sunlight that glinted against the polished wood. "He has not been seen here since. Although I imagine that he is quite determined to demand from you whatever payment he thinks is due him, there is a very good reason he has not returned now to exact it from you."

Katherine still said nothing. She leaned against the window frame, comfortable with the length of the room between them. Several of the windows were open. The breezes stirred in the room on hot wafts of air. Her heart was beating rapidly but not at the mention of Mauleon. After that night in the woods she had cherished the thought that she would be able to withstand better the Viking's effect on her own ground of the solar. She was mistaken.

As he stood before her, his strength and vitality and confidence filling the room, she suddenly realized that all her wisdom had fled. She would not, could not, resist his attraction. He had come to take possession of her personal chamber, just as he had so thoroughly captured her thoughts, and she feared for that last territory, her body, that he had not yet invaded but was sure to conquer if he desired it. A corner of her sanity remained to reason with her that she must at all costs keep her heart well guarded. She must keep her heart her own.

"My best guess is that he is already in London," her partner was saying, "protecting far more vital interests. Those lie at the moment with Louis in the south." He paused. "Louis has successfully landed on the Kentish coast with some thousand ships. He bypassed Dover, where John sat confidently awaiting the invasion, and has marched into London. Many of the rebel barons have now sworn fealty to the prince and his wife, who is, so the reports go, riding the streets as if she were already queen."

"Blanche of Castille," Katherine said, speaking at last. "A haughty woman if ever there was one." She asked, almost distractedly, "What does John do now?"

The Viking nodded, not surprised by Katherine's knowledge of Louis's wife. "He moves north," he answered, "probably with York in mind, to break communication between the invaders and the rich county of Yorkshire where opposition to John is strongest."

His eyes were resting on her. She felt their force like a physical touch. She tried to keep her mind on the important matters that he was telling her, but she did not think that the reports of Louis's and John's movements were the essence of what they had to say to each another.

"Will John achieve his purpose?" she asked.

He shook his head slowly. "I do not know. John has made a smart move and a daring one, after having been such a sorry general when fighting the French on their own land. But his troops are few. John's ultimate success may well depend," he said without taking his eyes from her, "on the sentiments of the York citizens."

"Which are well known to be with Louis," Katherine replied.

"A poor choice, to my way of thinking."

"Oh? And what has John done lately to recommend himself to his subjects?" she asked.

"Nothing. But Louis is more than proving himself a worthy son of his grasping father, Phillip of France. Louis has confiscated every castle between Kent and London and awarded them to one of his own followers."

Katherine considered the information. "That is of little interest to our local townsmen, although I can see that it would be of some concern to the barons who have lost their land."

"One or two of them belonged to rebel barons at whose invitation Louis has come."

Katherine made a move of distaste. "Louis has a strange way of doing business. But beyond that, I would only say that those rebel barons apparently managed very badly and are out their castles. How does that concern York?"

"Louis holds chains behind his back and is not to be trusted."

"And John is?" Katherine countered with a laugh. "Why do you tell me all this?"

"Because you have become a rich woman in the past months and have something to gain—or to lose—in this play for power. I only mention Louis's treachery so that you will think well before taking any kind of action."

Katherine opened her mouth to protest. The Viking held up his hand and interrupted with the ghost of a smile. "Do not cry poor with me. I am capable of sums and can calculate the fine profits we have reaped, you and I, over the summer. And I recall well enough that you sank one hundred marks some time ago in the now thriving wool guild. Robert Webster reports that the guild will soon be distributing remarkable profits among its investors. It seems that your speculation will provide you with the handsome return you had hoped for. I congratulate you on your farsightedness."

"On my luck, rather," Katherine replied. "But what kind of action do you think I will be taking?"

"Naturally I am not in a position to answer that."

"What kind of action do you advise me to take, then?"

"You would take it?" he said with a suggestion of humor.

"I don't know," she replied, matching his manner for all the serious matters they were discussing. "You were inclined to berate me at the very beginning of our partnership on my rash investment in the guild. Now it seems I did the right thing. So, too, might it prove best to support Louis, which is what I must guess you will advise me against doing."

He looked her up and down. "You have spared me the trouble of giving you my opinions. You shall have to make up your own mind for your own goals." His eyes rested on her at length, and she wished that she could read his inscrutable face. "Yes, you have done well," he said. "Very well. Your investment in the guild originally left you indebted to me, but then, our partnership has also enriched you, so you have profited doubly in the end."

Katherine's heart began to beat again, at a quickened tempo. Was this the prelude to the dissolution of their partnership? She should have welcomed the news, but it left her rather at sea. Too many things were crowding in on her. It was happening too fast.

"You have profited as well," she said, a little breathlessly, in an effort to gain time, "and have your own stake in the matter."

He nodded. "And to that end you will understand that I am leaving York on my own business."

Dismay flickered in her eyes. She did not want him to leave her, but she answered almost at once, "Yes, of course. You are free to go." Nothing could prevent her from inquiring, with as much dignity as she could command, "Will you be returning?"

"In a week or two," he answered. "Perhaps more, perhaps less. We'll have much to discuss upon my return."

"I see." Her composure threatened to desert her, but fortunately there was nothing more to say. She nodded her head slightly, lowering her lashes, and turned back toward the windows.

She knew the moment he left the room. A chill ran up her spine, as if she had been standing in the sun and it suddenly darted behind a cloud. The room was lifeless, and she had a compelling desire to leave it. Then the main portal was heard to open and shut, meaning the Viking had left her house. When she turned around much later, she found Emma at the door, watching her.

Katherine said her words carefully so that her voice did not tremble. "I must see the lord mayor without delay."

"Is there trouble?" Emma asked.

Katherine shrugged. "Trouble?" She tried to concentrate on business. It was a painful effort. She felt discontented and dissatisfied. "No. No trouble. All of our plans will soon bear fruit. No, there is no trouble at all."

"Why do you need to see the lord mayor?" Emma asked.

"About our investment in the guild," Katherine answered

somewhat distractedly. "The time has come to take our profit."

Emma nodded silently. "So this is it."

"This is it."

"You don't seem very happy about it," Emma ventured cautiously.

With effort Katherine took hold of herself. She made an attempt to smile. "Oh, I suppose that, having come to the point, I am apprehensive. Or perhaps I don't want my happiness in the forthcoming events to be premature. What is the rest of that phrase you are fond of, Emma, about not counting your chickens?"

"Before one of them sits on the throne," Emma finished. "So, is it Louis you'll be backing in the end?"

"I am not sure. That is why I want to speak with the lord mayor," Katherine replied.

Godric Fitz Osbert, however, was very sure where he was putting his own money. "Louis of France," he said to Katherine at the castle scarcely an hour after her conversation with Emma. "It will be Louis of France."

"But must it?" Katherine asked, finding it difficult to believe that the Viking would not see the issue so clearly and also be backing Louis.

"My dear Mistress Broiderer," Godric said languidly, "I am no soothsayer and have, when all is said and done, very little stake in the matter. Excuse my mild disinterest in the contest, but you are aware, my dear, that I have the advantage of you with my vast experience in this man's world. Take, for instance, cockfighting—a pastime I naturally deplore, yet as mayor I like to keep abreast of my fellow citizens' interests. But in any event, cockfighting has taught me an invaluable lesson: to back my cocks reasonably and both ways."

"Both ways?"

"Of course," Godric said with his feline smile. "My public and civic self supports John and the Angevin line, in the off chance he remains ruler, while my private self will channel my monies into Louis's pockets."

"I am not afforded the luxury of backing both contestants," Katherine said. "I have but one self and one chance."

"A decided disadvantage," Godric remarked.

"One that I must live with," she said a little sharply.

"My dear, I understand. Truly I do! I wonder only that it is so important to you," Godric said mildly.

Katherine met Godric's curious light-brown eyes directly. "You can guess that it is," she said simply. "And I must choose between the two. Quarter day is coming, and the guild will be making you a return on my investment—"

"Quite a nice one, too, if my painful efforts at calculation should happen, for once, to be correct," Godric interpolated, holding up the counterfeit prayer missal that Katherine had just delivered to him and which held the secret accounts.

"I shall give you the exact figure next week," Katherine said, smiling pleasantly and wondering if the book held the last accounts she would do for him.

"I am sure that you will. I take no offense, of course, that you must supply me with the figure. I am sure that I could not cheat you, even if I were of a mind to do it, you know, which I am not," Godric said with his own version of a pleasant smile.

"So many words to be assured of each other's honesty, sir," Katherine said with a laugh.

Godric nodded, acknowledging the hit. "My dear," he said in an altered, less playful tone, "you have asked me my opinion, and by my admittedly limited lights I am compelled to tell you in all honesty that King John is a doomed man and that Louis is as good as on the throne."

"Are you so sure?" Katherine insisted.

"Very. John runs hither and thither now in the north. A not entirely unsuccessful compaign, I admit, but he would do far better to be in London, one would think, taking care of his own back courtyard. Instead, Louis holds sway over most of London, making the ultimate, inevitable outcome only a question of time."

"But Louis has confiscated property in the south—in some cases from the very barons who sought Louis's aid in the first place! If he continues in this fashion, he may lose support among the rebel barons."

"I would be repeating myself unnecessarily," Godric said lightly, "to say yet again what a well-informed young woman you are." He smiled. "And being so well informed, you are certainly aware that Louis has the blessings of the pope for those confiscations. The rebel barons were foolish enough to ride against an anointed—although incompetent (one cannot help but sympathize with the strong feelings of the rebels)—king at Runnymede, and they are to be punished. When the sentiment has grown sufficiently against Louis, I am afraid that it will come, my dear, too late."

"No crown is ever perfectly secure," Katherine argued.

"Ah, but then the richest and most powerful barons will surely find it advantageous to support Louis."

"If they do not lose their castles and land to Louis's French followers," Katherine observed. "There cannot be many in that privileged circumstance."

"There are more than you think," Godric answered, "and you would be most unwise to underestimate the determination of those few to see Louis on the throne." Godric paused. "But this is not the time for wavering, my dear. Surely you can see that. When the time comes—and I've no doubt that it will be soon—you will have to let me know how I am to place your money for you. It is entirely up to you."

"I know that," Katherine replied, "and you will be hearing from me again soon. Nevertheless, I cannot believe that Louis's path to the crown is as clear as you present it."

"So cautious a young woman?" Godric rallied her.

"Not once I've made up my mind," she retorted.

"Then allow me to assist you in deciding the matter. Louis enjoys the support of a most unlikely man in the kingdom, a man who, like myself—but of an entirely different character, I assure you—has also absorbed with interest the lessons of the cockfight. This man is most determined to see Louis on the throne—and he will stop at nothing to see the Frenchman there. I am persuaded to support Louis on the strength of this man alone." Godric's slow, charming smile curved his lips. "You will be surprised, I think, to learn that my dear and titled brother, Mauleon, likes to consider himself Louis's secret weapon in the very heart of John's administration."

"But I am not surprised," Katherine said with no change of expression.

"Not surprised? You are a very clever woman, I own! However it was that you guessed, you must know as well that Cedric is a man who lets nothing keep him from his goals and desires. You, my dear, are one of the very few things he has not been able to have at the drop of his gauntlet. It would amuse me no end for you to continue to elude him—but, ah, well! I am afraid you are not that clever. Or perhaps, in Louis's administration, you would consider accommodating him willingly?"

The frozen look on Katherine's face answered Godric's unasked question.

"No, I quite see that you are not prepared to go that far in the accomplishment of your goals—whatever they may be. However, Cedric de Mauleon is capable of going to any length, my dear, to attain his desires. He would, for instance, certainly not hesitate to eliminate any man so foolhardy as to get in his way. But I hardly think the warning necessary. You know his potential for danger as well as anyone. And he lets no one stand in his way forever!"

Katherine's heart lurched but not in fear for herself. She would need the good luck to ward off Mauleon, but she was rather more worried about her partner, should he meet up with the villain Mauleon in the course of the next weeks.

"Do make free to call upon my services if you need them," Godric continued, "but in all good faith I advise you not to hesitate too long before placing your money. There is no time like the present!"

She left the mayor not much later, confused and afraid and indecisive. She was happy to have the time before her to come to terms with her doubts and fancies without having to face her maddening, elusive, attractive, and dangerous partner. She marshaled her considerable strength of will to fortify herself against his eventual return. In the relative calm of his absence she was able to convince herself that she felt nothing for the tall, blond shipwright from the coast, and once having arrived at that meritorious conclusion, it was much easier for her to see that she had been a fool to have doubted, even for a minute, the wisdom of backing the obvious choice for the throne in Louis of France. She had heeded Godric's warning against hesitation; but her own instincts counseled her to wait, that it was too soon to place her money, and so she later told Godric that she would have to think about it and let him know.

She felt once again as strong and as resolute about this decision as she used to feel about the many decisions she had made during the time in her life before the Viking had come to turn her mind upside down. In this poised state of equanimity Katherine went about her business for the next several weeks.

Then, when she least expected it, she had a disastrous encounter with the Viking that threw her delicate balance radically off-center.

It was two weeks to the day from when she had last seen her partner. September had come, but the weather had not cooled. In town it was decidedly hot, and Katherine liked to get out of her house and circulate. While still ruminating when might be the best moment to invest in Louis's cause (if she were indeed going to do so), she capriciously decided on this day to follow up on a special wool purchase she had heard about. She made an unprecedented journey to the vicinity of the wharf, the groin of the city, to check into the purchase. The afternoon was steamy, the tang of the air pronounced.

Katherine rounded the corner of a side street that led to the quays and chanced upon nothing less than the sight of her partner, the Viking, deep in conversation with a group of men who looked foreign to York. She also caught a glimpse of the redheaded Maria, just then leaving the scene. Katherine had not known of the Viking's return to York and so was unprepared for the fierce stab she felt in her breast. He had returned and had apparently spent his first hours in York in another woman's company.

Katherine turned quickly away, her heart beating irregularly, hardly able to comprehend that his unexpected appearance at the wharf and in company of strange men might mean something quite dangerous to herself and her security, knowing only that she must leave the area as quickly as possible.

She ducked down a side street. She heard her name called out from around the corner she had just left but did not stop. A moment later she heard again, in a voice whose deep rumble there was no mistaking, close at her back, "Mistress Katherine."

She hastened her steps until she was almost running. The next thing she knew, a strong hand had bitten into her arm and she was whirled around to face the snapping, angry gray eyes of Master Eric. He had rarely touched her in the course of their partnership. She felt now as if she had been burned.

She would not be undone by him. She would outface him. Her anger rose to meet his. She shrugged her arm to loosen herself from his grip, as if not suffering that touch, and found herself so quickly released that she stumbled against the wall of the house crowded up against the street. Her gesture of physical aversion toward him touched off the fire that always sparked between them and that was soon to be mightily fanned by the sharp words that sprang to both their tongues.

"Mistress Katherine," he said again, his low rumble roughened with anger. "I called you."

"And I heard you," she replied, her voice barely level. "But you apparently are too dull to understand that I do not care to speak with you."

"I would think, on the contrary, that we have a good deal to say to each other."

"Do we?" she returned very coldly. "But not here. Why you have accosted me in this public place is beyond me!"

"Just as your presence here is to me!" he retorted.

He was plainly angry. She could only interpret that to mean that he did not like her having caught him, unawares, in York. She knew in the pit of her stomach that he was involved in some intrigue that ran contrary to her best interests. She had found him out at it, whatever it was, and he was riled. She would never have guessed that his temper was roused from the fact that he did not, under any circumstances, want her to be seen by the men that he was with.

"I had some business here," she answered pertly, "as it is obvious that you have."

"Aye, business," he repeated slowly. "I thought that that part of the business was left to me."

"Oh, are you here on *our* business?" she asked with patent disbelief. "I could not have guessed! If you want to discuss it, you may meet me in my solar, this evening after sundown."

She turned to go. His next words stopped her feet and raised the hairs on her neck in a thrill of fear.

"I do not like talking to your back now, any more than I did a moment ago," he said in hot accents. "If I have to force you to face me, I swear to you, mistress, that I shall not be responsible for my actions."

That was all the warning she would get. She took it. She turned back around. "Excellent idea! It will spare you a stop later in Jubbergate Street. Now, what were you doing here?"

"I might ask the same thing of you."

"A very nice price on some wool," she replied. "When did you get here?"

"This morning."

"Ah, yes. That must be so, since you have not yet come to see me," she said with unmistakable irony.

"Just as you have so obviously come to the wharf about some wool," he replied with matching irony.

"Why else would I come?"

"I wouldn't know. I have thought a great many things about you, but not that you were foolish."

Those were fighting words. "Yes. You may spare me your opinions of my character. My foolishness is apparent from the fact that I have come—somewhat—to trust you!"

"You may still do so! Nevertheless, this foray to the wharf is beyond foolishness."

"But I have come to inspect the wool of our next run," she repeated unnecessarily.

"Do you think that now is a good time to undertake another shipment?" he demanded.

He had doubted her judgment. It needed nothing more than that to snap the slenderest of threads that kept Katherine's composure intact. She, herself, had doubted the wisdom of trying for any more shipments in the next month, with the political contest being so heated, but at his question the alchemy of their relationship took over, stripped to its barest essence of day and night, fire and ice.

"An excellent time," she retorted, defying him. She had lost control of her self-possession, and she found that she was having difficulty finding her words in English. "I have the best price yet, and there are good markets right now in the south."

"Dangerous markets," he said.

The emphasis on her syllables was falling all wrong. "When has that stopped you? If I am to trust you, I would think you would be ready for another run and more profit."

It was a red rag to a bull. He came toward her so that he was stock against her. "I don't dance to the tune of your piping," he growled.

"Do you not?" she taunted.

That was the drop that made his cup overflow. He pinned her shoulders between his two arms against the wall. "By Thor, woman, you're a burr under the saddle," he thundered low. His deep voice rasped like a file. "I've a mind to take you in hand this very moment, for you are surely asking for it."

Katherine realized full well the import behind her brazen taunt, and she wished to show him just how well she controlled him. "You may take your hands off me," she said coldly.

The matter swayed in its precarious balance. Anger blazed from his eyes. Her shoulders hurt under the pressure of his strong hands.

"I do not care to repeat myself any more than you do," she said in arctic accents. "Take your hands off me."

With a supreme effort he pulled himself together. He would not allow her to jerk at will the strings of his desire for her. She would not have the satisfaction of getting what she had coming to her.

"Arrange for the shipment, then," he snapped with fire. "I'll leave on the morrow, if you will have it so. Do not expect my return before the month is over, however. I hope it will not be too late for you and your purposes. You'll see a profit, mistress, a very good profit, and I shall wish you joy of it, for it shall be your last from me!"

He released her and stalked out of the alleyway, hardly trusting himself in her presence another second. He was suddenly assailed by a ravenous, visceral hunger that neither one of Geoffrey Taverner's copious meals nor the forthcoming sea voyage would entirely satisfy.

He arrived at the Blue Swan in the full grip of his temper and demanded of the astonished taverner a supper of raw chopped steak in the Norse fashion and a bottle of Scots whiskey. His appetite was basic, stark, and he would have in his mouth nothing that smacked of civilization. He wanted Katherine, and she would be his, but for the meantime he would eat blood and fire.

Katherine fared much better at first than her partner immediately after the stormy interlude in the alleyway. She regained her house in a mood that approached a purring self-congratulation. That buoyant humor presently expended itself, however, and she was left in a state of corroding dissatisfaction. It had fully dawned on her that he would be leaving her on the morrow without seeing her again and that she would not see him again for a good, long while.

Emma came to Katherine's solar with something quite different on her mind. "Mistress Katherine! Something has happened!"

"What is it, Emma?" Katherine asked listlessly from the window through which she was brooding.

"It's Maria."

Katherine suddenly remembered having seen Maria at the wharf. "Maria? What about her?"

"She was here in your solar earlier today."

"And so? She is often here with the others."

"No, she was alone. You had just finished the accounts for the lord mayor and put them away, I would suppose, and you went downstairs to check on something, and then I found Maria in here. Snooping, I would call it."

Katherine tried to drag her mind away from the misery in her heart. "Snooping? What is there to find?"

"Why, the accounts!"

"Maria can know nothing of them."

Emma looked doubtful. "I don't know. I didn't like it, that is all."

Katherine considered this information. "She did not take anything, for I went to the lord mayor's with both prayer missals this time. I am happy to be rid of them, I can tell you. But what do you suppose Maria could make of them, even if she did see them?"

"I don't know, but I still don't like it," Emma insisted. "Just her knowing about them is bad enough."

Katherine shook her head. "I cannot worry about it now, Emma. Thank you for telling me, however."

"And when is Master Eric returning?" Emma ventured.

"He's not."

___ Chapter 15 ___

Katherine had ample opportunity in the ensuing weeks to ponder the question of Maria, and she did not at all like where her thoughts led her. Maria had indeed been acting very smug of late, slanting sly looks and secret, satisfied smiles at Katherine. It could only mean one thing, and Katherine was amazed at herself for not having come to the obvious conclusion much earlier.

Maria's presence in Katherine's solar earlier the day of the Viking's reappearance in York was only one part of the problem. Maria, Katherine was convinced, had known nothing of Katherine's clandestine business activities; and in any case, Maria could not have interpreted what she might have found in the hollowed-out prayer missal that Katherine had handed over later that day to the lord mayor. Nevertheless, Maria's uninvited visit to the solar and her appearance at the wharf with the Viking, as well as the Viking's association there with a group of suspicious-looking men, caused Katherine some unwelcome doubts.

However, her mind was absorbed, for once, by interests very different from money and business and politics. She examined in excruciating detail every scrap of information she possessed about Maria and the Viking. She dwelled at length on the midsummer fair, when Maria and the Viking had spent the day together. Katherine wondered if they had spent the night together as well. Katherine recalled Maria's chance meeting early on with the Viking in the courtyard, when it had been clear that the two had seen each other earlier in the day in town. From there Katherine's mind leapt back and fastened on the first day the Viking had entered her house, when Maria had shown with a flash of her large, seductive eyes what she had in mind.

What was it that the Viking had said once on the very subject of Maria? Katherine struggled to recall, but her memory of the conversation was imperfect. It had something to do with his policy never to tangle business and pleasure. The comment had been made in overt reference to Maria and to her relationship to Katherine's household. By some strange twist of feminine logic, which Katherine had previously imagined did not afflict her thought processes, she had interpreted the comment to mean the Viking would not pursue a pleasurable relationship with Maria as long as he had a business partnership with Katherine. It simply did not occur to Katherine, by that same inexplicable twist of reasoning, that the Viking could possibly have been referring to Katherine herself, warning her that he would not be duped by her feminine wiles.

So the man did not mix business and pleasure. Why should he, after all, when he did not have to? He and Maria could have whatever arrangement they chose, and it had nothing to do with Katherine's business with him. Certainly a man as vital as the Viking would have established in York at least one woman who would be there for his pleasure. Katherine should have understood that long ago, but she had never given it a thought. The thought, once imagined, took instant root. She easily conceived, but not without a wrench of her heart, that he must have many women strewn around

the various ports he frequented, with whom he did not engage in business.

She could not rid her thoughts of him. How had the man
managed to get under her skin? It had happened almost
without her noticing it; but now she was exquisitely aware of
how much she had come to depend on him, how alive she
felt in his presence, how she lived to see him again. But
when had it happened? That night they had spent together in
the woods, or at the shipyard in Scarborough, or even that
very night when he lay so still and ashen and wounded in the
bed at his sister's house? Was it Easter morning when he
deftly repaid her in clever words on the subject of the tides
in the Ouse, or was it the very first moment she had opened
the door to him, thinking to find Josef?

No answer came, but the fact remained that she had fallen
in love with him. It was a most lowering, depressing realization. With it came the equally unpleasant confrontation with
her own vanity. Never having been attracted to a man, she
had thought she was simply immune to vanity, jealousy, and
love. But as she came to the slow, painful understanding of
her feelings for one man, she discovered in herself a silly,
most outrageous conceit: She had become so involved with
him that she had assumed that he would be equally involved
with her. Purest feminine fancy!

She forced herself to broach the subject of Maria with
Emma. It was agreed between them that Maria might make
an excellent addition to Mistress Olivia's team of broiderers,
although Emma was inclined to take a dark view of all the
circumstances that surrounded Maria's departure from Katherine's house.

Mistress Olivia was only too glad to receive the skilled
needlewoman and conducted the negotiation with a very
modest smile that informed Katherine that Mistress Olivia
could guess very well the reason why Katherine was turning
Maria off and that she, Mistress Olivia, was too well mannered to mention it.

Katherine happened to cross Maria's path once in town a
few days after Maria had been engaged at Mistress Olivia's.
Maria did not look the least put out to see her former mistress, and thus Katherine was determined to prove to herself

that she was capable of trading an amiable word or two with a woman whose face and figure had caused her a quick stab of jealous pain.

Katherine could only describe Maria's attitude toward her as triumphant, and the brief exchange with Maria produced a profound change in Katherine's plans. Something knowing and pitying in Maria's smile had given Katherine pause. She knew enough of the Saxon woman to believe that Maria would not take these attitudes toward her without just cause. Katherine reasoned that if Maria had succeeded in betraying Katherine to the Viking or someone else, a clever woman would have carefully guarded her triumph in order not to arouse suspicion. Maria was not so clever and had effectively alerted Katherine to some unknown danger. Katherine was wise enough to take heed. She decided that there was no immediate need to support Louis. Her good instincts advised her to bank the money.

In September she received a hefty five-fold return on her investment in the wool guild, which, added to the fine profits she had consistently turned throughout her partnership with the Viking, made her a rich woman. She took three-quarters of that cash and put it in the safe, secret hands of Baruch of Coney Street, to be drawn upon when the right moment presented itself.

Then the rains came to York. For the first several days the sky spluttered and spit on the city. A wet, weepy week passed, the heavens cleared for an afternoon, but the next day, torrents of water swept furiously inland from the east. They lashed, strong and steady, against the rooftops, they thundered the cobbles clean, they swamped the construction site of the minster in a pit of soggy mortar and cement.

Katherine was restless. She called on customers, attended the dripping market huddled under makeshift canvas canopies, and contrived any conceivable errand to keep her mind off the Viking. She was not successful. Everywhere she went, she heard the same thing. Everyone agreed that the inland gale drubbing the city was worse than the storm of the Michaelmas almost exactly the year before. Everyone also agreed that the merchants of York had learned their lesson. After the fine returns of the summer few businessmen chose to risk the September seas and the heavy losses they had endured the year before.

Hearing this time and again, Katherine's heart would sink like a plummet. She had sent the Viking into such weather. She, alone, of all the merchants, had not been satisfied with her enormous profits; but, no, she had not been motivated by greed. It had been feminine caprice, pure and simple, to have insisted on risking another run, and she had been enormously pleased with herself at the time to have provoked the Viking into undertaking the entirely unnecessary venture. Now, however, she was consumed by remorse and could not hide from the uncomfortable fact that she had only her foolish self to blame.

The Viking had suffered the year before along with everyone else, but he had survived. She was not, however, reassured. He may have survived last year's storm, but this year's was far worse, by everyone's reckoning. Had she sent him to his watery grave?

The thought was hardly to be endured. She took to spending long minutes contemplating the flames crackling on the hearth in her solar, moody and withdrawn. Emma could not fail to notice her mistress's flagging spirits, but no words concerning Master Eric passed between them. Emma was seen on frequent occasion shaking her head and muttering dark prophecies under her breath.

September plodded along in all its wet dreariness. A month had passsed since Katherine had last seen the Viking, and the more days that passed, the more his image came to be an obsession from which she was not released. By day his strong features imprisoned her mind, and by night she was haunted by the memory of his strong arms on her shoulders as he pinned her against the wall in the alley by the wharf. How angry he had been! How forceful had been the current that charged between them! How she longed to recapture that moment and to beg him not to go to sea this one last time!

Katherine could stand it no longer. If one person in York might know something of the Viking's whereabouts, it would be Geoffrey Taverner. Katherine suggested to Emma that they pay a social call at the Blue Swan Inn, and thus

Katherine and Emma entered Master Taverner's establishment one dismal afternoon. The familiar room was neat as wax and cheerful, with long benches at the rough tables, well scrubbed, and a floor of polished wood, newly swept. There were strings of onions on the walls and a half mutton-ham and bunches of herbs hanging from the rafters. Earthen pots of autumn asters lined the sills of the leaded windows. A bright fire crackling on the large hearth cast wavy lines across the room and gave a coziness in welcome contrast to the bluster outside. The inn smelled of aromatic meat on the spit and boiled greens.

The tingle of the bell above the door brought Mistress Petronella from the scullery and mine host, himself possessing the contours of a barrel of ale, from the depths of the cellar. Mistress Taverner greeted the two dames, and when she learned that Katherine and Emma had come only for some company, Mistress Petronella smiled and nodded her understanding but said she could not stay and visit, for she had a roast to dress for the evening meal and was in the midst of an egg dish which threatened to collapse due to the miserable weather outside. "Much worse than the Michaelmas gale of last year, don't you think, Mistress Katherine?" she added, and bade her friend Emma follow her back to the kitchens where she would put Emma's wrist to work with a wire whisk.

Master Geoffrey was always ready for a chat and so poured out a beaker of cider for Katherine and commenced to busy himself with wiping the pewter pitchers and plates lining the broad-beamed shelf that ran the length of one wall.

They spoke of this and that, mostly the weather, which banged against the windowpanes, until Katherine was able to steer the discussion around to the subject uppermost on her mind.

"Well, we haven't had much custom of late, mistress," the taverner replied to Katherine's query, "and though you might think it peculiar that I'm not regretting that circumstance, I can tell you that a few weeks of repose has done me and my missus a world of good after the boom times of the summer. And so it is. We're still happy to welcome our friends at any time, like yourself and Mistress Emma. The townfolk have taken to coming to the Blue Swan of late to get out of their own four walls. We're flattered by the visitors, and so we're enjoying friendly company after the custom of the past six-month."

"But you're not expecting any of your summer customers to return?"

"Why, as to that, I can't say. Once a person's been to York and stayed at the Blue Swan, I can't imagine that they'd go anywhere else upon their return. There are a queer lot of people on this earth, I'll grant you that, but none so strange that they'd go to Lemoine's after having sampled the Blue Swan. Now, let me tell you that—"

Katherine avoided a lengthy discussion on the deficiencies of Norman innkeepers by strategically tossing out at this point the name of Eric Shipwright of Scarborough.

Master Geoffrey's attention was effectively diverted, and he brightened considerably. "The shipwright from Scarborough! Now there's a splendid appetite," he exclaimed, reducing his most favored customer to his notion of essences.

Katherine smiled at that, but her mouth went a little awry. "Surely he has more to recommend him than his appetite," she said.

"Well, now, he did prime work down at the wharf, so I was told," the taverner said with a sapient nod, "and has something of a skill with the longbow, isn't it so? But, beyond his appetite, what is there to know about a man?"

"Whether or not he said he is returning, that is all," Katherine answered. "Just an idle question."

"Do you know him?" the taverner asked, surprised.

"A little. He said some time ago that he might do some repairs at my house, but he's never come around," Katherine improvised.

The taverner nodded. "Handy with a hammer, I'll wager, the shipwright! And with a good heart, too, to do work for your home for orphans. Come to think of it, Master Shipwright indicated once that he knew you. But I don't recall what he said. Well, as to his return, he said nothing of it upon his departure last month," Master Geoffrey continued, seriously considering the matter of the shipwright's possible return to York, "and as it happened, he paid me handsomely right then and there for everything and even cleared the few possessions from his rooms—I gave him a double room, what my competition calls a suite, but I'm not one, as you'll be knowing, to stick up my nose and use a Norman word—and now I remember thinking at the time, with regret, that I'd seen the last of the shipwright. A fine man to my way of thinking."

Katherine's spirits sank to their lowest ebb in the days that followed. Late one howling night, far past the din of the compline that advised all honest folk to say their prayers and to seek their beds, Katherine stood before the fire in her solar, awash with misery. She had tried to retire for the night, but sleep would not claim her. Her practical self had demanded that she close her eyes and find the peace of innocent sleep, but the intensity of her treacherous longing for something that was not hers and might never be hers was too strong to submit to slumber. So, having given up the unequal struggle and conceding defeat to her restless, unassuaged desire, she had risen from her bed. She cast a warm robe about her embroidered night rail and slipped into leather scuffs before going into her adjoining solar. There she stood motionless in contemplation of the fire. Her hand was bound in one long thick braid down her back, rumpled from her tossing and turning. Capturing the light of the bright flames leaping in the fireplace, her deep auburn hair aureoled her pure ivory face.

She poked the fire absently, suddenly startled by the realization that she had not once, in the month past, thought of her mother or Castle Roncevaux or the events that had brought her to York and whose memory strengthened her in her daily quest for Sybille's reinstatement. When she tried to recall those painful, inspiring memories now, she was arrested by her inability to do so. She was engulfed instead by thoughts of the Viking and by the prospect that her partner might never return to her, that she might be condemned to a lifetime of never knowing whether he was alive or dead.

The pounding of the weather outside became pronounced for a minute or two and then subsided but was still strong enough to obscure noises within the house. The door to her solar opened. Katherine turned, expecting to see Emma with a hot posset in hand, but what Katherine saw made her heart stop, flip over, and then soar to unknown heights.

The Viking filled the doorway, vivid and vital and dripping wet. Katherine closed her eyes against the wonder of his presence, and when she opened them, she saw that it was not a trick of the light or of her overwrought imagination. He was there, watching her closely, flesh and blood and very much alive. The hood of the cape circling his broad shoulders was pushed back to reveal the dampened mass of uncut curls. Without a word he let the sodden cape drop in a puddle at his feet and shoved the cloak aside with the toe of his boot.

Katherine found her voice at last. "I should have known that a foul wind would bring you back," she said. The scolding of the words was belied by the quiver in her voice, betraying all the hurt and anguish she had experienced in the past weeks and the trembling, unsure happiness she felt at the sight of him before her in her solar.

He shook his head. "Fair winds," he replied. She had forgotten the sound of his voice. The deep, gravelly tones produced a shiver down to her toes. "The weather is clear on the coast and has been for some time. The storm has been stalled over York these past several weeks, but I've not been hampered by it. Did you think that I was in it?"

"Yes," she admitted shakily. "In it and drowned, abominable man! How was I to know that the weather had subsided on the coast?"

The shadow of a smile played around the corners of his hard mouth. "I thought you had better sources of information."

His eyes, steady on her, had set her pulses to leaping unbearably. A rapt moment of silence stole into the room, and Katherine felt the few feet of space between them as an aching abyss.

She took a hesitant step toward him, unable to resist his pull, and said breathlessly, "My wits have fled, I fear, and no one in York could speak of anything save the horrible storm, so I did not even think to discover whether the news from the coast was any different."

"Did the oversight cause you uncertainty?"

Her laugh was a groan at the understatement. "Uncertainty? Aye, a bad moment or two in the eternity of your delay."

"I told you when I last saw you at the wharf that I would not return before the month," he said. "Five weeks have passed since then, and I'm not but a seven-night behind schedule. The initial bad weather on the coast delayed me the extra week."

By the apostles, had it only been a week that he was overdue? Katherine willed herself to steady her voice. "I should have checked into my sources better. A regrettable error."

"Certainly not your first," he replied, his eyes still on her face, the smile still flirting around his mouth, tempting her, tantalizing her with the promise of the feel of his lips against hers, "and not beyond your ability to repair." He did not move. "Now."

Katherine's deep hazel eyes widened. She could not possibly mistake his meaning. She gathered her courage, which was, at that moment, as delicate and tenuous as the fine silken embroidery curling around the neck of her night rail.

He had come this far. He had braved the rigors of the inland storm to come to her house but would come no farther. She, herself, would have to bridge the rest of the vast gulf yawning between them. She took another step toward him, then a farther step, and it needed only one more hesitant, heart-pounding pace to find herself at last in the harbor of his arms.

He leaned against the half-open door, closing it with his back and the weight of his body and hers as he drew her toward him, shutting out the rest of the world, and she learned at last the secrets of his lips against hers, soft, whispering kisses that spoke of longing and security and warmth. She murmured protest when his lips left hers to trail to her eyes, then her ear, down over her neck to the swell of her breasts that lay hidden and alluring beneath a wisp of lace, and back up to the corners of her mouth where he spoke to her with his kisses, a long-deferred, lingering, most fascinating conversation of well-stated and mutual desire.

The anguish and uncertainty and despair and ambition of the past days and weeks and months and years ran out of her as she clasped her arms about his neck and answered his kisses with abandon. She felt an extraordinary longing to be in his arms, desired and cherished, as if his kisses were a charm against all that had gone before and all that would come after. The Viking could not know her thoughts, nor was he in the least interested, but he did feel the tiny smile that curved her enchanting lips when she returned kiss for leisurely kiss. She was as beguiled as he that the antagonism and violence of all their past meetings should resolve itself so naturally in this encounter of lips and hands and bodies. By mutual consent they laid down the weapons that they had used to protect themselves from each other over the past months and gave themselves over to a dialogue stripped down to its elemental opposites, as old and powerful as fire but with the unexpected liquid rush of newness, surprise, and magic, a combining of the sun and the moon, an unprecedented union of the fiery sky of twilight and the streaky, bright horizon of the dawn.

It was no truce but a negotiation of position that could only be stated in the intranslatable language of lovers, and Katherine was most willing to carry out her part. Then something more powerful took command, the attraction of soft flesh to hard body, and she was swept away into something over which she was powerless to control. It was as inevitable and irresistible as the pull of the moon on the heavy, unfathomable depths of the ocean, churning up its hidden currents to produce pounding waves on the shore. Once begun, the tide of this passion could not be broken until it had crashed upon land, and Katherine was swept up in it and eager to follow that wave until it had spent itself and she was awash in it. She was exhilarated and alive to be in his arms, and he smelled so fresh and clean and masculine that she could not pull herself away.

The Viking was no less affected, but he was too experienced a sailor to cast off into her uncertain waters, to be caught up in the strong, unpredictable undercurrents of their attraction. He would demand that she meet him again, in the full light of day, to consummate the relationship that had driven them together and apart for so many months.

He had one hand in her thick, luxurious hair and the other inside her robe against her back, pressing her to his length. She smelled of dewy roses, an intoxicating scent, more seductive and haunting than the salty spray of sea. He kissed her hair and eyelids and nose and lips and withdrew his hand from her robe. He took one of her slim, white hands from his neck and held it in a firm clasp between them.

Very much against his own will, he drew his head away from her and looked down at her, his eyes stained with desire. She looked up at him, desire shining in her eyes, too, wondering, questioning, adorably hesitant, very beautiful eyes, but full of courage, the courage to tell him that her desire was surely the equal of his and that she was not afraid of it.

A lazy, languorous smile curved his mouth, and the look in his eyes caused her to draw back a little from him and a shadow of uncertainty to cross her brow. He shook his head slowly. "It is a habit with you, mistress, to underestimate the danger in which you constantly place yourself." His rough voice was a caress. "I have remarked on it before."

Katherine was unexpectedly and enormously pleased by this observation. "Have I placed myself in danger, Master Eric?" she whispered.

His hand came around to possess her breast. Her heart leapt to his palm. "Grave danger," he replied.

"But you have saved me from coming to grief on one or two occasions before," she said shakily.

"When was that?"

"Perhaps in the alleyway with the drunken muckraker," she said. "Perhaps on the return trip from Scarborough in the shelter from the rain."

He laughed low. "It is something that you admit it," he remarked. "I had thought you an independent young woman with no use for my help on those occasions."

"None whatsoever, and I only said perhaps," she answered, and made so bold to add, "But I had not thought you so gallant to save me yet another time."

The glint in his eye took her breath away. "If I shall save you now, it's not out of gallantry."

"No?"

He disengaged himself a little from her silken softness and shook his head again. "No. I am a sailor and must be guided by the stars. There are none out tonight."

She drew back, in turn. "What do you mean?"

"I mean that I shall return when the weather clears."

Katherine narrowed her fine eyes and said, a little coolly, "But the storm has stalled over York."

The wind and rain whipped at her windows to punctuate her statement.

He picked up a heavy auburn curl which was lying against her white breast. "The storm will be moving on soon, by my reckoning. We have other matters to clear first."

He was a maddening man who never failed to provoke her. She tried to calm the throb of blood beating at all her pulse points. She could not quite look at him, for fear that she would ignominiously throw herself into his arms again, only to be rejected again, as he seemed to be doing now.

"Then let us discuss them now without delay," she said with a hint of pique.

He shook his head again. "No. We can review everything on the morrow."

She thought that she would never understand him. She contemplated the neck of his tunic. "On the morrow? You are returning?"

"You may depend upon it."

She dared to look up at him. "But will the storm be over and the skies clear by tomorrow?"

He nodded toward the windows. "Aye. This is the last gasp. The sky will be clear by morning."

"I don't think so," she said, and repeated, "I don't think so. It might be worse and then—and then—I do not think that you understand me very well!"

This drew his most attractive smile. "I know you better than you think. And I will only say at this point that I am, on certain selected topics, as farsighted as you can be at times. I am only looking ahead."

"I don't understand," she complained, and unconsciously laid a hand on his arm to keep him at his side, her eyes beseeching.

"You are making this very difficult, Katherine," he said, and gently eased away from her. She released his arm and he turned away.

With that he left her, to her cold, empty bed and a hollow, bereft feeling in the pit of her stomach.

___ Chapter 16 ___

"He did *what*?" Katherine demanded.

"Ordered the midday meal here," Emma answered, repeating her earlier statement.

"That is what I thought you said," Katherine replied with a spurious calm. "Can I safely assume, since you did not consult me first, that you denied him the request?"

Emma cleared her throat. "No, mistress, that would be a bad assumption," the serving woman ventured.

"Ever-cautious Emma!" Katherine rallied the older woman. A militant sparkle lit Katherine's already very lively eyes. "Tell me, what *should* I assume?"

"Well, now, I thought when Master Eric told me last night upon leaving the house—I let him in, you know, and then waited up to let him out—that he would be returning today at midday and bespoke a meal for the two of you, giving me to understand that it was *just* the two of you. Alone in your solar! What was I to think, other than that you had already discussed and decided the matter between you?" Emma met her mistress's skeptical eye and amended, "That is, under normal circumstances—"

"Which these are not!"

"I thought there was a possibility—"

"Remote!"

"That you had discussed it between you—his having the midday meal here, as it were," Emma continued, ignoring the interruptions. She managed to keep her countenance admirably straight but took an absorbed interest in a point just beyond Katherine's shoulder. "Or so I inferred!"

"And just how *did* Master Eric put the matter to you, to allow such an inference?" Katherine asked, a suggestion of false sweetness in her voice.

For all her roundaboutation, Emma was no coward. The time for temporizing was over. She squared her shoulders and met her mistress's eye. "He said something about today being his time and his terms," she said stoutly, "and assured me that you would understand what he meant."

Katherine understood precisely what he meant and experienced the strongest surge, at once frightening and delightful, course through her veins. "Oh, he did, did he?" she said with a dangerous look.

Katherine had spent a night fraught with conflicting emotions. After the Viking's departure she had sought her bed once again, only to return to her tossing and turning, her restlessness, caused this time by feelings very different from the remorse and anxiety that had racked her earlier in the evening. Lying alone in her bed, she had sternly refused to credit that she had thrown herself into his arms upon the sight of him and had responded so wantonly to his kisses and caresses; and when she eventually sank into the softness of sleep, she was visited by the most delicious dreams of being in the Viking's strong arms and did not want to awaken. But the honest and proper light of the morning sun had eventually crept through the shutters at her windows and insisted that she rise to meet the day.

· Katherine had found herself, until this exchange with Emma, in a flutter of emotions so new, so strong, so upsetting to her usual calm self-possession that she hardly knew what to do with herself. She had been distracted all morning and unable to answer the simplest of questions that any of her broiderers or Cook or Nurse put to her. Emma's disclosure of Master Eric's very specific intentions for the day had the paradoxical effect of throwing Katherine into a further confusion, at the same time steadying her jumping nerves. She was excited with the prospect of seeing him again so soon and what might happen between them; she was calmed by the knowledge that he would return to make complete her understanding of what he had meant last night.

She had tried to prepare herself for the eventuality that he did not desire her and would not return to her to finish what he had so tantalizingly broken off the night before. She should have been flattered that he had weathered the rigors of the storm to reach her side and to assure her of his safety, but she could not allow herself to believe that he truly cared for her. Perhaps his desire came from his long weeks at sea. Or perhaps he did desire her as much as she desired him, and that thought was delicious and intoxicating and dangerous.

"That he did, mistress," replied Emma. "And I've already instructed Cook to prepare the meal. It's hard on to noon now, and I would have difficulty changing the arrangements at this late hour. You know how Cook objects to unannounced change!"

Katherine knew nothing of the sort. Looking out her solar window, she could see that the heavens had cleared of the storm (as her partner had predicted) and that the sun was almost straight up in the sky. Katherine agreed, with a quizzical lift to a fine eyebrow, that the sext of midday would ring from parish church towers at any moment but added that the business of the meal bespoken for her and Master Eric without her prior consent was far from decided.

Before Katherine could descend to the scullery in order to countermand to the Cook any orders Emma had given earlier, she was halted in her progress around the wooden balcony by the stormy entrance of Sybille and Marta into the house. Katherine paused to peer over the railing when the front door opened and to see Sybille fling herself into the courtyard and run across the cobbles. She took the stairs at a swift, most unfeminine pace, lifting high the skirts of her kirtle. She nearly ran Katherine down in her hurry to reach her own chamber.

When Katherine reached out an arm to catch her, Sybille spun around and cried out unhappily, "Leave me alone!"

Somewhat bewildered, Katherine looked down into the courtyard at Marta for some explanation of Sybille's extraordinary behavior. Marta's face mixed concern and love and disapproval for her beloved charge. She shrugged her shoulders slightly and held up her hands in a gesture of helplessness. Katherine hardly needed further explanation. She tried to coax Sybille into her chamber, so that they could discuss the matter in private, but Sybille cast her sister off angrily and stood her ground.

"Let me guess, Sybille," Katherine said, reigning in her own emotions. "Master Stephen has caused this unseemly outburst."

Sybille's pretty, angry face crumpled into beautiful despair. "You're very wide of the mark if you think that *Stephen* is the cause of my—of my *agony*," she replied with a sob in her voice. "Stephen has not caused me even a moment's unhappiness, nor a moment of uncertainty, since—since last spring at least. No! It is *you*, Katherine, who are responsible for everything. You and Stephen's mother between you." Sybille dashed a hand across her eyes. "And I hope you're happy about it!"

Katherine perceived that this was not the moment to repeat any of the usual arguments concerning Stephen Webster's announced engagement to Eleanora Brewer. Nor would it do any good to make light of Sybille's affections, which had certainly grown in intensity over the summer. It had been a bad business all around, and Katherine would be happy to remove Sybille from York to London the moment the political situation became clear.

"So," Katherine replied, "I see. I am not the least happy about your distress. Of course, it pains me to see you so troubled by your affection for Master Stephen. It pains me equally to see you so obvious about it as well. One would think you had no upbringing whatsoever, the way you are storming about. I only hope that you are wise enough to hide it from the rest of the town, unelss you desire to make yourself a laughingstock in the next few weeks!"

These cold words had the desired dampening effect on Sybille. She bit her lower lip with remorse but still mustered the energy to return, with spirit, "How can you lecture me when you know nothing about it?"

Katherine deliberately misinterpreted that statement.

"You are right. I have no idea what has just happened to have thrown you into such agony, I think you said."

"I have just seen Stephen in town squiring Eleanora about," Sybille explained.

"Ah! And Stephen looked quite content with the arrangement, I suppose?"

"Not at all," Sybille answered swiftly. "He looked quite *pained*, the poor dear. It was rather that Eleanora looked so—so—*triumphant*! And smug. Oh, it was all I could do to keep my hands at my sides. I've never been so angry in my life!"

Katherine made the tactical error of smiling indulgently at this point. She had gathered from this comment that her younger sister was suffering more from wounded vanity than from the loss of her love, and so Katherine felt prematurely relieved.

"You laugh," Sybille lashed out, with all the sting of youth. "You asked for an explanation, but it is only to make me an object of your amusement." She moaned in anger and hurt and frustration.

"That is not it at all, Sybille—" Katherine began, and had more soothing words of reassurance on her lips when she was interrupted.

"Well," said Sybille, searching wildly for an analogy to make Katherine understand, "how would *you* feel if you had just seen your Master Eric in town speaking cozily with Maria, as I have just done. Not that you care in the least for him—or anyone—but just supposing!"

Katherine's smile became somewhat fixed. "You have just seen Master Eric with Maria?" she asked.

"Yes, and in the center of town too. What do you think of that?"

"I think nothing of it. Of course, Master Eric may speak with whomever he chooses. It has nothing to do with me, my dear."

Sybille was still something of a willful child. She lashed out, with far better accuracy than she was aware, "Then why did you turn her off if you were not worried about her being with Master Eric?"

Katherine stiffened. "Because she was causing talk with

her ways," Katherine said evenly, "and I could not afford to keep her in my employ, given my position in town."

"Your position in town!" Sybille echoed derisively. "Is that all you think about?"

Katherine did not trust herself to answer that. She had placed her younger sister first in her thoughts for so long that Sybille's disparaging remarks were most painful to her. "I do not believe the present discussion is a particularly fruitful one, my dear. Please, let's stop it now."

"Oh, you don't understand," Sybille wailed. "How could you, when you have never felt anything for a man like I feel for Stephen? If you are wondering why I even bothered to bring up Master Eric, it was just that I had thought it possible that at last—"

Sybille never finished. Marta, seeing that Katherine had her hands full, had come up the stairs to take control of her charge, and Katherine was happy to relinquish the struggle to reason with her unhappy sister. Katherine bade Marta take Sybille to her own bedchamber to quiet her down, and Sybille, spent from her storm of emotion, submitted to Marta's gentle hand on her arm.

Katherine had had little time lately to attend to Sybille's emotional needs. Today was no exception. Her more immediate object was to leave the house. She did not pause to consider whether she was jealous of Maria. She simply could not bear the thought that the Viking had spent the previous night with the redheaded broiderer. She dashed across the yard and flung the door open.

Her passage was blocked by the large masculine form from which she was fleeing. So far from avoiding him, she just narrowly missed a collision with the Viking. She saw that his hand had been raised to pull at the bell. She drew in a sharp breath and took an instinctive step backward.

The Viking stood before her, a half smile curving his mouth, and Katherine remembered vividly the first time she had ever laid eyes on him, when she had thought that she was opening the door to Josef. Her heart stirred at the sight of him, as at that first meeting, but with a far stronger surge given all that had happened between them. The sun was high above him, and he was appraising her, as he had done on his first visit, but this time with a touch of amusement and desire. He did not miss the evident fact that she had been poised for flight.

At that very moment the church bells began proclaiming the noon hour. He said, with a hint of irony, "I am flattered that you were watching out your solar window for my arrival and have rushed down to meet me," he said.

He entered the house and closed the door behind him, leaving Katherine, color high, to follow him into the yard. He then, with a courtly gesture that was impossible to resist, swept Katherine before him and remained a half step below her in their ascent of the stairs. Their progress was checked midway by Emma's voice hailing them from the door separating the scullery from the yard.

"Master Eric," Emma said, advancing across the yard to the banister, "I have been awaiting your arrival and was hoping that it was you just now."

He halted his step, and Katherine's, with a light hand at her waist. "Yes, I have come, Mistress Emma," he replied, smiling disarmingly down at the serving woman. "But how charming to be awaited, and so impatiently, by two such delightful women."

Emma was agreeably flustered, and Katherine was beginning to perceive that she was in for a difficult time ahead with the Viking in such a mood. "Oh, yes, Master Eric," Emma replied. "Shall your meal be served now?"

"Not yet," he replied pleasantly. "But we can begin with two cups," he continued with a glance at Katherine's erect back, "of cider, I think. Come," he said, and prodded Katherine's back slightly.

Emma hustled out of the yard and disappeared behind the door, and Katherine, resuming the ascent, dared to look at the Viking behind her. His eyes were on a level with her. "Have you taken charge of my household?" she asked with a cool smile.

"For the day," he answered, and explained himself, "You've had far too many decisions to make these past weeks, and so I have come to help you. You shall thank me for it before the day is over."

Katherine flushed a little but managed a very even, "We shall see about that."

He merely laughed, quite charmingly, and led her around the landing to the solar, which was flooded with a bright filtered daylight. The storm had left a sparkling clean fresh world in its wake, and sun had firmly taken over possession of the skies. Several side windows in the solar were open, allowing warm breezes to circulate.

Katherine was not going to allow him such high-handed tactics. She sat down at the table and gestured for him to do so, as well, which he did, leaving the door open.

Katherine assumed her cool, businesslike manner, for she had already determined, earlier that morning and in some desperation, how she would open the conversation. "It seems we have an account to settle," she said, and reached for the ledger books that she had placed at her right hand.

"But, of course. That is why I am come" came the reply, bringing Katherine's head up sharply at the distinct and disconcerting note of humor in her partner's deep voice. "But it shall be quickly done, and I doubt that you'll have need of that," he said, nodding to the pen that she was paring and the pot of ink. He withdrew a slim pouch from his tunic and laid it on the table in front of Katherine.

She eyed it tentatively, then picked it up and weighed it in her hand. "It is very light," she commented. "Shall I hazard a guess that there are not more than, what, fifteen or twenty silver pieces in all?"

"Ten," he replied.

"Somewhat less than I had calculated" was her rather stiff reply.

"Indeed. You might have expected well over one hundred from this last run," he said with a nod that indicated, ever so slightly, that it had not been the worst financial decision on her part to have insisted on this last voyage that had caused her so much heartache. "But you have just bought me out."

Katherine blinked.

"Yes, mistress. This is where we began. Last March your debt to me allowed me to buy into your company, but our partnership has been a damnable business, and I want no further part of it. These last one hundred marks pays off your debt and dissolves the business relationship."

Katherine shut the ledger with something of a snap and tossed it onto the sideboard, along with the pouch. She hardly knew what to think or feel. "I see," she said. "I was under the apparently mistaken impression that our partnership has been very profitable for you."

"Moderately, but we've gone as far down that road as we can, and I do not care to travel any farther when there are far more interesting avenues to pursue," he replied, and added with a very effective smile to which Katherine was far from impervious, "I have mentioned to you that I never mix business with pleasure. Ah, here are our drinks. Thank you, Mistress Emma. You may serve the meal now, if you please, for we have settled our money matters, once and for all."

Emma bobbed and withdrew.

When Katherine had recovered her voice, trying with a modicum of success to keep her guard up against his disturbing presence, she said, "I am not entirely sure that the business between us, as you say, is settled."

"Depending on how one interprets that statement," the Viking replied reflectively, taking a sip of cider, "you are correct."

Katherine flushed. "You are determined to misinterpret everything I say. I was speaking of our trade, and I am not at all sure that I will let you end the partnership so abruptly. I have some rights to your services, after all."

The amused cock to the Viking's eyebrow only served to deepen Katherine's blush, but he merely said, "Should I be, once again today, flattered by your interest in me?" Meeting the militant sparkle in her eye, he continued, "No, I think not. Do you wish to continue the partnership then?"

"Not at all!" she said hotly.

"Then I defer to you the female prerogative of crying off," he replied, all politeness.

"Do not patronize me, Master Eric."

"I know of only one way to handle you, mistress, but you shall have to wait until after the meal."

Emma entered then with the first course, a platter of freshly dressed fish and herbed beans. Katherine felt it more becoming not to answer his highly impertinent remark and so replied to all his conversational openings in a manner that conveyed a cool composure she did not feel. They passed a very pleasant meal. She tried, without much success, to veer her thoughts away from the one topic that was uppermost in her mind.

Never before had the presence of a man so absorbed the whole of her being. She could not think of business or money or Sybille or the contest for the crown, any more than she could really concentrate on the light topics introduced by the Viking. The food was good and plentiful, the talk ran along, and almost before Katherine knew it, Emma had come to sweep away the remains of the almond and honey cakes that Katherine suspected had been prepared especially for the occasion.

Apparently in league with the Viking, Emma left the solar for the last time. The Viking rose and went to the door to close it. Then he came back to Katherine's chair, took both of her hands in his, and drew her to her feet. She looked up at him, questioning and apprehensive and entirely beautiful.

"No," she said in a voice that shook.

He smiled down at her and gathered her, unresisting, into his arms. "Business is finished. It is time for pleasure," he said.

She tried to pull away but was no match for the iron bands of his arms. "You cannot mean what I think you mean."

"Can I not? You are a stubborn, beautiful thorn in my flesh. Since I no longer hope to pluck you out, the least I can do is to ease the pain."

"But you do not—you do not—" She could not form her lips around the word *love*. "You have done everything possible to make me think that you dislike me."

"I dislike you intensely. And you dislike me at least as much. Admit it!" he commanded.

"I have disliked you from the moment I laid eyes on you," she obliged him with feeling.

His fingers sought out the pins that held her hair in place, and the heavy tresses tumbled down her back. He slowly began to kiss her forehead, then her eyes, her nose, and her ears.

"No," Katherine tried again. "It is not right. It may be one thing for you, but quite another for me, to defy the conventions of society."

"You, mistress," he said, kissing the pulse at her throat, causing desire to flame up her breast, "have broken almost every law devised by society, except this one." He laughed. "Despite the fact that you tried to convince me that your experience in pleasure," he amended, "equaled your experience in business. Never shall you have me dance on such a string again."

"But it is still against the law!"

He responded by continuing to kiss her. From their very first meeting they had been governed by laws very different from the ones that ruled men and women in day-to-day society. Their own laws had nothing to do with money or politics or anything else beyond the two of them together in the intimacy of her solar. He desired her, she desired him, and that was law enough to bind them.

"No," she moaned. "You know I have no experience in such things. It is not fair! You have no right to do this to me!"

He loosened her kirtle and dropped it at her feet, telling her quite forcefully that he had every right. Through her thin undershift she was exposed to him in her pearly loveliness. Behind the closed door was her bedchamber, and she found herself propelled through it, powerless to resist. The window was open, but the shutters were partially latched, permitting a half-light to enter the room.

"It's indecent! In the middle of the afternoon!" she protested. "Broad daylight!"

"Which only adds to the lawlessness. And it's the very best time of day," he said. "I much prefer it to the cover of night, and we've nothing to hide."

She managed to draw away from him enough to move her hand to the bellpull that was near her bed. "This cannot continue," she said. "I shall have to summon Emma."

He held her eyes, his lit with desire and laughter and the challenge that was always there when he was with her. "Do you really care to humiliate yourself by summoning a servant who won't come?"

Katherine hesitated. "As usual you have arranged everything so that I submit to your wishes!"

"I don't want your submission," he said, stripping off his tunic.

"But you've said from the beginning that our positions are not equal," she argued.

He shook his head. "I maintain that our positions are not comparable. But I expect them to be equal—particularly now."

Katherine gasped slightly. "Are you—could you really be *daring* me to do—to do this?"

He had unlaced his chemise and cast it aside. He managed to do away with her shift as well. "You catch on quickly. Clever fellow that I am, I know that you have never yet refused one of my challenges." His lips found the rosy tips of her naked breasts, and with his next breath he said, "You are very beautiful."

She was finding it entirely impossible to resist being desired by such a man. Engulfed by his nakedness, she breathed in the scent of his skin, which smelled of sunlight, and the drowsy, lemony breezes wafting through the window made her respond with ardor to his kisses and caresses. Suddenly she was as shy as any maiden on her wedding night.

"You cannot force me," she said, using her last shaky defense. "You cannot wish to force your attentions on an unwilling woman."

"Tell me honestly that you are unwilling," he said huskily, throwing back the covers of her bed and gently laying her down on the crisp sheets, "and I shall stop on the instant."

"Would you?"

"No."

"But I am afraid," she blurted out.

"Try again," he recommended, thoroughly unconvinced by her argument. "I have never known you to lack an often very foolish courage."

"This is surely foolish," she said. "I simply refuse to fall into your lap like every other woman you've had at the wave of your hand."

He laughed at that. "Many's the time I've wished to throttle you with my hand and may yet, woman, if you keep me waiting much longer."

That was the last he spoke. She responded then to the force of the law of his passion for her. She willingly gave herself over to the tide of his kisses, and it was not, as he had stated, a submission but rather, at first, the coming together of two breathtaking, opposing, and equal liquids, the confluence of two currents, the marriage of the Rivers Ouse and Foss.

Once opened, the floodgates of this passion too long dammed caught them up and swept them together in a soaring wave, frightening at first in its intensity, leaving behind all their arguments and hard words like flotsam bobbing on the surface of the sea. The wave bore him far, far inland where the swirling waters of an unknown, underground river burst forth into sunlight and flung him high. She, too, felt the force of this sparkling, ecstatic sea, and soon she was no longer drowning in the caressing blue-green waters of a safe lagoon but far above the surface, responding to him with every particle of her being. They were strong currents, fighting one another for the pure joy of it, swirling and merging into a body of water, an irresistible current passing through bone and flesh and tissue. It raced through the blood to crash with the force of a tidal wave; and he made her irrevocably his.

The swirling currents resolved themselves into the gleams of sunlight caught by the floating motes of dust, and the pounding of her heart into the street sounds that wandered up and through her window: the happy sounds of children playing, the chirping of the birds nested in thatch and gutter, the occasional rumble of a pushcart over the cobbles. The world had swung back to normality. Or almost. Never had these sounds rung so clear and sweet. Never had she been so happy and content and full of life.

When his bright curls lay against her white breast, she lay watching the beams of afternoon sunlight dance on the ceiling beams. She fetched a heavenly, contented sigh from the depths, not fully aware of all that she implied in that simple exhalation of breath.

He lifted his head and looked at her. He was taken aback by the sight of her beauty, with her hair tousled and her mouth still rosy and rumpled from his kisses, for she looked profoundly familiar. He had certainly never met another woman who resembled her, and neither was Katherine merely the most immediate ultimate of the usual. No, it was Katherine that he saw, and that was the incomprehensible part: He felt that he had known her for a very long time.

Then he put his lips to her neck, and she obediently closed her eyes and nestled against him, entirely willing to tighten her bodily hold on him and keep, within the circle of her arms, all the peace and serenity that she had never thought would be hers. She allowed him every liberty until it seemed that he had finished fondling her, and they dozed, legs and arms entwined.

Much later Katherine was aroused by the hand that slid down her leg and back up to the smooth curve of her stomach and then came to rest on her hip. His lips brushed her hair, then her eyelids, and came to her lips, which were slightly parted. Breathing evenly in her happy slumber, she was gently awakened.

Her eyes opened slowly, as if her lashes were too heavy on her lids, and then she registered the meaning of the extraordinary scene that had just passed between them. She shifted slightly, as if to get up. She did not succeed in rising.

"You are in my bedchamber!" she exclaimed.

He propped himself on an elbow but kept her imprisoned with his other hand, which caressed her satiny breast. "Have you just now discovered it?"

She blushed and laughed and said again, "But you are here in my bed in my chamber in my house! I cannot have it this way!"

"Too late," he replied. "And why not? I find it very satisfactory."

"You would! But now that you've been here and taken possession of my room, I shall never be rid of you. No man has ever come this far."

"Again, something I find to my complete satisfaction,"

he commented with a glint in his eye, "and I even plume myself, not unreasonably, on your satisfaction, as well."

"Your conceit, sir, is matched only by your—your—" She groped for the appropriate comparison.

"My skill?" he suggested helpfully, adding provocatively, "It is a change to find you without a ready barb on your tongue."

"There is a first time for everything," she retorted, somewhat defensively.

He smiled. "How charming! Mistress Katherine at a loss for words!" He dropped a kiss onto her neck. "I much prefer you that way."

Her eyes narrowed into gleams of laughter. "I may be at a loss for words but not at a loss for questions. I have one in particular I would like to pose to you."

He rolled over onto his side and propped his head on his fist to look at her. "You have chosen your moment well," he remarked. "I am entirely at your command."

"That is an equally charming change in you," she retorted. "But if I ask you the question, do you promise to answer me truthfully?"

"On one condition: that you grant me a question as well."

She frowned quickly and then conceded reluctantly, "That's fair enough. But you first!"

He considered this opportunity thoughtfully. "Ah, yes," he said after a moment. "Who is your creditor in York? The one who, I must assume, you paid off Easter morning."

"But our business is over," she protested.

"It most certainly is," he agreed. "But it's a harmless, curious question. The last piece of York's business intrigues that I was never able to place." He picked up one of her heavy curls between his strong fingers. "You have done a remarkable job in covering yourself."

She realized that he could have asked her a far more searching question, and so in the spirit of the moment she replied, with an easy heart, "Baruch of Coney Street."

He fingered the curl pensively. "Very good," he said appreciatively. "The man who owned your house before the riots in 'ninety? I believe the taverner told me that he had left York and might have returned."

"He was done wandering," Katherine said. "He lost everything except his life in the riots, as did all the other Jews. He vowed then that he would never come back—so he told me—but in the end there was nowhere else for him to go."

He nodded gravely. "Did he teach you the secrets of the Arabic numerals, then?"

Katherine raised a brow, very much liking this game, and teased, "You have asked your one question, and now it is my turn."

He smiled. "I submit with deep misgivings to the query."

"Then my question is this: What did you tell your sister about me to make her so hospitable—and mysterious— about my presence in her house and my relationship to you? On our ride from Scarborough back to York," she reminded him, "you said that the weather was too hot and humid to permit an explanation."

"I perceive that my misgivings were well founded," he commented.

"No stalling for time," she admonished, and chided softly, "Lost your courage, as you accused me earlier?"

"Not at all." He met her eye squarely. "I summoned Gwyneth to explain to her that I could not let you be on your own in Scarborough because you were carrying something valuable of mine on your person."

"I did have one of the account ledgers with me," Katherine affirmed, "expecting to go over a little business while in Scarborough, but I would not have said that it was yours exclusively."

"As to that," he agreed coolly, "I explained further that it actually belonged to both of us."

Katherine seemed satisfied by that but unenlightened. "And so? What did that have to do with keeping me your 'prisoner,' I think it was, and with being related to your attack at the harbor and my part in it?"

He slanted her a rakish glance. "Gwyneth made her own interpretation of the whole, I believe. And once she got going, I was unable to persuade her that she did not have the details quite right. You see, love, she thought that my attack

was instigated by you as revenge on the loss of your virtue
—and your imminent motherhood."

Katherine being momentarily dumbfounded, he continued
easily, "Yes! You see, the explanation answered beautifully.
I did not say that it was probably Mauleon and his men who
set upon me, since mention of his name causes her to become quite upset. So in an effort to spare her feelings, I
allowed her to think what she so delightedly chose to think,
which was something on the order of our having had a
lover's quarrel, and I will say—"

Her face and voice were suffused with outrage. "Spare
her feelings!" she interrupted. "By the apostles! Did I fail
for words before? You are the most conceited, arrogant, un-
scrupulous, dastardly person I have yet to come across. Dislike you? How I *detest* you! You, you, you—*man!*"

He was deeply pleased by these unloverlike words.

Katherine ignored his smug demeanor. "You are hope-
less. Gwyneth thought that whole time that what I was carrying of yours was—what we had between us was—was—I
cannot believe that you had the audacity to suggest such a
thing. A lover's quarrel! I cannot believe that *she* allowed
you to get away with it—that she did not have you make an
honest woman out of me. At least I was spared that!"

He laughed. "She knows that circumstances at present
don't permit me making an honest woman of you," he said,
and left it at that.

Katherine would consider the significance of that statement only at a much later time. At the moment she was too
absorbed in a delightful mixture of emotions. "And all her
references to my embarrassment and the ride back and my
comfort and safety! You are—you are *truly* despicable!"

"Oh, no. Gwyneth made her own interpretation. I said
nothing explicit and tried to tell her how wrong she was."

"Blaming it on someone else? That is even worse. You
apparently did not do much to disabuse her of her misbegot-
ten idea. No wonder you did not want to tell me about it on
that hot, dusty ride from Scarborough. Coward!"

In response he bent to kiss her. "Merely wise."

"You are hedging," she accused, loving the touch of his
lips on hers but drawing away.

"It's as straight an answer as you'll get."

"I should have known. Just like you! You never have given me a straight answer on anything. Not even on the rival merits of John or Louis, come to think of it," she continued, meaning nothing deep or dark about it but simply giving another example of his behavior with her.

He momentarily halted his kissing and looked down at her. She was very beautiful, very desirable, and a shadow came into his eye. The fragile trust between them would take time to mature. There was no hurry to push things today.

She saw something cloud his face. "Well?" she demanded.

"Well, what?" he countered.

Simply out of exasperation she asked, "You are not really for John, but you are not for Louis, either. Why? Who are you for?"

He put his lips back down to her neck and caressed her breast. "I have already answered your one question," he quoted back to her, "and I much prefer you when you are not talking."

Katherine had nothing more to say, for she did not care about John or Louis or anyone else. She kissed him back with all her newfound fervor, so that he quickly lost himself in her silken softness and the limitless hours of a private, golden, delightfully lawless afternoon.

After a light supper served by Emma just before nightfall, the Viking left Katherine's house a deeply satisfied man, the memory of her parting kisses and his name on her lips still fresh.

He had devised some plans that he meant to put into action without delay that would insure Katherine's safety in the near future, and he intended to begin on the morrow. Circumstances, as he had intimated to Katherine, did not permit him to elaborate the nature of his plans or the reasons for them.

He turned the last corner before the Blue Swan, whereupon his feelings of satisfaction were instantly replaced by a wariness when he saw three men hovering outside the inn's door. The Viking had cause to know these men very well.

They were John's men who ran to Mauleon's bidding. He

had last seen them the year before, just before his first imprisonment.

They had spotted him. There was no turning back for the Viking, so he approached the inn with a leisurely stride and an air of unconcern.

He greeted them by name, but they did not offer him their hands to shake. The atmosphere boded no good.

"Well, lads," he said, maintaining his ease. "To what do I owe the honor of your visit?"

The Viking had already determined that he had no hope of besting the three of them if it came to a difference of opinion. It would be best to go along with whatever they were going to say and not draw attention to himself here in the very midst of York.

"Just the small matter of a beggar in York," said the brawniest of the lot.

"A beggar?"

"One of John's men, as if you'd not be knowing that. We have it on good authority that you were the one to report him and have him thrown out. A treasonous action if ever there was one."

"To be punished accordingly, I suppose. Shall I guess what you have in mind for me?"

"We're thinking," growled the brute, "that the Tower's the place for you!"

___ Chapter 17 ___

London, it was universally agreed, is a man's town. There's power in the air.

In the air of early October the power in London was unmistakably in Prince Louis's hands. He had camped his French followers in strategic locations on England's southern shore and had captured both large, important castles, including Westminster, and other lesser fortresses. The prince and his wife, Blanche, and their retinue had then taken to circulating the streets of the royal seat. There they accepted the unofficial homage of those barons and citizens who genuinely welcomed their presence or who found it prudent to lionize them openly.

Meanwhile King John and his band of marauders and foreign mercenaries where roaming the north country. Although the king's absence left London with a vacuum that Louis could only too easily fill, the ailing, unpopular, and unbalanced Angevin ruler was at last succeeding in demonstrating some capacity for leadership. John had managed to keep Louis's forces confined to the south by scattering a line of forces between London and Oxford and by placing his most capable captains at strongholds on the eastern seaboard. He had even retained possession, almost miraculously, of that most important of citadels, the castle crowning the cliffs of Dover.

John had accomplished his military aim, but being impatient and restless in his old age and pressed by Louis's presence on English soil, he did not return immediately to London as he should have done. Louis's presence also caused John to travel with all his gold and precious jewels, which legally were supposed to be stored in the vaults at Westminster.

When William, Earl of Pembroke, High Marshal of England, learned of the irregularity, he was highly displeased. However, William had more important worries than the whereabouts of the accumulated wealth of the Angevin rulers. With the entire monarchy swaying in the balance and with John out of reach of communication, William had had to take it upon himself to plan the forthcoming, and no doubt final, campaign against Louis. He had called together the last few trustworthy earls and knights to assemble at the Earl of Warenne's keep, at two hard days' ride north of London. Gaston Parmentier, the Earl of Warenne, was a seasoned, forthright chevalier.

In addition to Gaston Parmentier, the Marshal had summoned three other men. Robert de Burgh was an attractive, fastidious widower of nice but not fabulous means and came willingly at the Marshal's demand. Cedric of Mauleon sent message of his deep regret that urgent, private, and unspecified family matters would keep him from the meeting. He expressed his desire to be briefed on the proceedings of the meeting just as soon as he could extract himself from his entanglements. It was all prettily said, but Mauleon's defection, however justified, had irked the Marshal. William was all the more vexed by the fact that he had received no reports that would either confirm or deny Mauleon's excuse.

The third man, however, had not yet appeared, nor had he sent any message. In the best of circumstances the Marshal did not like to be kept waiting, but now that time was so critical, he was all the more vexed by the tardy man's delay because the Marshal had ample and growing reason to doubt the third man's good faith.

Seated at the table in the receiving chamber, the Marshal, Robert de Burgh, and Gaston Parmentier were discussing the unfolding of events in this month of October.

"Almost surely a lost cause as things are going now," Robert de Burgh was saying to the discussion at hand and shaking his head, "but your optimism is infectious, if misplaced, I own, William."

"It is far from a lost cause, de Burgh," William replied with heavy emphasis. "You're simply too young to have the experience to know that losing a few skirmishes is far from losing the entire war."

"A downy youth am I, now?" Robert answered with a laugh, rubbing his handsome, shaven chin. "I'm old enough to be a widower with sons vying to reach my shoulder. And if you are trying to flatter me, my man, you might know that you have already won me over to your cause."

"John's cause," William said. "England's cause! And I know *you* too well to be taken in by your smooth words. I did not have to try very hard to win you over, as I recall. The position is reasonable and speaks for itself."

"I agree, but then there seems to be a distinct shortage of reasonable men left in the realm," Robert said affably, and added the reflection, "The importance of getting Louis off English soil should be apparent to the meanest of intelligences. Why, any knight could be *reasonably* expected to support John, simply upon hearing the vows being taken by Louis's men."

Gaston Parmentier, at seventy, was more of an age with William Marshal than Robert de Burgh. Thinking that he had missed some innovation, he asked, "What are the vows, Robert?"

"Oh, the Frenchmen are swearing the usual things, Gaston," Robert replied, putting the older man's mind at ease. "Abstaining from cutting their finger or toenails, from the favors of women, from bathing until the conquest of England has been completed, this last vow being one that does not cause our French cousins to alter their habits much. Nothing out of the ordinary but really rather grim!"

Warenne waved away these commonplaces. "Bah! Much good did those vows do us in the Levant. Paltry stuff! Now, I'll never forget the Lion Heart's vow at the seige of Acre; not to descend from his horse until the walls were broken. Why, he was forced to sleep sitting up for no less than—"

These fond recollections were brought to a halt by the timely interruption of a page bearing the message that a lone rider on the horizon had at last been sighted from the highest turret of Warenne Castle. The Marshal responded to the news with a curt, "Show him to this chamber the moment of his arrival." He then disclosed the identity of the man they were awaiting. The announcement created something of a stir.

"Eric, Earl of Scarborough?" Warenne echoed, astonished and with a heavy crease between his brows. "Could that be Knud of Scarborough's son?" he asked. To the Marshal's affirmative Warenne replied that he had not know that Knud of Scarborough had had a son, or if he did know it, he had completely forgotten the lad's existence.

"Hardly a lad anymore," the Marshal pointed out.

"Well, no," Warenne said, performing a feat of calculation. "Why, Scarborough lands must have been handed over to King Henry's worthless cousin decades ago. But remind me why the lands were confiscated in the first place. I fear that I must have forgotten that as well."

The Marshal had no recollection, either. He remembered Knud as a proud, fierce Dane with the love of the sea in his veins. Perhaps Knud of Scarborough had offended King Henry in some way, or perhaps he had become uncomfortably powerful in Yorkshire where lived that brute, unruly race of men; or perhaps it was just another episode in the age-old conflict between Dane and Norman. Since both stocks shared the same blood of those roaming Northmen of centuries past, Norman and Dane were bitter rivals.

"God's Wounds, what must Knud's son have been doing all these years?" Warenne demanded.

Robert de Burgh was equally curious. "How does a man, whose father was stripped of land and castle, earn a livelihood?" he wondered. "Knighthood would certainly not have come easily if this Eric had aspired to it, although he might have achieved the rank with some hard work and a good deal of money. However, one would have heard of him if he had won his golden spurs."

To this William replied severely that Eric of Scarborough harbored no desire to climb the ranks of chivalry. The Marshal complained that Eric's plain style of dress did little credit to the noble, if impoverished, breed from which he sprang; and had Eric not been the spit-and-image of Knud, William would have said he had more the look of a common townsman—or even of a Saxon thane, God forbid—than of an earl. The man's behavior was, lamentably, no better than his dress, William continued, for Eric of Scarborough had been thrown in the Tower months ago on a charge of slander against the king. Then the Marshal had learned that the man in the Tower was reputed to be something of a sailor, and so the Marshal had ordered his release in order to press him into the king's service in Yorkshire.

However, Eric of Scarborough had recently been imprisoned a second time. The arrest had come on John's orders, through Mauleon, so it seemed. The Marshal had caught wind of it and had had Scarborough released this second time as well, against his better judgment.

"And the only reason for this second release," William went on, "is that Scarborough has undoubtedly gathered some bits of information that might prove valuable in these desperate times. The goings-on in York and Yorkshire have always been a mystery to me—blast the hardheaded Saxons!

But he was the perfect man for the job, and I had to take my chances. His blond head would arouse neither suspicion nor resentment among the natives there."

"Perhaps he's a Saxon sympathizer," Warenne commented.

"The thought has occurred to me more than once, Gaston," William admitted. "I have cursed myself a thousand times these past two days for having released him this second time, for he is likely playing a double game. And I even had the foresight to have had him followed, but he eluded my men, or he would have been here two days ago." William grunted. "At least he has come! But he's a thought too crafty for my tastes, this Scarborough. And without an ounce of proper respect for authority."

Robert de Burgh had taken a lively interest in this harsh recital of Eric of Scarborough's shortcomings and ventured the opinion that a man whose father had been, rightfully or wrongfully, dispossessed of his fortune might not have had proper respect bred into him. "But I shan't argue the point, for I do not know the man," Robert said. "But tell me: Was Scarborough the one who was charged with the slander against the king, as you say, oh, about a year ago? I did catch some wind of that episode and recall that it had something to do with a man from the North—a Dane, it was rumored—but I had not heard that he was the son of an earl."

"That's the one," the Marshal said.

De Burgh regarded his well-manicured fingernails. "I also heard—if I recall the rumors correctly, it was a hush-hush affair, after all—that Cedric de Mauleon was the principal accuser. Of course, *his* loyalty is without question. But there were unconfirmed rumors that Mauleon's dislike of the Dane had more to do with an incident involving the Dane's sister than with Mauleon's deep offense at the slander against John. But it was only so much talk, and I rarely put much store in garbled reports."

Marshal admitted that it was Mauleon who had caused Scarborough's first imprisonment. "As was his duty," William grumbled. "But the intrigues of the north—especially among those headstrong Saxons in York, as I have said—

have always had a way of escaping me, and if I was forced
to take a chance and employ a questionable man like Scarborough to apprise me of them, then I was prepared for
double-crossing. Mauleon knows his duty and did well to
halt as quickly as possible any loose talk against John."

"Quite right." Warenne nodded. "Mauleon did quite right
to make an example of the man."

De Burgh, who had never admired Mauleon, observed
that one man's imprisonment—and a not highly publicized
one, at that—had hardly persuaded any of the rebel barons
from their present, disastrous course of action. However, he
was no quibbler and invited the Marshal to proceed in his
explanation of the services that Eric of Scarborough had (or
had not) executed in Yorkshire in the name of King John.

The Marshal sketched Scarborough's activities, after
which he said heatedly that although he would be very surprised if Scarborough offered him any valuable information
at all, it was "something to be thankful for, after all, that he
has shown up without my having to set a search party out
after him. That is, if it is indeed he who has been sighted on
the horizon."

The confirmation of Eric of Scarborough's presence in
the bailey sometime later should have put the Marshal in a
better frame of mind. Nevertheless, when Eric was ushered
into the receiving chamber, the sight of him did not dispel
the Marshal's ill humor. William had been prepared to accept without comment Scarborough's undistinguished mode
of dress, but there was a glaring detail in the newcomer's
appearance which provoked William the Marshal into dispensing with the usual formalities and introductions.

"I was not aware, Scarborough," William said by way of
greeting, "that the Danish custom of waiting upon Norman
lords half bearded had spread so far south."

"It hasn't," Eric of Scarborough assured the Marshal.

Robert de Burgh was impressed with Scarborough's commanding appearance and did not think, as the Marshal had
suggested earlier, that there could be any possible confusion
between Eric of Scarborough and a "common townsman" or
"Saxon thane."

De Burgh leaned over and murmured to Warenne, "Perhaps Scarborough has taken a vow not to shave until John's forces prevail," and drew a quelling eye from the Marshal at the impudence of the remark.

Scarborough added, without apology, "I have only this instant ridden into Warenne keep and was led immediately here. I thought you wanted to see me."

"I have been wanting to see you these past two days and more. I made it very clear that upon your release you were to travel here without unnecessary delay," William said irascibly.

Eric of Scarborough was in no good mood himself. His second imprisonment had put him in a damnable position, and he had had ample time in his cell to consider the implications and consequences of his abrupt, unannounced departure from York. The second arrest, however, had produced one positive change in his plans: Upon leaving the Tower the week before, he had shed once and for all the ways of the master shipwright from Scarborough; gone, too, was the Viking. The time had come to assume his peerage and to meet the Marshal and his men on equal terms.

Scarborough took the chair that was offered him, opposite men he recognized as Robert de Burgh and Gaston Parmentier, and accepted the horn of ale presented to him by an attending page. He made no mention of his surprise at the absence of one man, Cedric de Mauleon.

"I would have been here yesterday," Scarborough said, without a pause, "if I had not had to lose the trail of men you had following me."

Robert de Burgh smiled at the brazen flaunt. The Earl of Warenne spluttered and coughed into his ale. William the Marshal did not bother with a denial but grumbled in awe-inspiring accents that he was far from amused.

"I was even less so," Scarborough answered in his own deep voice. "But I am here now and ready to get on with it."

William was exasperated. "But, God's Love, man! The delay!"

"It was hardly unnecessary. Could you think otherwise?" Scarborough replied with a lift to his thick, blond brow. "I had an errand or two to run after this second imprisonment."

"Apparently a visit to the barber was not among them," the Marshal snapped.

"I naturally depend on the hospitality of Warenne Castle," Scarborough replied gravely, with a slight bow of his head, "to repair that omission."

So the man has a tongue as well, thought Robert de Burgh, who preserved an admiring silence. Warenne immediately offered the best services of his castle, blustering slightly.

William performed brief introductions and malevolently eyed the newcomer a moment longer. He shifted heavily in his seat. "And the errands, Scarborough?" he demanded.

"At the very heart of our business," Scarborough replied. "I shall oblige you by telling the whole if you are interested."

"Not so fast," William warned, holding up the strong, broad hand that never lost a joust in a thirty-year career on the tournament field. "I would like to hear first your version of this second imprisonment if you please! If I have the facts correctly, it seems that you are at cross-purposes with the Crown—something to do with your having had one of the king's men ousted from York."

"If you are referring to the man who was disguised as a beggar," Scarborough replied easily, "I had him removed in June. He had begun to haunt York around March, a circumstance which coincided too neatly with my own arrival there. Your work, William Marshal?"

"A necessary precaution," the Marshal replied.

"So I imagined," Scarborough answered, and indulged himself in a long sip of ale.

"Then why would you have him removed," William asked testily, "unless you are playing your own game?"

"Because he was in my way," Scarborough answered, "and the citizens of York are far from stupid. They had your man removed the year before, did they not? What was he again? A poultry merchant? They would have fallen to your beggar sooner or later, and I didn't want one of your men looking over my shoulder. His departure from York was easily arranged."

"You gained the confidence of the York merchants so quickly?" the Marshal asked.

"It was not difficult to convince the right people to rid themselves of a spy," Scarborough replied, "but as far as gaining their confidence, merchants are in the habit of sizing up their fellow traders."

"You do not despise the Saxon townsmen of the North, then?" Robert de Burgh asked with a pleasant smile.

Scarborough fixed his gray gaze on the handsome face opposite him. "I do not despise the men among whom I have lived my entire life," he replied evenly.

"But that must mean that you know their tongue," Warenne interjected, in a manner that suggested that he did not think much of the ability to speak Saxon.

"Of course," Scarborough replied, indifferent to insult.

"I see," de Burgh said, and considered the Dane a moment. "Have our paths never crossed before?" he asked.

"Perhaps," Scarborough said. "I have been to London on occasion in the past few years, so it is possible that you have seen me somewhere. However, the Danish style may be seen almost anywhere in town or at court, and I am but one of many."

"Very true. I may be thinking of someone else," Robert agreed lightly, thinking it singularly unlikely that Scarborough would blend into a crowd. "You have been engaged in business affairs, then. What could it have been, if I may ask?"

"It's no secret," Scarborough replied, for he had come to this meeting with a sure purpose. "I am generally known as Eric Shipwright of Scarborough. To my family I am Eric Knudson."

"The Danes and their names!" Warenne interpolated.

De Burgh was mildly surprised. "But the name Shipwright," he said, "means in Saxon that you build ships, does it not? That you have earned the title and privileges of a master?"

"Yes."

"It is manual labor," de Burgh pursued.

"Yes."

The idea that a nobleman would have been instructed in

the use of his hands for something other than warfare, and that he would have achieved mastery of the skill, was entirely novel to Robert de Burgh. It must have seemed strange to Warenne, too, for he could be heard murmuring the word *shipwright*, forming it awkwardly around his lips.

"The Marshal has told us that you are a sailor as well," de Burgh said with a glance to William Marshal, who nodded his permission of this minor digressionary examination.

Scarborough assented to this and said that as such, he naturally preferred to sail only those ships whose construction he had personally overseen. He commented on steering techniques and on the superiority of lateen sails over oars.

No one present was qualified to respond, but the Marshal said, somewhat irritably, that if Scarborough was so well informed on the latest innovations in seafare, he might have lent his aid where King John needed it most: the patrolling of the coast from Dover to Land's End.

"I might have lent my aid to Louis too," Scarborough pointed out. "He seems to have needed it more, for he suffered heavily crossing the Sleeve."

"So you do not employ your knowledge or your skills for political ends. You simply sail, then," de Burgh ventured with a questioning lift to his shoulders.

"I am normally engaged in trading," he answered.

"This is quite extraordinary," de Burgh insisted.

"Not at all. The two occupations go hand in hand, as I am sure you can see," Scarborough said.

Robert de Burgh, an astute man, smiled. "Now I am curious, and perhaps you will be so kind to answer another personal question for me—my last one, I assure you. I have heard stories for the past years of a sailor named the Viking, who roams the north country. He is reputed to be quite rich, in fact. Can you tell us anything about him?"

Scarborough's composure was far from shaken. His smile was as disarming as his questioner's. "I've heard the tales as well. His rousing adventures make for good talk late at night over a tankard of ale." Meeting de Burgh's eye, Scarborough shook his head. "But one is hardly likely to meet the man. I think the Viking to be a pleasant creation of someone's imagination."

"Ah," was all de Burgh said, and left it at that.

"Back to the problem at hand," William said at this opening. "I had put the beggar in York to investigate the workings of the wool guild, because I had gained the impression the year before from the work of my poultry merchant that the wool guild and York's intrigues were one and the same."

Scarborough smiled. "That is very true."

"But that was as far as I got with him," William continued, "and now this year you put a stop to anything I might have learned from the beggar—who, by the way, I have not seen since—but his early missives to me suggested that he was close on to something. Now, just how did you so easily rid York of my man?"

"A word in the lord mayor's ear sufficed," Scarborough replied.

"Aha! I knew it had something to do with the lord mayor!" William exclaimed. "The lord mayor—a Fitz-something—is, by all accounts, an interesting fellow and must be the key to all that I need to know."

"Not at all," Scarborough said with a chilling smile. "He is not the key. Or rather, if you want to go to the source of York intrigues, you must go beyond the lord mayor. But you are entirely right that the wool guild plays an important part in the York economy and might well play a deciding role in Louis's success or defeat in England."

"The fat wool merchants are soaking up all the cash of the country!" William spat. "And shirking their taxes!"

"They can afford not to pay them, it seems," Scarborough commented.

"Has York become so prosperous?" de Burgh queried.

"It was a most profitable summer," Scarborough averred, "with the political havoc a perfect excuse not to pay the Crown. York does not yet have the reputation of London for the wool trade on the international markets, but it makes the most of its advantage of being far beyond the easy reach of the royal tax collectors."

"And on those international markets, how stands English wool with regard to the products of other countries?" Warenne asked.

"England produces first-class wool and runs a second-class trading economy," Scarborough stated.

"Hhmpf!" Warenne grunted. "But how has York established a rivalry with London?"

"Is it the facility of the sea trade? The ready availability of sailors, such as yourself?" de Burgh asked. "York is situated something like London, with easy access to the open sea. That must be the major advantage York enjoys."

Scarborough paused. "The waterway is, of course, important to getting the stuff to market. However, it is the quality of the water that makes for distinctive, regional cloth. York's has come into high demand in the past several decades on the continental markets and beyond."

"Do you know as much about the manufacture of cloth as you do about shipbuilding?" de Burgh asked.

"If I did not," Scarborough answered, "I would be cheated every time, both buying and selling. As I said, a good merchant likes to size up his custom."

"You must have profited nicely, then, in the past years," de Burgh observed.

"Times are hard, nevertheless," Scarborough responded.

De Burgh held up a hand. "I quite see. I never would accuse you of having become rich."

The Marshal had other things on his mind. He demanded bluntly, "And you being so well informed, Scarborough, I suppose that you shall tell us who is at the head of all the unpaid taxes and who organizes the support of Louis in the north?"

"That is why I am come," Scarborough replied.

"You've certainly taken your time about it. And not one message did I receive from you these entire six months!" William accused.

"I did not agree," Scarborough reminded him, "to reporting to you every month, as you requested. I told you that I would contact you when the time was ripe."

"I could have learned as much and sooner through the beggar I had placed in York last March—" William said.

"I doubt it!" Scarborough interpolated.

"—and who, I might add," William continued, "I have not seen since."

Scarborough considered this information. He was suddenly sure of how he was going to present his case. "Are you accusing me of disposing of the disguised beggar in a more permanent way? I had nothing to do with him beyond his physical removal from York. The true source of the royal problems in Yorkshire is in the identity of the man who does know the beggar's fate, the same man who prompted my second imprisonment." Scarborough looked at each man in turn. "You will recall that I was imprisoned in a similar fashion the year before."

Robert de Burgh's eyes narrowed keenly. The Earl of Warenne look cautiously blank. William the Marshal's brow lowered thunderously. "What precisely do you mean, Scarborough?" he demanded in ominous tones.

"I prefer to lodge my accusations face-to-face," he said. "I am surprised and disappointed that I cannot do so today. The man who stands at the center of your problems is not here, and I would have expected to see him."

"You may name the man in his absence," William said low.

Scarborough allowed a moment of tense silence to pass before saying easily, "The man you want is Cedric de Mauleon."

This pronouncement created a drama that would have deeply satisfied a man with a sense of flair—Godric Fitz Osbert, for instance. It was as if the air had crackled. Robert de Burgh chuckled softly; Gaston Parmentier was suffused with an alarming shade of red; William the Marshal sat forward and fixed his gaze on Eric of Scarborough.

"You are prepared to defend that statement, Scarborough?" the Marshal stamped out.

"I do not accuse falsely," Scarborough replied.

"You enter a serious charge of treason against King John," the Marshal said. "Surely you are aware of it."

"Entirely."

"Cedric de Mauleon rode with John at Runnymede," William continued.

"I am well aware of that too."

"Do you ascribe Mauleon with a motive?"

"He stands to gain valuable tracts of land from Louis, if

Louis prevails. The Frenchman has vowed to exile the rebel barons as traitors to an annointed king. It is rumored that Rome will support the exile."

"I, too, have heard the rumors," de Burgh interjected softly.

The possibility of such treachery smote William the Marshal to his heart. His ways always ran straight as an arrow, but he had lived in the world long enough to entertain most any idea that touched on loyalties and allegiances. "What is your proof?" William asked.

It seemed to Scarborough that he would be permitted a fair hearing. He had expected that much of William the Marshal. He grinned. "A series of prayer missals, sire."

"This is not a jest, man!" came the whipping reply.

"It is not intended as one," Scarborough said soberly. "The clandestine records of the wool guild, Mauleon's participation in the profits, and his investments in Louis's cause have been hidden in two hollowed-out prayer missals."

De Burgh looked ready to speak, but the Marshal held up his hand and took the reins of questioning firmly in grip. "Which are in your possession?" he asked.

"Not in my immediate possession, no," Scarborough replied. "My arrest a few weeks ago came at an inopportune time, to say the least! But I know where they are, and upon being released a few days ago, I sent a message to my man in Scarborough to get them."

"You think, then, that Mauleon had you jailed this second time as well?"

"Mauleon has intimate ties with York and has had for many years. He had no difficulty in discovering that I told the lord mayor that the beggar was a royal spy. It was easy enough after that to contact the king, lodge another complaint against me, and have me arrested in the name of the King John."

William Marshal said nothing but merely regarded Scarborough fixedly. "What exactly is Mauleon's connection to York?"

It was Scarborough's turn for silence.

"Well?"

"It is time to bargain," Scarborough stated.

William bit off his words. "You've the mind of a merchant, Eric Scarborough."

Scarborough laughed and said, "Indeed I do, and you have just shown me what an excellent bargaining position I hold."

"An insolent tongue and a good deal of effrontery," William added in disgust.

Scarborough thanked him kindly and said that those qualities had served him well over the years.

The Marshal was on the point of losing his temper in earnest, but then suddenly, irrationally, his mood snapped. A smile threatened at the corners of his mouth. He had an odd liking and respect for the Dane. Eric of Scarborough had met the test.

"You're your father's son," he said at last. "And I'll take no lessons from you!"

William stood up then and dismissed Warenne and de Burgh from the chamber. Scarborough rose, too, and the two men faced each other. The Marshal's thatch of silver provided a brilliant foil to Scarborough's gold.

"Give me the proof of what you say, and Scarborough lands shall be yours," William said. "Surely that is a good enough bargain for you."

"You are so sure that John will win?"

"When you put the fleet of ships you surely control at my command!" William countered. "I've a few ideas about sea attack that might interest you for sport. Oh, yes! I still know a thing or two about running a government. And now about Mauleon's purported ties to York . . ."

"I can prove only what is on parchment," Scarborough said.

"Which you will show me before too much longer."

"If all goes the way I expect."

"Meaning that you will show me only those parchments that you choose. Whom do you protect?" the Marshal demanded.

"Why, no one," Scarborough said innocently. "But we can hardly jail the whole of York, can we? Let us worry about only the one man at the top. In order to accuse him I need to be free for a few more weeks to gather together my proof."

"You are free to leave," William assured him.

Scarborough smiled. "Thank you. I shall leave on the instant, then."

"Where do you go?"

"I won't spoil your fun, William Marshal. You'll have your men trail me. Let them discover my destination on their own!"

___Chapter 18___

The road to London proved difficult in those early days of October. Katherine was not indifferent to the hardships on the rutted highways. In a curious way she relished the challenge of the physical obstacles. She was happy to displace her absorption in the misery in her heart with the more familiar struggle for mere survival. She threw herself into the contest between wagon wheel and the mire and the mud of the thoroughfares. She would rise from hard pallets each morning to welcome a chill world rimed with a frost that the wan sun, a tarnished tuppence at the end of the harvest, could not penetrate before midday.

She had chosen her route without consulting Sybille or Emma and according to the convents that could lodge them along the way, and she slightly preferred, since she had a choice, the mendicant Franciscan orders. These rather cheerless feminine refuges from the secular world were a salve to Katherine's spirit in those long days of travel. She found a measure of peace after each hard day's journey within small, poor walls where the sisters lived by alms and the labors of their own hands, spinning, making altar linen, cultivating vegetables. The fare one could expect to receive there was always rigorously meager but of good quality; the chambers kept for traveling women staying the night were always sparsely, pitifully furnished but painstakingly clean. Katherine found that these barren quarters suited her mood well.

No matter how hard the pallet, however, sleep constantly eluded her. Night after night she was tormented by the Viking's words to her on that last afternoon: "Circumstances at present don't permit me making an honest woman of you." She reminded herself sternly that those circumstances were of no consequence, that they were a device he reserved to get want he wanted from a woman, all the while preserving his independence. She wished that she could cut him brutally out of her heart, but she no sooner could do that than stop breathing. It had been an unequal battle from the start, and she had suffered a devastating loss.

As torn as she was with her love for him and her deep sense of abandonment, she did not truly regret the afternoon she had spent with the Viking. She could not honestly find in her heart any remorse for having given herself to him so completely. He had promised her nothing. He had asked nothing of her but what she had to give him, and that she had freely given. He had finished what there had been between them and had gone along his way. On that score he had not played her false.

On another score, however, he had played treacherously and stood now, quite possibly, in a position to destroy her.

Katherine had sought out the lord mayor on the seventh dreary day of the Viking's absence from her door, when she finally had realized that he would not be returning to her. Godric had further depressed her with the information that the merchants' money channeled to Louis had already left York for the southern coast. The lord mayor did not expect another payment anytime soon. Katherine knew that the merchants' names had been included in this transfer of monies, and she knew that she had lost a strategic opportunity to invest in the likely future king. She had been so deluded by love to have trusted the Viking's hinted support of John that she had hesitated to back Louis when it would have been to her best advantage. To make up for lost time she needed to go to London to transfer her money to Louis personally.

Her missed opportunity to support Louis had not been the worst of Godric's news. He had also mentioned that the prayer missals had been misplaced. He had suggested that Mauleon might have had something to do with their disappearance.

"For although I have not seen my dear brother since August," the lord mayor had said, "I was aware that several of his men recently came to York. They apparently made a very short stay, for I only caught a glimpse of them early one afternoon last week and then *poof*, they vanished into thin air. But I am quite sure that it was they who came."

"Could they have known where you keep the books?" Katherine had asked.

"It is possible. Certainly it is possible," he had replied. "Cedric was always so particular about knowing just where I kept the accounts and might have instructed his men accordingly. I hardly need tell you how disappointed I shall be if my brother, my very own brother, has sought to—how can I express it other than to use the ugly word itself?—yes, to *steal* them from me."

Katherine had immediately grasped the implications of Mauleon's possession of the incriminating prayer missals. They would be of no use to him if Louis prevailed, but he would certainly use them if John would remain on the throne. They would be wonderful blackmail, she realized, to enable him to get, at last, what he wanted from her.

Katherine had been understandably disturbed by the thought that the York accounts could have fallen into the wrong hands and had said something to that effect. Godric had replied with his most effective, disintegrating smile, "Yes, my dear, so many unaccounted-for disappearances of late!"

The unspoken name of Eric Shipwright hovered between them. Katherine had felt quite faint with conflicting emotions. She remembered full well that the Viking had chanced to see the parchments strewn around her solar table at the beginning of their partnership, but she had doubted that he understood their significance. Then, too, there was Maria's possible involvement with the prayer missals and the Viking. With a stab of emotion Katherine had realized how badly she had underestimated the Viking. She had let her guard down, little by little, and had been lulled into trusting him.

Was Godric worried? Katherine had asked with a ragged, little breath. Yes, Godric was worried, but he felt that the matter was, quite literally, out of his hands. His fate was York's fate. He was prepared to take the blame or reap the credit. Such were the consequences of assuming the job of lord mayor that the good citizens of York had entrusted to him. Godric had paused and smiled again and remarked that Katherine need not submit to his fate. She might take matters in her own hands, he had suggested, and thought a trip to London would be just the thing. Katherine had agreed. Godric had approved with a nod and the words, "Godspeed, my dear, and the best of good luck!"

Indeed, everything indicated that Katherine should leave York. The latest reports made Louis the sure winner. Katherine wanted to be there at the beginning of his reign to present Sybille to court. She had gone again to consult Baruch on the issue, and he had advised her to take the half of her investment with her to London. He had told her that she could send a messenger to him at any time for the other half. He was even prepared to lend her a rather fabulous sum, in addition, if she found that Prince Louis needed a further display of cash to reinstate the daughter of the Duc de Roncevaux.

Katherine would not, however, burn all her bridges in York. Since the Viking's arrival in her life, she had, for some reason, never felt more at home in York. Thoughts of the Viking, too, had made her stop, for once, to consider her own future. She had decided tentatively to return to York after she reinstated Sybille, to continue her broidery, and to keep up her home for the children. She found myriad reasons to return to York—her business, her friends, her lack of political ambition for herself in London—but she could not quite admit to herself that her principal interest in York was to be there when and if the Viking ever returned.

Katherine had paid a final visit to Mistress Mathilda. She

had told the webstress that she and Sybille and Emma needed to "ruralize" for a month or so after the boom business of the summer. Mistress Mathilda had enthusiastically seconded this very sensible idea. She had nodded with the perfect understanding that if Katherine were removing Sybille from York for the month of October, she herself would raise no objection. She mentioned how deeply her family would feel the broiderer's absence at Stephen's forthcoming wedding to Eleanora. To that Katherine had a ready response: The table linens being embroidered by Katherine's house as the wedding present were nearly ready and would be delivered to the Websters before Katherine's departure. Mistress Mathilda had smiled and said that she would personally see to it that all the friends attending the wedding celebrations would understand Katherine's removal from York at this time.

Katherine had had the archbishop assume the administration of her house in Jubbergate Street. She had turned off her prentice broiderers with a month's paid holiday.

Once Katherine had announced the impending trip to London, she had made very sure that Sybille would never leave the house unaccompanied by Marta or Emma. Even with this double guard Sybille managed to get a message to Stephen that bore the date on which she was being torn from his side and carried off to London. Stephen's rather dramatic plans to elope with Sybille were foiled when Katherine had decided to leave York two days earlier than originally planned. Sybille was consternated by this change, but she had confidence in Stephen and nourished romantic thoughts of being rescued by her love, which sustained her throughout most of the long journey to London.

En route the subject of Stephen Webster had arisen only once, and that was at Katherine's instigation. A frightening thought had occurred to Katherine. Given her own recent disastrous experience in love, she had asked Sybille if Stephen had, in his ardor, soiled Sybille's honor and ruined her chances for an honorable match among her noble peers.

Sybille had replied with great dignity that her love for Stephen (which she was not ashamed to admit openly) and his love for her was far above the physical plane, if *that* was what Katherine meant.

Katherine did, and she was reassured by Sybille's categorical, unblushing statement. However, in some tiny corner of her heart Katherine thought that perhaps Sybille and Stephen's love might be a lukewarm affair.

Actually, Sybille's thoughts were filled with passionate scenes of her rescue at Stephen's hands. These visions receded when all too soon, from Sybille's point of view, the small traveling party found themselves at the outskirts of London, and before Sybille knew it, they were paying their toll of admission at Aldersgate. Once within city walls, Sybille began to doubt that Stephen would be able to find her in the crowded streets where the bellicose throng of peasants and burghers and noblemen jostled one another cheek-by-jowl in the large, busy, buzzing, fashionable marketplace that was London.

Katherine came with a letter of introduction from the Archbishop of York so that she, Sybille, and Emma could be comfortably housed with the nuns in the women's quarters of the Priory of the Holy Trinity at Christ Church. Being located within city walls in the northeast sector of town, and being very rich and well guarded, the priory was a luxurious and safe lodging from which she could await events and plan Sybille's admission to Westminster.

Katherine was seeing London as if it were the first time. Since it was in fact Emma's first trip to the metropolis, she and Katherine were continually enthralled by the royal city and were eager to plunge into its mysteries. The skies of mid-October were cooperating, being clear and crisp, and Katherine reveled in this merchant's paradise.

Even Sybille permitted herself to be diverted by the sights. Not, of course, by the monuments, for she passed the Guild Hall, the College of St. Martin le Grand, St. Paul's Cathedral, and the Site of the Folkmote without a second glance. However, she studied in absorbing detail the colorful and beautiful ladies parading the streets on the arms of their equally well-dressed cavaliers. Sybille's attention immediately fastened on the ladies' shoes, small insubstantial things, hardly more than charming slippers really, and so

different from the clumsy footwear worn by the practical
housewives of York! The feminine fashionable of London
were invariably shod in pointed-toed slippers made of goat-
skin or leather from Cordova or Florence or Milan, dyed
fascinating, improbable hues, and so prettily stitched.

Katherine was more interested in trying her hand at trade.
She had brought with her some of her own wares and nearly
lost a small packet of money in a bad trade with a broiderer
who spoke so quickly and in such broad, flat accents that
Katherine could not keep the pace. Katherine was rescued at
the last moment by Emma, who knew a bad bargain when
she heard one and had to draw her mistress aside before the
disaster was concluded. Katherine laughed when Emma informed her that she had mistakenly heard a two for a twenty,
bought Emma a pretty trinket in thanks, and expressed an
almost pleased surprise that she still had a thing or two to
learn about bargaining in English. Commands and curses
resounded in several languages in the streets. She encountered French among the traders and fared much better, and
an occasional strain of what was Catalan could be heard as
well. Katherine guessed the rough Teutonic voices that rumbled out from enormous bellies to have come from any of
the numerous German principalities.

The choice of goods offered at every booth was prodi-
gious. The three women spent their first few days wandering
the spidering streets where hawked the shoemakers, the hat-
makers, the candlestick makers, the armorers, the urbanized
millers, the carpenters, the cartwrights, the coopers, the
smiths, the skinners, the oil merchants, the farriers, and the
beer sellers. As in York, the rich and cocky wool merchants
dominated the trading. Samples of wares were thrust upon
them from every counter, figures were called out to them in
invitation to bargaining from every trader, and everywhere
around them deals were argued and bargains sealed.

Katherine was exhilarated by what she saw and encouraged by what she heard. She was not entirely surprised to
find them not as enthusiastic about prince Louis as she
would have thought. "The lesser of two evils" was the
phrase that summed up the common feeling, and more and

more there were grumbles that the Frenchman might possibly prove a worse tyrant than John.

"Glad I am," professed a particularly friendly vintner with a startling variety of French wines, "that Louis has been called out of London with his haughty wife to tend to his troops instead of strutting the streets where he is still but a guest. And I hope that the ships that have reportedly sailed down from the North to harass his garrison on the coast give the Frenchy a run for his money! I may like to sell his wines," the vintner continued with a toothy grin, "but that doesn't mean I want him sitting but a stone's throw from across city walls. I'll mind my business, and he can mind his—in France! But we can't depend on our good-for-nothing monarch to rid us of the French plague—pardon my pun—for John has never come to any good in this world and surely won't in the next. It's said now that William Marshal shall look after us—but we'll see about that," he said with a heavy measure of skepticism, "and today it's the nineteenth of October with time frittering away, and who can forget the date when taxes are due in another few days?" After more in this style, he ended with the lamentation, rather cheerfully delivered, that the present turmoil would bring no better rule to the land, only sharply higher prices.

The very next morning, a day like any other, Katherine heard several more reports of the ships that had swept down the coast from the north. It was whispered that there were only one or two vessels involved; it was whispered that there were a hundred. The general feeling pronounced it good, for once, to have that pack of Danes sailing in defense of the English population rather than against it, as during the fierce Viking raids.

She had imagined Eric at the helm of one of those ships, but that very afternoon she caught sight of a blond head tipping the throng of marketers. It turned down a street half a block ahead of her and out of her vision. Her heart flipped over against her will, and her feet drew her irresistibly in his direction. No, it can't be he! she thought as she bade Emma and Sybille to await her at the corner and she wove her way through the milling crowds.

She had turned her head perhaps a hundred times since

being in London at the sight of any tall blond man that crossed her path. She had followed several for a closer look. Even without seeing them close-up she would always quickly discern that they were not the Viking. However, this man, even from the back, looked so very like him, with the familiar set of his shoulders and the particular curl of his hair, that her heart was filled with a conflicting mixture pleasure and pain. She had thought him at sea. What was he doing in London?

She rounded the same corner she had seen him travel down, keeping his head in her line of vision, waiting for some movement to betray to her that it was not her Eric. She both feared and hoped that it would not be he. Her suspicion grew into a certainty. She was sure of his identity, even at the distance she kept. He could be confused with no other man, and she felt quite weak. She made her way behind him through the busy streets, murmuring her pardon, never once considering what she would do when she caught up with him, knowing only that she must know where he was going and what he was doing.

He picked a quick way through several streets, penetrated the district of West Cheap, and stopped finally at the doors of what appeared to be a thriving hostel, called on its shingle the Crown Inn. It was well situated on the thoroughfare of St. Swithin's Lane. The double portals of the inn were thrown open to reveal a bustling courtyard.

Katherine stood in the shadowy doorway of a bakery opposite the inn. Her precaution was unnecessary. Master Eric did not appear to be interested in who might be watching him from the street. In full view of the yard and the lane, he held up what he had been carrying for the inspection of another man. It was a small sack, rather heavy-looking, and must have contained something compact.

Could it be the prayer missals? Katherine wondered, an icy trickle running in her blood. The sack was the right size. She would also have liked to have seen better the other man with the Viking, but from her particular angle she could see nothing of his face. After a few words and a vague gesture at the inn, the man took his leave of Eric and plunged out into the street in the opposite direction from Katherine.

Eric had kept the sack. Without a backward glance he crossed the courtyard of the inn and was lost from her view.

She turned slowly back into the street in the direction from which she had come and entered the hubbub, scarcely heeding her surroundings. She drew several indignant glances from passersby, who sniffed annoyance at her lack of attention, one of them saying, in rather plain language, that she should watch where she was going. Nothing penetrated her reflection.

Then the thought came from nowhere—He has not won yet, the Viking!—and she was suddenly heartened. The test of wits and wills was far from over, and she now held a small advantage in knowing his exact whereabouts. She could exploit that advantage. She had learned a thing or two about being a woman in the past months, had she not? She felt fresh winds blow over: she had at last been shaken out of the doldrums in which she had foundered for the past month since the Viking's abandonment. She let her sails fill with new life.

It was fortunate that the shock Katherine had received at the sight of her love and former partner should have resulted in so rapid a self-possession. Hardly had she turned off St. Swithin's Lane, in the direction of Emma and Sybille, than she ran, literally, into the arms of a new problem.

Katherine raised her beautiful hazel eyes, cool and calm and direct, to meet the narrow brown ones of Cedric de Mauleon.

Mauleon had grasped her forearms to steady himself at the force of the impact, not yet aware of the prize that had fallen into his hands. The sly, suggestive comment that rose of its own to his lips when he felt the prettily rounded feminine arms beneath his fingers died quickly when the identity of the young woman registered.

Katherine saw the way his lids lowered slightly to lend a human touch to his lizard's eyes. The moment was not well chosen to display her physical aversion to him. She willed herself not to flinch. She wanted to determine whether Mauleon possessed the prayer missals or if the Viking had them.

"So it is you, my lovely Mistress Katherine," Mauleon

said. "Providence must have brought you on this day to this quarter of London." Small, malevolent gleams darted in his eyes. "Or *is* it Providence?" He paused and looked around him briefly. He did not lower his voice, since French was current in the streets of London. "I wonder what can have brought you to this most interesting Lane of St. Swithin's today, at this hour and, I discern, unattended? But most likely you shall tell me it is business, *ma petite bourgeoise!*"

"Not entirely, sire," Katherine replied steadily. Had he been following the Viking, as Katherine had? "I have lost my way and am returning to the corner where I last saw Emma," she continued. "You remember my serving woman, Emma? London is such a big, bewildering place, and I am not yet used to it. I find that a familiar face, such as yours, in the throng of strangers a most pleasant surprise. Such a fortunate encounter!"

Mauleon chuckled softly with an evil undertone. He always liked to catch his victims a little off-guard, but he admired her poise. His hands had not yet released her. "I am happy to have surprised you . . . so pleasantly. And it is a most fortunate meeting but hardly fortuitous."

It would be fatal for him to associate her presence in West Cheap with the Viking. "Sire?" she questioned cautiously.

"I guessed that you had come to London. I even determined your lodgings." This with an airy gesture that permitted Katherine to free herself from his hateful touch. To the startled look on her face that she was unable to hide, he said, "Yes, I was back in York only days ago. It has become quite an important city of late, but I shall not bother you with all of that. I gathered from York's fine lord mayor that Mistress Katherine had gone to—what was the word?—"ruralize" in the event of a wedding or some such thing that was supposed to make perfect sense. I was indeed convinced until I heard from my men in London that three interesting women had arrived at the priory of the Holy Trinity at Christ Church with a letter of introduction from the Archbishop of York."

"Your men in London?"

He smiled his satisfaction, thinking her to be impressed. "I have told you that I am not without a certain power in the

town. Yes, my men are instructed to inform me of everything that has to do with York. I have arrived in London only
this morning, and I was quite put out with Godric for not
knowing where you were. All is forgiven him now. He is not
usually so ill-informed."

Katherine remembered clearly how Godric had been
present when the archbishop had scrawled her letter of introduction. Bless Godric for having tried to protect her, at least.

"Were you so anxious to see me, sire?" Katherine dared.

"A small matter of unfinished business, I think you would
call it," he said. His voice was unpleasantly waxy. "You
have had a habit of slipping out of my hands these past
months, and I have grown quite tired of your elusiveness.
You were not destined for life as a broiderer in York. I have
much better plans for you. You have something I want very
much."

If Mauleon was implying that she had possession of the
prayer missals, then that must mean the Viking did indeed
have them.

Katherine lowered her eyes and smiled modestly. "I do
not know what you are talking about."

"If you did not," he said in his flat voice, "you would not
have left York for London at this time. I am not a stupid
man, nor am I a patient one. The games are over."

Katherine looked up again. "We cannot discuss this
here." The words cost her something, but she was to say
with no evidence of the distaste she felt, "When shall I await
your pleasure?"

Mauleon reached out and caressed Katherine's slim white
neck. "That is much, much better, mistress. I would come
tonight, but I have another, more pressing, invitation. *Peste*!
I am forever preoccupied when it comes to you. I wonder if
you are my jinx. But no! You shall await me at the priory for
tomorrow night," he said firmly. "My rank allows me right
of entry, so you shall not be able to deny me. And if you
choose not to be there . . ."

Katherine held his gaze steadily.

His hand slipped down her neck to her shoulder and down
her arm. She shivered involuntarily.

"You understand," he stated. "Yes, you understand that if you are not there, I shall find you, and you shall be very sorry when I do."

__Chapter 19__

Katherine found Emma and Sybille patiently awaiting her at the corner where she had left them. To Emma's anxious question Katherine replied, "I found exactly what I was looking for and more." Then the three women returned to the priory for the midday repast. After the meal Katherine insisted that Sybille repose for the better part of the afternoon in her chamber. Katherine drew Emma aside in order to explain what she had found in the street and what she intended to do about it.

"I don't like the sound of it," Emma stated categorically after Katherine had mentioned her various encounters and stated her desire to leave the priory that evening.

"But there's no other way," Katherine replied.

"There's got to be another way!" she exclaimed. Then, "I'm coming with you."

"You must stay here with Sybille."

"Your safety is more important," Emma argued.

"Not at all."

Emma looked mutinous. "Now more than ever! You have never given a thought to your own safety—"

"We've been over all of that before. Please do not start in on me now," Katherine interrupted. "I must be allowed to circulate freely today, and you *must* stay here with Sybille. If Mauleon were to suspect who Sybille is—if he or his men were to come and do something to Sybille—" Katherine could hardly speak of such a possibility. "I cannot trust one

of the sisters here with the responsibility of Sybille, nor
could I divulge to them why it is so important to keep her
safe. Mauleon knows where we are staying, and he said that
he could not come before tomorrow night—thank the twelve
apostles! I have a little breathing room and have this evening
to act."

"Why isn't Mauleon coming this evening? I had thought
him so eager."

"He has a prior engagement with someone, and that gives
me the perfect opportunity to retrieve the prayer missals."

"Do you know where they are?" Emma asked.

"I have an excellent idea that they are at the Crown Inn in
St. Swithin's Lane and in Master Eric's possession."

Emma drew a long breath. "Are you sure it was Master
Eric you saw?"

"I'm sure."

"And there was no mistake?"

"No mistake whatsoever," Katherine replied firmly.

Emma heard her mistress's cool, composed tones. "Why
didn't you speak with Master Eric when you saw him?"

"Whatever for?" Katherine asked with a distinct note of
bitterness.

"But there must be some explanation for his abrupt departure from York," Emma countered.

"I am sure there must, and I hardly think it necessary to
delve too deeply to find it, my dear Emma," Katherine retorted. "It is a very old story, and I'm a day older and a day
wiser."

"I do not suppose that there is anything I can say to make
you change your mind—"

"You suppose correctly," Katherine interrupted, "and I
would prefer it if you did not insult my intelligence. Let me
see . . . you shall tell me that he is madly in love with me,
would never have parted from my side, save for some extraordinary circumstance beyond his control that prevented
his return to Jubbergate Street. That is the gist of it, no? You
may as well attempt to persuade me that fairies exist or that
guardian angels have protected my life until now. Let us
agree, then, that Master Eric got what he wanted—me, his
money, the prayer missals—and left York. But I am not

about to let him get away with it. He has not pulled the wool over my eyes! This means, of course, that I shall have to beard the lion in his den, but that is hardly a deterrent—rather a spur—and I intend to do my work tonight."

"You cannot go out at night. The couvre-feu bells toll at eight o'clock from All Hallow's Barking and St. Martin's le Grand," Emma argued.

"I shall not *go* out," Katherine explained. "I shall already be out. And thank you for reminding me to fill my purse with coins. I have not yet become accustomed to traveling about with so much money, and the watch will certainly demand their share if they see me in the streets." Katherine sighed, reminiscently, annoyed by thoughts of the curfew. "We certainly did not need to worry about such things or have so much ready cash in York."

Emma listened in silence to her mistress's plan. She fully realized that if Mauleon did not have the prayer missals and if Katherine could deliver them to him the next night, then she might still be able to fend him off. It pained Emma to think that the Viking might play Katherine false, if he indeed had the prayer missals, but she reckoned that Mauleon was still surely worse.

Katherine left the priory and traveled slowly, lost in thought, in the direction on St. Swithin's Lane in West Cheap. The sun would soon be sinking to die in a blaze on the horizon, and Katherine had provided herself with a heavy cape for the cool of the approaching evening. She was happy to see that the heavy doors to the Crown Inn were still flung open, providing an unobstructed view of the court-yard. She positioned herself in the half-covered doorway of the bakery opposite to await any movement her former partner might make in or out of the inn. Katherine had known enough to press a coin into the baker's hand, and he understood that he would ask no questions.

Katherine waited. The shadows lengthened. Church bells from all over town rang seven o'clock. Still she waited. She had no assurance that Master Eric was there, and she wondered if her luck was out.

Her luck was in. Shortly before the curfew, Katherine saw her quarry cross the yard in the direction of the street.

His hands were empty, his gait easy. Katherine drew herself back into the shadows. He looked neither right nor left before turning into the street where people were still milling. Then he headed purposely north.

Katherine trailed after him. He was easy enough to follow and never once looked behind him. Why should he think he was being followed, after all? After a few turns Katherine was surprised to find him make his way toward Cripplegate. It seemed that he was going to leave the city; and now that the sun had set and the curfew bells would soon ring, he would not be able to reenter. Since Cripplegate's exposure left no wall or door she could hide behind, Katherine had to keep to the shadows and was not able to witness his departure. She felt, nonetheless, sure that he had gone.

She headed back to the Crown Inn, took several wrong turns, got hopelessly lost, ran into some dead ends, and finally found her bearings again, rather far from the neighborhood of West Cheap. It took some time to make her way back to St. Swithin's Lane. Her progress was impeded first by several men of the watch who required a coin or two to allow her passage, and then by a few other, less official men whose bold advances she warded off with several pungent phrases.

After all her trouble Katherine wondered if she would find the prayer missals in the Viking's room, or if she were on a fool's errand. Much later she slipped in through the portals of the Crown Inn, which arrogantly disregarded the curfew, and she found the Dane's chambers with the ease of only one question and a key produced with a smile. It was easily done. Too easy, in fact, and if she had not been so desperate, she would have realized that she was about to fall into a neat trap. The trap had not been set for her, however, but for Cedric de Mauleon.

In the meantime Eric of Scarborough made his way back to West Cheap by a much more direct route than the one Katherine had taken. He was weary of this game he was forced to play in town. Every sundown for the past four or five evenings he had left the Crown openly and in full light of the dying day to make his way toward city gates. He had put the word out that he was in town and was sure that

Mauleon's men would eventually become aware of him. He was hoping, in fact, that they would take the bait tonight and be following him on his evening stroll through town, but he was to be disappointed.

Scarborough felt the bite of inactivity. He wished to be at the helm of one of his ships, where most of his men were now fighting the Frenchman. He was in town only because he could not trust the matter of bringing Mauleon to justice to anyone but himself. He was impatient to settle the score with his hated enemy so that he could get back to the more important matter of Mistress Katherine the Broiderer. Scarborough had gone straight from Warenne Castle to York, only to find that she had retired for the entire month of October at an undisclosed destination. He had initially taken the report of Katherine's departure at face value and had accepted Godric's hints that the Broiderer had wisely removed Sybille from York in the face of the upcoming marriage between Eleanora Brewer and Stephen Webster.

Second thoughts, however, had made Scarborough progressively more uneasy about the reasons for Katherine's disappearance from York. He had thought he had arrived at last at gauging Katherine's character, but the unwelcome suspicion that he might after all have been wrong could not entirely be banished. At no time did Scarborough care to find himself mistaken; in this instance he had found compelling reasons, entirely new to him, that his judgment of a woman should not be found to have been at fault.

Scarborough threaded his way back through town and headed for a particular tavern. Earlier in the day Robert de Burgh had contacted Scarborough, wanting to meet later that evening, and Scarborough had suggested the Mortal Man, the tavern just around the corner from the Crown.

Scarborough stepped into the long, low room some minutes before de Burgh. His eyes scanned the big wine tuns which rested on the plank supports against the brick walls, spigots attached and turning to the hands of the serving maids who ran between the bare wooden tables where men and women sat at benches. Straw, dirtied by thrown bones and the lees of spilled wine, covered the hard-packed dirt floor. In a cleared space a knife thrower performed, hurling wickedly sharp daggers at a wooden shield before which a pretty girl stood frozen. Each time a steel blade flashed close to her, she winced.

He commanded bread, sausage, and a pitcher of beer with two pewter tankards and paid for them in advance. The changemaker sat behind a fence of wooden bars perched on a high stool, a dozen leather bags propped open before him. Half of these were filled with coppers; a few held silver coins. From the scot rods in back of him dangled odds and ends of wearing apparel left behind by diners lacking coins with which to pay their fees. From the various other objects hanging from the hooks and propped against the upright rods, Scarborough judged the man to be also in the pawn-broking business, a not unusual sideline for tavern hostlers. He could see two shields, a long sword, a score of gold and silver brooches, and, in a leather bucket fastened to the wall bricks, a number of worn gold rings. There were a few precious scrolls tied to the hooks with cords, attesting to the fact that more than one scholar had purchased a flask of wine for which he was unable to pay.

Robert de Burgh entered the tavern minutes later, paused on the threshold for a moment, and cast a glance around the room with visible distaste. He could only describe the atmosphere as fetid. Upon seeing Scarborough amongst the unwashed throng, he came forward with a smile on his handsome lips.

"Charming," the Norman nobleman said low in greeting. "A perfect spot for our talk. 'Save you, Scarborough."

"Good enough, de Burgh," Scarborough replied indifferently, and gestured the newcomer to sit on a common bench at the rough table.

"Quite, but I fear that I have overdressed for the occasion," de Burgh commented humorously. "Do I attract unwanted attention to ourselves?" he queried, looking idly around them.

"My reputation will survive," Scarborough assured him.

Robert de Burgh smiled. He noted that Scarborough was clean-shaven now; and, as on the first occasion they met, the Dane presented a scrupulously clean appearance to the world. Since he did not wear his rank on his back, however, he was still not out of place in such a setting. "You shall retrieve it in any case."

Scarborough waved this away. "Well, de Burgh?" he asked bluntly.

Robert de Burgh was not as direct a man as Scarborough. "Just a friendly chat," the Norman parried. "You captured my interest when we met at Warenne Castle, and there remained many unanswered questions in my mind about you after you had left. Humor me!"

Scarborough was willing to humor the man. He signed for a serving woman to attend to them. A voluptuous maid with a wide, gap-toothed grin sidled up to them and was only too happy to run to their bidding. Scarborough then poured out a second tankard of beer for himself and then another, which he pushed across the planks to his companion. "What is it you wanted to know?"

"Simple things, really. For one, how you eluded the Marshal's scout men when you were released from prison—the second time, I believe."

Scarborough laughed and explained briefly how he had been able to hide a heavy bag of coins from his jailer, so that upon his release he still had the money to fling in the air to divert the men who were following him rather closely and clumsily. Scarborough had thrown three handfuls of coins in the air, and when the men stooped to scoop up the far-flung coins, Scarborough had made good his escape. "A child's trick," he concluded.

"Yet it worked," de Burgh observed.

"Whoever heard of a rich scout man?" Scarborough asked in return.

"Why, yourself, for instance," was de Burgh's reply, which only drew another laugh from Scarborough. "But I suppose that you must know that I have not come here to ask you idle and impertinent questions," de Burgh said after a sip of beer.

"At a guess, I would say that your visit to me has something to do with Mauleon," Scarborough replied.

De Burgh paused. "Indeed, it does. You appear to have the answers before I have posed the questions. But I have come with an offer of help."

"I need no help," Scarborough replied.

"I am sure that you do not. That is, you need no help from me to entrap him—if what you say about the evidence you possess against him is true."

"It is."

"Well, that matter is entirely up to you. You may entrap him how you want, but I merely offer myself as a witness."

"How would that serve you?"

"You are right! I have ulterior motives! Several, in fact," de Burgh said lightly. "How shall I say it? I've never liked the man Mauleon. As his equal in this world, I object to the way he assumes that he is more equal than the rest of us. He does nothing that is not politically motivated, has no thought for the common good, and is not quite as strong as he likes his reputation to claim he is. But I doubt that Mauleon's, ah, character defects are at the source of your problems with him, so I will not elaborate."

"I find the man easy enough to dislike," Scarborough agreed. "But why the need to help me or to witness anything?"

"My other motive." De Burgh smiled. "I have said that Mauleon has no feeling for esprit de corps, you see. If he wears your colors at a tournament, you never know that he will play on your side in earnest. He is out for himself. Having said this, I must confess to the virtue of being a team player. Not that I do not have other faults. But I do think of the common good. Now, I've spoken with William Marshal, and I have suggested your name as the king's counselor of trade and finance."

Scarborough shook his blond head.

"You are perfect for the position. Probably too perfect for your own good," de Burgh said after recruiting himself with a quaff of beer, "for the position would require that you stay more on land than you've been accustomed to doing these past years, unless I err? No? Good. As you know, the kingdom needs a few good men now, ones who have not been caught up in the struggles of the past years. Ones with unblemished reputations."

"You've come to the wrong address, then," Scarborough commented humorously.

The serving wench chose that moment to return to their table. She made sure to brush Scarborough invitingly with her breasts and hips. Scarborough obliged her by caressing her, somewhat absently, his smile indicating present preoccupation but a promise for entertainment later that night.

"Oh, I don't think so. We'll have trouble enough to put the rebel barons back in line once the worst is over."

"You are so sure that John will prevail?"

"Have you not heard the very latest?" de Burgh said. "Louis has suffered severely in skirmishes at sea of late. Danes sweeping down from the north, it is said. But you would not know anything about that, would you?"

Scarborough disclaimed any knowledge of battles at sea.

"Of course not," de Burgh continued affably. "How should you know anything about a roving band of Danes in wonderfully built ships who have come to scare the chausses off the Frenchmen? Their trick, by the by, has been to set fire to the enemy ships. Faith, but it takes a fearless and skillful band of sailors to travel with live fire as ammunition!"

"Perhaps they're foolhardy," Scarborough observed.

"Perhaps," de Burgh replied with good humor. "Now tell me about your wife."

"My wife?" Scarborough echoed with an inquiring cock to his brow.

"Do I tread on private ground?"

"Not at all. I have no wife."

"No?" de Burgh said, digesting the news. "I must beg your pardon for my vulgar curiosity. It is simply this: If you were to come into the government, you might want to consider bringing your household to London. Then again, perhaps not. You shall have to spend a lot of time here, and I thought that if you had an attachment to a wife or children who did not want to move . . . you see? Well, it seems we need not consider that aspect of things. Are you a widower, then, like myself, with sons?"

Again, no. Scarborough had never been married, and he had no sons.

Robert de Burgh was intrigued. He had construed that the enmity between Mauleon and Scarborough had as its source a woman. In any case he was heartened by Scarborough's single state. He thought a man could function better if he had no wife or at least a wife who could live comfortably in the atmosphere of the Royal Court. He had feared that Scarborough might have married some north-country townswoman wholly unsuited to live in London and the court.

"I can see that I need not have worried about any family entanglement," de Burgh said.

"Not at all. Worry rather about the fact that I am not sure that I am ready to leave the sea for land so permanently."

"Yes, well, there is that to consider. However, here you are now and not at sea with the other Danes," de Burgh pointed out shrewdly.

"This is different."

"Is it? What comes after you've entrapped Mauleon?"

"We shall have to see. I must get him first."

De Burgh nodded his head deferentially. "Tell me what I must do to help you to that end."

Scarborough came to a swift decision. He described to de Burgh how he had been leaving his rooms every evening, hoping to lure Mauleon's men. Scarborough had placed lookouts at various points in his evening route to detect any man that might chance to be following him. Nothing had happened that evening, so they would try again the next night. He would look for de Burgh's help then.

With that, at a quick close to the conversation, Robert de Burgh left the tavern.

Scarborough laid his coins on the table and made his way to the back of the establishment. The wench came up with the bold offer of herself. Scarborough considered her ripe charms, and although he easily could have been in the mood to sample her, he passed up the opportunity with no regrets. Only one woman would satisfy him now, and she was not available to him. He left the tavern, not by the front door but by a series of secret doorways in the back. In his own resourceful way Scarborough had discovered the existence of the communicating hallways between the Mortal Man and the Crown.

He made his way around the passageways and up the

back stairs to his room, so that no one would see him cross the inn's yard.

His footfall was at all times light, but the moment he turned down the hallway that led to his room and saw his chamber door half open, the sound of his boots on the planking became inperceptible.

Had one of Mauleon's men already come, then? Had the meeting he had just had with de Burgh in the tavern been planned by de Burgh and Mauleon together to give someone time to go through his room? Scarborough dismissed the thought. De Burgh had no reason to want to save Mauleon's neck.

Scarborough was hoping that it might be Mauleon himself in the chamber. He approached the door with extreme caution and reassured himself with the palm of his hand against the butt of the dagger in his belt.

He had left the shutters on his window open. The moonlight was streaming in, so that when he came to the door, he saw perfectly well the outline of a kirtle and cloak in woman's form, turned away from him and busy at the chest upon which stood the decoy prayer missals. Scarborough's lips curled as he took up a negligent position against the jamb. How like Mauleon to send a woman for the job!

"I am here now, wench," he said, "so there's no need for disappointment."

At the sound of his deep voice Katherine whirled to the door. Her hood fell back to expose her face, pale and beautiful in the moonlight.

Scarborough's sardonic smile became fixed. He straightened himself from the door and took several steps into the room. "Well, now," he said in his low, gravelly, nerve-tingling voice. "Mistress Katherine."

Katherine's wits had scattered upon the sight of him. She had thought him far beyond city walls. She was unprepared for the leap of her heart, a leap which was not entirely the result of fear. But the lump in her throat was, and she swallowed it painfully. "Master Eric," she replied. Her voice was hardly more than a whisper.

"Looking for something?"

The scorn in his voice was unmistakable. Her wits had

flown, but she was a woman in the presence of the love who had abandoned her. She obeyed her heart and said the first words that come to her.

"I came looking for you," she said with relative calm, but she could not raise her voice to its normal level. "I have not had long to wait." She turned to lean against the chest in what looked to be a casual gesture but which, in reality, provided her her only support. Her legs had buckled underneath her.

He glanced over her shoulder at the top of the chest. The missals were in the exact position he had left them. She had not had a chance yet to discover that they were fakes. Very well, then. His eyes narrowed into gray slits when they shifted back to Katherine. "You came looking for me?"

"Yes."

He came another few paces toward her until he could look down into her lovely wide eyes. They held his steady. He shook his head slowly. "London's a big place. How did you know where I was staying?"

"I saw you going through the market today and followed you here," she said faintly.

Did she expect him to believe that? After all the trouble he had taken to alert Mauleon's men of his whereabouts, it would have been far easier for her to have had the information from Mauleon. The only time he had crossed the market was that afternoon. The chances that she happened to see him then were one in a thousand, at best. She must have succumbed to Mauleon's power and promises. Mauleon must have sent her this night, knowing that if she were discovered in his room, she would have the perfect excuse to be there.

"Planning a pleasant surprise for me this evening, then, mistress? I am entirely captivated!" The savage irony in his voice was biting. "You did not think, of course, to catch up with me and simply speak with me—that is, when you say you saw me earlier in the streets?"

Katherine's eyes cooled. "Oh, yes. I should have hailed you in the marketplace and demanded to know, in full view of the interested, why you left York so abruptly. Should we have put on a show for the otherwise jaded marketers? I confess that my sense of drama does not lead me that far. I thought it much more . . . more appropriate and reasonable to come tonight, to find out from you alone and with a little privacy."

"And you thought to find me here, and when I was not here, you waited for me?"

"Here you are," she replied evenly, "and here I am, awaiting you and your explanation."

He laughed derisively, under his breath. "So you want explanations from me?"

The attraction between them was a physical force, never stronger or more potent, with memory firing anticipation where this meeting would end and nearness fanning desire. Yet the contradictory forces that drew them together also pushed them apart and were never more repellent in this moment of doubt and estrangement.

Scarborough moved a step closer. They were but a breath apart. Katherine's lashes flickered, but her gaze never wavered from his. "Yes, I want an explanation," she said shakily. Moonlight touched her hair and skin, making them glow.

Scarborough obliged her. "When I left your house several week ago, I was apprehended in front of the Blue Swan by three of John's men and was thrown into the Tower," he said.

Katherine drew in a sharp breath. Did he expect her to believe that? The timing of events was too much for her to allow.

"I see," she said. "Emma would relish the excuse." But she did not, and that much was obvious.

The moonbeams were striking right down into her eyes, green, luminiscent pools, like the limitless ocean at night. The whole of the heavens were reflected in her eyes, he thought, the stars that were so unattainable to him and the feathery wisps of cloud rack. He knew of only one way to break the spell she had over him. He reached out and caught her shoulders. His light touch was deceptive, for she was unable to shake herself free.

"I, on the other hand, was wholly taken in by Godric's explanation of where you were spending your time this month."

"You returned to York?" she asked, surprised.

"After I was released from the Tower," he said.

"But of course," she said. "You must have forgotten to take something with you when you left so quickly."

"I did," he said.

Katherine, looking up at him, saw him consider her just so and saw the desire kindle in the depths of his gray eyes. Reason counseled her to take flight but was impotent against the rush of an answering desire she felt well up in her. It had been just a little pebble at their first meeting, the attraction between them, then a stone gathering momentum over the months that instantly swelled to larger proportions that moonlit night to become a millstone that threatened to drag her down with it. She tried desperately to shrug it off. She opened her mouth to accuse him of having taken the prayer missals and, with them, all her safety and ambition, but the effort was forestalled when his lips imprisoned hers.

He wanted to hear no more lies from her now and encircled her with his arms to cajole each of her curves into its rightful place against him. A sailor subject to tides and the pull of the moon, he found that he could not resist Katherine. If she would not tell the truth with her words, then he would draw her secrets out in another fashion. Her passion did not lie, at least, and he would satisfy himself with that, if nothing else. They could speak later, or never, and if he never heard another word from her, it would be enough to have her in his arms.

She did not attempt to draw away. The torrent of desire, satisfied once between them, had become an urgent need. All other thoughts rolled away. Their partnership was over; the issue of money was gone between them. Only desire raged between them, far stronger than their distrust, and when his lips came down on hers to claim them, Katherine knew that she would not resist, could not resist, the seduction of his light, provocative, indulgent kisses that drew the breath from her body.

She allowed her cape to fall to the floor and wrapped her arms around his neck and responded to his kisses with the abandon and intensity of a long-awaited dream. He kissed the dimpled corners of her mouth, seeking their shape and their fullness eagerly and insistently, exploring their sweep and curve in delight, claiming the trembling softness once more, and she was totally lost.

His lips left hers to explore her neck and throat and breast beneath her dress. His hands roamed at will. This was how they best spoke with each other, with hands and lips and bodies; this was how they were meant to be, and Katherine did not protest further or try to deny her fate in his hands.

He pulled her toward the bed and she did not resist. She knew that he had it within his power to destroy her and all her careful plans, but she would not deny the needs of her traitorous body to find the satisfaction only he could give her. He quickly shed his tunic and chemise and slipped his hands inside the neck of her kirtle and gently pulled on the lacings so that it fell in a heap at her feet. Then he took her in his arms again, and they were both shocked and exhilarated by the feel of his skin against her thin chemise. This, too, was cast aside, and then he laid her down with him on the sheets of the bed. His thumb found the hollow beneath her jaw, sending waves of pleasure through her as his hand traveled down the length of her satin body. He did not hurry. He drew long kisses from her instead, an intimate mingling of lips and breath, and then kissed her yet again, hardly aware himself of how thoroughly she had come to obsess him, knowing only that he was determined to taste again the secrets of her body, how he must have her again and again.

The desire flared out in earnest and engulfed them with its urgency, and suddenly Katherine was overwhelmed by the force of their passions and was ready to give herself to him without reservation.

"Why have you come?" he asked into her ear before he would bury himself in her. "Tell me."

"For this," she replied, unable to formulate any other answer or remember why it was that she had come. It seemed impossible that she had not been bound to him body and soul from the moment she had laid eyes on him.

"I thought you a product of my imagination," he said, "when I first saw you here."

"No, I am very real," she said with a throaty laugh. "Never more so."

They were alone in a world of their own, on the verge of fulfilling the desire that consumed them both, so that they did not immediately perceive the heavy tolling of bells that had begun first in the northern quarter of London. The ringing of the bells spread, little by little, until all the bell towers were alive with it, and the tolling became a din that would awaken the dead and all sleeping souls.

Shouts started from the streets and in the courtyard of the Crown. The curfew was fully broken, and there reigned a pandemonium in the streets. Lanterns were lit and robes hastily donned as the city folk were roused from their beds and ran to windows to raise the sash and to hear the criers spreading the word "King John is dead! The king is dead! King John is dead!"

The flames of desire, far from quenched of their own accord, were suddenly doused by the shouts in the street. Scarborough lifted his head, his eyes dark with desire, and looked into Katherine's. It was as if he did not at first believe what he had heard. He ran a finger down her face to her throat and breast and to the curve of her hip. She quivered in exquisite pleasure that so minimal a gesture could keep the flames leaping between them. He bent to kiss her again, intending to complete what he had set out to do, but the cries from the street penetrated the room again: "King John is dead! The king is dead!"

Katherine struggled to her senses. "What?"

Scarborough looked down at her. "What we have all been waiting for," he said, his deep voice husky.

Katherine had not been hoping for John's demise.

Heavy bootsteps thundered in the hallways, in the courtyard and street. There came a pounding of fists on Scarborough's door and a recommendation that he rise and hear the news that was spreading like wildfire through the royal city.

"The king is dead! Long live the king!"

"What king?" Katherine dared to ask.

"Who is to know?" Scarborough replied. "Tell me instead where you are staying in London."

The fist beat a second time on the door. "Eric! Eric! Are you there?"

Scarborough answered quickly. "Here, Hardolf! I'm coming!"

"Good news, Eric! John is dead!" the man's voice answered.

"Where are you staying?" Scarborough demanded of Katherine again.

She hesitated. The moment of indecision would cost her dearly.

The flames in his eyes had cooled with her hesitation, but he still wanted her. He slipped his arm around her shoulder again to draw her to him, but then Hardolf, in his impatience, kicked the door in with his foot. What he saw made him grin, for Katherine had quickly snatched the covers up to her chin. The henchman commented crudely, cursed, and recommended that his master be quick on his feet.

Scarborough did not want to go, but his future was at stake. He did not ask Katherine again where she was staying, and because of the suddenly cold look in his eye she did not volunteer the information. Yet he knew that he would find her again and finish what had been started that night. However, for the moment, Scarborough hastily dressed and was quickly gone. Desire had to wait upon destiny.

___ Chapter 20 ___

Stephen Webster had been shocked at his first experiences in London. He had expected the elegance of the royal city to surpass what he dismissed as the unenlightened pretentions of York, but he had not quite prepared himself for the brawling, sprawling life within Londontown walls and all its attendant annoyances. First had come the numerous tolls. Stephen had been surprised by the numbers of coins he had had to dispense for passage in and across the city, then frankly scandalized by the audacious prices that were demanded for mediocre lodgings. The most common food and drink were, furthermore, not as well prepared or as copious as those same dishes presented to the traveler to York; and while the magnificent quarters of London were more magnificent than those of York, the dirty quarters were certainly dirtier. He quickly discovered that dishonest merchants could survive very nicely in the crowded anonymity of London. He had always been irritated that in York everyone knew everyone else, but he soberly reflected now that personal relations were far superior to unenforced laws as a way of controlling the quality and price of merchandise.

Stephen was a rich young man and had a ready store of coins to distribute as the occasions arose, but he had not spent the greater part of his life behind a cash counter for nothing. He was not as easily taken in as his open face and his expensive supertunic might have suggested to any number of sharp-eyed, sharp-dealing London merchants. Stephen found himself haggling (an activity he generally scorned) over pennies in a way that might ordinarily have made his father's chest swell with pride. However, not even knowledge of Stephen's newfound bargaining abilities would have alleviated the paternal rage that stormed in the senior Webster's breast since his feckless, disobedient offspring's disappearance from York in the week preceding his marriage to Eleanora Brewer.

Stephen had a vague notion that he would be in for the drubbing of his life upon his return to York, but he had thrust those highly uncomfortable thoughts to the back of his mind. Uppermost was Sybille: the fairest, rarest flower of beauty in all of England, and nothing—not the entreaties of his mother or the blusterings of his father or the beseeching, slightly predatory eyes of the plump and very rich Eleanora —would take him from his Quest for the Queen of Love. He had had to lower his dignity considerably in order to get on that noble road, however, by slinking out of York at the crack of dawn the day after he had discovered that his beloved Sybille had been swept from the city two days before originally planned. But once out of York, he was able to don his armor and raise his lance, figuratively speaking, and ride forth to London and to Sybille's rescue. His first few hours in the royal city alerted him to the fact that he had no very clear notion of how he was to go about finding her in the great throng crowding the streets, but he trusted to fate the discovery of a scheme to find her.

What he lacked in ideas he more than made up for in ardor, which was fired to new heat in any number of taverns in town frequented by the goliards, the footloose poets who strummed the viol and lived for love. He spent many hours in his first few days in London committing to memory valuable rhymes for *beauté* and *sagesse* and storing up new techniques to heighten poignancy (*Las! Las!*). These new arts would supply him with more than enough material to complete the several lyrics that were lying, half finished, on parchments under the counter of the till in Webster's shop on Petergate Square.

Stephen was savoring both his defiance of the curfew one night in a crowded tavern as well as one of the most beautiful canzonets he had ever heard sung by a trouvère, when the city bells began to toll ominously. The din was at first a nuisance to the audience hanging on every passionate warble from the trouvère's lips, but the continued ringing and the shouts in the street eventually drew the crowd out of the tavern to hear the stunning news that King John was dead.

Stephen was no more interested in politics than he was in the best prices on wool clips after the shearing. However, he knew his father's views well enough on the subject to guess that the demise of the hated ruler would be considered by Robert Webster a blessing in disguise. Sure enough, Stephen heard the first rumblings of sentiment in the street that night to the effect that although King John had not come to any good in this world and would not in the next, his dying was the very best thing he could have done for his people in the present circumstances. No need now for foreign intervention from the French, it was openly said, and the sooner Louis was off English soil, the better. John had an heir, a youth of some nine summers named Henry, and by God, had not the English people always liked the name Henry?

Stephen was not much concerned with such mundane matters as royal successions, but inspiration truly visited him

that evening. With the news of John's demise and the sense
he gained from the spontaneous comments he heard in the
streets, Stephen suddenly realized that Sybille's next move,
as dictated by her formidable sister, would most likely be in
the direction of William, High Marshal of England, whose
excellence Robert Webster had of late extolled. If Stephen
were to retrieve his beloved before her sister had married her
off to some unworthy nobleman, Stephen would find most
profit in searching in William Marshal's vicinity.

Stephen's intuitions ran true. Across town at the priory of
the Holy Trinity similar discussions were going forward in
this night of extraordinary news and more than one extraordinary encounter.

Far past the ten-o'clock bells, Katherine was making her
way back through a quickly torchlit London, rather dazed by
her own extraordinary and unexpected encounter with the
Viking. He had gone off with his men, leaving her incom-
plete and tantalizingly unsatisfied. On her way across town
she felt that a blazing torch had been thrust lit end into her
hand, and she did not know how to quench the flames. Then
she remembered Eric's cool slate eyes resting on her when
she had refused to give him her address, and she spent the
rest of the way back trying to put him out of her mind.

Katherine's musings came to a halt when she saw the
thicket of black-habited sisters milling with everyone else in
the alley in front of the priory. Beyond the nuns she saw
Emma and Sybille in company of a man she had not seen for
many months.

"By all that is wonderful!" Katherine exclaimed involuntarily. "Master Bar!"

"Aye, Mistress Katherine," the burly, blond Bar replied
"A long time it has been since we've seen one another in
York, and by Burgrune, if it's not fate that we meet again in
London!"

"A stroke of fate, indeed," Katherine concurred, and exchanged only a quick glance that read "no" with Emma
while Sybille stood sleepily at the serving woman's side
"But what brings you here? Why have we not seen you for
what, a six-month at least?"

"The sea swallowed me," Bar answered humorously

"and then not finding me to her taste, she spit me out again at the mouth of the Thames but not without my having first sent a few French ships to a watery grave!"

"Then you were amongst those Danes who sailed against Louis that we've heard so much about this fortnight past?" Katherine queried, and was conscious of the contrast between Bar's activities for the week and Eric's, and thus she had no reason to associate the two Northmen.

"That I was, and good sport it was too!" Bar answered. "The best I've had in the past five years," he added.

"Weren't you taking a chance, sailing against Louis?" she asked.

Bar shrugged cheerfully. "And so? What's the Frenchie to do if all his sailors are at the bottom of the sea? Besides, John is dead now, and Louis will find even tougher sailing ahead."

"I doubt that John's death will make much difference to Louis's activities. It might help him, in fact, what with the absence of a crowned head on the throne," Katherine reasoned.

Bar grinned. "But John's death leaves a clear and honorable path for William Marshal's plans. He's the one to follow, by England! You'll see. He wants to put John's son, Henry, on the throne."

Since Katherine had never heard William Marshal's well-known name on Eric's lips, she had, once again, no reason to associate Bar's sentiments or activities with her former partner's. She saw that before her arrival on the scene, Bar had been regaling Emma and Sybille with anecdotes of sea travel. In this happy reunion of old acquaintances politics was far from the most important topic at hand. Katherine let it drop while keeping mention of William Marshal's name in the back of her mind.

"How on earth have you met up with us now?" Katherine asked suddenly, still distrait in the wake of the quick series of events that night.

"Ran into Mistress Emma here and Mistress Sybille—straight into them!" Bar explained with an affectionate glance at Emma, who blushed. He went on to describe how he and his men had sailed into London earlier in the day and had taken to discovering London's pleasures. When the fuss and flap over John's death had begun, Bar went out in the streets with the rest of the world and, in his roaming about the warren of streets, happened onto the alley where stood the priory.

The crowds in the streets, restive but not unruly, displayed no inclination to disperse and seemed to want to make a night of it. The streets were alive with a buzz of activity. There was no telling, Bar stated after a while, when a mob could turn ugly. The people were not openly rejoicing the monarch's death, but they were not quite mournful, either. Bar decided it best if he stayed close by the women in the priory. He hustled off in search of the mother superior and explained to her that he and his men were going to stand guard in the courtyard of the Holy Trinity this night. Although the mother superior was reassured by Bar's bluffing good humor, she was given to understand that she did not have much choice in the matter of Bar's self-imposed guard. This rough seaman wanted his three women to have a peaceful rest, so he said, and he was going to insure that no one within priory walls would come into any danger. Bar recommended that everyone get back inside and that the heavy doors be firmly shut for the night.

Bar's concern for the ladies' safety was certainly gratifying to them, although his measures proved overcautious. The mood of the crowds that night and over the next few days did not grow ugly. The initial apprehension over the fate of the crown was too great, and the people had turned fiercely loyalist.

Before all else, the story of the Angevin ruler's demise on the nineteenth of October was on every Londoner's lips. The news had taken but a day to reach the ears of the royal city, so swift were the messengers. All talk that next day, the twenty-first, was consumed by the circumstances of John's death in the waters of the Wash, to the east of Newark. John had been traveling south at the time, on a raw and windy day, with all the royal regalia in tow, and had decided, impatiently, to cross the sandy fords where the River Glen and the Willestream flowed into a great basin of shallows known as the Wash, not far from Swineshead. John was convinced that they could safely cross, and he was the first to plunge his horse into the ankle-deep waters and to splash and gallop through the sands to the higher ground beyond. The rest of the troops had followed as quickly as they could, and it had seemed a certainty that the whole train would get over before the tide imposed any serious barrier.

However, what the king did not know, nor apparently did any of his advisers, was that the meeting of fresh and salt water often produced a swift and furious wall of water when the river met the inward thrust of the sea. When John had shouted the order for the wagon trains to advance into the waters, he had chosen the exact moment for the tide on the rise to swirl into a flash flood of enormous proportions.

With John was also swept out to sea the crown and scepter and orb of England, along with the cups of gold and white silver numbering nearly two hundred, the goblets and flagons, the rings, the jeweled belts, the pendants and the innumerable crosses, the clasps, and the unset rubies and emeralds and sapphires. This loss had been the very last wickedness of John. The Londoners proclaimed that he was so avaricious that even in death he had taken with him the great accumulation of England's wealth.

The consequences of John's death could now be confronted. It seemed at first, as Katherine had suspected, that the king's death would not interfere with Louis's claims on the English throne. The rebel barons supporting the Frenchman had sworn openly that they would not accept any of John's heirs as ruler of the land. Nevertheless, a few of the rebel barons began to perceive a change in the situation and found themselves in a tricky dilemma. Bound to the French prince by their oaths, they were realizing in the past weeks and months that they had sold themselves to a master as autocratic and unyielding as the dead John. Louis had already let them see that they would gain nothing if their efforts placed him in John's seat. Louis had not hesitated to hand over their lands and castles to the French knights he had brought with him. The whispers had become stronger that, once firmly in power, Louis would treat the rebel barons as traitors to an anointed king.

Robert de Burgh, as William Marshal's right-hand man in

town, had formed a fairly accurate idea of the grave obstacles that lay ahead, but he was convinced of the chances of success for John's son Henry. There were difficulties. Westminster Abbey, just outside the city walls, was still in the hands of the enemy. It would be a long job of detaching support from prince Louis. It would have to go man by man.

The first man that Robert de Burgh wanted out of the way was Cedric de Mauleon. De Burgh was looking forward to Mauleon's undoing, and he certainly did not want to miss the event. He hoped that Mauleon's removal would strike a telling blow to the heart of the rebel monster.

Mauleon was running scared. John's death, the open spark of sentiment against Louis that could be heard in the streets, and the perfectly legitimate successor to the crown in young Henry had made Mauleon's position precarious. He devoutly wished Louis to be on the throne and with as much haste possible. In the event that this did not come to pass, Mauleon knew for a certainty that he must retrieve the damning evidence against him in the York accounts. If they ever came to William Marshal's attention, this aging knight still wielded enough power to make Mauleon's life long in the Tower, or very short on the chopping block.

Being arrogant, Mauleon underestimated the intelligence of his enemies; being rattled by the implications of John's death, Mauleon became imprudent. He had threatened a visit to the lovely Mistress Katherine for the night after he had seen her in the street, the night of the twenty-first. He guessed that she did not have the prayer missals, but that was of little importance. If she did not in fact have them, he would make sure that she retrieved them for him.

Mauleon had had his little plans for doing away, once and for all, with his hated enemy, Eric of Scarborough, who had, Mauleon felt quite sure, the evidence against him. Then John's death changed everything. Mauleon needed to act swiftly if he were to insure his good name in the next government.

A number of Mauleon's men had fled London upon hearing the news of John's death. These cowards could not have been depended upon, anyway, Mauleon thought scornfully, to execute what needed so desperately to be done. Thus

Mauleon went himself, in company of two men, to the priory of the Holy Trinity early that evening. There, to his unpleasant surprise, he found the priory guarded by a pack of rough-looking, blond-haired thugs and wondered if Mistress Katherine had put them up to it.

Mauleon found none of this to his liking. Normally he would have demanded entry to the priory on the authority of King John, but he could not know in whose camp these crude fellows guarding the portals might be. If they were Louis's men, then that would be very well indeed. But if they had been installed there by William Marshal . . . Mauleon would not want to be identified later with anyone or anything having a connection to York. In this instance Mauleon chose caution.

He congratulated himself on his prudence and avoided thinking that his reluctance to enter the priory had anything to do with the fact that he was vastly outnumbered. Yet once again, Mistress Katherine had eluded him, and he was most displeased.

His irritability grew. He proceeded with his two men to the neighborhood of West Cheap, only to find that the men he had on lookout at the Crown Inn were no longer at their posts. Various possibilities for their disappearance occurred to Mauleon. Chief among them was the likelihood that they had been swept into some revelry or another. It did not enter his arrogant brain that Scarborough had effected their disappearance. He was operating at half the force he would have liked for the night he had ahead of him. If he had been of a less power-hungry nature, he might have noticed that the odds in his favor had been steadily dwindling and that he had more cause now than ever to be wary.

Mauleon was not sufficiently wary. Just as Katherine had done the evening before, he installed himself in the bakery across the street from the Crown and placed his two men at either end of St. Swithin's Lane. Like Katherine, he was highly pleased when Scarborough left the inn, empty-handed, a little before the curfew bells rang. Mauleon motioned for one of his two men to follow the Dane. The man came back quite a long time later and informed Mauleon that Scarborough, after taking a circuitous route through the city,

seemed to have left the walls through Cripplegate and could
not be expected back before the morning.

With a cock of his arrogant head Mauleon motioned that
the two men should follow him through the still-open gates
to the yard of the Crown. As before, Scarborough had taken
a quicker path back through town and had made his way
through the maze of passages that led from the Mortal Man
to the Crown's main hall. Scarborough had also bought the
entire inn for the night, which meant that there were no
longer any ordinary customers about. The people milling in
the courtyard through which Mauleon and his men crossed
were in Scarborough's employ. The two hostlers who closed
the portals behind them were not simply doing their nightly
duty but were rather closing the trap; and in the main hall
there would be no innkeeper. Scarborough, himself, was
there in company of some burly Danes; and Robert de
Burgh, with several of his men, was waiting as well, expectantly, in a brightly lit, low-rafted room.

It was on this unexpected scene that Mauleon and his two
men crossed the threshold of the door to the inn.

Mauleon heard the door shut behind him and the click of
the key in the lock. Across the room from him, leaning in-
solently on his unsheathed sword, was Eric, the deposed and
most unworthy Earl of Scarborough, smiling at him in a way
that Mauleon read in an instant. He turned rigid for one
frozen moment and tasted fear in his throat. He swallowed
and then advanced a pace into the room.

There were other faces, too, that Mauleon recognized.
With a curl to his lips he groped for the jewel-encrusted
ivory-and-gilt handle of his own sword. The ice-cold gems
against his sweating palm reassured him.

To this gesture Scarborough said in his deep, chilling
voice, "How well we understand each other, Mauleon."

Mauleon said nothing. He had momentarily lost his
tongue.

"But, naturally, I am flattered by your visit," Scarborough went on cordially. "I assume that it is in my honor that
you have come to the Crown."

All was not lost. "Why would you think that?" Mauleon

responded, the waxy, whiny character of his voice pronounced.

Scarborough straightened himself and reached over to the top of a nearby sideboard. He lifted up a thick, black book and waved it at Mauleon. "At my best guess I would say that you have come for this."

Mauleon's hatred leapt out of his face. He saw that the trap had been set very neatly. Witnesses abounded. Well, John's son was not yet on the throne, and Louis's forces were far from routed. "Why should I care about some book? —a prayer book, no less. I'm a God-fearing man and have my own breviary."

"I'm sure you own a score of them. But this one here, and another one," Scarborough said, pointing to the second missal, lying out of Mauleon's reach on the sideboard, "should interest you most particularly."

"Indeed? My only interest is to know why."

"In them are concealed the records over the past year of your financial support for Prince Louis of France through the intermediary, no less, of your half brother, Godric Fitz Osbert, Lord Mayor of York," Scarborough said carelessly.

The circle of faces surrounding Mauleon looked expectant. "At that statement I would be quite foolish to acknowledge them, would I not?" Mauleon pursued.

"It would be an open admission of treason," Scarborough concurred with a pleasant smile, "and surely deserving of strong censure once John's son succeeds to the throne."

Mauleon tried to shrug it off. "He is not yet on the throne, and I will maintain that you have entrapped me."

"Acute of you, Mauleon, to recognize entrapment," Scarborough returned. "I have taken a leaf out of your psalter and cordially return the favor you paid me on the very subject of slanderous treason against King John—for which I spent several months on holiday in the Tower."

"Revenge, Scarborough?" Mauleon chided. "I had not thought you so petty a man to stoop to it!"

The taunt fell wide of its mark. Scarborough replied promptly, "May I read that as a challenge?"

Mauleon was not yet prepared to go that far. "So quick to take offense, man," Mauleon replied with a snide chuckle, and tried to hit Scarborough at what Mauleon hoped would be a sore spot. "But so it is with a man who has no station in life."

"A sad circumstance I hope to alter soon," Scarborough answered, unruffled.

"The man's ambitious," Mauleon commented derisively to the room at large. His strategy, pitiful in its desperation, lay in swaying the men present against their acknowledged leader in Eric of Scarborough.

"You, Mauleon, fault me for that?" Scarborough laughed.

Mauleon attempted an equal lightness. "Upon my honor, Scarborough, you are determined to provoke me."

Scarborough's pleasant face turned into one of cool resolution. His gravelly voice scraped across Mauleon's nerves. "You have no honor, Mauleon."

The room stiffened expectantly.

"Now it is you who challenge me," Mauleon said, his eyes narrowing, his mind calculating rapidly. Scarborough had spent his time at sea and not training his sword arm on the field of battle. "But the odds are not good against me. I have but two men at my side and you have a dozen or more."

This drew another laugh from Scarborough. "Never fear, Mauleon. I challenge you to a fair fight. Your blood for mine! Do not think that you shall be set upon by four of my men, just as four of your men set upon me in Scarborough. I am recovered from the stab in the back, by the way, thanks to the ministrations of my sister, Gwyneth, and in fine form for a fight."

Mauleon's brows snapped together. He was certainly not going to admit to the ambush he had planned in the village of Scarborough, but mention of the fair Gwyneth and the insult Mauleon had suffered so long ago at Scarborough's hands drew Mauleon's anger, as it was intended to do.

Mauleon's lips writhed with a bitter, scornful smile. "It's a long list of grievances we have, Scarborough," he said waxily. Suddenly finding his own deep, vengeful urge to fight, he added with an undertone of savagery, "My God, how I've waited for this. I am glad that I am come, in sooth, if you offer me your blood."

The two men faced each other from across the points of their swords, two men in whom hatred, long ignited, burned still with a steady strength, too great to admit to half measures. It was to be the final fight between them; of that each man in the room was certain. Scarborough had no interest in killing his opponent. His revenge would be all the sweeter for bringing Mauleon to public justice.

The swords flashed a brief salute in the candlelight. The two combatants engaged one another with the scrape of steel on steel. Mauleon was the more experienced swordsman and the better trained. He opened with deft feints and parries and lunges and had the footwork to back them up. He was encouraged that he was going to have an easier time of it than he had at first hoped. His best thrusts, however, in those early minutes, did not take his opponent off-balance, but this was no affair of official rules or polite swordplay.

It was a grim fight, dangerous in its hard swiftness and brutal in its strength, where raw determination counted for more than skill. For each antagonist the world fell away. All their grievances leapt to the tips of their swords. There were no sounds but the ringing and clashing of steel, the scuffling of boot against wood, their breathing rasping and labored. Their eyes were on each other's, their faces set with the hatred that fired them both. Time after time Mauleon's feints and parries were met. Time after time his lunges passed just wide of the mark, and the determined fight went on, untiring.

Mauleon was beginning to fear that Scarborough was the stronger of the two combatants. The Norman nobleman had the advantage of practice, however, and used it to deliver a lightning thrust in a small opening Scarborough gave him. The point of Mauleon's blade caught Scarborough's sword arm and traced a bright red slash across the muscles that were standing out on it, ribbed and hard. Scarborough had no answering thrust. He disengaged his blade.

In spite of the wound there was no moment of check, which Mauleon had hoped to use to deadly advantage, and this was not a quarrel that would be decided by first blood. Scarborough's red slash was absorbed first by his chemise, which soon became soaked. His blood began to drip slowly on the floor.

"Had enough?" Mauleon jeered with deep satisfaction and obvious reference to Scarborough's gash.

"A flesh scrape only," Scarborough answered, "no depth." Indeed, Scarborough showed no signs of debilitation but maneuvered deftly around the sticky pool on the floor. "If you slip in it, Mauleon," he continued, "you have yourself to blame."

Rather than being impeded by his wound, Scarborough suddenly became more alive. Mauleon perceived this with his first feeling of real fear. Mauleon was not yet winded, but the meeting of blade against blade was relentless, and the pool of blood posed as much a hazard to himself as to his opponent. Mauleon attempted yet another thrust that barely touched Scarborough's side. Scarborough countered it swiftly and furiously, so that it was all Mauleon could do to protect himself against the fierce and deadly lunge. Mauleon did recover, but he was left panting slightly.

Mauleon kept to the attack, trying every trick he knew to draw Scarborough into exposing himself, every lure failing. Experience was on Mauleon's side; savagery on Scarborough's. After some long minutes of blade against blade, Mauleon's arm began to flag. His initial hatred of Scarborough had transformed itself into animal fright. He dimly recognized that a change had come. Scarborough was beginning at last to press the attack.

Great drops of sweat began to roll off Mauleon's forehead. He heard Scarborough speak, breathing very hard, yet his words were clearly spoken. "Did you come here for the prayer missals?"

"I came for your blood," Mauleon answered between breaths.

Scarborough was aggressively on the offensive. Mauleon could do naught but defend himself now, and even that was becoming increasingly difficult. Scarborough's point flashed in under Mauleon's guard but withdrew before it could do any damage.

Scarborough's intention was to demonstrate to his enemy

that he was controlling the match and would continue to control it until he had gotten Mauleon's confession.

"Did you come here—for the prayer missals?" Scarborough demanded again.

"I know nothing—of prayer missals," Mauleon panted in return.

With the response Scarborough attacked again, but in the opening he had created he deflected his blade from doing Mauleon harm. Mauleon comprehended in a flash Scarborough's intention. He understood that he was being spared, would be spared again, until he had answered the query. Did Scarborough think him a fool?

"You—know something of—Fitz Osbert," Scarborough said, "Lord Mayor of York."

Mauleon shook his head. He had little struggle left to waste in words or in attack. He was defending himself from force of habit now, his arm heavy and aching.

"He's your half brother, Mauleon," Scarborough said again. "You kept—illegal accounts—with him. Against John."

Mauleon grinned unpleasantly. "Why ask—me, then? When you—know—everything."

Scarborough had Mauleon cornered. The circle of men watching had fallen back to allow the movement of the two combatants. Mauleon saw the ring of faces before him. He saw Scarborough's object. The Dane wanted Mauleon's confession. He wanted Mauleon to admit in full hearing of a dozen witnesses his treason against John. He did not want to end Mauleon's life in this room. He wanted the satisfaction of public justice.

Mauleon, understanding revenge as well as the next man, had labored through Scarborough's motives. He had no desire to fall in with Scarborough's wishes or leave this room to be the object of a public execution, if Louis's forces were routed. At this point, even if Louis were to prevail, Mauleon would not be well regarded by the French prince for having his duplicity exposed in such a fashion by Scarborough. Mauleon would rather die in this room than remain alive at Scarborough's mercy, only to be later executed.

Mauleon was backed into a corner. The point of his blade was becoming extremely heavy. He could hardly keep it in front of him. Scarborough knew this. Instead of taking advantage of Mauleon's defenselessness, Scarborough ground him down.

"Admit your—duplicity, Mauleon."

"Never."

Scarborough lunged in but not to finish Mauleon off. With a quick feint of his sword Scarborough managed to fling Mauleon's weapon out of his hand. The metal clattered on the floor with a deadly sound. Mauleon's arm dropped, his shoulder sagged. He was looking directly on the point of Scarborough's blade.

"Admit it," Scarborough demanded.

Defeat brought out the worst in Mauleon. He and Scarborough were old enemies, always in each other's way, always wanting the same things. The idea that had been dancing around the edges of Mauleon's brain suddenly, and in the face of death, jelled into perfect form.

Mauleon sobbed for breath. "I am not—the only one—involved."

"You're at the—head" came the reply. "We—the Marshal and young Henry—cannot prosecute—all of York."

Mauleon shook his head. "Not—everyone. But there is one—person who should be—implicated with me."

The room was hushed. Into the expectant silence came Mauleon's gasping words, "Mistress—Katherine the—Broiderer."

The murderous look that sprang into Scarborough's eye confirmed the accuracy of Mauleon's verbal thrust. The Norman had no steel at his command, but the poison in his tongue was alive and flowing.

"So," Mauleon stated derisively and with deep satisfaction. He had caught a second wind and a means of his ultimate revenge against Scarborough. It had come, as it had always come between them, to the same desire. They both wanted the same woman. Mauleon had never been able to have his little broiderer, and now he knew why she had managed to elude his charms for so long. With death imminent, Mauleon would derive a measure of gratification by poisoning Scarborough against Mistress Katherine the Broiderer.

"She's played you for a fool," Mauleon said with malice aforethought. "She thought as much."

Scarborough's blade chillingly touched the wild pulse at Mauleon's throat, bringing another spurt of venom to Mauleon's tongue. "At last I surprise you, Scarborough," he said.

"No, you never surprise me," Scarborough replied, and appended an assessment, stated in explicitly crude terms, of Mauleon's character.

Mauleon merely laughed. "You had thought her so pure, your little broiderer. Her name is Katherine, after all. How sad for you to discover from me, of all people, that she does not live up to her name or her saintly reputation. Or do you already know differently—as I do?"

"You know nothing, Mauleon," Scarborough said. A deadly chill had frozen his voice.

"Do I not?"

Scarborough's blade itched Mauleon's throat. Mauleon had a foretaste of death.

"I know enough to have seen her last night," Mauleon lied.

Scarborough shook his head. "You don't know where she's staying in London," he said.

Mauleon smiled. "She's at the priory of the Holy Trinity," he said with great confidence, adding an inspired thought, "Planning when and how to place all her money behind Prince Louis of France." Mauleon paused, pleased to see his venomous lies biting deep into Scarborough's veins. Mauleon drew a long breath and, for his last, vicious words on earth, said, "She made me a happy man last night, Scarborough. An exceptionally happy and satisfied man."

For an answer Scarborough thrust his blade deep into Mauleon's throat, but sudden death did little to alter the smile of sly triumph that had come to rest on Mauleon's twisted lips.

___Chapter 21 ___

Knowing nothing of what had happened the night before at the Crown Inn, Katherine set into vigorous motion her plans for Sybille's reinstatement. The time for hedging her bets was over; the time for action had arrived. Prince Louis had the advantage of occupying Westminster, and he still held sway over London and a good part of the south of England. Anyone banking on sheer force of character would have had to back Louis. He was austere and tenacious, and once roused to the notion of the conquest of England, he was unlikely to leave before a long, well-organized pitch of battle, and once engaged, he was not the sort to hesitate draining the coffers of his father, Philip Augustus, to achieve his goal. Nevertheless, Katherine decided instead to channel all her money in support of the late King John's nine-year-old son, pretty little Henry Plantagenet.

Katherine's decision had been growing on her for some time, but the impetus came from several of her conversations with Bar, who, during the day and a half of his unofficial guardianship of his three ladies at the priory, assured her cheerfully that the strength of Louis's forces would be slowly but surely dissipated by an "incompetence among the rebel barons unmatched even among John's chief functionaries" and that the man to back was William Marshal. She had long been for Louis on the strength of York sentiments, but with John's death she knew that all that had quite possibly changed in York and that one had to look to the greater good of England now.

In choosing to support the Marshal, Katherine satisfied her innate political sense and appeased her emotional preferences. She saw the wisdom of supporting the man whose name was synonymous with that of England. She had come to love the island home that the twists of fate had thrust upon her, and since she cast her fortunes with that of England, her political intuitions counseled her that the Marshal would make the best man behind the throne. At the same time, if the Frenchman did ascend to the throne and recognized the daughter of the Duc de Roncevaux, he might make an alliance between her and one of his noblemen in France. The unexpected thought came to Katherine that too much had happened for her to consider ever returning to France. Neither could she bear the idea that her sister might reside so far away.

Katherine thrust to the back of her mind Master Eric's possible motives for having desired John's death, or that the backing of William Marshal was what he had had in mind all along; and she stoutly refused to consider what might be the fate of the prayer missals in his hands.

She naturally mentioned none of her misgivings to Bar, nor did Bar, who was mindful of his earlier orders to stay away from Mistress Katherine, have any reason to enter Eric of Scarborough's name into their talk. When Bar removed himself from his guardianship at the priory of the Holy Trinity to regain Eric's company across town, he said nothing to Eric of his associations of the past days with the Mistresses Katherine, Emma, and Sybille. Bar said merely that he had been carousing with the rest of London since his return to land. In any case, Bar's attention was immediately taken by the details of Mauleon's death, which his cohorts were only too happy to relate to him with relish.

Katherine acted swiftly. She had little difficulty determining William Marshal's whereabouts. Among the people in London who were turning so fiercely royalist, Katherine learned quite easily that the Marshal had designated the ancient Roman city of Gloucester as the temporary royal seat and would, most probably, be stationed there himself. Accordingly, Katherine sent forth two strategic missives, one to William Marshal, Earl of Pembroke, at Gloucester; and another to Baruch of Coney Street. She also made swift preparations for removal from London to Gloucester. Emma approved but Sybille groaned. Once again Sybille had seen her hopes of being rescued by Stephen in London come to nothing.

In her lovesick state, Sybille underestimated the resourcefulness of her swain in those days following the news of King John's death. Stephen Webster, guided by his intuitions and abreast of affairs of state, also removed himself from London in the direction of Gloucester. Stephen was not the only one heading in that direction, either. Most of the advisers of the late king were on their way to Gloucester, at the Marshal's behest, from Newark where they had seen John buried, and all of them were aware that the greatest haste was necessary to keep the reins of government in English hands.

William the Marshal was already in Gloucester with Henry and Henry's mother, Isabelle, when the advisers arrived. It was decided that in spite of the difficulties which stood in the way of a proper coronation, the boy Henry should be crowned without any delay. With the crown swept out to sea with all the royal regalia, and with Westminster in the hands of the enemy, it was apparent that the crowning would have a preliminary character, with an eye to a more regular and properly imposing ceremony later. First, however, the young prince had to be knighted, and it was agreed that the old Marshal, who had performed the service for King John, should officiate. The coronation, performed on the twenty-eighth of October, scarcely a week after King John's death, was held in the presence of a small group of bishops and earls instead of an assembly of all the great men of the kingdom in their finest robes and glittering jewels. In the stead of the proper crown a plain gold circlet was placed on the head of the third Henry of England; and once this necessary and symbolic transference of power had been carried out, the Marshal breathed a sigh of relief and called for the real business of the government to begin.

The Marshal called a meeting in the beautiful Royal Court of neighboring Lancaster the day after the coronation. The Lancaster court was an imposing and rather elegant jumble of stone buildings whose crowded gables rose above the mellow gray walls of the city and whose stained lozenge windowpanes caught and reflected the late October sun from every conceivable angle. A cloistered chapel of noble proportions sat upon the waterfront that snaked through the court grounds, and somewhere in the maze of buildings there stood the countinghouse where the banking of the country had been carried out since the days of the young Henry's grandfather, Henry II, and great-grandfather, Henry I.

On the day after the coronation the new counselor of trade for the fledgling government, Eric, Earl of Scarborough, could be found in this countinghouse. With a heavy frown between his brows, he was reviewing the economic disaster of the last years of John's rule. His men, hailed and well met after the satisfying victories over the French at sea, were roaming the hallways, sauntering and swaggering with their newfound importance and engaged in comradeship with the likes of the men who owed allegiance to such notables as Robert de Burgh and the Earl of Warenne.

An assortment of bishops and earls could be identified in the hallowed hallways. One unmourned absence was often remarked upon, and that was the absence of Cedric de Mauleon.

The Marshal was eager to draw to his cause any and all names of wealth and worth. He had received a most interesting and intriguing missive from the House of Roncevaux, with a pledge of money of rather splendid proportions that could not be ignored, and made arrangements for an audience with this slightly mysterious party for that very afternoon. With the flurry of movements and activities the Marshal had not had a chance properly to inform his inner circle of men of the forthcoming audience.

Having finally arrived at the moment she had been planning for over six years, Katherine's misgivings threatened to engulf her. She was invaded by a dull, lifeless feeling. She relied heavily on Emma for equilibrium during that morning, and Emma had done a masterful job of coaxing Sybille into her most obedient manner. The three women were led up to an antechamber to await the Marshal's summons. Emma was dismissed with the assurance that she had free access to the various public hallways of the building. Katherine was left to wait with Sybille.

Emma went on her way. To her profound surprise she
crossed paths with Bar not many minutes later. When they
had both sufficiently recovered themselves from the shock of
this highly unexpected encounter, they began to unravel the
identities of the players of the scene that would soon be
taking place in one of the upper rooms. In the receiving
chamber sat Eric of Scarborough in company of William the
Marshal, Robert de Burgh, and the Earl of Warenne, awaiting the admission of Katherine de Lunais and her half sister,
Sybille de Roncevaux.

"But let me see if I understand you correctly, Master
Bar," Emma said to the first disclosure. "Your master is the
reinstated Earl of Scarborough and a newly appointed king's
counselor?"

"As good as reinstated," Bar said. "Counting on Young
Henry's eventual success."

Emma continued with trepidation. "And he is the one we
have known for the past six months as—as— No! I cannot
credit it."

"The Viking," Bar supplied, and added with pride, "Aye!
Knud's son, or Eric Shipwright, if you prefer. A fine
shipwright, too, I might add, and an even better sailor and
trader. My master!"

Emma felt affronted. "And you say that you have known
this the entire time that he was in partnership with Mistress
Katherine?"

"Eric ordered me to stay away from York," Bar affirmed
with a wink. "And I'll admit to missing my Emma, but it's
not as if there is any harm done now. I always knew that
there was something special about Mistress Katherine, think
on! I'm not a bit surprised."

"Not surprised? I'm entirely overcome," said Emma, who
was absorbing with difficulty the revelation of the Viking's
identity and envisioning the possible outcome of the meeting
between the former partners in Leofwyn Shippers.

Bar rose manfully to the occasion by permitting himself a
comforting arm around Emma's shoulder and a quick
squeeze. "Well, now, if anything's changed, it's for the better. The ban on my movements in York will be lifted, and

I'll be coming to see you again. Maybe on a more regular basis," he added, with a hopeful lift to his brows.

Emma shook her head. "I don't know that we'll be returning to York. Mistress Katherine seemed reluctant to pull up stakes, I'll admit. But that was before, before—well, I'm thinking that she might not want anything to do with York, or London, or England, when she finds out who the new counselor is! I wonder if it will be too late now for her to back Louis?"

Bar laughed. "Far too late! And I don't think the Frenchman is long for England now. The betting in the taverns give him three months at most! He'll pursue a winter's campaign, but it will scatter his forces, and by the springtime, we'll see him take to what ships he has left and leave the island forever."

Emma was not appeased. "Are you so sure?"

"With Eric of Scarborough behind the Marshal, Young Henry is as good as king!"

Emma admired this confidence of man to master, but she shook her head again. "It is not good," she said dourly.

"They're on the same side now, your Mistress Katherine and my Eric! It will all turn out for the best," Bar predicted.

"I do not think you fully understrand how it stands between my mistress and your master," Emma insisted. "Or exactly what has happened in the last months."

Bar grinned. "Mayhap I do, mayhap I don't. But I do know my cautious Emma, and she's a worrier," he said with gruff affection. "I assure you that there is nothing to fret about. From here on out it will be smooth sailing. You'll see."

Bar's optimism was misplaced. Although the details eluded him, he did have a fair idea of how matters stood between Eric and Katherine. With regard to the imminent meeting between Katherine de Lunais and Eric of Scarborough, however, Bar had underestimated the depth of feeling that ran between the former partners and uncertain lovers. He could not guess at the strong, often repellent chemistry between the two. He could not predict the force of the clash when sun and moon would come to inhabit the skies at the same time. He had reckoned without two powerful factors:

Katherine's fierce determination to accomplish her goal and Cedric de Mauleon's perfidy, which still reached out from his ignominious grave to poison Eric of Scarborough's thoughts.

Unaware of what awaited her on the other side of the heavy door, Katherine sat on the settle in the antechamber with apprehensions crowding in on her. A glorious autumn sun warmed the chamber and fell with divine luminosity on the perfection of Sybille's face and figure, partially dispelling Katherine's fears.

Sybille, more beautiful in her misery at the prospect of a brilliant, undesired marriage but unable to withstand the strength of her elder sister's convictions, was suitably demure. She was dressed in a heavenly blue kirtle that matched her eyes and which was caught at all her curves by a lighter blue bliaut. Over her hair she wore a brief lace-and-linen wimple, and her throat gleamed with the gold Roncevaux signet on a thin gold chain.

Katherine had chosen for herself a magnificent green watered samite, rich in hue and elaborately embroidered by her own skillful fingers, with slippers of a matching fabric that she had had made for herself in London. A simple caul of seed pearls held her heavy auburn hair. She was otherwise innocent of jewelry.

The Marshal ran an efficient operation. There was little time to wait before Katherine de Lunais and Sybille de Roncevaux were sonorously summoned and ceremoniously announced to the small party assembled in the counting chamber.

The two young women were ushered, eyes properly lowered, into a stately room of quiet proportions, heated by two blazing fireplaces and with a beamed ceiling from which were already hung the new green-and-gold silken banners of the young Henry's reign, satisfying the Marshal's vigilant eye for symbolic display. The masonry walls, covered with bright tapestries which rustled and arrested the drafts of winter, were broken by long, arched, mullioned windows. The mellow light of late October streamed in to gild the deep oak parquetry of the floor and gleam in the depths of the dark, aged ash table and chairs upon the raised dais which occupied center place in the room.

The table was set impressively with two silver ewers and six weighty silver chalices, heavily embossed and chased, and several branches of tall candlesticks, as yet unlit. In addition to the Marshal, who came instantly forward to receive the women, were three other men whose standing forms Katherine glimpsed upon entering.

The two women were made known to Gaston Parmentier, the Earl of Warenne, whose besotted expression indicated that he had fallen instantly and indifferently in love with both beauties, and to Robert de Burgh, who smiled and bowed to their graceful curtsies. The young widower had not been looking forward to this routine, possibly dull session, but upon sight of the two women, he suddenly could not have imagined any place on earth he would have rather been just then than in the counting chambers of Lancaster Castle.

"Les demoiselles de Lunais et de Roncevaux," the Marshal repeated a third time, continuing his introductions. "Eric, Earl of Scarborough. The king's Counselor of the Exchequer."

Katherine curtsied low to the third man, and when she raised her eyes again, it was to look straight into the flinty gray eyes of the Earl of Scarborough.

She felt an undeniable jolt at the sight of him, but in the split second that their eyes met, she was aware only that she had seen that look from him before. Her immediate thought was the calm reflection: *So now we're quits.*

His appraisal of her was as remote and considering as it had been that moment so long ago at her house in Jubbergate Street when he had announced to her his identity as the Viking and his intention of collecting on her debt to him. Now, of course, it was necessarily different: she was a Norman noblewoman, and he the king's counselor and an earl. With their new identities came new territory, and all her questions now had answers which fell wonderfully well into place.

Rather than being shattered by this encounter, Katherine felt instead anchored, as if an essential piece of her being had been missing and was suddenly supplied by his presence. A candle was lit inside of her at the sight of him, and the cold weight of her uncertainties vanished in this new light. The strength of her resolve, which had quavered before coming into the room, came to new, fiery life in that instant of recognition. She knew herself to be equal to the occasion.

She willed her knees to obey her, and when she had executed her curtsy, she straightened and murmured his name and title in greeting, as was expected of her.

"Demoiselle de Lunais, a pleasure," he replied. His voice, in Katherine's native tongue, was exactly as she might have imagined it to be. The deep resonances streaked across her nerves. "And Demoiselle de Roncevaux, your servant."

Katherine glanced at Sybille, who had also suffered something of a shock at the sight of the man they had known as Master Eric, but fortunately for Sybille, nothing more than a graceful curtsy was expected of her, and her stricken silence went unnoticed.

The Marshal bade everyone be seated and opened the meeting on a congenial discussion of the previous day's coronation, appending some observations of the prospect that one day Henry III would be seated on the proper throne in Westminster and that the troublesome Frenchman would once and for all be driven from the island kingdom to which he could not, the Marshal insisted, legitimately lay claim.

Katherine recognized her opening. "And it is to that end that I am come," she said with a straight look at William Marshal, "in that you and I, as supporters of King Henry, now share a common purpose."

"Why, yes, Demoiselle de Lunais," the Marshal agreed. "You wrote me to that effect. I confess that the new government is in sore need of sums of money, and there is hardly a moment to waste. You have contacted us at a very opportune time, for we shall be moving into a major campaign in a matter of days. But we shall come to all of that presently," he said, then continued, "However, I had imagined you somewhat different, demoiselle, and now that I have seen you, I would like to hear something of your story. I gather that you have been in England for some time, although your family lands are in Languedoc, are they not?"

"Not my family's," Katherine corrected with a nod to Sybille, "but my sister's, the daughter of the Duc de Roncevaux. And, yes, the lands are—were—in Languedoc, though no doubt now in the hands of Simon de Montfort. I have received no word as to the fate of the Roncevaux demesne, as much as I have tried to learn of it in the past years. I do not hope to retrieve them. But to answer your question: We have been here six years, almost seven now."

"Such a long time!" the Marshal exclaimed. "I would not have thought it. I had imagined—but that is of no moment. Where have you been all this time?"

"In York," Katherine answered steadily. "For four of the years."

William Marshal shot a glance at Scarborough, who was regarding Katherine impassively. "But do you not know each other already?" the Marshal was surprised into asking.

"We might have met once or twice at the market," Katherine said.

"Perhaps at the summer fair I saw Demoiselle de Lunais," Scarborough interjected in unison.

Robert de Burgh smoothed over the suddenly charged moment by asking Katherine if she had not felt out of place in Saxon York.

Katherine smiled charmingly at the handsome widower. "Not at all," she replied. "York was a decent place to settle down, and I have nothing but good to say of the Saxon citizens of York."

"A sentiment shared by our counselor of trade, I believe," Robert de Burgh commented with a nod to Scarborough.

The Earl of Warenne was heard to mutter something about the horrid fate of living with a lot of Saxons, but Katherine ignored this by smiling again at Robert de Burgh. "Indeed?" she said.

De Burgh, an undemonstrative man, appeared to be affected by the smile, for his fingertips began to drum very gently on the arm of his chair. He did not have an opportunity to pursue inquiries into Saxon York, for the Marshal was not going to let the reins of this particular conversation leave his capable, old hands.

"And you have been quite alone all this time?" William asked.

"Absent of male company, if that is what you mean," Katherine replied, not mincing matters. "My sister and I, that is. The two servants we arrived with in England have since died, but upon arriving in York, I found and engaged another woman. She accompanied us this morning, in fact."

"Why, yes, I see," the Marshal said, not seeing anything at all. "How came you to settle, as you say, in York?"

Katherine explained, calmly and clearly, that she had fled Castle Roncevaux after the massacre of her family and folk during the early days of the Albigensian Crusade. Since Roncevaux was under the formal jurisdiction of John of England at that time and at war with Philip Augustus, Katherine had not thought it prudent to seek refuge at the French court. Seven years ago, with the admittedly limited political lights of a girl of seventeen, she had decided that the salvation of what was left of the Roncevaux name lay far across the Channel of England. Sybille had been coached to supplement Katherine's recital of the family's misfortunes at various intervals.

The losses suffered by Katherine and Sybille during the Albigensian Crusade struck a sympathetic chord in Gaston Parmentier. He had seen a good deal of his own land holdings swallowed up in the bitter fighting and ruthless destruction that marked the sectarian differences between the Abigenses and the orthodox papists.

"Heretics, all of them!" Parmentier exclaimed, with a sweeping condemnation of both sides of the religious issue. "The fighting has been going on already, what, seven or eight years now, and there's no end of it in sight. Why, one would have thought that the Church Council decree last year condemning the Albigenses might have done something to abate the fighting, but no! It goes on worse than ever." The earl caught his breath and asked the direction question, "What religious position did your family hold, demoiselle?"

Katherine folded her slim white hands on the tabletop. "We—my mother and my mother's husband, the Duc de Roncevaux—were true followers of Pope Innocent the Third, sire, and did not hold with the principles of the Cathari of Albi. We believed in One Being. However, since the Albigensian invasion of Roncevaux, I have had occasion to ponder their belief in the existence of two supreme beings, one good and the other evil. If one accepts this Manichaeism, one might then identify the Albigensians as the embodiment of their own principle of evil in this world."

Parmentier smiled at this sophism. "Something of a student of philosophy, are you?" he asked.

Katherine shook her head. "Not at all, sire, but as you know, Languedoc—before the plague of the Albigensians—was known for refined learning and culture. My mother's husband was particularly interested in the great learning of the Arabs as transmitted by the Jews, as were many of the noblemen since the days of Queen Eleanor of Aquitaine. He had engaged a resident scholar at Castle Roncevaux, a student of Maimonides of Cordova, in fact, to live and work among us. It was merest chance that I had some tutelage with him."

"Maimonides?" the Marshal repeated, the mention of this name stretching William's knowledge of things other than chivalry, warfare, and politics.

Scarborough chose to enter the discussion. "The physician at the court of Saladin," he supplied, by way of information. "He fled from Cordova after the fall of the city to the Almohads and settled in Cairo."

The Marshal raised his brows. "How came *you* by such information, Scarborough?"

"Trade, as I have often said," he replied, "is more profitable than war. Maimonides was also known for his skill with ciphers," he added with a rapier glance at Katherine, "and so, must one assume, were his students also skilled with numbers and that they trained their pupils accordingly."

Before Katherine had an opportunity to reply adequately to the highly provocative statement, the Marshal nodded to Scarborough and said to Katherine, "Something of a wizard with ciphers on pen and parchment, Scarborough is!"

Katherine smiled prettily. "Really! Then I have a bit of advice for him, sire. I have been told that parchment is sadly out of fashion and that for ciphers one should use paper, the

Arab's paper, which is far superior. Or perhaps the Earl of
Scarborough is already aware of this advantage?"

Scarborough did not respond but regarded Katherine
through cool gray eyes. Moving along, the Marshal said,
"Yes, well. Paper is very expensive, demoiselle, and you
have hardly begun with your story. How extraordinary that
you should settle in York and not in London."

Katherine veered her thoughts back to the matter at hand.
"We did come to London first, of course," she continued. "I
even managed an audience with King John."

"And?" the Marshal prompted.

Katherine said evenly, "He was not interested in receiving
or recognizing penniless noblewomen, even ones with very
illustrious names."

Katherine omitted a recital of the indignities she had suffered at John's hands and the highly improper proposals he
had put forward to her and Sybille, who was then only a
tender thirteen. It was not necessary for Katherine to mention such things. John's penchant for lechery was infamous,
and the two unusually beautiful women could not have failed
to arouse John's lust. De Burgh and the Earl of Warenne
looked instantly sympathetic and ready to take up cudgels in
defense of the two brave and beautiful women; what Scarborough thought of this disclosure could not be read on his
face; and William cleared his throat meaningfully.

"So you left London to find your future elsewhere," the
Marshal pursued.

Katherine readily accepted the change of subject. "London did not seem to hold any promise for us," she said.
"I—we—did not know English ways, and having lived our
entire lives in a castle, the city of London's ways were entirely foreign to us. So we did not stay. I suppose that I felt
the devil on my heels. Perhaps I still felt the pursuit of the
Cathari. In any case I was not able to spend time in any one
place. Then we came to York, and it seemed, for a variety of
reasons, that our roaming was at an end. We have been there
ever since."

"Simply living in York?" the Marshal asked.

"Yes," Katherine answered. She was wary of what was
coming next, and she would have to be very careful.

With the mention of York a spark lit the atmosphere again, a small charge that could be felt by everyone present and that could, with little difficulty, be fanned into something more brilliant.

The Marshal kept it in check. "But what, may I ask, does a young woman—that is, two young women—do when confronted with life in a foreign city?"

"I applied to the lord mayor with a sum of money and to the broidery guild with samples of my work to obtain the status of Mistress Broiderer," she said.

Robert de Burgh had a sudden memory of the name of a certain woman on Cedric de Mauleon's lips, one that had incited Scarborough's blood lust. De Burgh remembered the woman's name with startling clarity. His eyes widened momentarily with surprise and delight at the situation. Admiration for the woman opposite him was there too. Then he shifted a curious glance to Scarborough and allowed his eyes to rest there a moment in speculation. Eric met de Burgh's eyes blandly.

"Very resourceful," the Marshal said.

"If you choose to call it such," Katherine said. With that she dared to look Scarborough directly in the eye. "It was the only skill I had available to sell, and even at that, it took me some time to realize that the needlecraft I learned as a girl growing up in a castle could be a commodity that would have a market value in a commercial town such as York."

"You prospered?" Again, the Marshal.

"I like to think that my broidery," Katherine said with a measure of dignity and simple pride, "far outstrips for quality that of my main competitor. My house is reputed to produce the best work in York, and it attracts the best prentices. Of course, I charge accordingly, but the townswomen are willing to pay for what they get."

Robert de Burgh smiled. "Why, yes, I have heard that York is a rich enough burgh."

"It has become so," Katherine agreed.

De Burgh had become bewitched by Katherine's smile, and he found himself angling for it. "But," he continued in the genial manner that had proven effective amongst the court ladies, "could you have prospered so well as a broiderer? That is, I imagine that you must have made money in these past four years to come now with an offer of a contribution to young Henry's cause? You must produce superior broidery, indeed."

Responding unawares to his manner, Katherine obliged him with her smile. "I invested some silver last year at an opportune time in the wool guild," she replied. "It yielded a fivefold return."

This disclosure came so unexpectedly to three of the four men present that they could not think quickly enough to question the aberration of a woman investing in a guild. In any case, neither the Marshal, nor the Earl of Warenne, nor Robert de Burgh was much interested in tedious financial details. Not one of the three of them was equal to the task of determining what must have been Katherine's initial investment in the guild to have returned the thousand marks for her sister's title. Nor did they have a moment to wonder how she had amassed that much capital in the first place or to question whether she had any other sources of money.

The Marshal did, however, have his suspicions about York's independent spirit when it came to the matter of taxes, and it was on the strength of those suspicions that he had released the Earl of Scarborough from prison the year before and set him to work for the crown.

"A wise investment, as it turned out for you, Demoiselle de Lunais," the Marshal said, "and now that the subject of York economy has arisen, I will freely admit how much the wool merchants have vexed me over the years. The irregularities in the accounts from Saxon York seemed to elude me to a maddening degree. A vexatious situation, you must agree, which is almost resolved, and I, for one, would be happy to have the last mysteries of the York tax accounts explained to me."

Katherine blanched. Was this to be her trial? She paused to swallow the ache in her throat and said steadily, without looking at Scarborough, "Surely your doubtlessly well-informed Counselor of the Exchequer should be able to offer an explanation."

"Oh," the Marshal said with a wave of the hand, "he's just newly engaged—just newly reinstated as Earl of Scarborough, too—this week past. Before that, though, I sent him up to York to find out what was going on. He found out—well enough, I would say—and while I would not say that all the details have been put forth on the table, I would say that he got right down to the source of the problem."

Katherine felt faint. She found no words of response.

"It's all taken care of now," the Marshal was saying, apparently oblivious to the change in Katherine's face, suddenly a pale ivory sculpture. "Yes, it was an elaborate set of tax records, it seems, though I'm no judge of the numbers, with which almost all of the merchants in town were involved. Or at least those wool merchants, the ones with the most to gain. But we've gotten to the heart of the problem, so I say."

Katherine would not be condemned without a fight. She said with as much calm as she was capable, "The merchants, particularly the wool merchants, were unhappy with the taxes. They're a law-abiding folk, the citizens of York, but King John's reign—if you'll beg my pardon for speaking forthrightly—was a financial disaster. If there is one thing that I have learned as a townswoman, it is that hardworking burghers will do almost anything to keep from throwing their good money after bad policies."

"Your sentiments do you justice, demoiselle," the Marshal replied affably. "You make a compelling advocate for the unruly York merchants, but they must be brought into line in the future, or we'll have chaos in earnest. But as I was saying, we've got the problem well in hand. That is to say, we can't prosecute the whole of York, and in any case, John's passing effects a kind of absolution, you might say, on past conditions. The important matter is that the career of the leader of the tax business is over."

"Oh?" was all she could manage.

"It might surprise you to know," the Marshal said, "that the proper culprit in all of this was one of John's most open supporters. Scarborough did excellent work in uncovering this man's clandestine support of Louis of France. It is something of a blessing and a tragedy, then, that Cedric de Mauleon met his end a week ago."

Katherine's surprise was genuine. Had her former partner indeed spared her? "Met his end? Sire de Mauleon?"

"Why, yes. But we need not speak of the sad details now," the Marshal continued. To the Marshal's way of thinking, talk of Mauleon's perfidy and the bloody end of his life were not fare for a lady's plate. "And we consider the incident over and done with, and along with that, the end of York's misbehavior."

The emotions that chased across Katherine's face were irresistible to Robert de Burgh. "You knew Mauleon, demoiselle?" he was fascinated into asking.

"A little," she admitted weakly. "He was something of a personage in York, after all."

She was still trying to assimilate the good news that Cedric de Mauleon was dead, and that she, along with the lord mayor and the rest of York, would be off scot-free. She saw now that clemency for York was the only possible way to start afresh in the reign of the new Henry. Nevertheless, it came as something of a relief, and she could not help but feel some joy at the news of Mauleon's demise.

"You did not know this news, demoiselle?" Scarborough asked, asserting himself at last.

Katherine turned to look at him. "This is the first I have heard of it," she said evenly. "How should I have learned of it?"

"I would not know, of course. Sources of information, I imagine," Scarborough returned. "You have always enjoyed excellent sources of information, have you not?"

It was a direct challenge. The sparks were crackling in the air, and the fire that smoldered between the two of them could no longer be contained. "I have not had access to the general run of information this week past," she said.

"Were you not in London?"

"Of course I was in London," she returned. "But the priory of the Holy Trinity, where we were staying, would not be considered by most to be a particularly good place from which to learn any interesting items of news, save for King John's death, which could be heard on any street corner."

"You resided at the Holy Trinity?" Scarborough queried with keen gray eyes.

"Yes, the priory of the Holy Trinity," Katherine affirmed.

The look in Scarborough's eyes was distinctly unpleasant. Katherine could not miss it. Her eyes narrowed in response and glittered militant green. "A most respectable place, I assure you. Does something trouble you in my particular choice of lodgings in London?"

"Not at all," Scarborough replied, his gray eyes as cold as ashes in a winter fireplace. "And I am sure that it is most respectable. Why, even Cedric de Mauleon remarked upon its respectability when he informed me that you were residing there. And speaking of Mauleon, I suspect that upon learning of his death the next day after King John's demise, you switched your allegiance, which was first to Louis of France, was it not?"

"Like everyone else in York," Katherine interpolated.

"And thus having lost in Mauleon your most valuable conduit to Louis's cause, you immediately contacted William Marshal to put your support behind John's heir, Henry," he finished.

Katherine was on her feet. Wrath flamed in her cheeks and eyes. "Are you accusing me of having been in league with Mauleon at this late date?" she flashed.

Chapter 22

It was steel to magnet. Scarborough was on his feet, too, his arms propped against the table. They had ceased speaking French, but neither could have said at what point they had reverted the conversation to English. Nor did they pay the slightest heed to the astonishment on the faces of their entirely captivated audience.

"I am, indeed," Scarborough replied with equal swiftness. "How else should I interpret Mauleon's knowledge of your whereabouts in London, when I myself did not know and you would not tell me?"

A pulse throbbed at Katherine's throat. Her eyes were slits of green light. "You may interpret that any way you please!" she answered defiantly. "But I can certainly make my guesses as to how you shall choose to read it. Despite anything I say to the contrary!"

"Do you have something to say to the contrary, mistress?"

"Not at all," she tossed back carelessly.

"You do not deny having seen Mauleon in London, then?"

Katherine knew that he was not asking whether she had chanced to see Mauleon in the streets but that he was accusing her of intimacy with her hated enemy. "I deny nothing."

"You told me once that Mauleon was not at all to your liking," he flung at her with disdain.

"And you believed me, I suppose?" She mocked him. "Mauleon was a Norman, like myself," she continued, picking her arguments for a purported alliance with Mauleon from thin air. "So there was a bond, after all. You must find some satisfaction, in the end, at having your original interpretation of my character so thoroughly confirmed. But it would interest me to know how you came to discover my involvement with Mauleon in London."

"From Mauleon himself," Scarborough answered.

"An impeccable source of information, to be sure," Katherine replied with a laugh of withering scorn. She continued with irony, "Thank you so much for having now reminded me of something that, in the press of my many engagements in London, I confess that I had forgotten. Perhaps Mauleon was so obliging to have also informed you of *when* he and I were supposed to have had our meeting."

"He was," Scarborough said. "He told me quite distinctly that you and he met on the night the news of John's death reached the city. You will remember that I have reason to think that you met him much later that night."

Katherine could scarce credit her ears. Did he imagine that she could have left his arms that same night to conspire and consort with Mauleon? Did he truly think her capable of it? The implication left her speechless.

"Yes," Scarborough continued bitterly, interpreting her silence as an admission of guilt. "You miscalculated in Mauleon, mistress, and should have known that he would divulge, at the point of a sword, what you would least like the world to know."

Katherine laughed again. "A woman always takes her chances when it comes to men, Master Eric, and if I have learned nothing else in the past six months, it is to know that one man is no different from the next!"

Scarborough's anger was unreasoning. "And I have learned that a woman will go to any length to reinstate herself!"

"To reinstate my sister," Katherine corrected swiftly, for she would not compromise on this point. "And yes," she went on angrily, and never more beautiful in that anger, "I would go to any length to see my sister, Demoiselle Sybille de Roncevaux, reinstated. That is, after all, the reason I am come here today, for that reason and none other."

William Marshal, on whom the essentials of this exchange were lost, caught mention of Sybille's name. Guessing at his opening, he half rose from his chair and interjected firmly, and in the civilized French tongue, "Why, Sybille de Roncevaux, yes, indeed. Let us discuss the matter of your sister with no further delay. Pray, be seated. Demoiselle, Scarborough," William invited cordially, setting a precedent himself by settling back into his chair. "If I recall correctly, I believe that the discussion digressed with mention of Cedric de Mauleon."

Katherine's eyes strove with Scarborough's for a moment or two longer before she took a deep breath and sat back down. Scarborough also subsided to his seat in something of a silent ill humor.

If Scarborough did not feel the least need to excuse himself in the wake of their unseemly outburst, Katherine did. "I beg your pardon, if you please, sire," she said, recovering her composure, although her eyes still glittered. "I fear that the Earl of Scarborough and I have fallen into an inconsequent quarrel. I recall now on the one or two occasions, when he and I might have met previously in York, that he took delight in exposing my most unbecoming temper."

"It become you well, demoiselle," de Burgh interjected, against his better judgment.

The Marshal ignored this interpolation, as well as the passionate exchange between the lovely young noblewoman and the Counselor of Trade. He did not think it wise to delve too deeply into the reasons for the fire between them. He sought only to keep the peace. "I have been on the receiving end of Scarborough's tongue as well, demoiselle, and so you have all my sympathies. Permit me to compliment you on your apparent ability to withstand attack. But we wander from the issue, which is the reinstatement of your sister, is it not?"

Katherine put a strong guard on her emotions and hoped that she would refrain from any further unseemly displays with the Earl of Scarborough. She nodded deferentially at the Marshal's question.

"The reign of Henry III will make an effort to redress past wrongs, as in your case," the Marshal continued. "The new reign is also in need of new blood and, as you are well aware, new monies. In short, your plea on your sister's behalf falls on timely, sympathetic ears. There are, however, a few preliminary obstacles. You realize, of course, that we must first verify Sybille de Roncevaux's lineage."

Katherine readily assented to this and agreed to a further meeting in which the details of Sybille's lineage might be confirmed.

"May I suggest that we pursue that inquiry on the morrow, then?" the Marshal said. "But in the meantime, tell me what you have in mind for your sister."

"A marriage that is the equal of her birth," Katherine replied with a satisfied look at Sybille, who, eyes lowered, was a very beautiful sight to behold.

"Yes, of course! You are aware that the sum of one thousand marks is considered customary for a title—in this case, the reinstatement of a title?" When Katherine nodded, the Marshal pursued, "And the sum of her dowry, since she is landless?"

Katherine wanted to avoid the appearance of bargaining, reckoning quite correctly that the Marshal would have no taste for it. She would stop at no figure to dower Sybille.

Still, she did not want to endebt herself unnecessarily to Baruch, who had generously offered to extend her credit, if a further sum should prove advantageous to Sybille.

"That would depend, of course, to whom she was betrothed," Katherine said. "And my sister, I am sure we all agree, is a treasure in herself."

The Marshal nodded and mentioned no less than three eligible, titled, and landed noblemen who would be suitable. He then named a rather enormous but not unheard-of figure that would represent the necessary dowry for Sybille's betrothal. He mentioned the young (and very agreeably handsome) heir to the Earl of Langley.

There was method in the Marshal's mention of the Langley estate, for it was one of the demesnes to the south presently occupied by a French follower of Louis. The elderly Langley, a rebel baron, had forfeited it upon Louis's arrival on English soil. The Marshal had visions of using Sybille's much-needed dower to launch a strategic attack to regain it for the Langley family. He could heal one rift with the rebel barons by a marriage to a supporter of the young Henry.

Katherine said that she was agreeable to that match, or any other of similar station, but insisted firmly that Sybille's approval of the young nobleman was necessary.

The Marshal replied that these introductions could begin on the morrow as well, after their meeting to establish Sybille's lineage.

"There are the usual homage fees to be paid, in addition; and quarter-day to the crown, in advance, I am afraid," the Marshal continued congenially.

Katherine's rapid mental calculations of the expenses all told was beyond her ready cash in hand. She did not hesitate, however, to assent to the demanded sum. She smiled and verbally committed another hundred marks to the Royal Treasury in a grand gesture.

An appreciative murmur ran around the table. Only the Earl of Scarborough seemed unimpressed.

The Marshal nodded. "Very well, demoiselle. Allow me to express my delight that we have so easily come to terms. Now, as I stated at the opening of this discussion, time is as valuable a commodity in these times as money. My men and

I shall be leaving Lancaster for the troublesome south within the seven-night, and so, I am sure you will agree, the seal on Demoiselle de Roncevaux's future should be set before then."

Katherine agreed again wholeheartedly to this, saying that she could put all of the initial fees in the Marshal's hands but that the remaining five hundred marks would have to wait several days until her banker in York had had time to transfer monies to his London agent and to the Royal Exchequer, as the established customs of banking were transacted.

A shadow crossed the Marshal's face. He was put in mind of some detail but could not think what it was. "You shall have to discuss these particulars with the Earl of Scarborough, I believe," he said with a gesture to his Counselor of the Exchequer, "for I claim no expertise in such matters."

Katherine turned to face Scarborough directly. "I trust there shall be no difficulty in a small delay in payment of the balance, my lord?" she queried as neutrally as she as able.

Scarborough's face was grim. "The matter need not be settled at this moment," he said. "The five hundred marks can wait until after the campaign in the south, as well as Demoiselle de Roncevaux's immediate future."

"Not settled?" she repeated with a skeptical ring in her pleasant voice. Was he trying to buy time to maneuver her out of her excellent position? She had not thought him vindictive, but she could see no other motive for a delay than an attempt to foil her. "I see no reason to defer the matter," she said coolly. "I will be more than happy to supply the necessary funds that William Marshal has indicated must be respected for our deal to be set and sealed."

"I repeat, demoiselle," Scarborough insisted, "that haste is not indicated in this particular matter."

"Time is of the essence," Katherine countered, keeping now a firm rein on her temper. "William Marshal has said so himself, and I am very determined to see my sister reinstated and have no desire to wait another month when, as we all know, anything can happen to overset the present arrangement. I do not understand why you should enter an objection at this point, my lord. I have arranged everything, and barring some extraordinary circumstance, I do not know why the sum of my fees should not be paid within the week."

Before Scarborough had a chance to reply to this, the Marshal suddenly remembered what it was that had teased him a moment ago. "Ah, yes," he said rather impetuously, unaware of the storm on Scarborough's brow. "It has come to me."

"Leave it be, William Marshal," Scarborough said, low and rasping.

The Marshal was as surprised as Katherine by this implied threat, and he wrongly supposed, as did Katherine, that Scarborough's objections were not in Demoiselle de Lunais's best interest. "But I can't let it be, Scarborough. Why, just a few days ago—a week perhaps—in any case, before Gloucester, I sealed the order sequestering all of York's banking funds. The order that you, Scarborough, instituted yourself and had sent directly to the lord mayor, a Fitz Osbert by name, I believe. I stamped the parchment myself."

Katherine remained puzzled, and the Marshal went on. "The king's envoy was sent posthaste, and you sent another man whose job, if I recall correctly, was to intercept all messages directed to official lending institutions. Why, that must have been your first act as the Counselor of the Exchequer! A good job it was, too, to have brought the wool merchants so quickly into line, but I wonder now if that order might present something of a problem with Demoiselle de Lunais's transaction?"

Katherine was about to smile and say, with confidence, that her banker would not be affected by a Royal Writ when she suddenly, and with anguish, remembered the warm, sunlit, sinful afternoon when she had divulged to the man seated across from her her the name of her creditor and unofficial banker in York.

He would not have failed to remember the name of Baruch of Coney Street, and one look at his face informed Katherine that he remembered the address very well indeed and that his essential purpose in trying to defer the present discussion was to avoid exposing the restraining order he had put on the flow of York's cash. She would not have thought that anything could hurt so much.

Stripped of all her defenses, Katherine rallied her forces for the last time. "There is no need to sidestep the matter here or to make my sister wait any longer," she said to Scarborough. With an inspiration born of desperation she began a line of questions. "So you directed the king's envoy to close York's official banks?"

To this Scarborough answered in the affirmative.

"A very wise move," Katherine commented. "And you also concerned yourself with the unofficial bankers?"

"By placing my man in the streets I thought most likely to experience some activity," Scarborough answered. He did not say that he had placed that man for Katherine's own protection, so that she could not withdraw money to unwisely invest in Louis's cause. He had put all his plans into motion the morning of his meeting with Mauleon, the night after he had seen Katherine in London.

"And did you glean anything from having surveilled those streets?" Katherine asked.

"I received word that a messenger was intercepted at Coney Street," he answered, for it was pointless now to avoid the central issue.

"Ah," Katherine replied calmly. "Did you say 'messenger'?"

Scarborough affirmed this.

"Not messengers?" Katherine pursued.

Scarborough cocked a brow.

"Well, then! I shall take leave to inform you, my lord minister, that I sent *two* messengers to Coney Street—just in case. You should have known by now that I leave little to chance," she rebuked, and found puny satisfaction that she had momentarily gotten the better of him.

"The Counselor of the Exchequer can count the five hundred marks," she said, turning once again to the Marshal, "within the week. I have no desire to delay my sister's reinstatement any longer."

Katherine had no idea where she was going to obtain five hundred marks in a matter of days, but it was enough to have thwarted him, if only for the moment. It was all she could do to keep her countenance through the mercifully rapid finalities and courtesies. Within minutes she was able to sweep out of the room, happy to be gone to nurse her wounds in private, feeling spent and exhausted, unable to appreciate fully the fact that she had all but succeeded in her long quest, satisfied only that she had kept face before that man. Nor could she, in her own hurt, understand the effect of the meeting on Sybille, who was dutifully at her side.

When the door to the receiving chamber closed behind Katherine and her sister, the Marshal pronounced himself well pleased with the turn of events and was eager to bend his energies on the next order of business. The Marshal had one or two things to discuss with his new Counselor of the Exchequer. When the Marshal attempted to engage Scarborough in discussion, the Earl of Warenne bowed himself out in the direction of a side door. Robert de Burgh, however, moved in the direction of the door through which Katherine had exited moments before.

Scarborough rudely quit the Marshal in mid-sentence and planted himself between de Burgh and the door. "Don't go near her, de Burgh," he stated with an unequivocal challenge.

Robert de Burgh affected some surprise. He was forced to look up, but only fractionally, to meet Scarborough's eye. "Whatever are you about, Scarborough?" he asked.

"You heard me," he stated flatly.

"Are you perhaps referring to the most charming Demoiselle de Roncevaux?" de Burgh ventured.

"No."

"But, Scarborough," de Burgh replied, "there seemed to be nothing but animosity between you and the lovely Demoiselle Katherine. Surely you do not presume any sort of cordial relations with her."

"Don't go near her," Scarborough reiterated.

Robert de Burgh could not pretend to misunderstand. He had a sudden, vivid memory of Scarborough's savagery in the face of Cedric de Mauleon's well-practiced sword arm. Still, Demoiselle Katherine de Lunais had mightily captured de Burgh's attention. He smiled and was about to take up the challenge by saying that Demoiselle de Lunais seemed to be fair ground when the Marshal intervened.

"My lords! My lords!" William said with a determined cheerfulness. "No use standing about. We've work ahead of us. Were you not going to gather your men for the campaign in the south next week, de Burgh? And, Scarborough, you must finish the tax records from East Anglia for me!"

The Earl of Warenne had wandered over to the little scene, rather intrigued by it all, and inadvertently aided the Marshal in breaking up a potentially dangerous rift between his chief advisers. Warenne linked arms with de Burgh and, leading him toward the side door, said, "Why, yes. I've several men for your campaign, Robert, that I've been wanting you to look over."

Robert de Burgh flicked a last glance at Scarborough and inclined his head. In all honesty, the look on Scarborough's face made de Burgh rather happy that a meeting with the Dane had been avoided or at least deferred. He accepted Warenne's escort gracefully.

"Well, now, Robert," the Earl of Warenne was saying, "what is it you mean to do?"

Robert de Burgh, allowing his companion to precede him through the door, said, quite blandly, "I mean to brush up on my Saxon. I fear, Gaston, that I never anticipated it being of any use and am rather rusty."

"Saxon!" Warenne ejaculated, balking at the thought, and then chuckled. "I own that the little Lunais is extraordinarily beautiful, and such a tongue! While the sister . . . Ah, Robert, if I were only twenty years younger!"

"Forty, Gaston," de Burgh replied. "Rather more like forty!"

The Marshal had turned back to Scarborough and, with a quick reverse of his intentions, excused him from the room. The permission to leave was merely a formality, since it was perfectly obvious to the Marshal that the Dane had other things on his mind and had every desire to leave the chamber, with or without the Marshal's invitation.

With a last look at de Burgh's retreating figure and with only the curtest of valedictions to his superior, Scarborough flung himself out of the receiving chamber, in the grip of the most violent emotions he had ever experienced. He stalked down the stately corridors of the countinghouse with no very real direction in mind, imagining with a murderous pleasure the venting of his fury on Robert de Burgh. He presently discovered that his anger was misplaced and realized instead that it would afford him an exquisite satisfaction to be able now to resuscitate Cedric de Mauleon and to strangle him. Scarborough was heartily sorry that he had ended that worthless Norman's life with cold steel, and so he dwelled at some length on the far more satisfying vision of having Mauleon's neck between his fingers and of choking the life out of him with his bare hands.

These thoughts, however, did little to assuage the real source of his violence, and as he continued to pace restlessly through the hallways he was torn between a desire to kill Mauleon a second time and a desire to have his hands around Mistress Katherine's lovely neck. Enraged all over again at the thought of Katherine, he told himself that he had known all along that she was something rather different from what she claimed to be and that he had done very well to have ordered the momentary halt to the flow of York's cash. He gratified himself with elaborate plans for putting all of the king's men in search of that second messenger and spun thoughts of an appropriate punishment for the heartless, unprincipled Katherine de Lunais, who had gambled so badly on her choice of champion. He settled on the perversely fitting punishment of first supplying the remaining five hundred marks for Sybille's reinstatement himself and then legally barring Katherine from any further trade in England, thereby putting her in his debt for the rest of her life.

He arrived, hardly before he knew it, at his large suite of rooms in the adjoining castle proper with the idea of shutting himself in it for the remainder of the day. In this painful mood of corroding disillusionment and hungry for prey, he happened onto Bar, who, occupying the antechamber, was busy with the arrangement of some gear for the forthcoming offensive in the south.

"Why, Eric, I hadn't expected to see you so soon!" Bar exclaimed, only glancing up briefly. He then muttered some rather innocuous remarks about the poor prospects of a cam-

paign loaded with an excess of materials, recommending
Eric to tell the Marshal to "travel light," and got his head
bitten off for his pains.

Scarborough's blighting response brought Bar's head up
for a good look. Thinking that there had been some misun-
derstanding, Bar decided the moment opportune to divulge
the most extraordinary encounter he had had earlier in the
hallway with Mistress Emma of York.

"Just let me tell you who I saw—" he began.

"Don't!" Scarborough interrupted with threatening feroc-
ity, and took several steps toward Bar. "For your sake and
mine get out!"

Remarkably impervious to his master's wrath, Bar shook
his head and said with a deprecatory humor, "You don't understand. I saw Mistress Emma a while ago. You remember
that I mentioned the Mistress Emma? Mistress Katherine's
serving woman. Of York. Why, I was a mite bit surprised to
see her, I can tell you. And I would have thought that you
were in an audience with the Mistress Katherine—"

"I was"—Scarborough bit off his words—"and she is
more correctly called, I believe, Demoiselle Katherine de
Lunais."

"Just as you're the Earl of Scarborough," Bar pointed out
cheerfully, and won only a scowl from Scarborough for his
efforts at levity.

"Don't try me too far," Scarborough warned, striding past
Bar to the window. "I am in no mood for it."

A simple creature, Bar had guessed that all would be
right between his master and Mistress Katherine when their
true identities were disclosed, but he did not need remarkable powers of discernment to understand that such an easy
coming to terms had not occurred.

"And so I see that you lost no time and fell into a quarrel
with a fine young woman," Bar had the audacity to say with
a hint of reproof, "who has had a hard time of it all these
years. So my Emma told me. And with quite a head on her
shoulders, Mistress Katherine, if all I heard is true."

"It is. And the whole story is very affecting, I grant you
that. But clever as she is, the Demoiselle de Lunais out-
smarted herself in the end." Scarborough laughed unpleas-

antly, having appended an observation on the character of the woman Bar had always held in highest esteem, which quite shocked and angered the burly, blond bear.

"Eric!" Bar exclaimed. "You don't mean that!"

Scarborough tore himself away from the window and came nose-to-nose with Bar. "I do, indeed," he said with fire, "and know it by her own admission. Do you care to take issue with me?"

Dimly perceiving that his master had a brutal case of it, Bar read murder in his master's eyes. However, Bar did not back down from the most openly violent threat on his life he had experienced to date. Bar was feeling fine and feisty after his encounter with Emma and ready to wrangle. He met and held Scarborough's eyes fearlessly. "I do, man, and challenge you in turn to explain yourself."

"I mean precisely that your saintly Mistress Katherine openly admitted to a liaison with Cedric de Mauleon in London on the night the news of John's death reached the city. Do you challenge me?"

Bar absorbed this information with a blink and then threw his head back and laughed. With a rather pungent reference to the combined heroes of Valhalla, Bar exclaimed that he would gladly fight that one out.

Such a reaction understandably threw Scarborough off his stride. He grasped the neck of Bar's tunic and pulled him slightly off the floor, causing Bar to explain hastily, "Mistress Katherine was with me that night!"

"Thor's Blood, man!" Scarborough thundered, ready to drub his henchman senseless.

Recognizing that his life truly might be in danger, Bar suppressed an inclination to snap that his master not make a bigger fool of himself than he had done already. Bar attempted to shrug himself free and thrust his own fist into his master's face, saying, "I'll tell you the whole story only when you have come to your senses enough to listen."

Mastering himself with effort, Scarborough expelled a long breath and slowly let go of Bar's tunic.

Bar twitched his tunic into place and flourished his half-whiskered chin pugnaciously. "That's right," he said, not flinching under the quelling gray gaze. "I saw the Mistress Katherine with my own eyes that night."

"Where?"

"At the priory of the Holy Trinity. Do you know it? It's in the northeast quarter, and even with the whole of London emptied into the streets that night, I happened onto the Mistress Emma in company of the Mistress Sybille."

"And Mistress Katherine?"

"She came later. Not from inside the walls of the priory, though, but from somewhere else in town, and I'll wager your entire fleet docked in London that she was *not* coming from a tryst with Mauleon."

"She wasn't."

Bar appraised his master. So that was the way the wind blew, was it? "And she didn't see him later that night, either." Bar went on to explain how he and the men he was with that night had thought it best to guard his three women, as he had phrased it, from the uncertain crowds milling the late-night streets. Thus he could say for a certainty that no man had entered the priory and dared his master to challenge that.

Scarborough seemed to experience some difficulty responding to Bar's disclosures, but after a moment's silence he managed to speak with merely a vestige of the fire that had been consuming him only moments previous; and his face was somewhat paler. "I am still somewhat in the dark. How came you to find Mistress Emma in the streets?"

"It was entirely by chance, and so I tell you."

"But London is a large place, and accidental encounters are difficult to credit, at best," Scarborough commented. He was not thinking of Bar's meeting with Katherine; rather he was working through in his mind the possibility that Katherine had truly chanced to see him cross the marketplace a week ago and had thus discovered on her own that he was lodged at the Crown Inn.

"Are you doubting me?" Bar grumbled, availing himself of his turn for a threatening challenge.

Scarborough laughed for the first time in several hours. "Not so fast, Bar!"

"You're one to talk!"

"I believe you," Scarborough continued, ignoring Bar's interpolation. "But tell me: How came you to neglect to mention to me this most interesting circumstance with the three women from York?"

Bar was not mollified by his master's sudden good humor. "You dare ask me that, Eric?" he growled. "After what you said about the Mistress Katherine months ago and telling me not to go near her?"

Scarborough patted Bar's shoulders. "I remember. And if ever you were to countermand my orders, you could not have chosen a better time to do it. I must thank you."

Bar snorted his response. "I doubt that the Mistress Katherine will thank *you* for the slight I am sure you did not hesitate to thrust on her in your latest meeting."

Scarborough paled a little more at that. He was suddenly impatient to be away, to find Katherine in her rooms in order to beg her forgiveness. "God's Wounds, it was a sorry day's work, Bar," he admitted, and added that he would repair immediately to Katherine de Lunais's chambers, once he had discovered from the Marshal where she was lodged.

"Well, it won't surprise me if she doesn't receive you, Eric. Or if she does, she'll send you away with a flea in your ear," Bar called out after the retreating form of his master, who could not get away fast enough.

This time Bar had the right of it. Scarborough had directions to Katherine's rooms within minutes and was on his way, striding the corridors, casting aside strolling groups or couples in his haste to reach Katherine. A few turns, a flight of stairs, the length of a freshly beeswaxed parquetry corridor, and he was knocking authoritatively at Katherine de Lunais's antechamber door.

A moment or two passed before Emma cracked the door open and gave a slight start at sight of the Earl of Scarborough. She shook her head slightly.

Scarborough did not take the hint. "I am come, Mistress Emma," he said, "to pay my respects to Demoiselle de Lunais."

Emma shook her head again. "I've orders to prevent you from crossing the threshold," she said low, in almost a whisper, adding as an afterthought a bobbing curtsy and the title of respect, "my lord."

"I intend to see Demoiselle de Lunais," Scarborough repeated in normal tones and pushed his way through the door.

"Not a good time, my lord," Emma repeated with a hiss, jerking her head meaningfully toward the closed door that apparently led to Katherine's chamber.

"I must and will speak to Mistress Katherine, and I will not be kept waiting. Have the goodness to announce me to your mistress, Emma."

Emma looked highly doubtful. She was in something of a quandary whether to respect her mistress's orders or to follow the forceful Earl of Scarborough's command, but in any event, she was spared the impossible decision.

Katherine emerged at the door to her chamber, having heard the exchange in the antechamber and instantly recognizing Scarborough's voice. She was paler than Scarborough had been and still visibly shaken from the recent audience and wore the slightly rumpled appearance of someone who had been lying down. She had never looked more desirable to him.

"No, sire," Katherine said, responding with her most formal French to the intimacy of his conversational English. "It is you who shall have the goodness to remove yourself from these chambers."

"Demoiselle Katherine," he replied, following her lead in French and moving several steps toward her. "Grant me a few moments to explain myself."

"Explain yourself?" Katherine replied haughtily, taking a step back. "There is not the slightest need to do so."

"But there is. You know there is." He tried to grasp her hand, but she flung it away.

"Your boorish manner has been known to me from the start. Keep your hands and your most unpleasant behavior to yourself."

"I have come to beg your pardon. I was wrong," he said.

"Were you, indeed? Wrong about what, pray? My character, my motives, my lineage, my business?"

"Everything. Please forgive me."

"I shall not go to the trouble, for your being in the right or the wrong is a matter of utter indifference to me."

"No, you misunderstand. You allowed me—nay, you goaded me—into believing that you had a liaison with Mauleon."

"Oh? It is my fault, then? What a charming apology." She laughed. It was not a warm sound.

Scarborough shook his head. "Do not you see that I never would have said what I did, had I been in my right mind? But I was not. I was eaten up out of jealousy for you. You must forgive me!"

Katherine was still very pale. Her voice shook pitifully. She was struggling to maintain a certain dignity. "There is nothing that I *must* do for you, sire. Especially not forgive you. Your accusations were beyond anything I have ever had to suffer before in my life, and if I never hear another word from you for as long as I live, it will be a rare blessing!"

"Katherine," he began, and saw her stiffen. "Demoiselle, I love you!"

"Such a time to declare yourself. But I have no desire to be your paramour."

"My wife. I am asking you to marry me." He took another step toward her.

"Not another pace! I shall go distracted if you ever attempt to touch me again!"

Scarborough was at a complete loss. "It was Mauleon. He poisoned my thoughts against you. Katherine, listen to me. I was jealous and angry that, clever as you are, you had put your money on the wrong man. I could hardly believe that you could not see who was the bigger prize."

Katherine's green eyes flashed magnificently. "The bigger prize?" she echoed scornfully. "Yourself, I suppose! No, I thank you. The honor is too great for my indecent self. The only prize I crave, that I have planned for seven years, is the reinstatement of my sister. I hope that you will have the goodness to do nothing to jeopardize her future and that you will have the sense to leave me and my family alone from now on. I had never thought to hate anyone as much as I hated Mauleon, but I find that I was wrong. I hope never to see you again. I am entirely satisfied that you understand me."

"I do," Scarborough replied with distant formality. He bowed and said, "I will quit you now, so that my presence will afford you no further pain. Pray, accept my sincerest wish that if you should ever need my help, you shall not hesitate to call upon me. In writing, if you desire it so. I shall be at your disposal, and your sister's, for whatever you may need in the years to come. You may rest assured that Demoiselle Sybille shall receive all the considerations due her."

Katherine could not speak for the angry lump in her throat and the tears ignominiously threatening to spill over. She remained immobile. He bowed again, and Emma closed the door behind him very softly. Katherine heard the strong echo of his steps slowly die as he strode down the corridor.

Katherine dashed a hand across her brow and retreated to her chamber, giving Emma the order that she was not to be disturbed for any reason whatsoever. She waved away, with every evidence of loathing, Emma's suggestion for dinner, saying instead that Emma could spend the evening with Sybille. Then Katherine shut the door behind her and went to her window, where she gazed sightlessly out across the slate rooftops of the crowd of castle wings and the tangle of chimneys spiking the evening sky.

She wished that she could cry and give vent to all the turbulence in her breast, but no tears came. She felt, for all of that, limp and listlessness and with a melancholia she had never before experienced. She thought of all she had done over the past years since she had come to the sceptered isle but could find nothing in her accomplishments upon which she could attach to her life any particular importance.

A spark of liveliness came into being when she dwelled savagely on the Earl of Scarborough. Her unusually sluggish brain took only a few imaginative turns in thinking out a fit punishment for the hateful man; but she came at length to the conclusion that a vigorous stretching on the rack and a year's hanging by the thumbs would be far, far too good for him.

Katherine's mood presently expended itself, leaving her

exhausted and empty. Still, over the hours, she hardly moved from her position at the window. With her forehead against the cool diamond-shaped pane she witnessed, with no apparent interest, the moon riding fitfully from cloud to cloud across the vast wastes of the night sky and registered, quite impassively, the magnificent silvering of the distant, unattainable domes and spires.

___ Chapter 23 ___

Sybille left the chambers immediately after the interview with the Marshal. She made her way to the gardens, only to find them stripped of leaf and flower and poignantly desolate in their autumnal barrenness. She wandered aimlessly among the high hedges, sighing often, and languished in her unhappiness.

Sybille was glad of this time alone. She had thought, now that Katherine's goals for her were so nearly accomplished, that she would be more jealously guarded than ever, but Emma had given her a welcome reprieve by shooing her out of the chambers, almost at the very moment that she and Katherine had arrived back at them.

Sybille gazed wide-eyed at the lily pond, turning up her pretty little nose at the green film covering the murky water. Thoughts chased one another in her unhappy brain, confused musings on Master Eric, the new Earl of Scarborough; on Stephen Webster; and on the unknown nobleman to whom she would soon be betrothed. Katherine's pale face intruded upon Sybille's thoughts on occasion, only to be hastily dismissed. When Sybille thought of all that Katherine had done for her in the past years, she felt guilty twinges. Not, she reminded herself, that she had ever asked Katherine to do all those things for her. In fact, on more than one occasion she had let Katherine know that her efforts were unnecessary. Nevertheless, Katherine had fed and clothed and housed her in excellent style all these years, and Sybille could not help but feel ungrateful now that she had a deep-down desire to throw it all back in Katherine's face.

As she gazed out glumly over the pond she dreamed of the blissful, comfortable and certainly less magnificent life she could lead as a married woman in York, preferably as the wife of Stephen Webster. She sighed again, heavily and in deep self-pity, knowing that Stephen was already married to that hateful Eleanora Brewer. It would be Eleanora who would have the handsome house on Petergate Square; Eleanora who would supervise all of the household's shopping; Eleanora who would direct the preparation of all of Stephen's meals; Eleanora who would sew and mend Stephen's clothing. It would be Eleanora. Eleanora, who could not even set a decent stitch, much less embroider with Sybille's loving skill.

Sybille sighed again in her misery and sank down onto a cold stone bench overlooking the blank wall of apartment windows. She stared around her at the naked branches and at the cold blue sky above. She heard the plaintive cries of hungry starlings and inhaled the crisp air of the dying year. It was a scene without solace, and one she was at a loss to describe. Only the poetic powers of her Stephen would be able to put her feelings into words and alleviate her anguish.

Then she heard the crashing of a winter rabbit through the bushes. But no, it must be something rather larger than a mere rabbit to make such a racket. A human form must be making her way toward her. She stood up, poised for flight. Then, as if she had conjured him out of thin air, Stephen Webster thrust himself through a brambled hedge (cursing very softly under his breath) and greeted her with the exasperated words: "God's Foot, Sybille! There you are at last! I've had the devil's own time catching up with you. It's a devilish big pile of stones they've got here, curse it all, and I was just now thinking that perhaps I'd been misled this entire week past and that you weren't here after all."

Sybille's eyes widened and shone with love. She clasped her hands to her bosom. Her sense of the enraptured beauty of the situation more than made up for Stephen's prosaic entrance.

"Stephen," she breathed happily. "Oh, it's you! It's truly you, Stephen!"

The sight of Sybille's transformed beauty brought Stephen to his poetic senses. "Sybille!" he breathed in return, falling in love with her all over again. "Sybille!" he repeated, finding no other words adequate to the occasion. All the enchanting lines he had picked up during his stay in London seemed to have flown right out of his head.

Without further speech the two star-crossed lovers fell into each other's arms and embraced, thoroughly, for the very first time in the course of their true love. Stephen's ardor surprised Sybille as much as it frightened her. After the first, dizzying seconds, she struggled to free herself from his passionate embrace.

"No, Stephen, no," she protested between kisses.

"Yes, Sybille, yes," he answered, showering her with mute tributes from his lips. "I cannot help myself," he continued, and added on the somewhat peevish complaint, "And curse it all, considering what I've been through to get here, I'd not think you'd begrudge me a few kisses now."

Sybille submitted meekly to this persuasive argument and found that his kisses were really very pleasant, though not at all the ethereal things she thought they would be. Then the fire on her side caught as well (for Stephen was truly a handsome, well-set-up young man), and she returned his passion with a shy but, for all of that, equal fervor.

Stephen, shocked now in his turn, broke off for air and unwound Sybille's arms from his neck.

"My love," he began in mild reproach, and then stopped, his tongue having become tangled at the sight of the stars shining from his very own Sybille's eyes. "I'm glad I've come," he said in all honesty, and took his due from her in the form of longer, more lingering kisses, bethinking himself, quite spontaneously, of wild honey and nectar and the fresh dew of roses at dawn.

"Stephen, we must talk," Sybille managed to say at last.

"Talk, what good is talk?" Stephen responded, finding

the pulse at Sybille's throat and brushing its fluttering motion with his lips.

"Stephen!" she exclaimed when he became somewhat bolder in his lovemaking. "Stephen!"

Sybille's stern tones brought her swain back to earth. He cleared his throat. "Yes, my love. Yes, indeed!"

"I said we must talk."

"Oh, all right," Stephen conceded, allowing himself to be led to the neighboring stone bench, but he did not relinquish his hold around Sybille's waist. "What do you want to talk about?"

"Everything," Sybille cried, taken aback. "To begin with, how did you find me?"

Stephen was rather proud of himself on this point. "I figured it out. First I went to London, but when news of John's death broke, I reckoned that you would be found where the next government was forming."

"How did you know we wouldn't be seeking refuge with Prince Louis?" Sybille queried.

"That Frenchie?" Stephen said scornfully. "Begging your pardon, Sybille, but I don't think he has a chance now, and I don't think of you as French."

"I'm not anymore," she said with satisfaction. Then she paled suddenly, remembering that she had been fervently kissing a married man and feeling a delicious little thrill at that sinful thought. "But I am not sure what I am," she said again with a catch in her voice, "if you're married to Eleanora."

Stephen bent to kiss away the tiny frown marring Sybille's brow. "I didn't marry her."

Joy and disbelief warred in Sybille's breast. "Was the marriage called off?" she asked, scarcely waiting to hear the response.

"I suppose it must have been, now that you mention it. You see, I wasn't there," Stephen explained.

"You ran away?"

Stephen did not like the sound of that. "I wouldn't say that, Sybille. You make it sound like I slunk out of town under the cover of night. Well, actually I did leave just before dawn, because I couldn't very well chance one of the gatekeepers—all of whom have known me since birth—betraying me to my father. So I had to manage . . . well, never mind that," he said, for while he had contrived a very ingenious escape from York, he did not think the retelling of it would raise himself in his True Love's eyes. "The important thing is that I went on the quest for my Sybille, and by the angels, I've found her!"

"Oh, Stephen." Sybille sighed, not for the last time in this happy meeting. "You are so brave and good and my own true knight in armor. To have done this all for me. I never thought it possible. All the obstacles that stood in your way!" The pretty vision of Stephen's impassioned pursuit was chased away by a sudden, uncomfortable pang for Eleanora Brewer. Since Sybille was a very sweet-natured young woman, her earlier pique toward her now vanquished rival was slain in light of what she could well imagine to be Eleanora's very real distress. "Poor Eleanora! How hard it must be for her. Think of it!"

"I'd rather not," Stephen said practically.

"But I know just what she is going through now. Oh, it was agony to think of her marrying you. It must be very hard for her to have loved and lost you."

Stephen puffed himself up, just a little.

"And to be left at the altar like that—or almost," Sybille added, looking at it from the point of view of friends and neighbors and guessing well enough Eleanora's humiliation. These considerations inevitably led her to name the other most important personage in this drama. "And your father, Stephen. Think of your father!"

Stephen shuddered. Thoughts of his father appealed to him even far less than the contemplation of the jilted Eleanora. He blanched a little but said manfully, "My father will just have to accept the situation as it is."

"Do you plan to return to York?" Sybille asked, rather round-eyed.

"Of course, where else would we go?"

"We?"

"You and me, Sybille."

Sybille's face suddenly crumpled.

Stephen felt a stab in the region of his heart. "No, Sybille. Don't tell me that I'm too late—that you're already married."

"I'm not, Stephen. Don't look like that. I'm not! But Katherine and William the Marshal have already mentioned some earl or another and—and I hope you would know that I'd rather not marry him."

"I should rather think not!" Stephen exclaimed, affronted. "I can't very well have come all this way for *nothing*, can I?"

"Well, I don't know what we are to do about it," Sybille said. She was put happily in mind of the subject which had been among her confused thoughts just before Stephen's arrival. "Did you know that Master Eric the Shipwright is the Earl of Scarborough?"

"No, really? Earl of Scarborough? Well, now!" Stephen replied, diverted and rather awed by this unexpected tidbit. "I'm not sure that I understand. How does a shipwright become an earl?"

"I don't have the most distant guess, but it seems that he did not become one, he always *was* one."

"A shipwright an earl? You go too fast for me, Sybille," Stephen said, shaking his head. "But if it is the case, then I can tell you that Master Eric must be the most important man in the area for miles around. Why, the Scarborough estate comes inland almost as far as York and commands leagues of coastline. Important to all sailors and traders in the area!"

"Maybe that is why Master Eric—the Earl of Scarborough, that is—was such a skillful sailor," Sybille suggested. "Since he already knew the coastline. But that is of no moment. I was thinking that he and Katherine do not see eye to eye. They never have, as far as I can tell. He might be disposed to barring my marriage to anyone of Katherine's choosing. It's worth a try, you know."

Stephen sat up straight, struck by this particularly brilliant thought. "And if he *is* the Earl of Scarborough, then he quite possibly could use some of his influence to help us. I'd like to think that he always thought well of me. Why, I'll be dashed if it isn't just perfect! Sybille, you're a wonder!"

"You like the idea?" Sybille said, sighing yet again.

"Like it? I love it!" Stephen said enthusiastically. "I wonder if I might seek an audience with the Earl of Scarborough," he said, still shaking his head over the unexpected elevation in the status of the master shipwright from Scarborough, "to see if he'll support a marriage of—er—rather unequal status."

Sybille shook her head. "No. It won't do. I should never actively go against Katherine. I would like it only if he were to take it upon himself to bar my reinstatement, just to thwart Katherine, if you see what I mean."

"But someone must put the idea in his head, after all," Stephen said. "I shall take it upon myself to do so."

Stephen was to have the opportunity far sooner than he could have expected. Not a minute later the Earl of Scarborough himself, taking a turn in the gardens, came face-to-face with Sybille and Stephen.

Scarborough was not in an approachable mood after his unsuccessful apology to Katherine. His frown, already heavy on his stern face, became deeper at the sight of the two young lovers.

"G-good e-eventide to you, s-sir!" Stephen stammered, remembering a bow and trying hard not to look guilty.

"What the devil are you doing here, Webster?" Scarborough demanded, apparently feeling no greeting in return to be necessary.

"What am I doing here?" Stephen repeated blankly. "Oh! You mean me, here! What am *I* doing *here* in Lancaster! At court! Me!" Stephen laughed nervously, and something in the situation warned him that he should give his strange presence in the gardens with Sybille the cachet of parental approval. "My father sent me."

The look on Scarborough's face was not encouraging.

Stephen continued, improvising rapidly, "Oh, yes! My father sent me on a buying trip to London." He then became entangled in a rather involved story about John and Louis and the fate of the English government when he remembered that he should have thought of the excuse of the political situation in the first place as a far better reason for his presence in Lancaster.

To this highly dubious account of Stephen Webster's activities Scarborough regarded the young man with penetrating eyes. He then turned to Sybille, to her profound discomfiture. Scarborough would have liked to have removed Stephen from Sybille's side without further ado, knowing what Katherine's thoughts on the matter would be; but the memory of her rejection of his apology still stung, and he was sure that Katherine would not appreciate any intervention from him.

"I see," Scarborough said slowly. "I see. Let me give you a word of warning. Do not, I repeat, *do not* do anything rash or foolish if you can possibly help it."

Stephen instantly dashed the idea of disclosing to the Earl of Scarborough his intention of marrying Sybille. Stephen tried, with limited success, to appear in control of himself and the situation. Since the Earl of Scarborough looked in no mood to countenance an unequal match, Stephen felt he could burn his bridges.

Stephen dared to respond to Scarborough's annihilating recommendation with a sniff and the words: "I do not think it any of your business what we are doing here or what we intend to do! And if you mean by doing anything rash and foolish, Master—er—my lord, to follow one's heart instead of one's head, then I shall take extreme pride in following my heart."

Scarborough's face became positively murderous. Stephen was not to know (and would have been gratified to learn) that he had flicked Scarborough on the raw. Scarborough's thoughts had turned to his own foolishness with regards to Katherine during their interview, knowing it to have been one time that he should have listened to his heart.

Stephen added hastily and with extreme ill timing, "Not that you would know about that, for although you have always rather liked my poetry, I am not sure that you possess a heart."

Scarborough snapped, "Get thee gone from Lancaster, Stephen Webster. I can see that you are determined to fly in the face of all common sense, and while it goes against the grain for me to exercise my newfound authority, I can have you removed from the castle grounds by morning light if you are not already gone by your own volition. I shall leave the both of you to say your good-byes. I shall see Demoiselle Sybille on the morrow in William Marshal's chambers, as we agreed earlier. Good day to you, Master Stephen and God's Speed. I trust that the next time we meet will be in York."

With the briefest of bows Scarborough was gone, the gardens suddenly having lost any restorative effect they could possibly have had on him. His departure was witnessed by Emma, who had a corner of the garden available to her eye from the window of Katherine's antechamber. Emma could not, however, see Sybille and Stephen from that window, nor could Emma have dreamed what was happening between the two thwarted lovers.

Stephen and Sybille were both stunned and pale at Scarborough's exit. Stephen, recovering first, turned toward Sybille and said, "We must go away together and with no loss of time, Sybille."

"I do not understand you," Sybille said in a pathetic little voice.

"We must leave Lancaster together, tonight, immediately."

"And leave Katherine? Without telling her?"

"I see no other way if we are to be together. Another day and you'll be betrothed to some nobleman or other, and then it will be the end for you and me." Stephen paused. "We must do it!"

Sybille was torn between wild fits of hope and despair. "Leave Katherine?" she repeated. "To travel together, unmarried?"

"Well, that does pose a problem," Stephen conceded. "We wouldn't have to tell any innkeeper on our way back to York that we're unmarried, you know. We're both of age."

"We'd go back to York and get married there?" Sybille inquired.

"I don't think we could do that, either, for we would have already traveled a good many days together and alone, and I think that would quite shock my parents," Stephen explained, and added as an afterthought, "On top of everything else that I've done in the past month."

"We must get married on the way, then."

"Yes, that's it. We'll get married on the way," Stephen seconded happily, glad that Sybille had suggested it.

"But that was not at all what I had in mind for my—our—wedding, Stephen."

"Well, curse it, Sybille, you can't have everything your own way," Stephen said practically. "It's not what I had in mind, either, but there you have it! And now that I think about it, there is something appealing about doing it on our own and without anyone's help. We've been treated as babies long enough, you know. I've made it this far, God's Foot, and I've a mind to finish the job!"

The stars came back into Sybille's eyes when she contemplated Stephen's heroics. To complain now at a less-than-perfect wedding would be foolish in the extreme.

"You're right, Stephen. Let us not fall into a senseless quarrel over what is not our fault. After all, the important thing is that we are together—and shall stay together."

Stephen looked a little brighter at that. "You mean that you will defy your sister and leave with me?"

Sybille gulped. "I shall go to her and tell her about us," she responded at last.

"And allow her to make an end to us?"

"Well," Sybille conceded, "I should at least write her a note."

Stephen preserved a silence.

"A message to Emma, perhaps?" Sybille suggested.

"As if that wouldn't be worse!"

"A note to William the Marshal, then, informing him that I will not see him on the morrow," Sybille said in the spirit of compromise. "It is only the proper thing to do."

Stephen agreed to this sop to their feelings for propriety.

"And what about my clothes?" Sybille continued. "I should at least go back to my chambers and get a fresh kirtle, for I cannot career around the countryside in all my finery!"

Stephen considered these very real problems. After a few moments he said, "If we don't leave soon, you won't be needing a change of clothes, for your sister will have discovered you here with me, if the Earl of Scarborough hasn't already told her about us!"

Mention of the Earl of Scarborough had a powerful effect on Sybille. His dismissal of Stephen still echoed forcefully in Sybille's mind. With the exact opposite effect of the intention of his recommendation not to do anything rash and foolish, Sybille decided that their only course was to pursue something extremely rash and foolish. Naturally, Sybille did not think of her imminent actions in that light. She considered rather that she was being brave and adult. In the very back of her mind lurked the stray thought that if Katherine had been able to take responsibility for the long journey from France to York, then she, Sybille, should be able to make it from Lancaster to York, albeit in the company of Stephen.

"Yes, Stephen," Sybille agreed at last. "We should not waste any more time." She surveyed her clothes critically and decided that it might not be the worst thing to travel in such fine clothes. It surely would give their fellow travelers a better opinion of them.

Stephen had no particular feelings on the subject of Sybille's clothing. He did have at his disposal the one thing that would insure the respect of anyone they crossed, and that was a heavy bag of coins. "But let us stick to the back roads, Sybille," he added, "for London was frightfully more expensive than I ever would have imagined. An awful place, if there ever was one!"

After having devised and left a message to the Marshal, the eloping couple left the gardens and the castle and Lancaster itself in a fashion that was perhaps not worthy of the daughter of the Duc de Roncevaux.

Sybille did not give it a second thought. Once on the road for points north, she felt immeasurably better, leaving the burden of her heritage and Katherine's plans for her behind. She allowed Stephen to place her tenderly on the stack of hay in the back of a cart which Stephen had waved down. The two fell into a happy, companionable silence.

With the descent of night came a grumbling in the stomach. No town or little village appeared on the horizon. Stephen became rather less sanguine about their adventure and the reception they would be receiving in York. His face fell accordingly.

Sybille, perceptive in her own happiness of Stephen's growing agitation and state of mind, knew just how to humor her love. Making imperfect and rather laborious communication with the poor villein with whom they were riding, Sybille achieved an invitation from the man to share his evening porridge and a bed of straw in the stables for the night.

Stephen was rather shocked to think of his Sybille in such humble surroundings, but Sybille merely said that anywhere was a grand castle as long as they were together. The villein's home was indeed very humble, but Sybille showed no tendency to hold herself high and helped the weather-beaten wife prepare as tasty a meal as possible with the meager materials at hand. Before they bedded down (separately and chastely) for the night, Sybille had given Stephen an excellent impression of just what a very good wife she intended to be.

___ Chapter 24 ___

Katherine could not have guessed the frenzy that Emma had fallen into much later that evening. Nor was she informed of the cause of Emma's real distress until it was far too late to remedy it.

Emma's late-night anxiety could not have been predicted from her state of mind earlier, toward the end of the afternoon, when her concern had focused solely on Katherine herself. When Emma saw Katherine immediately after the interview with William the Marshal, Emma's fears for her mistress had been more than fulfilled. One look at the pallor of Katherine's face told Emma that she was suffering deeply.

Emma had seen her duty very clearly: to attend to Katherine's needs first and to let Sybille take care of herself for a while. Emma justified herself with the very judicious thought that Katherine had devoted far too much attention to Sybille already and that now was the time for Katherine's problems to take precedence. Emma had deemed it wisest for Sybille to take a turn in the gardens. It would have been preferable for Sybille to have been chaperoned, but Emma could not in her wildest imaginings conceive that Sybille would come to any long-lasting harm for the few hours she might spend in the gardens alone. Besides which, Emma reasoned, Sybille owed Katherine something, after all, and she could now start repaying her elder sister by removing herself from the chambers for a bit and by keeping out of trouble.

Emma had silently congratulated herself for her foresight in having sent Sybille away when the Earl of Scarborough came knocking on Katherine's door some time later. That heated exchange ended, however, with no improvement in her mistress's mood. If anything, it had worsened. Katherine looked in need of a good cry after the encounter, but no tears were visible on any of the various occasions when Emma cracked open the door to the bedchamber and saw Katherine, immobile, at the window. Furthermore, her mistress shook her head violently at all mention of food. The only words she had uttered after Scarborough's unsuccessful reconciliation visit had been in response to Emma's suggestion that she lie down.

"No, Emma," Katherine had said in a distant voice. "Bed is something to be avoided at all costs."

Katherine had indeed no desire to seek her bed. She knew that she would only lie agonizingly awake. The pattern of her life had been radically cut by the events of the day, and no signs of a fresh pattern had taken shape. When she asked herself the question "Now what?" all answers were equally empty and devoid of meaning. Standing at the window, she lost track of time.

Not so for Emma. With each passing minute she became more aware of time and of Sybille's prolonged absence. As the afternoon shadows lengthened, Emma's worries transferred themselves from Katherine to Sybille. Sybille had been gone a good while. Emma had not made explicit when she expected Sybille to return to the chambers. She had assumed it would be well before nightfall. Emma did not at first want to leave the chamber, on the chance that Katherine would desire some service of her. However, with the passing time, Emma became acutely conscious of the need to go in search of Sybille.

Emma peeked into Katherine's chamber just after the sun had set and saw that her mistress had not moved an inch. Emma, more exasperated at Sybille than worried, decided that now was the time to go fetch the girl, who was no doubt mooning over whatever it was that Sybille thought was wrong with her life. Emma found the gardens with no difficulty. It was only when her search up and down the pathways became more frantic that a sense of Sybille's disappearance was borne in on her.

It was unlikely to Emma that Sybille was simply wandering the hallways of the castle. Emma needed to reach into all possible corners and crannies before she would truly consider the idea that Sybille had left the castle grounds.

Emma finally determined that she needed assistance. She found a discreet serving maid who went in search of Bar. Later, in a darkened hallway, Bar listened to Emma's now fearful account of Sybille's apparent disappearance, and they discussed her possible whereabouts.

Bar agreed that the circumstances surrounding Sybille's absence smelled of something not quite right and opined, "If that reptile Mauleon weren't already dead, I'd suspect him of having whisked her away, just out of devilry. He's caused more trouble than you can imagine."

"Oh, I can imagine it, all right," Emma replied. "But something else is afoot here, and it's as sneaky as two left shoes!"

Emma mentioned that she had seen the Earl of Scarborough in the gardens and wondered if perhaps he had seen Sybille. Bar admitted that his master had been in the gardens late in the afternoon after having seen Mistress Katherine, but Scarborough had returned to his apartment in such a fierce state that Bar had not dared speak one word to him. In any case, his master had shut himself up in his chambers and had not seen Bar or summoned him since.

The evening progressed with no developments. Mindful of Emma's admonition not to spread the news that Demoiselle de Roncevaux was missing, Bar ran here and there in search of the wayward young noblewoman. When the night became very late indeed, he finally sought counsel of William the Marshal, whom he had the temerity to rouse from bed.

The Marshal was instantly concerned by Bar's report. After groping for his dressing gown he lit several tapers in his antechamber, whereupon he discovered a missive addressed to himself that had been shoved under his door. It was written by an inexpert and apparently trembling hand and was marred by several blotches that might have been caused by teardrops. Nevertheless, the message was clear and to the point: "To William, High Marshal of England. I shall be unable to attend our meeting on the morrow." It was signed, unmistakably, "Sybille de Roncevaux."

William looked up at Bar and handed the parchment over to him with the words, "Take it to Scarborough."

Without waiting for an explanation, and unable to decipher the message himself, Bar did as he was told. Scarborough read it minutes later with a heavy frown, commenting briefly that Demoiselle Sybille must have flown with Stephen Webster, whom he had seen earlier in the gardens. He recommended that the missive be passed immediately to Mistress Emma to show to Demoiselle Katherine, to do with as she saw fit.

Thus it was in the blackest hour of the night and with the aid of a hastily lit taper that Katherine read Sybille's message. She blinked, unbelieving, and put out a hand to the cold stone coping of the window for support. She ran her eyes again over the spare words and could make no sense over the implication that Sybille was gone. It took an effort to comprehend.

Then it was as though scalding water poured through Katherine's brain. Sybille was gone. Compromised by now, so it would seem, with Stephen Webster. Sybille would not be making a brilliant marriage. Sybille had thrown everything away. All Katherine's gold had turned to dross.

She turned, distraught, to Emma and demanded clarification. "Bar said that Scarborough had seen Sybille with Stephen in the gardens earlier today, or rather," she said, putting a shaky hand to her brow, "yesterday afternoon?"

Emma nodded.

Katherine shook her head, trying to assimilate the few facts she had at her command. Then, suddenly, "I need Eric."

A very short time later Emma had escorted Katherine through the cold, black hallways to the Earl of Scarborough's door. It was opened to her by Bar, and Emma told him she desired for her mistress an audience with Scarborough. Bar did not look much surprised at this request, and he held the door open and stood aside to reveal the antechamber lit and Scarborough himself dressed and emerging at that moment from his chamber. He waved Bar and Emma from the room. When the door had been shut behind them, Katherine and Eric regarded each another in silence.

"Do you think that there is a chance to prevent a scandal?" Katherine asked in a voice that quavered pitifully.

"Perhaps."

"If we went after them now," Katherine continued, holding precariously onto her self-control, "before they have spent the entire night together ... before ... before Sybille has compromised herself beyond redemption ... before the whole castle knows of her flight ..." She drew an unsteady breath. "You say you saw them in the gardens earlier today, Sybille and Stephen?"

"Yes, I told them to do nothing foolish and was apparently the unwitting cause of their precipitous departure together." He paused. "You may hold me responsible if you like."

The matter was too serious to permit senseless quarreling. "As if that would alter things!" Katherine exclaimed, and then shook her head. "And, anyway, it's not your fault. It was Sybille's doing, I warrant. Or Stephen's. The both of them together. The fools!" Katherine took a long breath. "I do not know what you could have done to prevent it, save to escort Stephen personally to the castle walls."

"I considered it," he replied, "but I did not think you would care for my intervention."

Katherine laughed a little, half in pain, half in amusement. Then she asked again, anxiously, "Do you think that we can get her back before it is too late?"

"That depends on the direction in which they have gone and when they started out."

"They only have a few hours' head start. And no doubt they have gone north, to York," Katherine said. Her self-control was slipping away. "It is so important to get her back. She knows how important it is. She has known her entire life. How could she do this to me? All my plans, all my work, all my efforts! She knows that it was for *her*. She knows that it was for the memory of our *mother*!"

Scarborough said nothing. He was regarding Katherine intently and very gravely. When the tears began at last to roll down Katherine's cheeks, still he made no move toward her.

"It was for our mother," Katherine went on, seemingly unaware of the tears now coursing plentifully down her cheeks. "It was for the duke, who was always so dear and kind to me and who loved Sybille to the bottom of his heart. It was for Gaston the Gameskeeper and Marie-Lisette, our nursemaid, and Juliana and Harold and Michael"—she was sobbing now—"and Elias and Christina and Philippe and Elisabeth, who died before my very eyes. And then there was Bernard in the courtyard and his wife, Blanche, and their five children, not one of whom had turned seven, and even *they* were mercilessly slaughtered. All the children! All of them! You cannot imagine the horror! With God in His Heaven allowing the Cathars their day!" She swallowed hard. "And Jeanne the Cook and her husband, Jacques, at the portals and—and—" She faltered. "And Illiana and Etienne and all the pages and villeins, and then, in the end, no one was spared but Sybille and m-me . . . and the old and crippled Odette, and Elisa, both of whom have since died, anyway!" She choked over her words. "It was for Mother, who died in my arms!"

Finally the mention of the host of names of her beloved family and castle folk, accompanied by the vision of their faces and the memory of that brutal scene of carnage, welled up inside and overcame her. She covered her head with her hands and wept.

After a long moment came Scarborough's harsh words. "Bury them, Katherine."

She sniffed and stopped crying and lifted her head slowly at the blighting command.

"Bury them," he said again.

Katherine struggled with his words. Scarborough crossed the small space separating them and calmly laid both his hands on her shoulders in a firm grip. "Put them in their proper graves, my love," he said, and this time his stern tones were tempered, just a little, with tenderness.

"Don't you understand?" Katherine cried in agony.

"I understand."

She shook her head emphatically. "My mother died in my arms. I had to cross the whole of the castle to get to her solar. She was not—she was not, thank the Holy Mother mutilated, but she was severely wounded and only hanging on to life as if . . . as if she were waiting for me to come to her!" She was looking up at him earnestly. "But Mother had suffered for so many long hours—waiting to die—and I think she was even beyond pain when I gathered her into my arms." Her eyes were very wide and wet. "She had me promise to take proper care of Sybille. And then it was over." Katherine stopped and could speak no more.

He nodded his comprehension and took her chin in hand. "You have kept that promise, my heart. There is nothing more for you to do. Let your ghosts lie in peace." He kissed her brow very gently. "Bury them once and for all. Let them lie, let them rest."

She stared at him and then formed her words, very slowly, as a child would. "It is too difficult . . . to let them go."

He took her arms and put them around his neck. "Let go, my love. It is not so difficult. You have done what you could, and you have a right to your own life now. I predict that you will survive nicely without self-pity."

"Without self-pity?" she echoed in disbelief. The glimmer of a watery smile dawned in her eyes. She said in a low challenging voice, "How *dare* you take that away from me?"

"I dare."

The pain she had so stoutly refused to allow to vanquish

her all these years diminished slightly. The bitter taste of loss became less acrid. She relaxed against the comforting expanse of his chest and remembered the peaceful times of her girlhood without an accompanying anguish. There came suddenly a clear vision of Castle Roncevaux, still strong and whole and uninvaded. The memory caught at her heart wistfully, like the muted vibration of a mandolin string when lightly touched. The pieces of her life fell together. She suddenly found herself accepting that yesterday was over and done with, that it had become today, just as today would become tomorrow.

She was dazed in the light of this new lightness of heart. "But what about Sybille and Stephen?"

His bodily hold on her became tighter. "I shall go after them if that is what you desire."

Katherine wrinkled her brow in thought. "Can it be done with no scandal?"

He caressed her neck with his lips. "I am sure that I can contrive it."

She found it impossible not to respond to his kisses. Nevertheless, she cried, "Eric! We must be serious."

"I am very serious."

She attempted, halfheartedly, to disentangle herself from his arms. "Sybille is ruining her life!"

He looked down into her eyes. "Is she, Katherine? Where is her life? Not, I venture to say, under your thumb." He waited a moment. "What? No fiery retort?" He smiled. "But I shall agree that Sybille has a complete disregard for her sense of duty."

Katherine made a wry mouth. "Duty," she repeated. Then, "But Sybille *does* know her heart, does she not?"

"I do not know, nor do I care," he said. "At a guess, I would say that Sybille and the Webster are perfectly suited."

"But Sybille of Roncevaux a townswoman? A tradesman's wife?"

"She has been that for most of her life."

"Yes, but engaged in business?"

Scarborough laughed. "Your skepticism is well founded. She doesn't have a grain of your business sense, more's the pity! At least she will be marrying into money!"

"And Master Webster!" Katherine gasped. "Whatever will he think?"

Gently unlacing the neck and sleeves of her kirtle, he answered, "When Master Robert has recovered from his initial apoplexy, he will be delighted to receive his new daughter-in-law and discover that he had thought the match perfect all along."

Katherine retained a stray vestige of reason. She was not going to let him handle her so easily. "One moment," she said, not without quivering deliciously at his touch as his hand slid down her hips. "I demand, before you do one thing more, that you beg my forgiveness."

"Beg your forgiveness? Good God!" he said in savage accents. "I have already tried that and had it flung in my teeth!"

"Try it again," she suggested. "I'm more receptive now."

His eyes narrowed to gray slits of laughter. "Not a chance. I intend rather to make you pay for the rest of your life the way you have had me dance on your string for so long."

"Is this—could this truly be a proposal of marriage?" Katherine asked, suddenly coy.

"No, not a proposal," he said, "for you don't have a choice in the matter. You shall marry me on the morrow."

"Marry you? No, think of our lives together. Impossible!"

"A horrible prospect, I agree. But I don't have much choice in the matter, either," he confessed, "for Gwyneth has told me in no uncertain terms just what she thinks of me."

"At least you got what was coming to you."

"Yes, my love," he said, "marriage to you."

"I'd as soon lock myself in a cage with a lion," she said.

He smiled. "Our marriage will be far worse than that," he assured her lovingly.

After several long moments Katherine broke off a highly satisfying kiss and looked up at him. "Eric," she said. "I must tell you something."

He raised his brows.

"There was only one messenger," she said.

A second elapsed before he absorbed the meaning of her

words. Then he murmured something that sounded like, "You are magnificent," before he crushed his lips on hers and made sure, with some bolder actions, that it was the last she spoke.

Much later, when the wan light of the dawn struggled to splay its fingers through the slats of the shutters, Katherine and Eric stood at the window in a comforting embrace. The large bed was in the next chamber, still warm and rumpled and far from forgotten. Katherine sighed at the unexpected and so natural turn her life had taken. She had never thought that anything could replace her passion for her sister's rein-statement, and she marveled afresh at the peace and comfort of her love's arms.

At length, Katherine lifted her head from Eric's shoulder to look into the depths of his gray eyes.

"Will it always be like this?" she asked, sighing again with perfect contentment.

"I will not deceive you, my love," he replied easily. "It cannot possibly remain like this between us for long. We shall be at dagger-drawing before you know it. Shrew!"

Katherine laughed. "Such hard names you have always thought to call me!"

"But I did not address you by the worst of them, much as I would have liked. You drove me very hard."

"Very true," she said with a reminiscent smile. "Eric, I think we can do better in the future."

"Do you, my heart?" he queried. "I am not as confident."

"But will you at least *try* not to put me into a rage every time we speak?"

"I will if you will," he replied, keeping all trace of a smile from his face.

"Oh, but I *will* try," she answered readily. "Or at least I will, on one condition."

"Always bargaining, Katherine?" he asked with a glint in his eye.

"Why, yes, now that you mention it. But you see, I have had some time to consider our lives together, and it seems we must set up residence in London, no?"

"Most of the time," he answered. "I shall want to spend some time at Scarborough, of course."

"Well, yes. But for the times we shall be in London it will be imperative for me to own a broidery shop."

"Imperative?"

She nodded.

"You shall have it," he said.

"In Watling Street," Katherine pursued.

"Ah, the most fashionable! Of course! And do you have a particular shop in mind?" he asked. To her nod he replied, "I shall write the deed and stamp the official seal on it this afternoon if that is what you would like."

Finding him so acquiescent, Katherine could not resist adding in a quiet, but provocative, voice as she moved away from him, "And, Eric," she said, "I do not intend to pay a penny's tax."

The king's Counselor of the Exchequer put his hands on his hips and looked fiercely at his wife-to-be. "I intend to audit your ledger at the end of every working day!" he informed her forcefully.

They gazed at each other, and at length his hard regard softened under the spell of the laughter and love in her eyes.

"Katherine," he said at last.

It was a command. He had stretched out his hand imperiously, and when she laid hers in it, he drew her to him.

from Dorothy Garlock . . .

__WILD SWEET WILDERNESS *(D20-011, $3.95, U.S.A.)*
(D20-012, $4.95, Canada)

Berry was only eighteen when she left the wagon train to find her father's claim in Missouri. She was determined to prove that she was a match for them all—even the brave trader who fell in love with her.

__ANNIE LASH *(D20-037, $3.95, U.S.A.)*
(D20-038, $4.95, Canada)

When her parents died, Annie Lash was left alone in St. Louis till a young frontiersman, Jefferson Merrick, offered her a chance to escape to a distant settlement. But how would she cope with the trials of a hostile frontier and the young man who tried to tame her as he tamed the wild country around them?

__LONESOME RIVER *(D20-362, $3.95, U.S.A.)*
(D20-363, $4.95, Canada)

Liberty fled New York to the wild wilderness when her father demanded she marry Stith Lenning. Rampaging Indians awaited her and Stith pursued her till Farr Quill rode into her life, offering his protection even as he demanded her total surrender.

WARNER BOOKS
P.O. Box 690
New York, N.Y. 10019

Please send me the books I have checked. I enclose a check or money order (not cash), plus 50¢ per order and 50¢ per copy to cover postage and handling.* (Allow 4 weeks for delivery.)

_____ Please send me your free mail order catalog. (If ordering only the catalog, include a large self-addressed, stamped envelope.)

Name _____

Address _____

City _____

State _____ Zip _____

*N.Y. State and California residents add applicable sales tax.   199

27 million Americans can't read a bedtime story to a child.

It's because 27 million adults in this country simply can't read.

Functional illiteracy has reached one out of five Americans. It robs them of even the simplest of human pleasures, like reading a fairy tale to a child.

You can change all this by joining the fight against illiteracy.

Call the Coalition for Literacy at toll-free **1-800-228-8813** and volunteer.

Volunteer Against Illiteracy. The only degree you need is a degree of caring.

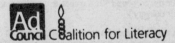

Ad Council Coalition for Literacy

Warner Books is proud to be an active supporter of the Coalition for Literacy.